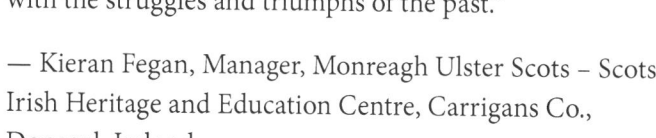

" Margaret's approach to h[istory goes] beyond mere facts and dates. [She infuses] moments with emotional and [depth,] humanizing historical figures [and creating a sense] of empathy and connection, allowing [readers to engage] with the struggles and triumphs of the past."

— Kieran Fegan, Manager, Monreagh Ulster Scots – Scots Irish Heritage and Education Centre, Carrigans Co., Donegal, Ireland

" 'Max' McLaughlin's book tells the story of how Irish patriots—both men and women—are found in many ordinary families. Starting in 1820, McLaughlin weaves the histories of four, interconnected families through time with the likes of Parnell, de Valera, and Collins. As with Irish lace, the reader learns of the complexity of the pattern that twists the Irish independence movement into knots. The families and their members take sides and suffer the consequences. However, throughout the story, the wives and mothers take on the role of conciliator, balancing freedom with justice. This historical novel provides a human visage to the Irish saga. McLaughlin's poetic writing style, in keeping with the Irish tale she is telling, enchants the reader to turn the pages of a history that consumed three centuries of a people in search of their independence."

— John McWilliam, author, *African Travels 1967–2010*

"A compelling, intimate read! These characters, many based on real persons and conditions, come alive with Margaret McLaughlin's capable hand. She gives us a glimpse not only into their hearts and minds, but also their souls. After reading *Beloved Reconciliation* I now feel I have friends in 19th and early 20th century Ireland."

— Jeannie Martin, author, *Shaped by the Sun*, Bottle Rockets Press, Windsor, CT

Beloved Reconciliation
Book 2: 1918–1923

Margaret Maxwell McLaughlin

All cover photos © Margaret McLaughlin. Front cover: Annie Smiley Douglas (1894–1925), unknown Smiley brother standing, John Alexander McAfee Smiley sitting (1883–1944). Back cover (from left to right): Three Smiley brothers—David (1882–?), William (1885–1942), and James (1889–1960). Photo circa 1910; Heywood Crawford Irvine Smiley (1884–1967), maternal grandmother of the author; William Smiley (1885–1942) and Nathan Irvine (1882–1950). Photo circa 1920.

© 2024 Margaret McLaughlin. All Rights Reserved. Rights reserved in worldwide, in all languages and formats, including print, audio, and electronic; and all adaptations to other media including radio, television, film, and theatre.

No part of this book may be reproduced or used in any form, or by any means, electronic or mechanical, including photocopying and recording, or by any information storage and retrieval system, without first obtaining written permission from the author. Requests for permission to make copies or reuse of any part of this work should be sent to:

Margaret McLaughlin
10 Lady Slipper Ln.
Forestdale, MA 02644
margaretmclaughlin50@comcast.net

This is a work of fiction. Names, characters, businesses, places, events, locales, and incidents are either the products of the author's imagination or used in a fictitious manner. Any resemblance to other actual persons, living or dead, is purely coincidental.

Cover design and interior formatting: Vanessa Moore
Publisher: Moore Media, Inc., Plymouth, MA
ISBN: 979-8-9852789-9-6
Printed in the United States of America.

Contents

Preface .... *ix*
Acknowledgments .... *xii*
Cast of Families .... *xiv*

Una's Introduction to Part IV. *1*

Part IV: May 1918–December 1921
War of Independence

Chapter 1	My Name in the Heart of a Child—May 1, 1918	3
Chapter 2	An Arrogant Man, Loved and Admired—May 1, 1918	7
Chapter 3	To Act Justly—May 5, 1918	11
Chapter 4	Zoot Monday—May 20, 1918	15
Chapter 5	Outside Insight—October 19, 1918	19
Chapter 6	Coalisland Tale—December 7, 1918	23
Chapter 7	Eve's Revenge—December 18, 1918	27
Chapter 8	Resurrection Evening—January 18, 1919	32
Chapter 9	The Hunter after the Mountain Cat—January 23, 1919	36
Chapter 10	The Ethics of a Just Life—January 25, 1919	40
Chapter 11	The Other Side—January 25, 1919	44
Chapter 12	The Women's Franchise Meeting—January 31, 1919	48
Chapter 13	Crossing—February 3, 1919	52
Chapter 14	An Exchange—February 5, 1919	56

Chapter 15	Confessional—February 12, 1919	61
Chapter 16	Transatlantic Plans—February, 1919	65
Chapter 17	More Black Cats—February 20, 1919	69
Chapter 18	The Skunk and the Cat—February 20, 1919	73
Chapter 19	Righteous Justice—February 20, 1919	76
Chapter 20	Wordless—February 20, 1919	81
Chapter 21	The Master Trio—April 27, 1919	84
Chapter 22	Ashes, no coffin. Ale, no whiskey. Laughter, no tears.—April 27, 1919	89
Chapter 23	The Gift of Memory—June 30, 1919	93
Chapter 24	Circling Around the Carpet—July 10, 1919	97
Chapter 25	Train of Thought—July 11, 1919	102
Chapter 26	The Falcon and the Dove—July 11, 1919	105
Chapter 27	Silent Listening—July 12, 1919	109
Chapter 28	Farewells—July 12, 1919	112

Una's Epilogue to Part IV: Passages—December 1921............115

Part V: July 1921–April 1922
Anglo-Irish Treaty Deliberations

Chapter 29	Façades—August 1921	121
Chapter 30	A Just Decision—Early September 1921	125
Chapter 31	Below the Surface—Late September 1921	129
Chapter 32	On the Surface—Late September 1921	132
Chapter 33	Rising Mists—Late September 1921	136
Chapter 34	From the Bench—First Week of October 1921	140
Chapter 35	Righteous Revenge?—First Week of October 1921	143

Chapter 36	Enlightened Perspectives— Second Week of October 1921	147
Chapter 37	Ploughing the Mind— Third Week of October 1921	151
Chapter 38	The Beastie King—Third Week of October 1921	154
Chapter 39	Irish Wine—Early November 1921	158
Chapter 40	Dancing with the Devil—December 8, 1921	162
Chapter 41	A True Friend and Patriot—December 20, 1921	168
Chapter 42	The Unraveling—Sunday, January 15, 1922	171
Chapter 43	Choosing Sides—Monday, January 16, 1922	175
Chapter 44	The Hungry Tree Revisited— Wednesday, January 18, 1922	178
Chapter 45	Jumping into Puddles—Friday 3, February 1922	181
Chapter 46	Louisa and Lester—Friday, February 10, 1922	184
Chapter 47	Cows and Clover—Friday, February 17, 1922	191
Chapter 48	St. Jude's Prayer—Friday, February 24, 1922	195
Chapter 49	The Souring—Friday, February 24, 1922	199
Chapter 50	The Warning—Saturday, February 25, 1922	202
Chapter 51	The Oasis—Sunday, March 5, 1922	205
Chapter 52	Playing an Innocent—Friday, March 10, 1922	208
Chapter 53	The Magic of Fairies—Friday, March 31, 1922	212
Chapter 54	A Tapestry of Family Threads— Friday, March 31, 1922	216
Chapter 55	The Philosopher and the Activist— Saturday, April 8, 1922	221
Chapter 56	The Macroom Spirits—Sunday, April 9, 1922	224
Chapter 57	Naming a Better Ireland— Monday, April 10, 1922	229

Una's Epilogue to Part V:
A Call for a Better Ireland—April 8, 1922 .... *232*

Part VI: 1922 | The Civil War

Chapter 58 Serving Two Masters—Saturday, April 15, 1922 ... 235

Chapter 59 The Surprise Reunion—Saturday, April 15, 1922 ... 238

Chapter 60 A Tangled Web—Saturday, April 15, 1922 242

Chapter 61 The Spirit of Truth—Monday, April 17, 1922 247

Chapter 62 Understanding by Inference—
Wednesday, April 19, 1922...................... 251

Chapter 63 The Assumptions—Wednesday, April 19, 1922 256

Chapter 64 Coming Home—Friday, April 21, 1922........... 258

Chapter 65 Stepping Backward and Forward—May, 1922 261

Chapter 66 Opening the Gates—June 26, 1922............... 265

Chapter 67 Behind the Gates—June 26, 1922 268

Chapter 68 Natural Revenge—June 26, 1922 273

Chapter 69 Catching the Fox—June 26, 1922 276

Chapter 70 Riddles—June 27, 1922 279

Chapter 71 The Muddles—June 28–July 3, 1922 283

Chapter 72 Good News?—August 1, 1922................... 288

Chapter 73 Resting on an Unassured Axis—
August 18, 1922............................... 291

Chapter 74 Let Us Pray—Sunday, August 27, 1922 294

Una's Epilogue to Part VI:
Let Us Rejoice for Now—Tuesday, May 1, 1923................. *299*

Endnotes *302*

Preface

For those of you who have read or listened to *Beloved Reconciliation Book 1: 1820–1916*, forgive me for repeating myself here. For those of you who have not, I hope you will find the following helpful in understanding why this work was written. Many of us actively seek what in our past may inform our current beliefs and actions—or inactions—in being peacemakers. Many of us don't seek why, yet wonder nonetheless. As described here, I hope my journey will help you wonder more, seek, and maybe even take action.

My father, Edward Nelson Maxwell, was born in Belfast, Ireland, in 1908—before the Easter Rising in 1916, the partition of Northern and Southern Ireland in 1921, and the Free State civil war in 1922. He never talked to me about the impact these historic events had on his childhood before emigrating to America in 1929. He rarely talked about his personal life either, except that he graduated from Belfast Royal Academy, proselytized on soapboxes outside Fisherwick Presbyterian Church, fought boys who were harassing his older brother James, and lacked funds to go to college so ironed men's suits in the laundry room of a Belfast linen mill.

It was my maternal grandmother, Heywood Crawford Irvine Smiley born in 1884, who was my first formal teacher about Irish life. Living with my family throughout the 1950s and '60s, she would enthrall me during our afternoon "teas" with stories of tours around the Belfast Lough in the family sailboat, *Snow Pea*, and her courtship with my grandfather after she caught his eye while singing in a Bangor Presbyterian church choir. They emigrated to America in 1918. Rarely did she share historical events from "back home."

Fast-forward to 2017 and a study carrel in the U.S. Library of Congress. I had just retired from a thirty-year career in international development with a focus on girls' education and women's rights. I was determined to move beyond those topics to write a biography of my father. Once I learned that his father, Robert Maxwell, had signed the 1912 Ulster Covenant to take up arms against all Catholics if Home Rule passed, I was resolved to understand the attitudes supporting such a stand.

It was a small book by Tom Hartley on the Belfast Milltown Cemetery that convinced me to embellish the biography with a few historical facts about Irish history. I quickly realized there is no such thing as a "few historical facts" about a family, or about Belfast, or about Northern Ireland, or about the Republic of Ireland that do justice to six hundred years of conflict.

Sitting in the library's neoclassical grand reading room, next to the U.S. Supreme Court and across from the U.S. Capitol, the biography transformed itself into an historical fiction about the Irish struggle for independence from Great Britain. For the past seven years, I have read Irish books, plays, and poetry—I must regret, however, not in Gaelic Irish; I've studied research papers, speeches, scholarly histories, and newspaper articles; and, I've gathered information from conversations with friends and family members in the U.S. and Ireland. All these resources helped me imagine and reimagine—with a modicum of facts—life in Ireland for families facing social, religious, economic, and political challenges between 1820 and now—and how women have been instrumental in the independence and peace movements despite those challenges.

I recognize, more now than when I wrote *Book 1: 1820–1916*, that this is a story not only about the strength of Irish women, but of women throughout the world who stand up right next to their male colleagues for justice and equality. They are inspired for the sake of their children and their children's children to reconcile differences and bring peace to their homelands. Ironically in my retirement, I have come back full-circle to speak, if possible, on behalf of women with whom I had worked in the U.S. and overseas.

I can only hope the writing in this series—which now includes *Book 1* and *Book 2*—honors their wisdom and courage as beloved reconcilers.

It is because of this hope that profits from the books in this series will go to the The Monreagh Ulster Scots – Scots Irish Heritage and Educational Center in Donegall, Republic of Ireland (visit monreaghulsterscotscentre.com to learn more). Now with *Book 2*, Monreagh will share those profits equally with my undergraduate college, Wilson College in Chambersburg, Pennsylvania (wilson.edu). Monreagh conducts conflict transformation workshops throughout Ireland and invites visitors from around the world to learn of their work. Wilson College offers scholarships to single parents seeking to be ". . . honorable leaders and agents of justice." The work of both institutions is a model for any peace and reconciliation effort. I hope you will agree and support them.

— Margaret Maxwell McLaughlin, Ed.D.
  Forestdale, Massachusetts, 2024

Acknowledgments

This historical fiction is based on research, imagination, and literary critiques by numerous readers. Each resource was essential in creating factual contexts, believable plot progressions, and character attributes—factual or fictional.

For the facts, I am grateful to Irish historians, writers, playwrights, and poets who lived in or wrote about the time period described in each chapter. The writers who contributed substantively to factual contexts include, but are not limited to, Robert McKee, Carlton Younger, Desmond Ryan, Tim Pat Coogan, John Dorney, and John O'Neill. Highlighted poems were found in various anthologies including Brenden Kennelly's *The Penguin Book of Irish Verse*, Anne Enright's *The Granta Book of The Irish Short Story*, and Thomas Kinsella's *The New Oxford Book of Irish Verse*. Plays by Anglo-Irish playwrights were located either online or in reference books. Numerous visits to Irish museums and centers in both The Republic and Northern Ireland, as well as Scotland, helped find facts within their relative time capsules. Of particular assistance were the Michael Collins Museum in Macroom and the Monreagh Ulster Scots-Scots Irish Heritage Center in Donegall. I would be disingenuous in not mentioning that some historical details and literary quotes came from online resources such as Wikipedia, irishfolklore.wordpress.com, Queen's University, and Vasser College since I wrote several chapters during the COVID pandemic and thereafter. I have made every effort to confirm all primary sources.

Imaginary characters came solely from my own reflections on experiences with family and acquaintances in the U.S., Canada, and Ireland. The relationships and conversations between imagined and factual characters are solely products of my imagination after reading the biographies, personal writings, and public speeches of those historic figures.

In addition, though, I cannot thank enough new-found friends in Donegall—Una and Ian McCracken and Kieran Fegan. Their "reality testing" perspectives and encouragement of this first generation Irish-American daring to write about Irish history remain invaluable. They are present in key fictional characters who represent the best of Irish courage and honor.

As for the many folks who offered literary critiques of these works, I am truly grateful for their acumen, generosity, and commitment to bear with me over seven years—and their willingness to continue with me on this journey. First, the clutch of friends in a short story writing group that provided constructive critiques every Friday for three years was outstanding. While often seated in front of a Zoom screen or around a small table in our local chamber of commerce, these people include Barbara Berelowitz, June Calendar, Sheila Place, Ellen Nosel, and John McWilliam. Avid book reader and friend Greg Case also provided thoughtful feedback. Poet extraordinaire Jeannie Martin and writer Susan Thompson were key advisors on the art of writing and publishing. I must also thank my editor and designer, Vanessa Moore, whose understanding of what reads, sounds, and looks well on the printed page was as equally extraordinary as her patience with this first-time author.

Finally, the burning questions around purpose, logic, and grammar were offered by my two life-companions—my dear friend of more than fifty years, Gayle Kelly; and my life partner of forty-five years, husband Stephen McLaughlin. Every week for the past five years, these two have served as first-line editors and supporters, providing triage on every aspect of verbiage, character development, reality setting, and overall plot progression. Their brilliance, attention to detail, and philosophical queries have enabled this work to be what I hope the reader will find fascinating and informative, passionate and inspirational, and resonant with the spirit of equality and justice.

Cast of Families

McCann Family

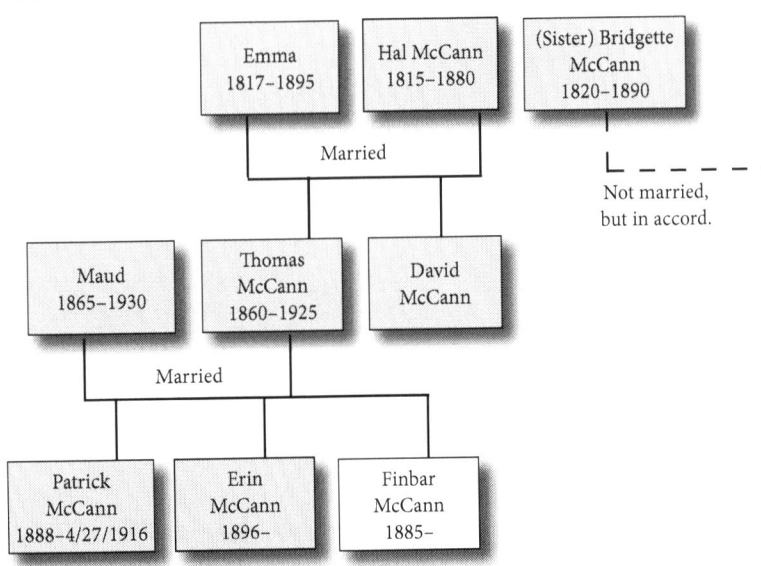

Gallagher Family

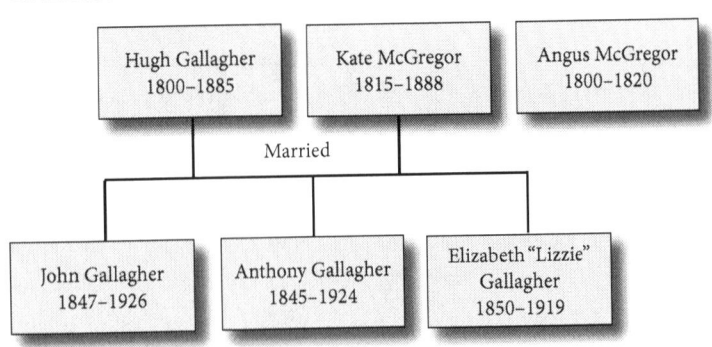

BELOVED RECONCILIATION, BOOK 2   xv

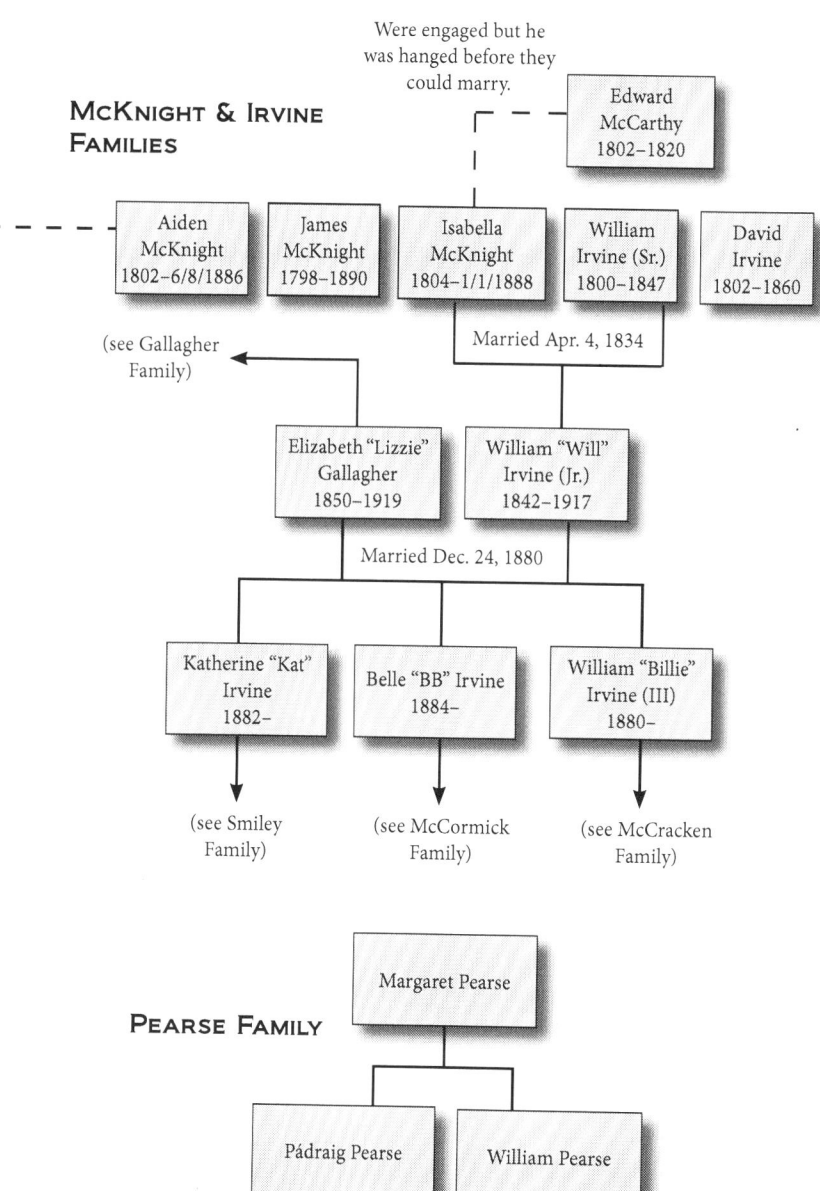

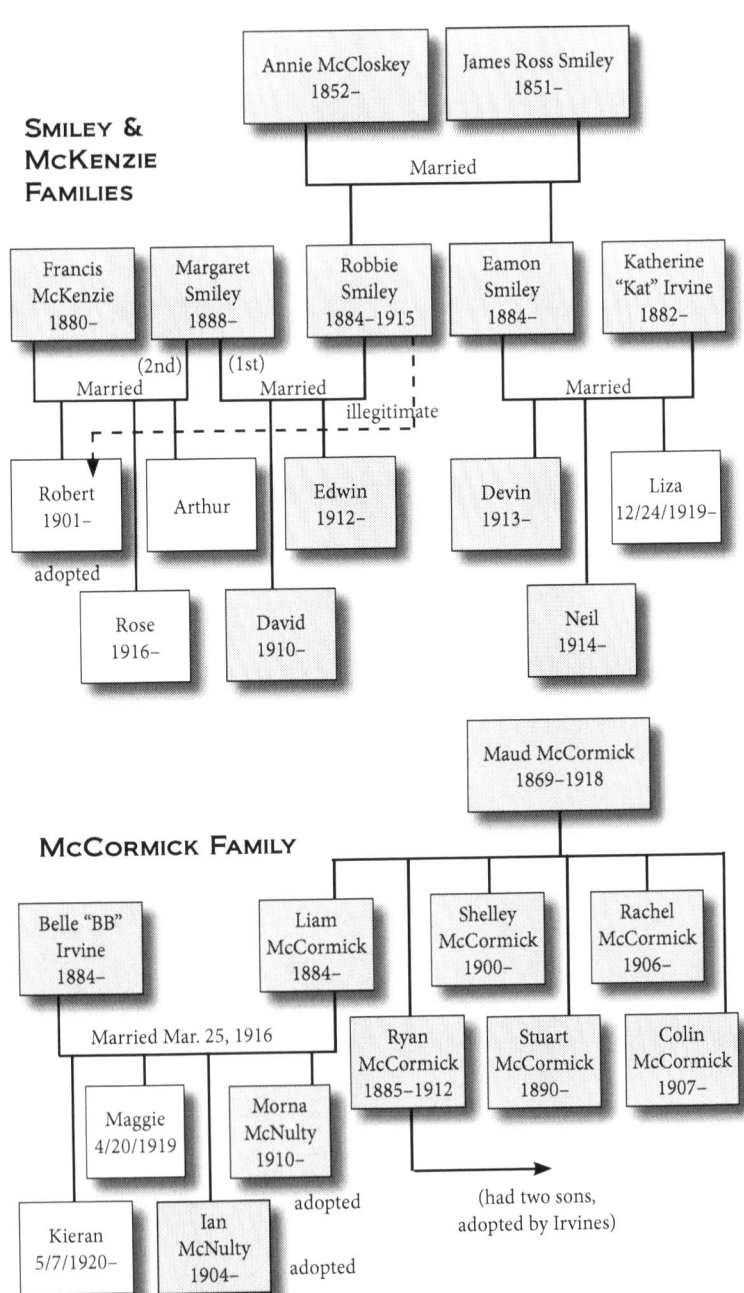

BELOVED RECONCILIATION, BOOK 2   xvii

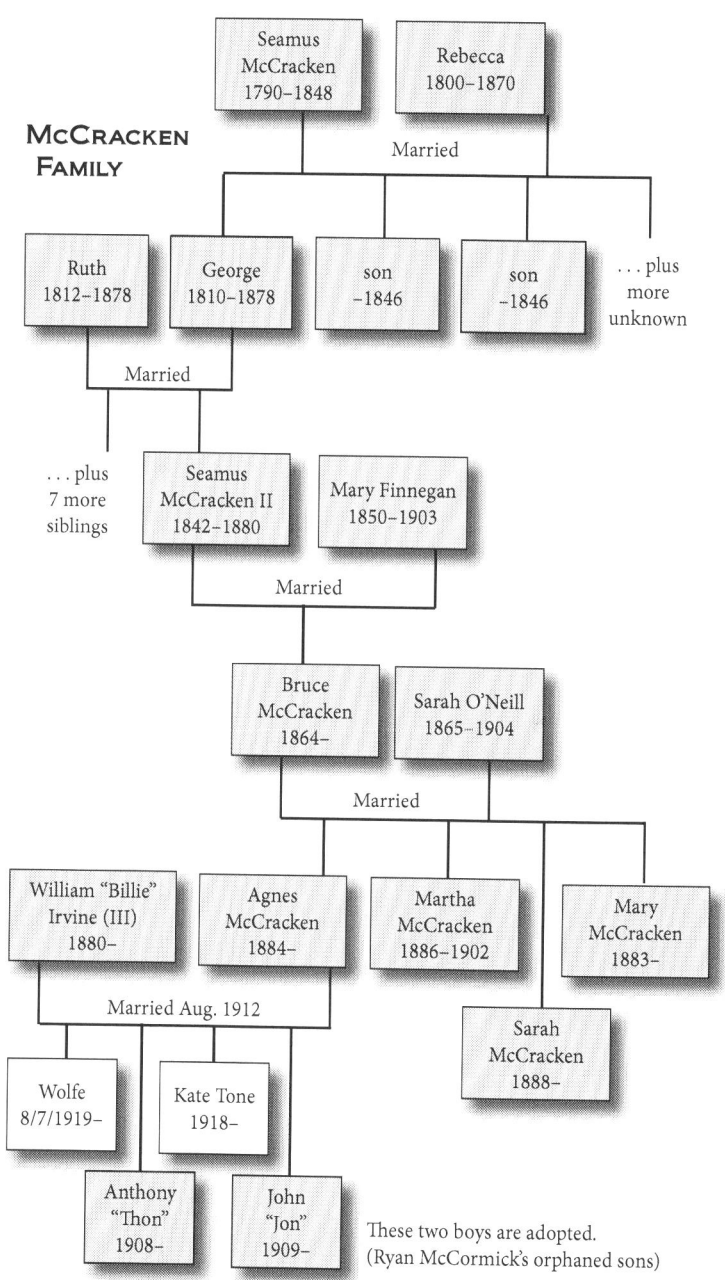

Dedication

To the children of Ireland—past, present, and future.

An Irishman [woman] is "merely a man [woman] who has had the good or bad fortune to be born in Ireland, or of Irish parents, and is interested in Ireland more than any other country in the world."

— Robert Lynd, *Home Life in Ireland*, 1909

"Yet, reading all thy mournful history,
Thy children, with a mystic faith sublime,
Turn to the future, confident that Fate,
Become at last thy friend, reserves for thee,
To be thy portion in the coming time,
They know not what—but surly something great."

— John Kells Ingram, *Sonnets and Other Poems*, 1900

Una's Introduction to Part IV

I am not of this world . . . well, not in the physical sense. I have been, am, and will be of many worlds.

Archaeologists would say I am an ancient vessel that holds an era's social, economic, and cultural remnants. Historians would say I am an interlocutor of fact and fiction—the witness to whoever won the war. Scientists would say I'm a genome made of three billion base pairs of DNA arranged in forty-six chromosomes. Spiritualists would say I am a ghost caught between the veil and the afterlife.

I'm not exactly sure who or what I am. Nor am I interested in finding out. What I am interested in are those with whom I have traveled over the last hundred years. They fascinate me, and, perhaps, they will fascinate you, too.

These are members of my family, an illustrious clan of Scots Irish with a smattering of Celt and Finnish genes. They are farmers, seamstresses, tanners, maids, jewelers, accountants, ministers, soldiers, doctors, engineers, nurses, and artists. They are mothers, fathers, grandmothers, grandfathers, sons, daughters, aunts and uncles. They are heroes and villains, anarchists and pacifists, novitiates and agnostics; they are saints and sinners.

Alexis de Tocqueville said, "History is a gallery of pictures in which there are few originals and many copies." Each member of my clan deserves a picture in the following gallery of stories. Because I know I will be traveling with them for another two hundred years and my current cerebral capacities are beginning to slow down, I must capture their originals before copies compromise their being.

Join me as I travel through this gallery.

And, by the way, you can call me whatever name you like. I'm most comfortable, though, with the one by which these clan members have known me—Winifred, or Una for short.

PART IV:
May 1918 – December 1921
War of Independence

Part IV: May 1918–December 1921

Chapter 1

My Name in the Heart of a Child—May 1, 1918

"Ye're a cackling goose!" Ian shouted at Rachel.

"Ach, ye're a brawling bull!" the young girl yelled back.

The two, red-faced youth—Ian age fifteen and Rachel twelve—sputtered at each other on the cobbled walk in front of the two-story, row house they called home on Leinster Road in Rathmines. Book bags precariously dropped between them mimicked a lopsided barricade, foiling the physical barrage their words anticipated.

"Ye're a mockingbird flying without wings nor compass!" Ian yelled.

"And ye're the blind cat that can't even tell I'm on the ground in front of ye!" Rachel retorted.

The front door of the house swung open and BB Irvine McCormick swiftly alighted from the top steps to the front line of this verbal battle. She was followed by the scampering Bigger, wagging his tail and barking in rhyme to her rapid pace.

"Good heavens above—and ye know where below—what are ye two arguin' about now?" BB inquired, her legs straddling the book bags, as she stepped between the two young folk. On her hip, she balanced an infant, joining the fray with a gasp that quickly escalated into a high-pitched wail.

"Now, look what ye both have done. Maggie was just about to nod off and ye two have awakened her peace. Ach, stop this fussin', pick up yer books and get inside before yer blessed da finds you out here in the dark keeping the entire neighborhood awake."

Frowning, Ian begrudgingly picked up both book bags, traipsed up the front path onto the stairs and into the house. Rachel, also frowning, took the crying Maggie in her arms and reluctantly followed her nemesis. Bigger sat and looked up at BB; she, in turn looked down at him, their heads equally cocked toward the left. Bigger's eyes seemed to smile and BB returned the same expression.

Leaning down and scratching the dog's left ear, BB sighed, "Ach. Did ye ever think ye'd be the only sane bein' in this wild and woolly household, dear Bigger? May God grant me the gift one day to see life in the same amusing way ye do." Bigger wagged his tail and led his most favored mistress back into the house.

Once all were inside, BB set up the afternoon tea table of bayberry scones and warm milk in the kitchen. She added a third place setting for Morna, Ian's eight-year-old sister who was out of school this day recovering from a severe cold.

Maggie had finally fallen asleep in Rachel's embrace. Under the kitchen table, Bigger had curled himself into a ragged ball of fur.

"Now, let's be civil, conciliatory, and concise. Tell me what this verbal fisticuff is all about," BB asked as she leaned back in a worn, wooden-spooled chair and adjusted the cushion behind her. She took the dozing Maggie from Rachel, wrapped the infant in a plaid blanket and nestled her into the rocking cradle near—but not too near—the stove.

"She—"

"He—"

The two youth vociferously began at once, interrupting each other.

"Ach, my loves. One voice at a time," BB cajoled.

Out of the circular, porcelain bowl in the center of the table, she drew a tiny coin and flung it in the air. All watched it descend and spin like a top before falling flat upon the table's well-waxed surface. BB quickly covered it with her hand.

"Whoever guesses the upside of the coin goes first," said BB.

"The crown," said Ian.

"The lyre," said Rachel.

BB uncovered the coin and all three, including Morna, leaned in from their respective chairs around the table to see who was the victor. The lyre appeared. The victor was Rachel.

Part IV: May 1918–December 1921

Quickly, she described how earlier in the day, during her class on Irish literature at St. Ita's—the girls' school accompanying St. Enda's for boys—Margaret Pearse had entered to see how the students were progressing. Mrs. Pearse had asked a pupil to recite her son Pádraig's December 1910 poem "Níor Cruinnigheadh Liom-sa Ór," or "I Have Not Garnered Gold," and discuss its meaning.

BB asked Rachel if she could calm herself enough to recite the poem. Rachel stood and slowly spoke the lines,

"I have not garnered gold;
The fame I found hath perished;
In love I got but grief
That withered my life.
Of riches or of store
I shall not leave behind me
(Yet I deem it, O God, sufficient)
But my name in the heart of a child."

"Very good, my dear," BB acknowledged.

Rachel went on to explain that while walking home together from their schools, Rachel had told Ian what she thought the poem meant, and he had immediately disagreed with her.

As a student at St. Enda's, Ian had studied the poem, too, the previous year. Now, they once again continued the debate at the table, here before BB.

"It's about a poor man who has nothing to leave the nation's children except his name. No wife, no riches, no fortune. Nothing. What is in a name?" Rachel insisted.

"Nay, it's about a man who died rich because he was a humble hero who loved his country. He wants all the children to know that no material wealth nor fame nor sire can better provide for a nation than having an honored name and the patriotic values that name represents," Ian rebutted and continued, "If we remember and cherish in our hearts why he died, then he has left the most valuable of riches."

"How can a name be worth anything?" Rachel insisted, turning her bright red, puffed-out cheeks toward Ian. She screwed up her nose and pursed her lips in frustration.

"It is worth gold if a family and a nation repeat it with respect and honor and carry it in their hearts as their own, acting out its values," Ian quietly responded.

Rachel, too, became quiet. "You mean Pearse is a name of honor we should always cherish by doing what he did?" she asked.

"Aye," he said. "No matter what anyone says about him, he set us on the path to independence and will be known for that. My da did that, too. So I'll honor the McNulty name and keep it in my heart. All of us young ones who lost our das in the Rising should do the same."

"Maybe I should change my name to McCann?" Rachel sighed, and turning toward BB said, "I wish Patrick McCann had been my da."

BB wanted to reach over to take the young girl's hand, but hesitated. Rachel had never talked about the Rising day when Patrick McCann had saved her life by taking on the bullet meant for her. Ian and BB stared at Rachel, but their thoughts took on no action.

The porch door at the back of the kitchen suddenly opened with a flurry of noise. Liam McCormick and two stately men entered with a flair of laughter and bravado. Their energy ignited the contemplative mood into excitement.

"Aye, my good lad and lassies!" Liam declared. "Turn up the stove and evening lights, for we are in for a night of much debate and amusement. Are ye ready?"

The children and BB rose from their seats in astonished joy, knowing immediately who their da's companions were. They were Michael Collins[1] and Arthur Griffith[2], names Liam and BB already held in esteem, and Rachel and Ian would someday hold in their hearts. Tonight, the two youth would begin learning why.

Part IV: May 1918–December 1921

Chapter 2

An Arrogant Man, Loved and Admired—May 1, 1918

Quiet embraced the Leinster Road home as the piano fell silent, the violin was encased in its leather carrier, and the young ones were kissed on their foreheads in true Irvine, now McCormick, tradition. There had been a fine meal and frolicking ceilidh offered before the moon began to rise and young heads to nod.

Ian now nudged his sleeping sister Morna and guided her wobbling legs to the second-floor bedroom she shared with Rachel. He, then, took the ladder up to his tiny room in the attic.

Liam had led his resistant, yet exhausted, sister Rachel to her room, admonishing, "get thy sleep."

Knowing Ian all too well, Liam called up to him from the bottom rung of the ladder, "Now, don't wear out yer eyes on that Wilde play. What's it called again?"

Ian called down from his crow's nest. "*The Importance of Being Earnest*," Ian replied.

"Ach, why waste yer time on such a read, me lad?" Liam teased. "Ye already know the import."

Both youth and elder chuckled as Liam strode down the stairs and entered the parlor. Upstairs, Ian relit his candle, opening to page thirty-four of the play.

"Ye have a commendable group of patriot scholars in yer abode here, Mr. and Mrs. McCormick," offered Collins, once settled onto the velvet settee next to BB.

"The wee lass Rachel and lad Ian know their history, for sure. I only regret that it is not just knowledge from their studies at St. Enda's and St. Ita's. But—" Collins sighed and continued, "it might just be that they are the kind of warriors we need for this next effort.

Sorrow and revenge are powerful partners in securing the legacy our martyrs have left behind."

BB, rocking the infant Maggie's wicker bassinet, turned away. She could not bear seeing any more of her wards suffer the loss of loved ones nor resort to violence in the form of retaliation.

Liam McCormick did not turn away. Instead, he offered Collins and Griffith a refreshed glass of whiskey and directly asked, "Tell us what that effort now requires. Ye both have come tonight not just to enjoy me darlin' BB's fine cooking, Ian's fiddle playing, and Rachel's melodic voice. What is next for us?"

Arthur Griffith calmly faced Michael Collins, not Liam McCormick. As a writer and philosopher, Griffith had experienced many a dilemma in his three decades of translating words into action when creating the Sinn Féin party[3] out of its predecessors—the Society of the Gaels and the Sinn Féin League—both of which he had been influential in founding in 1900 and 1905, respectively. Now, the British blamed Sinn Féin for the Rising, although neither Griffith nor the organization had anything to do with its planning. However, being labeled as such had actually advanced Sinn Féin's membership, for it soared after April 1916. This was in response to both the executions of Pearse and other leaders, as well as the recent April 1918 Irish Conscription Act, which was sending Irish lads involuntarily onto the war's battlefields.

Little did those around the table tonight know that the Irish population would soon strike back during the upcoming December 1918 general election. Sinn Féin candidates—including Michael Collins, Arthur Griffith, and Eamon de Valera[4]—would win the majority of Irish seats as Ministers of Parliament in the House of Commons. Adding more peat to the burning fire of politics, those same MPs would refuse to go to London. Instead, they would declare their own Irish Parliament, the Dáil Éireann, on January 21, 1919 to be located in Dublin.

Part IV: May 1918–December 1921

Prior to this election, however, much needed to be determined within Sinn Féin and IRB leadership. Griffith's current role was problematic. Tonight's gathering in the neutral setting of the McCormick's household would allow Griffith and Collins to discuss their differences privately and hopefully see their common goals.

"I read yer editorial in *Nationality*, Arthur," said Collins. "Ye still are sticking to the hope that we can reconcile our differences with Ulster, aren't ye?"

"Aye, Mick. We have to bring the Ulster Nationalists and Republicans together with the Unionists for a united Ireland. Otherwise, we're going to lose all of Ulster to the Unionist side." Griffith held up his whiskey glass between two hands and twirled around the liquid inside. "Like the separate malt barley and corn in this wee pint, we need all our citizen ingredients to distill into a formidable and digestible nation."

"Nay, Arthur, ye're delusional," Collins responded, holding up his own glass. "Ye know that distillation requires taking out the sickening sulfur to produce the finest whiskey. Those Ulster Unionists don't care one grain for us Republicans nor their Nationalist neighbors. Look at Carson's Ulster Covenant and Ian Paisley's congregants. They are the poisonous ingredient of your imaginary whiskey. Together with the British, they will do all they can to destroy the movement, even if it means turning on their own family members and friends. We must mobilize and use physical force quickly or all the sacrifices of our martyrs and those interned after the Rising will be for naught."

Griffith rose from his seat and started to pace behind Collins. "Ah, good friend. Mick, I know you suffered greatly witnessing those whom you led that week die before ye, and those they followed executed without justice afterwards. I see that yer time of internment in Frongoch has never cooled yer passions. I merely want ye and de Valera to stick to the compromise we agreed to last October at Ard Fhies[5] whereby we strive for a republic first and, then, let the Irish people decide if they want that or a monarchy."

"I say 'nay' again," Collins snorted. "Ye're going to need more than just sympathy with all so-called patriots to convince me that you truly understand the battle ground ahead. I warned you and de Valera; my lads have clear evidence of the pending arrest of us Sinn Féin MPs by the Black and Tans before we win our Parliamentary seats and create our own first Dáil. You should go underground tonight, the sooner the better." Collins' exasperation began to show as he rose and turned toward BB.

"I thank ye, Mrs. McCormick, for yer fine grace and hospitality tonight. I am grateful that at least someone in this room has taken my advice as ye did in wearing the Red Cross arm band that safely let ye leave the Post Office clinic that fateful night. As a result, ye have brought great joy to yer family and a new weein into our nation's future. Both are victories."

He turned to Liam.

"I'll take my leave, Liam. Ye know where I am bound, and I will expect ye there next Monday night. Arthur, unless ye heed my warning, I won't be seeing ye for a time. Know I will be making every effort to carry on our movement in your absence. And, if ye're lucky, I may weave a miracle and rescue ye and de Valera on the other side of the channel. Take that message to him."

Arthur looked shocked and, then, amused. As he heard the kitchen door close behind Michael Collins, Arthur Griffith rose and turned to Liam.

"In all my days, I have never met such an arrogant man whom I have loved and admired so much," said Arthur.

Rachel and Ian, who had secretly been sitting upon the landing above the staircase, listening to the leaders, began to quietly debate what that meant.

Part IV: May 1918–December 1921   11

Chapter 3

To Act Justly—May 5, 1918

The four Smiley family members walked briskly along Belfast's University Street on their way from Stranmillis.

Kat's right hand was neatly tucked around husband Eamon's left elbow, her left hand clasping the Sunday liturgical bulletin of Fitzroy Avenue Presbyterian Church. Eamon was tightly holding the hand of rambunctious, four-year-old Neil, who was trying to race ahead rather than maintain the measured steps of his parents. After all, his five-year-old brother Devin, whom Neil aspired to match in spirit and form, had charged ahead of the family, independent and free.

"Hold on, Neil," Eamon cautioned. "Yer legs aren't quite as long as yer brother's. Wait until we reach the green in Botanic Gardens. There ye can run after him as fast as ye want and are able." Neil puckered up his lower lip but refrained from any verbal complaint, abiding by his mother's next words.

"Ye must conserve your energy for the sport ahead, Neil. Remember last night when we were reading *Peter Pan* In Kensington Gardens? Ye're a boy, not a bird that can fly," Kat cautioned her precocious second son, whom she knew was sensitive yet determined, well beyond his years. Kat mused that Neil was certainly Eamon's son, given his curiosity and intuition, and just as his name denoted, he was always somewhere in the clouds observing all below him.

"Mama, I know I can fly. When we get to the park, I'll show ye." Neil pouted, turning his face toward his brother's back, and still pulling on his father's hand to speed up the elder's pace.

Kat noted that she also saw Eamon's stubbornness in Neil, thinking to herself, "He'll be a lawyer or diplomat, no doubt, resolved to convince any adversary of his views. I pity the recipient of his perseverance and imagination."

The threesome followed Devin and turned north, then left into the garden just beyond Queen's College. It had been two years since Eamon had been confronted by Patrick McCann sitting next to Kat's mother Lizzie and claiming he had seen Robbie Smiley's ghost. Today, as usual, the family would avoid that exact spot and, instead, venture to the verdant lawn in front of the Palm House.

Upon arriving, Eamon released his son's hand. Neil raced to Devin, already engaged in an impromptu rugby match with several boys a good tad older than he. Eamon and Kat sat on a bench abutting the improvised playing field. They had much to discuss after the morning's sermon and yesterday's visit from Michael Collins.

"What are ye thinking, my darlin'?" asked Kat, as she straightened out the shin-length skirt of her navy, Sunday walking suit. Her fingers twisted the section of her grandmother Bella's long streamed, pearl necklace that rested upon Kat's heart. She remembered what Dr. Chadwick at Craigmaddie Hospital and her mother Lizzie had advised about asking Eamon first about his thoughts before asking about his feelings. War memories still haunted him at night, but less frequently since he had recovered not only his place in the family but his position at Queen's College in the philosophy department.

Eamon looked out at their sons. "We must do as Michael asked us, Kat. This morning's sermon confirmed that for me, although Reverend Colguhoun surprised me in being so adamant about justice for a united Ireland. I fear many of his congregants will not be happy with his guidance."

"Aye," Kat mused. "There was no hidden message in that reading from Micah today upon which the Reverend based his sermon. She unfolded the bulletin and read,

> "What does the Lord require of you?
> To act justly, to love mercy and
> Walk humbly with your God."

Part IV: May 1918–December 1921

Eamon nodded. "Indeed. And Michael's request is the same, although he may not know that. We must act justly, love mercy, and walk humbly."

Kat again tucked her arm around Eamon's elbow and nested his hand in hers. She placed the palm of her other hand on top of the two joined together, anchoring her own roiling emotions rapidly skipping upon froth-capped waves of doubt.

"Our Belfast community is torn apart among the three adversaries: Unionists, Republicans, and Nationalists. We cannot ignore the influence of additional allegiances—Catholic and Protestant, rich and poor, male and female. In my Irish Women's Franchise League meeting last week, the chair read a message from Hanna Sheehy-Skeffington[6] herself from Dublin. She asked us to recruit women of age thirty and over who can now vote and support Sinn Féin in this December's election. I will enlist those women on the tasks Michael gave us. For certain, they have influence over the men in their lives."

Eamon laughed quietly, as was his way when witnessing Kat's excitement as she quickly made decisions. He raised her hand to his mouth for a gentle kiss. "Ach, and if those lassies are anything like you, my dearest love, their lads will soon follow."

The two fell silent, watching the immediate future of their sons play out figuratively before them. The ad hoc rugby match had found its purpose within the circular huddles of boys, shoulder to shoulder moving furiously around a beleaguered ball.

Eamon broke their thoughts with his characteristically, figurative wordage. "The next year will tell if, like our sons there, we too are coursing across a land pushing against each other over an oblong, brown leather ball or forming a national huddle that, arm in arm, wins a common victory. Like you, I must find my place in that huddle."

He turned toward her and, uncharacteristically, said, "Here is what I feel." Eamon quickly told Kat his response to Michael's request. He would cautiously assess the opinions of his fellow faculty members and students as they considered candidates for the upcoming elections. He would collect the names of those who supported Sinn Féin or were against the Home Rule amendment separating Ulster from the south. Those names he would pass on to Michael when he returned to Belfast in June. In addition, Eamon would join the Ulster Sinn Féin unit and attend protests opposing the Irish Conscription Act.

"It is time I did what the Lord requires, Kat. But I fear it will jeopardize our family's safety if the elections favor a separation from the south." Kat felt his arm tense.

As she comfortingly patted it, she said, "We will deal with that possibility if it arises. For now, we have each decided our next plays on the field and will act on them." Neither had to approve of the other's.

And with that, a cheer arose from their sons and playmates—a goal had been made. Eamon and Kat joined in the applause. Silently though, each prayed more cheers would arise in their future.

PART IV: MAY 1918–DECEMBER 1921

CHAPTER 4

Zoot Monday—May 20, 1918

"Zoot! Zoot! Zoot!" exclaimed Billie, throwing down the message handed to him by Erin McCann. "How can this be?"

"Ach, Master Irvine. You know how it can be," responded Erin, sitting himself down in the worn-cushioned, straight-back chair before Billie's desk. His faculty office at St. Enda's was the size of a double lean-to, like a stall in a Saturday farmer's market. Rather than potatoes and cabbage covering the wooden planks of a seller's cart, however, four distinct literary piles were on Billie's desk: student papers, journals, newspapers, and hardcover books. Erin took the most recent edition of the Republican *Nationality* journal from the second pile, opening it to page four and stretching his crippled leg out to the right of the desk.

"Aha. I see—and now hear—you still use that baffling expression 'zoot'! Will ye ever tell your students, or alumni, from whence it comes?" asked Erin, always the thespian.

"When you tell me you have read *Othello*, I will perhaps give you a clue. For now, dear Erin, we have more important sources of words to consider. Why in God's name did de Valera and Griffith not heed Collins' warning of the arrests?"

Billie stood up from behind his desk and started to pace between it and the stained glass window beside him, its colors dulled by the greyness of a rainy day outside.

Billie continued, "The leadership of our movement has now been sorely diminished. De Valera, Griffith, Cosgrove, Plunkett, the Countess, Clarke's widow Kathleen—all ensconced in God knows which prison. How I pity Michael left behind as both Sinn Féin's only executive and the commander of the Irish Volunteers. Tell me more about what ye are hearing from him."

Erin became uncharacteristically pensive. His belief in the rebellion had grown much since the death of his brother Patrick. Every time he visited the McCormicks and saw Rachel, he felt such a sweep of regret and grief, quickly tempered by an impassioned determination. Could he ever match his own brother's sacrifice? Would he, Erin, give his life for another in the struggle? He thought so, but feared his proclivity was to play a role, not actually perform it in the real world. Still, he had succeeded well enough in the art of camouflage to benefit the movement and move quickly, during the year of the Rising, into the center ring of the IRB leadership to serve in disguise as his mentor Pádraig's eyes and ears.

Despite Erin's inability to save Pádraig's life from the execution squad, he had increased his value as both a storyteller and committed rebel while interned from 1916 to '17 in Frongoch prison. Billie had heard about Erin's memorable recitation given across the inmates' cells on one cold night. In his deep-throated brogue, drawing out every lilting tone, he recited "The Combat of Ferdiad and Cuchulain" from *The Táin*, or *The Cattle Raid of Cooley*. His fellow inmates had wept at Erin's telling, for it described the last minutes of the mighty leader Cuchulain, regretting his inevitable death by his childhood friend, now adult opponent, Ferdiad. The prisoners knew it portrayed the same fate as Pádraig's and the conflicts that would soon set Irish men and women against each other. Billie now thought of those lines, spoken by Cuchulain:

> "We were heart-companions once;
> We were comrades in the woods;
> We were men that shared a bed,
> When we slept the heavy sleep,
> After hard and weary fights.
> Into many lands, so strange,
> Side by side we sallied forth,
> And we ranged the woodlands through,
> When with Scathach we learned arms!"

Part IV: May 1918–December 1921

In one of those Frongoch cells was Michael Collins, who had not wept hearing Erin that night, but rather knew this young man and his message were critical to the future of independence. As had Pádraig Pearse, Michael Collins placed Erin, upon their release, close at hand within the Sinn Féin inner circle. He was a trusted spokesman.

Thus, Erin shared with Billie this day the intent behind Michael's message. "Ye know that Michael will do all he can to keep the momentum going for Sinn Féin in order that it win as many seats as possible in the upcoming December elections. Griffith and de Valera will run for office from their prison cells and you must run from Rathmines, but only if you leave Redmond's Irish Parliamentary Party and join our party. The IPP will die if it doesn't support a Republic of Ireland, not a divided one. We need every seat to secure Home Rule and establish a Dáil Éireann in Dublin, devoid of London control. Ye know Redmond won't support that. Are ye with us or against us?"

Billie turned his back on Erin and gazed out the single, clear pane in the stained glass window before him, the result of a rock thrown at St. Enda's by local constabularies during the Rising. His loyalties had always been with his father Will and the IPP. But since Will's death in 1917, Billie had rethought his positions.

He had been livid at Agnes for disobeying him that Easter week of the conflict. He thought she had endangered the stability of the entire family—he, Thon, Jon, and Rachel—by her priority of country over family. The two elders had had their first vociferous argument after the burial of Patrick McCann, resulting in a compromise: Rachel had to move to the home of BB if Agnes were to continue her IRB work with the Countess Markievicz. Billie could not tolerate two passionate females at his dinner table proposing "revolutionary" ideas. Nor did he feel he could protect both at the same time when the inevitable events coming would turn neighbor against neighbor. There had been a silent truce between the two elders as their love for each other rivaled their love of the cause. Billie knew the truce would have to be renegotiated.

"I will consider Michael's wish," Billie finally said, turning toward Erin. Erin rose. The two faced each other, eyes matched in intensity. Suddenly, bright sunshine streamed through the stained glass, illuminating brilliant greens and oranges, blues and yellows. From the single, clear glass pane, a stream of light crossed the desk.

"Zoot!" exclaimed Erin. "Look at who's with us today." The light's beam had landed on a book, Pádraig Pearse's play, *The Master*. "Perhaps it is a sign from him telling ye to believe in what God has set out for us."

Erin turned toward the door, but not before the curtain closed on his last word and action. He threw a copy of the *Sinn Féin* newspaper back onto Billie's desk, as he said, "Here, better yet, read Griffith's essay on page four, and let it make your decision."

Part IV: May 1918–December 1921

Chapter 5

Outside Insight—October 19, 1918

Lizzie had always loved the Linen Hall Library. She admired its stately entrance on Donegall Square North across from Belfast City Hall. Equally, she felt its grandeur every time she ascended the narrow, marble staircase that invited the public to leave the hectic street below and enter a hushed second floor. That space greeted every person, regardless of means, to shelves of tightly packed books dating back to 1788. Over a century later, the scent and sense of antiquity and gravitas still lingered in the air, inviting all to savor its original and current mission: The Belfast Society for Promoting Knowledge.

All of these visual and mental enticements Lizzie had cherished over her seven decades when, regardless of the year or book in hand, she would take her favorite seat near the north wall below a beveled window. As a young child, her father had led her by hand every Sunday afternoon up the worn steps. She would sit next to him as he conducted research into early Irish history and that of Ulster and the Catholic faith. Occasionally, after Lizzie would peruse the picture books of mythological characters, he would place her on his lap and read to her in his quiet, bass-timbre whisper. He would always ask her to repeat the three or four syllable words he encouraged her to memorize. In her early teens, as a student at St. Patrick's under the tutelage of Sister Bridgette McCann, Lizzie would return again on weekends to this sanctuary of thought to study various scientific and medical journals. They, plus her devoted advocates, convinced her that she had the mind and heart to become one of the first women doctors in Ireland.

Familial encouragement and her own confidence, plus her father's sense of history and justice, had also led her to become an unpretentious, yet sought-after, leader. Many women from all backgrounds in Ireland—religious, economic, medical, feminist—regarded her as their model. Her writings in Griffith's formerly titled *United Irishman* newspaper, now renamed *Sinn Féin*, shared not only news about the women's suffragette movement, but essays about the independence and peace movements. Today, however, Lizzie saw her most critical role more personally. She would be the elder teacher of the youngest generation of Smileys, Irvines, and through the marriage of her daughter BB to Liam, the McCormicks as well. She would focus this morning on the precocious, twelve-year-old Rachel McCormick.

The main hall of the library was uncharacteristically abuzz with the voices and actions of over forty women and young girls, members of various organizations such as the Irish Women's Franchise League, the National Aid and Volunteers Dependants' Fund, Sinn Féin's League of Women Candidates and its Cumann na mBan. After the February 6 passage of the Representation of the People Act 1918, in which women thirty years of age and over were granted the right to vote, their presence in public protests exploded.

On this Saturday, the Linen Hall contingent was preparing for a massive march supporting women candidates against the Conscription Act. In addition, some women were present to protest the fact that the People Act 1918 had been tempered by another act—the Parliament (Qualification of Women) Act. It restricted voting privileges only to women who owned property or had university degrees.

Lizzie and Rachel were writing protest signs on a table by Lizzie's favorite window in the area she now called her "outside insight" corner. Rachel was asking Lizzie what she meant by those words when the two were interrupted by the loud voice of a woman approaching them. It was Christine O'Leary.

"Ach, I see ye're still promoting peace within the movement, Dr. Irvine." Christine's voice had lowered and hardened after two decades of choosing the arms of revolution over those of a beloved partner or children. Lizzie and BB had felt sorry for Christine in 1916 after

Part IV: May 1918–December 1921

her rejection of Patrick McCann's proposal to escape from the movement's violent ways. However, learning later that Christine belittled Patrick's heroic death, the two Irvines had replaced their sorrow with a determination that she be shunned by the family. Christine was too wedded to violence as the sole independence tactic, and Rachel needed to be protected from any false revision of Patrick's sacrifice.

"Aye, ye are correct in that, Christine," responded Lizzie, placing her arm around Rachel's shoulder and drawing her near.

"And who is this young lass?" Christine queried. "She has a familiar look with those red curls and rosy cheeks."

"I'm Rachel McCormick. And who are ye?"

Christine halted for a spark of a second, then, quickly regained the aim of her verbal weapon.

"I'm Christine O'Leary. Haven't you grown, little Rachel? The last time I saw ye was at St. Stephen's Green during the Rising. Ye were with your Auntie Agnes and that crazy boy and dog."

Rachel frowned and turned her face up to Lizzie. A moment of silence permeated the visceral triangle of emotions.

Lizzie's arm slipped off Rachel's shoulder. The elder matron stepped toward Christine, but Rachel was too fast for Lizzie to restrain the youth.

Rachel advanced before Lizzie and confronted Christine. "I remember ye, now. Ye were Master McCann's woman, weren't ye?"

Christine leaned back from Rachel's confrontive stance and query.

Then, regaining her stature, Christine spoke with a veiled generosity. "Ach, child, that's nothing ye should think about. I see ye have a spirit we need in the movement. Perhaps I'll recruit ye for a new group of Cumann na mBan girls I'm forming. Here's my calling card. Join me tomorrow afternoon at the Palm House of the Botanic Gardens. Bring a picnic lunch. Ye'll learn much and have a jolly time."

Christine handed the card to Rachel and swiftly turned away. There was no acknowledgment of Lizzie.

Rachel watched the back of Christine disappear into the crowd of women, now growing in number and voice. Lizzie moved up next to Rachel and, again, put her arm around the girl's shoulder.

"I don't like that woman, Nanna Lizzie," Rachel stated. "There is something about her that gives me chills." Raising her hand up to Lizzie's, Rachel tightly clasped Lizzie's index finger.

Lizzie swiveled Rachel around to face her directly. "Aye, dear Rachel. I fear, yet am glad, ye are so perceptive. Ye asked what 'outside insight' means? Ye have just experienced it. Ye can learn just so much from books, journals, and newspapers about facts. But truth is always found from taking the knowledge those paper sources give your mind and letting it be nurtured within your heart. I fear Miss O'Leary has lost the connection between the two. Ye must never let that happen, dear Rachel. After ye consider all that's outside ye—the facts, the opinions, the arguments—when yer heart cleanses them with a bath of justice and compassion, follow its insight. Our family has learned that, and ye're part of us now."

Lizzie placed a kiss on Rachel's forehead. Rachel tore up the calling card.

Holding each other's hand, the two returned to their placards.

PART IV: MAY 1918–DECEMBER 1921

CHAPTER 6

Coalisland Tale—December 7, 1918

"Liam Macanisius McCormick! What were ye thinkin'? I . . . I . . . I . . . just don't understand ye!" sputtered an exasperated BB. "Hasn't the boy endured enough in his short life? Ye treat him like the man he has yet to become. He's just a youth who needs to study, play, and enjoy the gift of life instead of what ye have just put him through." BB took a breath and was about to continue her tirade when Liam pulled her toward him. Instead of raising her fists in frustrated emotion, she started to weep.

"Ach, BB dear. Yer heart and fear are overwhelming your ears and mind tonight. Let those tears flow, instead, in gratefulness that we are home safe with ye. I'll tell ye the details of what happened to calm ye." Liam led BB to the edge of their single-mattressed, alcove bed, tucked into the back corner of their narrow, second floor "two-up" bedroom. They sat hip to hip, he steady and she shaking between sobs.

Since the 1916 Rising, he had seen her act this way only twice—that Saturday evening at the end of the Rising when he had come safely home with Ian and Bigger in hand; next, the evening of her father Will's wake. Liam knew that any loss ignited her memories of too many deaths—familial and familiar, innocent and evil, preventable and destined. She had seen too much in the war, the Rising, and now in the clinic of the National Aid and Volunteers Dependants' Fund. Usually, she was able to tame her emotions; but recently, he noticed her nursing and religious practices could no longer comfort her about the inevitability of death or its redemptive afterlife in Heaven. Liam sensed that, with the birth of their own weein, BB felt her life now slowly diminishing with the passing of any living creature. Thank goodness, he reasoned, that their ward Ian and scruffy

Bigger were sleeping safely in the adjacent room and that Maggie was such a sound sleeper in her basket next to the bed. Rachel, too, was asleep.

But reason was not useful in what he would now tell BB. Liam had to convince and comfort his life partner in ways he was constantly learning and refining. Tonight, he needed first to relate to BB the purpose of his Sinn Féin assignment in Coalisland and why he had decided to take Ian and Bigger with him. Then, he would embrace her and listen to her heart, not telling her any of the danger they experienced. Perhaps tonight, he could temporarily ease her fear and angst before both would reoccur during their next struggles for independence.

He began his tale.

"I could not tell ye, dearest, that Mick, while on the run, had visited me here last Thursday night. He asked me to travel to Coalisland to assess the presence of the Black and Tan battalion and their Auxiliaries, the Brits' special forces. Mick also needed to deliver a command to our newly formed Irish Republican Army—the IRA Volunteers. With only a few days left before the parliamentary elections, he wanted to be sure that Sinn Féin could secure as many seats as possible in the County Tyrone region. If any candidates or supporters were intimidated by the Brits or local constabularies, there could be a worrisome setback to the movement. Our people need to know Mick's Flying Columns are there to address any barriers, be they verbal threats or physical attacks."

Liam continued, hearing BB's sobs diminish. "We both know that Ian misses his Coalisland pals. After all, he's gone back only once to get Morna and that was more than a year ago. I thought it would give him a chance to return safely if he traveled with me."

Liam was not going to add that he and Mick had actually planned for the boy and dog to accompany Liam as a good cover. Nor was he going to share that the young man Ian himself had suggested this ruse after he had overheard the kitchen conversation between Collins and Liam.

Part IV: May 1918–December 1921

"Ye're a good man," Mick Colllins had said to Ian, after Ian had approached the two with his plan. At age fifteen, Ian did, indeed, consider himself a man and was anxious to display it as a newly recruited member of Sinn Féin's IRA brigades. Neither Liam nor Ian had told BB about that. Such news could wait.

"We arrived in good time at the McLoughlin farmhouse in Coalisland. The sun was just setting and the cows were venturing down the back shed's pathway. You should have seen the grin on Bigger's face and the frowns on those cows as he nipped their heels. Ye would have thought he was their shepherd, herding them home. I truly believe that imp is much happier on country lanes than on paved streets."

BB turned to Liam. "Don't ye distract me from yer tale, Master McCormick. Much as I love the antics of our pal, talking about a dog will not lessen my questions or concerns about mankind. Keep talkin' about people, now."

Liam was grateful BB used the word "concerns" rather than "anger" or "frustration." He knew he was succeeding in easing her angst. And her sobs had completely ceased. Now, the couple sat left knee to right upon the bed's edge. He continued his tale.

"Martha McLoughlin and her four girls set a grand meal for us and the other men who had come to learn about Mick's plans and share their reconnaissance. I reported his support, and, in return, they related the number of battalion members and types of arms employed by the Auxiliaries. We chatted long into the wee hours of the morn'. At dawn, Ian and I gathered Bigger up and began our march home, none the weary. Ye'll be proud of Ian as, on our way back, he recited a sack load of poems written by Pearse and told me of a new play written by, believe it or not, Erin McCann. We must go and see it when it's performed at St. Enda's College."

BB knew her husband all too well, particularly when he was making light of serious events and taking a divergent path from the truth. He was the master of extemporaneous avoidance.

"Is there anything more ye're not telling me?" asked BB, looking him directly eye to eye.

"Nay, my love. Nothing ye need worry about," he replied.

And with that, the two embraced and relived their marital night.

Of course, there was much more Liam did not share about which BB would worry. He and Ian had pledged not to tell BB nor Rachel how the British military vans that trundled down the McLoughlin's row became stuck in cow's manure on the rutted path, how the soldiers' boots had slid on the square slates leading up to the house and exacerbated their fierce shouting and pounding at the front door. Fortunately, these natural barriers had given Liam, Ian, the McLoughlin men, plus their Sinn Féin supporters, enough time to escape out the back door into the woods behind the shed.

The McLoughlin women also had time to hide the meal's uneaten remains and cutlery in wooden cupboards beside the dining table. The only remaining male, Bigger, barked ferociously at the intruding soldiers. One attempted to kick the canine protector but fell back onto his rear when his muddied boot gave way under him. The McLoughlin girls began to laugh at the plight of the soldier, but his sneers cut them up short. Mother McLoughlin quickly went to the cupboard and offered the shamed soldier and his frustrated peers what she claimed were stored delicacies. Within a half-hour, the foiled battalion members, their trucks, and the danger had departed.

The McLoughlin men, Liam, and Ian returned safely to the house. Before leaving the next morning, they had determined who had betrayed them to the Brits and what would follow.

Only then, with Bigger in tow, was Liam's version of the tale created.

PART IV: MAY 1918–DECEMBER 1921

CHAPTER 7

Eve's Revenge—December 18, 1918

Two weeks later, Liam and Ian traveled back to Coalisland without telling BB of their true mission. The excuse they used—which actually wasn't an excuse after all—was that Ian and Morna's Great-aunt Eve had passed away the month before, and they needed to attend to her last wish. On the night before her demise, she had demanded that her husband Angus postpone any celebratory gathering after her wake and funeral to the Wednesday night of December 18, election day.

"I'll leave this earth as I came in—fightin' to raise the Irish flag, to farm me fields as I like, and prayin' for banshees to plague those who don't support either. What better day to send me out than the 18th when, even if I won't be there to vote for the first time as a lass, I'll still be fightin' from beyond the veil."

Great-uncle McNulty had never refused a wish—let alone a demand—from his life partner of sixty-five years. Family and friends weren't sure if Angus' acquiescence was from devotion or fear or both. On this election day, after a few pints, he now confessed to Liam and young Ian that he had obeyed this last demand out of fear. He didn't want Eve returning in death with fuller force than she had exhibited in life. "She was a mighty lass, that Eve. I hope the Lord above knows the handful he has to deal with at those Pearly Gates. He better not deny her entrance!"

At the Hawk Tavern, during the lull between gentrified citizens lunching and hard laborers drinking their respite, Liam, Ian, and Angus McNulty sat at a corner table. Just off the circle of Coalisland's main juncture of three dirt roads, the tavern served as a focal point for Coalisland news—gossip and truth often combined to make up the mythology of the town as a covert capitol of Irish rebellion. The

McNulty family had owned this bastion of whiskey and beer, leading to rebellious whims and bravado, for over three centuries. The pub had born witness to many a celebration of births and deaths as well as surreptitious plans for Irish justice. Tonight, Eve's celebration would host another tribute to the family's longevity and its gift of guise.

"I hear, thank God, ye've come on behalf of Mick." The elder McNulty spoke in the somber, drawn-out lilt of an octogenarian-plus-five. His voice had been tired by the peat-field labor of his childhood, followed by years in the musty Coalisland B&T coal mines of his youth and adulthood. Though it had been more than twenty years since he left the mines at age sixty, his voice nonetheless belied a local doctor's prognosis of imminent death from lung disease. Angus reigned as the town's spokesperson and soothsayer, reporting daily from his perch in the Hawk while watching Eve manage the tavern with their four sons and two of their six grandsons.

Tonight, Angus knew this gathering would serve as more than just a celebration of Eve's life. It would bring justice to the recent death of two boys, betrayed by the same rogue who had alerted the Brits and local constabulary of the recent meeting at the McLoughlin's farmhouse. Only a week after that foiled reconnaissance, the two McNulty grandsons, as members of the IRA's Flying Column, had been taken from their beds and shot.

"Ach, tell me ye're here to set things right," McNulty scowled as his right hand tightly clutched a worn, woolen tam while his left lifted the pint in front of him. He took a full swig, glaring at the two messengers before him. He didn't bother to brush the liquid foam from his wizened beard as he growled, "Their das are ready for whatever instructions ye give them, Liam McCormick. And, if ye haven't the ones I want, I'll take the task into me own hands."

"Now, Angus," cautioned Liam, "there's no need for ye to worry about what will happen here tonight. All will transpire as ye know Mick wants. I beg ye to trust me and young Ian to do right by your

Part IV: May 1918–December 1921

grandlads and by justice. Ye just need to keep the crowd focused on yer dear Eve, with stories about her going strong and long. I hear ye've gotten the McLoughlin lassies to sing Eve's favorite songs, and McGregor is playing his fiddle with them. That's a grand plan. And, young Ian here will read a letter from the Countess Markievicz herself in Eve's honor. Mick wants ye to know the Countess wrote it right from her prison cell in Holloway. Rest assured, all those goin' ons will let us find the Judas."

Liam paused, hoping he had calmed the old man's agitation. Mick had warned McCormick about McNulty's notorious reputation over seven of his past eight-and-a-half decades for taking matters into his own hands. Often, he disobeyed a planned operation agreed upon by the movement's leaders and went out on his own. Both McNulty and Eve were unfettered rebels, Mick had told him—never willing to listen to distant, nor local, leaders. Tonight's plans must not go astray, Mick had stressed, because of an impassioned and reckless action by the widower or his sons.

McNulty nodded and turned his eyes to the tavern's door which, past the afternoon lull, now opened to several men coming from their work at the mine and ready to drink.

"Aye, laddies," called out Angus. "Come and sit with me awhile before we start the laughs and tears." Liam and Ian stood up and, like dismissed school boys, left the headmaster's presence.

Three hours later, after the men from the mine had been joined by their wives, their children, their mothers' mothers, and grans accompanied by the remaining Coalisland elders, there was little room in the tavern for anyone to raise an arm, let alone stomp a foot in rhythm to the music. Small tables had been arranged throughout the pub's open space with multiple chairs around and between them. These, plus the benches that abutted the walls, found family and friends closer to each other than during a Sunday mass.

In front of them all, on a makeshift platform next to the bar, stood three of the McLoughlin girls accompanied by the renown fiddler, Andy McGregor. He was tapping his feet and burning his bow to the girls' harmonic rendition of the song "Kate O'Brien," in which the girls had changed the title name to Eve McNulty: ". . . not a jewel that money can buy . . . a warm-hearted creature . . . her name was Eve McNulty, my bright-eyed Colleen."

When they finished, there wasn't a dry eye in the gathering, except for one. Liam, the McNulty sons, and Angus knew who it was. Slowly, the four began to move toward the man standing near the entrance door, face smug and arm slowly moving toward his pants pocket.

Fiddler McGregor noted the movements and quickly invited the gathering to sing Thomas Moore's poignant song "I Mourn the Hopes." The room began to reverberate with the community's chorale praise of spirits gone, present and yet to come.

"I'd mourn the hopes that leave me,
If thy smiles had left me too;
I'd weep when friends deceive me,
If thou wert, like them, untrue.
But while I've thee before me,
With heart so warm and eyes so bright,
No clouds can linger o'er me,
That smile turns them all to light."

Before the four reached the man, he clutched his chest, stumbled and fell to the floor, face ashen and mouth gasping for air. No cry was heard from him as the crowd, ignoring his plight, continued to bellow out the remaining lines of the song. They knew Eve had joined them.

"'Tis not in fate to harm me,
While fate leaves thy love to me:
'Tis not in joy to charm me,
Unless joy be shared with thee.

Part IV: May 1918–December 1921

> One minute's dream about thee
> Were worth a long, an endless year
> Of waking bliss without thee,
> My own love, my only dear!
> And though the hope be gone, love,
> That long sparkled o'er our way,
> Oh! We shall journey on, love,
> More safely, without its ray.
> Far better lights shall win me,
> Along the path I've yet to roam—
> The mind that burns within me,
> And pure smiles from thee at home."

Angus nodded his head toward Liam as he and the two fathers of the murdered sons lifted the body and took it out the entrance. Not one other person looked in their direction. They knew what had happened.

Eve had, indeed, returned—in, as Angus had predicted, fuller force than in life. Defying the physical world, the rebellious fighter had taken the life of the betrayer. Eve could now follow Heaven's light.

As the Coalisland mortals finished their song, they heard her avenged voice joining them in its final words.

> "Thus, when the lamp that lighted
> The traveler at first goes out,
> He feels awhile benighted,
> And looks round in fear and doubt.
> But soon, the prospect clearing,
> By cloudless starlight on he treads,
> And thinks no lamp so cheering
> As the light which Heaven sheds."

CHAPTER 8

Resurrection Evening—January 18, 1919

"Halt, who comes here!?" The first line of Erin's play resounded around the spacious Hall of the Innocent at St. Enda's school in Rathmines.

The main actor, playing the deceased Pádraig Pearse, was seated in a single chair at a small table, stage center. His head was bowed. His eyes were closed. He leaned into his hands that were placed around his ears. He was alone in his world, acknowledging the internal, yet sensing something external. Seven single chairs and single tables were positioned in a semicircle behind him. Individual characters, each seated with heads down and eyes closed, were illuminated by glowing kerosene lanterns, each placed at the center of his respective table.

The audience was silent like those on the stage, but heads were up and eyes open. They awaited the next phrase, pensively anticipating the play's message that would soon unfold before them.

Agnes and Billie, with Liam and BB, sat together in the third row of chairs, placed in arcs like those on the stage. Mother Lizzie sat next to Margaret Pearse in the front row. Toward the rear, camouflaged in clerical garb, sat Michael "Mick" Collins next to Father Sullivan, a priest from the nearby Mary Immaculate Refuge of Sinners. The semblance of a wake was in the musty air of this enclosed gathering on this frigid evening, warmed by candles, woolen shawls, and tweed jackets. Like a wake, emotions heated the minds and souls of the watchers.

In the previous month's general election for the House of Parliament, Griffith's Sinn Féin party had won an astonishing seventy-three seats, defeating John Redmond's Irish Parliamentary Party.

Part IV: May 1918–December 1921

The IPP had retained only six of its previous sixty-eight. Collins, de Valera, and Griffith had won seats, despite Collins being on the run and de Valera and Griffith residing in jail. The formation of an Irish Republic seemed more within reach than ever. Tonight, at this hour, the congregants and followers of Pearse awaited a sign from him. Perhaps, as the play's title insinuated—*Resurrection*. His or theirs, they would soon realize. Erin had intentionally written this play to convey that sign.

"Halt, who comes here!?" Pádraig repeated the question, now raising his head and opening his eyes, hands down from his ears to grip the sides of his table. In response, came the ethereal sound of a violin bow crossing its fourth string. The mellow note of low G filled the air. Then, behind the first character stage right, a woman's figure appeared, carrying a beveled kerosene lamp. She was draped in a shimmering white night-dress, tufts of curly gray hair circling her visage, the rest flowing over one shoulder in a knotted braid that reached to her waist. The violin faded into silence.

"It is I, Pádraig," the woman said, in the sing-song lilt of ancient Gaelic, mellow toned like a fine, honey-like whiskey.

Pádraig rose from the table. He approached the figure, while carrying his lamp. She raised hers. The beams of light now connected them—lamp to lamp, her to him.

"Who are you?" Pádraig challenged, his voice mixed with apprehension and curiosity.

"Ye need not know who I am, son. It matters more that you know the folks around ye. Come. Greet them." She took his lamp in one hand, balancing it with her own.

As the play continued, she led him to each seated character, one at a time. The violin repeated its resonant G seven times as he stood before each table, once before each soul. During the pregnant few minutes he stood before each, a head rose and eyes opened to focus directly on the increasingly astonished Pádraig. The violin ceased and began again six times, once for each soul except the last.

The first was Cuchalain, the mythological warrior hero. Pádraig bowed his head. The second was Wolfe Tone, revolutionary founder of the United Irishmen. Pádraig knelt. The third was the commander of the Rebellion of 1789, Henry Joy McCracken, whom Pádraig saluted. The next three were Thomas Clarke, John Plunkett, and James Connelly—all executed leaders of the recent 1916 Rising.

Pádraig attempted to embrace each, but each time the accompanying figure put a gentle hand on his shoulder to constrain his touch.

Pádraig knew them all, except for the two sitting at the seventh table. There, a mother was holding a tiny lass on her lap. Both appeared emaciated. He stared intently but did not recognize them. Neither raised her head nor opened her eyes to acknowledge him. No violin played.

"Who are these two pitiful souls?" Pádraig asked the figure.

"Ach, ye don't know them?" she questioned.

"Nay," replied Pádraig.

"They are the innocents who died in all of the uprisings over the last four hundred years. The mothers and children who will never see their kin. And yet, here they are with you tonight," she replied.

Pádraig lowered his head and began to weep quietly.

The figure glided to the front of the stage. She faced the audience and reached out her hands, still holding the two lamps. They illuminated her entire body.

She continued, "These departed ones are with us tonight. They have always been with us. They will always be with us. I, Morrigan, the ancient Phantom Queen, ask you: What will ye do to honor their names, known and unknown? Will ye save this suffering world as Christ did through his death and victorious Easter rising? Like He, will ye transform our struggle into a resurrection and the eternal life of freedom?"

Leaving one lamp now unlit at the edge of the stage, she turned away and walked toward the back of the stage. The violin played its resonant, single note.

Part IV: May 1918–December 1921

One by one, the characters took up their lamps, walked along their respective paths leading to the door behind them, and departed.

Going toward it as well, Pádraig turned to face the woman figure. She placed her remaining lamp on a mantel next to the door and leaned forward to cup his head in her hands. She kissed him on his forehead, then they left together. The stage went dark, except for the door, which remained open, illuminated by her remaining lamp.

There was silence in the hall. Then, one by one, each audience member rose and started to clap. A thunderous applause exploded. They had heard the play's message. They were prepared to resurrect the entire nation.

In just four days, they would know what Michael Collins already knew from his seat in the last row: the Irish representatives of Sinn Féin will refuse to sit in Westminster. Instead, they will form the first Dáil Éireann—the Assembly of Ireland—and, repeat Pádraig's words of April 24, 1916 from his Declaration of the Republic of Ireland.

This "resurrection" will begin the Irish War of Independence.

CHAPTER 9

The Hunter after the Mountain Cat—January 23, 1919

The afternoon, winter sky was as speckled gray and white as the coat of the Irvine's newly adopted Irish Wolfhound, Boru. Aged by years hunting large-game animals and retired from serving alongside the Irish Guards, he was at rest on the woolen, hooked rug before a blazing fireplace. The sky outside that resembled the aging canine's tumultuous history also reflected the ponderings of the man inside regarding his own. Billie Irvine was in turmoil.

"Ye took a grand stance," voiced Lizzie, preparing afternoon tea in the small salon of her son's home in Rathmines. "As a returning MP, you refused to go to Westminster, sitting instead two days ago in our new Dáil Éireann here in Dublin. That took courage, me son, and I am proud of ye." Lizzie handed him a cup of steaming, Irish black tea, as he paced back and forth before her. He refused it.

"Mother, ye have no understanding of what now lies ahead of us." Billie turned to face her, cheeks flushed with anger and frustration. "Like father, I was elected to represent the Irish Parliamentary Party, but it no longer has any mandate from the majority of Irish people. We only retained six seats of our former sixty-eight, and our leader John Dillon has lost his seat.

"And consider Sinn Féin. It won seventy-three seats. Despite never having contested in a parliamentary election before, it now reflects the decisive message of what our people want—a free, independent, and unified island of Ireland.

"What am I supposed to do representing a party that is even less popular than that of our nemesis Sir Edward Carson's[7] Irish Unionist Parliamentary Party? His is a party that pledged an Irish covenant that fosters arms against anyone—Protestant or Catholic—who supports independence from Great Britain. What must I stand for

Part IV: May 1918–December 1921

in this limbo between a united Republic of Ireland formed through defiance and, inevitably, physical force far more ardent than that of the Easter Rising, versus a divided Ireland formed through prejudice and counter-violence? What would father do?"

Billie turned away, shoulders bowed, and strode over to the beveled windows that stretched across the entire back wall of the salon. Looking out at the ominous clouds above him, he heard the rumble of thunder. Or was it the slow growl of Boru asleep at Lizzie's feet, dreaming perhaps about bounding across some French battlefield?

"Billie, come, sit ye down. Let me tell ye a story about yer grandfather, William Irvine." She placed his rejected teacup on the circular top of the tri-pedestal end table next to her armchair. Smoothing the lap of her black, silk skirt—worn almost daily since her husband Will's death six months before—she gently unfolded a beige, linen napkin, placed it upon her lap, and nestled her teacup upon its width.

Billie reluctantly returned to the sofa next to his mother's armchair. Ever since he was a child, he had been sensitive to the political debates among family and friends, particularly those members of the IRB, but, more so, to the heated emotions of his mother, sisters, and recently his wife, Agnes. There was something about his mother's voice, however—the mix of Scottish sing and Irish song—that best captured his perception of truth and, thus, calmed him. He needed both tonight.

Lizzie looked directly at her only son as he arranged the sofa's pillow behind his back, retrieved his teacup from the tabletop, and crossed his right leg upon his left.

"Let me take you back to the year 1847," she implored.

"Ye know that your grandfather William was a member of parliament like your da and ye. Ye may not know, though, that he was also a member of the Irish Confederation in 1847, formed by John Blake Dillon of Young Irelanders fame and father of your own friend John Dillon who just lost his seat and will, most probably, be the last leader of the IPP. John Blake didn't believe in violent insurrection, but when it came time to take a stand with the Young Irelanders, he changed his mind. Because of that, he had to flee from the British soldiers to America. Only when he gained amnesty in '55 was he able to return to Ireland and, again, represent us in London in '65.

"Your grandfather admired John Blake Dillon. He also loved what Dillon stood for—freedom from Great Britain through peaceful, political means. But, like Dillon, your grand knew that there comes a time when the belief in such a strategy by one side is mocked by the other and is seen as weak and senseless unless it physically stands up for that freedom and the ultimate peace to benefit the next generation. Your grand never told your grandmother Bella that he was on a mission for John Dillon the night her beloved died in '47 outside Macroom. Instead, the word came back to her from her brother—your late uncle Aiden—that William had died of typhoid after visiting the starving evicted. Decades later, she learned that, in truth, he had been shot by the plantation manager Dickson who suspected your grandfather of spying for Dillon.

"I tell ye this because there are choices ye need to make that require a unanimity between a man's mind and his natural instincts. Like the hunter after the mountain cat, or the mountain cat after the hare—there is a time in the pursuit of survival that begs one to cease worrying and to act, to set aside caution and fear, and instead, resolve to pursue a greater good.

"Your grandfather, like the hunter, did not want to condone, let alone participate in, violence. But he knew he had to for our independence. Like the mountain cat, he may not have wanted to cause harm to the hare but, for the sake of his family and pride, he had to. And God only knows whether your grandfather, or even God for that matter, ever considered what goes on in the mind of the mountain cat or the hare. All four—God, your grandfather, the cat, and the hare—must be hearing us chat tonight and wonder, in Heaven's name, what story is the old Dr. Lizzie weaving for that lad?"

Part IV: May 1918–December 1921

She laughed and saw Billie's lips form a half-moon grin. He chuckled, and then, became somber.

"Mum. I know ye mean to guide me with your tale of Grandfather Irvine. I hear ye and will take it into advisement. Perhaps it is time, as you say, that I cease pondering and start acting. For the sake of our family and our future, I promise I will consider what ye have shared."

Just as he said that, there was a rush of bodies racing through the front door and into the salon. Thon and Jon dropped their school bags and, one by one, embraced their gran and, then, their da. Agnes followed them.

"Ach, I bet ye two have been discussing the city, countryside, nation, and world. Are we all at peace now?" she asked, first kissing Lizzie on her forehead and, then Billie.

Billie laughed and reached up to grasp one of Agnes' hands.

"Ach, I think ye'll have to ask old Boru here," he said.

And, at that, the dog opened his eyes, raised up his head, perked up his ears, rose and stretched his long body. He vigorously wagged his graying tail, as if saying to himself, *Aye, we are.*

CHAPTER 10

The Ethics of a Just Life—January 25, 1919

The note read, *Ye better watch yer back, Dr. Smiley. A bullet there is just as good as a bullet in your chest.*

Eamon crumbled the note within his unsteady hand and continued toward the classroom auditorium of Lanyon Hall, Queen's College. When he was reinstated in 1916 as a professor within the philosophy department, he was still recuperating physically and mentally from the battlefields of France. Three years later, after many a therapeutic session on both his leg and his mind, plus the love of his dear wife Kat and her supportive family, he was at peace.

It was a peace of sorts, however, as he had chosen to join the newly formed Sinn Féin party and its military ally, the Irish Republican Army. Not that he wanted to participate in any overt attack, but rather, in the creation of its intelligence.

Having successfully identified key Ulster-based residents sympathetic to the Republican cause during the Easter Rising, he had been accepted as a critical resource for espionage activities. His ability to understand the makings of men's souls led him to propose ways and means to subvert those opponents acting in the Ulster Unionist Party and in the British Black and Tans brigades.

De Valera himself, before being recently arrested and imprisoned in Lincoln jail, had visited Eamon a number of times for his advice. The two men had similar intellectual prowess, but totally different egos. Having been raised in poverty by a loving, yet destitute mother, Eamon was grateful for her faith in him and the assistance others had offered. De Valera, also raised in poverty but abandoned by his mother, had credited his advancement solely on self-reliance. Eamon had no lust for praise; de Valera had more than enough for both.

Part IV: May 1918–December 1921

It was Michael Collins who had convinced Eamon to disregard his dislike of de Valera and join Collins' newly founded Invisible Army as an intelligence agent. Collins was particularly appreciative of Eamon's ability at Queen's College to garner information from opposing partisan faculty under the guise of being an academic.

As Eamon tucked the threatening note into his vest pocket, he was grateful that, in the back of this particular classroom, Mick would be seated. The two would meet afterwards.

The amphitheater was crowded with second-year students waiting to hear Eamon's lecture on *The Ethics of a Just Life,* a course designed by Eamon with considerable input from his mentor and Kat's uncle, Anthony Gallagher, now age seventy-four. It was Anthony, after all, who had recognized Eamon's acumen in that introductory philosophy class back in 1912. Uncle Anthony had also introduced Eamon to Kat. How Eamon's life had changed because of both. This afternoon, he knew it would change again.

"Let us contemplate the ethics of a just life through various lenses," began Eamon. "What are the lenses through which we may define such a life?"

Eamon placed his hands on the lectern to support the balance he still had to secure upon his damaged leg. He looked out at the seated students before him, approximately sixty fanning out and up the tiered rows. He knew them all, but nodded only at a new one leaning forward in the fourth row from the top. That "student" grinned back, clutching the lapels of his oversized academic robe that hid his rough—and typical IRA—clothing. Eamon could just make out Michael Collins' wink and boyish grin forming from cheek to cheek. Obviously, Mick could not wait to hear the students' answers. They would determine whom he could recruit as members of the IRA's Flying Columns.

"I say the lens most appropriate today is the political lens," spoke out a young man in the third row from the front.

"I say the lens is a cultural one," proclaimed another, seated in the second row.

"Nay," exclaimed a young woman poised directly in front of Collins. "It must be economic."

"Aha," said Eamon. "We have three lenses offered already. Let's hear from their spokesmen as to what rationale undergirds each."

Over the next hour, the respective spokesmen—including the woman, the other classmates, and Eamon—debated the value of each lens. Several other lenses—such as legal, religious, and genetic—were offered, often presented as variations or subsets of the original three. By the end of class, no one had convinced another of the sanctity of just one lens. Rather, there was a long list of "just life" characteristics under and, surprisingly, across each lens. Absolutely no consensus arose on the ethics that could prioritize one over the other.

"I see we must continue to discuss what determines a just life before we apply any precept of ethical guidance." Eamon paused. "Let us continue that study after you have examined your own lenses. For next week, I ask you to write a brief, yet succinct, two-page description of your lens and how it guides you to live a just life today. Think about six of the major philosophers you have already studied—Saint Thomas Aquinas, Aristotle, Descartes, Hume, Kant, and Emerson. Each primarily uses one of the lenses we have offered today, although sometimes embellished by variations. If you were to have a conversation with each man, with whom would you agree the most?"

There was a rustle in the class as many students readjusted their seated positions and papers. Some wrote down the assignment. Several just stared into the air. Eamon could see the division growing between activists and thinkers in the room. Mick saw it, too, quickly noting five whom he thought he could approach. He was particularly pleased that the young woman in front of him, who suggested the lens of economy, appeared to him to be part of the activist group. He also studied two thinkers.

Part IV: May 1918–December 1921

After all the students had left the auditorium, Eamon folded up his lecture notes and waited for Mick to descend the stairs to his right. When he reached the front of the hall, they first shook hands and, then, embraced.

"Ye look well, Dr. Smiley," posed Collins.

Eamon blushed and nodded his head. "Aye, I am. Thanks be to Kat, me boys, and colleagues like ye, Commander." Now, Collins blushed.

"That was quite a coming of minds," Collins continued. "How I wish I had been a student of yours decades ago."

"Ach," replied Eamon. "It is I who regrets not meeting you then and following your path, rather than the one I did."

"Nay, you chose the right path as now you are living the just life about which these students need to learn." Mick put his arm around Eamon's shoulder as they left the hall. They stopped under the darkened arch before the street at the back of the college courtyard.

"I thank ye for letting me come to hear your wisdom and to seek out new recruits. Let me quickly depart as one never knows who will recognize me and turn me in. A final question, though, through what lens do you think I now view a just life?"

Eamon smiled. "I'll await your paper next week." The two laughed and Collins, turned quietly away, clutching his academic robe around him to continue walking the streets as a student of the illustrious university.

Eamon took the threatening note out of his vest pocket. He had wanted to share it with Mick, but hesitated. Unlike the activists that Mick and others in the Invisible Army predominantly were, Eamon was still a consummate thinker. Perhaps, next week, he would share the note with Collins along with the students' papers. But tonight, he would share it only with the one activist he loved and trusted so dearly, his Kat.

CHAPTER 11

The Other Side—January 25, 1919

While Eamon's students were dispersing across the Belfast cityscape, a gathering of approximately one hundred fifty Irish was settling in for the evening—albeit one hundred thirty of them were dead and, thus, permanently settled. The Belfast City Cemetery was the perfect site for a meeting of twenty, living, unionist Ulster Volunteers, called forward this evening by one of its founders, Sir James Craig.[8]

The Protestant section of the cemetery, cordoned off from the Catholic and Jewish sections by sunken walls, offered a foolproof cover for political gatherings recently considered illegal by the British. With dusk falling and the moon in its first phase of darkness, Sir James Craig had chosen the place and time well. It had also helped that the contingent of men whom he would now lead in discussion had actually attended an afternoon internment of one of their own: a man from Coalisland who had been killed in the town's pub by members of Collins' Invisible Army a month before. Secret alternatives to meeting locations were the mainstay of tactical planning.

"Come lads, we must garner our thoughts and forge ahead," remarked Craig as he unlocked the wooden door of a mortuary chapel tucked behind the cemetery's central, winter garden of blackthorn bushes and furze. Symbolically, the spreading limbs of stately oaks, the Celtic tree of life and strength, protected the chapel's roof.

The twenty men followed Craig into the stone-floored sanctuary and took their seats on wooden pews facing a primitive altar. He stood before them, in hand a prayer book remaining from the afternoon service. As a long-time parliamentarian and military leader during the Boer War, he knew how to move both sedentary and mobile units. He began his secular preaching.

Part IV: May 1918–December 1921

"Despite our Ulster Covenant pledged seven years ago, we have not been as organized in our offensive activities as have our opponents. Yes, we have our Ulster Unionist Council, our Orange Lodges and the Covenant, but you know that the Catholics and Republicans are gaining ground every time one of our lads dies. Those traitors have escalated their actions with assaults and murders unlike any we have seen in years. What shall we do?" he implored his companions.

Craig was not an idle planner as such a question might presume when posed to those whom he was leading. Written upon his cerebral slate of counteroffensive tactics, he had his own ideas. But, as an experienced leader on either the battlefield or in parliament, he knew he could not lead men into policy-making and war unless they believed and trusted him with their minds and lives. Tonight, he would solicit their answers and, then, by garnering their agreement on future actions, secure their allegiance. Knowing his opposition—de Valera, Griffith, and Collins—Craig knew this War of Independence would be a battle to the death—the death of Irishmen and of a united Ireland. Loyalty was paramount.

"We can, at least, save our Ulster from becoming part of a Republic. Then, we can move on the South. Let's hear your ideas, boys."

He waited.

"I say we buy as many weapons as possible and attack any Catholics we see," shouted one man. The comment echoed off the stone walls.

"Let's burn down their houses so they have nowhere to live," exclaimed another. A collective "Aye!" came from the twenty.

"Arrest them, put them on transits, and boot them out of the country to Australia and America," sounded a third, a tussled-haired youth seated in the back of the chapel. Applause followed.

The growing passion in the sanctuary was palpable. Instead of saints being beckoned, banshees had taken their place.

"All of these are good ideas, my friends. But may I ask how we reach such admirable goals?" Craig started walking up and down the short nave between the parallel pews, turning in time with his steps to address each of the seated men. He wanted to connect with and ensure he honored each one.

For every suggestion, he asked a tactic. "How can we gain the funds to buy such weapons? How can we know which Catholics are truly against us? Not all are, you know. What might happen if we burn down the houses of those who feed our own families? Remember we need Catholic women and children in factories to make our linen and produce our whiskey. Who will do our labor if we boot them all out of the country?"

At that last remark, the accompanying men chuckled.

"'Tis true," remarked the man that had suggested the burning.

"Aye, that's not such a good idea," stated the second.

Men's heads started to nod in agreement.

"So, what must we do?" asked the youth seated in the last row of the chapel. His dark hair, hung down from under a worn, tweed tam and nearly covered his ears and eyes. A thick woolen scarf was tucked up around his neck as were his jacket lapels.

Craig stopped his pacing up the aisle and returned to the front of the church. He placed the prayer book on the first seat in the pew next to him, and smiled, and said, "Here's what we will do."

For the next hour, he described various actions: raising funds to purchase weapons from the Germans with whom the Ulster Volunteers were already in contact; training counter-espionage agents to infiltrate the Sinn Féin party and its mobilized Invisible Army; conducting planned or sporadic attacks on individuals living in Ulster and in the South. All who were known to be part of the Republican paramilitary, be they women or men, would become targets.

Once the men agreed to these, Craig picked up his prayer book and read from Psalm 52, Quid Gloriaris. "Here are God's words against our enemy and in support of us."

Part IV: May 1918 – December 1921

> "Why boastest though thyself, thou tyrant, that thou canst do mischief;
> Whereas the goodness of God endureth yet daily?
> Thy tongue imagineth wickedness, and with lies thou cuttest like a sharp razor.
> Thou hast loved unrighteousness more than goodness, and falsehood more than righteousness.
> Thou hast loved to speak all words that may do hurt, O thou false tongue.
> Therefore shall God destroy thee for ever; he shall take thee and pluck thee out of thy dwelling and root thee out of the land of the living.
> The righteous also shall see this, and fear, and shall laugh him to scorn;
> Lo, this is the man that took not God for his strength; but trusted unto the multitude of his riches, and strengthened himself in his wickedness.
> As for me, I am like the green olive-tree in the house of God; my trust is in the tender mercy of God for ever and ever.
> I will alway give thanks unto thee for that thou hast done; and I will hope in thy Name, for thy saints like it well."

He finished by adding, "Now, let us be righteous and root out the evil, the wicked enemy."

All men except one said, "Amen."

They proceeded out the chapel's door and dispersed along the crooked pathways of the cemetery.

Most went home, as did Craig, satisfied that they had a plan.

The long-haired youth was also satisfied, but he did not go home. Instead, he went directly to Michael Collins', Belfast-based safe house and reported what he had heard.

"Good work, me lad," said Mick to his newest recruit, Ian McNulty.

CHAPTER 12

The Women's Franchise Meeting—January 31, 1919

There was a buzz in the meeting hall, like that around a Langstroth beehive. Parallel rows of Unionist and Republican women were lined up such that the combs formed by numerous honeybees in attendance would not have to "rub wings." They would only have to decide the next actions as members of the Irish Women's Franchise League. Seated in one row was Cecil Craig, wife of Sir James, and adamant Unionist. Seated three rows behind Cecil were Lizzie and Kat.

"I cannot tolerate that woman," exclaimed Kat, nodding toward Mrs. Craig, known formally as Viscountess Craigavon. "She is like a queen bee ready to exploit her workers. Look at them swarming around her. Why is she here? It's impossible that she would support expanding the vote for Catholic women who are under thirty and don't own land."

"Ach, Kat, do not presume. Cecil," Lizzie continued, addressing Mrs. Craig by her first name rather than her nobility title of Viscountess nor her husband's last name, "is a wise politician, ready to infuse her Ulster Women's Unionist Council mission however she can into any other organization's efforts. For certain, you will hear her preach eloquently and convincingly, offering her nectar about the role women can play in saving the Irish family. She will insinuate, not state, that it doesn't matter their background or political belief.

"In actuality, however, it is all hypocrisy. Once she gets a recruit in her grasp, she'll force that woman to pledge allegiance to a Protestant Great Britain. If not, like the queen, Cecil will destroy the worker bee. I wouldn't trust anything she says tonight despite how much she touts the right of women voting. For her, they must vote only as the UWUC requires."

Part IV: May 1918–December 1921

As Lizzie finished this last word to Kat, Cecil rose to face the crowd. At age thirty-six, she personified stateliness, wrapped in a short fur jacket, long black skirt, and pheasant-plumed, velvet hat. The intricate lace around her neck began to vibrate with her voice.

"Ladies," she began in a posh English accent. "It is our duty to protect the Irish family by continuing to expand the voting privilege to which we are entitled. We must speak out on this mission and engage even those who do not agree with us. We must organize rallies, protests, and marches. Let us pledge tonight to go back to our homes, our neighborhoods, and our community organizations to do just that." She sat down with her back to the rows behind her.

Lizzie could see several women around her nod their heads. Others began to clap in agreement.

Both unnerved Lizzie. She started mentally to form her response. As the well-known wife of a former parliamentarian who had supported Home Rule through diplomacy and Redmond's Irish Parliamentary Party, she knew her words would have credence. She would have to parse them carefully, however, in order to expose the ulterior motives behind Cecil's words, but not alienate the women who might be aligned with the Republican cause. Lizzie also knew there were women members of the IRA's Invisible Army in attendance this night. Already, she had seen Christine O'Leary sitting toward the rear of the hall.

Lizzie rose from her seat. Most knew her through her fifty years within the various Belfast communities as a doctor, teacher, and mentor. She knew most of the women by their first names; she knew their families' illnesses—both physical and emotional—as well as the births and deaths of their loved ones, and their dreams. The buzzing faded away as the hive went silent.

"My friends," she began. "I greatly appreciate the words of our sister Cecil tonight. She has long been an advocate for women's responsibilities as mothers, wives, and protectors of our cherished island. It behooves us tonight to also consider our rights as women— the right for us to choose whatever role we believe can best support and protect our families. Like our men, we do have the right to choose our professions, our faiths, our loyalties. No one should require us to follow a path which we have not thoughtfully and morally considered. Each of us has the gift of a working brain, body, and conscience to learn from each other and, then, decide for ourselves how we must act. Don't you agree, Cecil?"

There was a gasp among the Loyalists who could never imagine addressing the Viscountess by her given name. Among the others, there was a quiet mummer of glee.

Cecil began to blush, or was it redden in growing anger? Throughout Lizzie's speech, Cecil had remained seated with her back to the woman behind her. Now, she rose again, turned, and faced Lizzie, saying, "It seems that the good lady here has a specific role for women that does not account for their partnership as wives with their husbands, nor daughters with their fathers. I would suggest that she discuss what she is proposing with her father or husband and reconsider the premise upon which womens' rights is founded. Yes, we have the right to our professions, faith, and loyalties, but what we choose must be done in cooperation with our men. After all, they are our sole guide for daily actions. Don't you agree, Dr. Irvine?"

Lizzie sighed, smiled, and spoke to the entire audience, turning around in a circle so to address everyone.

"Aye, ye are correct. We should listen to Him who is The Sole Guide for daily actions. As we pray every Sunday, be it at St. James or St. Mary's, we ask for guidance from Him, the One Writer of that guide, who teaches us love, compassion, and respect for all people. As a child, I particularly remember the sacred beatitudes He gave to Matthew. I hold those in my hand and heart tonight."

She raised a small prayer card up and read from it to the gathering.

"Blessed are the poor in spirit: for theirs is the kingdom of heaven.
Blessed are the meek: for they shall possess the land.

Part IV: May 1918–December 1921

> Blessed are they who mourn: for they shall be comforted.
> Blessed are they that hunger and thirst after justice: for they shall have their fill.
> Blessed are the merciful: for they shall obtain mercy.
> Blessed are the clean of heart: for they shall see God.
> Blessed are the peacemakers: for they shall be called the children of God.
> Blessed are they that suffer persecution for justice sake, for theirs is the kingdom of heaven."

Lizzie closed by saying, "I hope tonight you feel these words take precedence over whatever any of us espouse individually."

Cecil sat down, as did Lizzie. The room broke out in a loud applause. The meeting carried on with actions that followed the beatitudes when respecting the rights of women to expand their voting franchise. They all agreed to share those rights with whomever they felt would benefit, including their fathers, husbands, brothers, and sons.

Kat sat in awe of her mother throughout the rest of the meeting. While the daughter knew her mum was powerful, Kat had forgotten by how much. As they rose to leave the hall, Kat faced her mother and exclaimed, "Mum, I never knew you to be so religious."

Lizzie smiled. She handed Kat the prayer card with The Beatitudes scripted in Spencerian cursive and rimmed with Easter lilies.

"I'm actually not, but your sister BB is. She asked me to read this tonight. How prescient she was. Now, with much humility, I will have to debate her on whether it was divine intervention, a banshee spirit's presence, or the nature of queen bees that aroused me to read it."

The two women were laughing when Christine O'Leary approached them from the back of the hall.

"Ye were spot-on tonight, Dr. Irvine. And, Kat, good to see ye."

Christine passed Kat a folded note, as she whispered, "Read this when ye arrive home."

CHAPTER 13

Crossing—February 3, 1919

He never liked crossing the Irish Sea from Dublin to Holyhead. It was a dangerous journey, particularly in the winter months. Rough seas and wild winds hindered the mail steamer, tossing it from aft to bow, port to starboard—just like the British Parliament Billie Irvine was about to attend in London.

As one of only six members of the Irish Parliamentary Party (IPP) who successfully were elected in the 1918 elections, Billie knew he could be facing seas and winds much more turbulent than those during this night sailing.

He had considered Erin McCann's proposal to join the Sinn Féin party before running for office, but did not want to betray his father's memory nor his own loyalty to Griffith's original intent to unite Unionists and Republicans, Catholics and Protestants. Between man and nature, he wasn't sure which would unbalance him more; but, for the moment, he would sit in both the Dáil and the London House of Commons. After all, there was another, more surreptitious and strategic reason for this duality.

"It's a rough sailing tonight," came a baritone voice behind Billie, as a man settled near him into a worn lounge seat in the cramped passenger section of the steamer's enclosed cabin. Sleet was pounding the eight round windows on each side while a howling wind mimicked banshees peering in ominously.

Billie looked up at the speaker and faced his Rathmines neighbor, the seventy-nine-year-old Sir Maurice Pickering, one of the few members of the Irish Unionist Alliance elected outside Ulster.

"Aye," responded Billie sensing that one particular banshee had just succeeded in permeating the glass window behind him. Picker-

Part IV: May 1918–December 1921

ing was a close companion of Sir James Craig and had refused to sit in the Dublin Dáil Éireann. He was obviously on his way to London to secure his place in the House of Commons, instead.

"May I sit with ye?" Pickering asked, leaning forward upon his wooden cane.

"Aye," repeated Billie, as the wide girth of the older man lowered itself onto an accompanying chair. Pickering was a stately man, large in waist and long in gray moustache—both awarding him a presence of considerable substance. Billie, in contrast, was slight, clean shaven, and with blue eyes of such clarity that even *The Irish Times*, a Unionist paper, described him as "possessing strong intellectual prowess despite physical slimness and misguided loyalties."

The two men presented a deceptive picture of a collegial grandfather and grandson. Like the ship they were on, their many compartments were engineered to steer their conversation carefully through a storm of divisiveness. Each would take a turn at the wheel of this exchange while the other would pull at the anchor. Billie braced himself. His new role as a Sinn Féin informant made him uncomfortable.

"And what, pray tell, are ye venturing off to tonight, me good lad?" asked Maurice. "Now that yer IPP has failed so spectacularly to secure a majority of votes for its moderate stand on Home Rule, ye must feel somewhat disorientated."

Billie bristled at Pickering's label of "lad," but he was not going to let such dismissiveness steer his own course. Instead, he focused his mind on the various responses he could offer this man whom he considered backward in thought and forward in malevolence toward the working people of Ireland. Billie knew he had to employ the skill of calculated tacks and turns exactly as he had learned from his grandfather on their sloop the *Snow Bird*. He would not let Maurice know the real purpose of his voyage—collecting vital information for Erin and Mick on the Unionist Alliance's offensive tactics against Sinn Féin. While feigning allegiance to the House of Commons, Billie would suss out the nefarious, Unionist intentions.

Despite knowing he had to assume a diplomatic role with Pickering, Billie could not yet bring himself to call Maurice by the formal title of *Sir* Pickering. Instead, Billie used the term by which he addressed all of his students at St. Enda, "good sir."

"As ye know, good sir, my party and the people of Ireland look forward to a peaceful resolution of the current conflict. We trust ye, too, will guide yer Unionist Alliance members and those of conservative and labor allies in London toward such. We must resolve the current crisis facing our country."

Pickering grunted, like a walrus beached upon the rocks of Inishmore off the coast of Galway Bay. Quick to anger, he raised his voice.

"Ye mock me, laddie. There will be no peace until all of Sinn Féin's rebels are subdued and Ulster is on its own united with Great Britain. How do ye define yer peace?"

"Ah, good sir." Billie turned to face his companion. "Ye're a man of good faith, as am I and my father before me. Let us take guidance from Isaiah who recommends that the wolf and the lamb graze together and be unafraid of each other. If the Lord requires that of His people, then should we not require that of ourselves and live congenially together?"

Pickering smiled at Billie.

"Ach, ye're yer father's son after all. He was a good soul, and I miss him very much. Why ye have turned away from our party, I don't know. Perhaps it's that wife of yers. Agnes is her name, isn't it? I hear from my wife, Margaret, that ye have a handful when it comes to yer fair young lady speaking her mind at those suffragist meetings."

Billie smiled as well. He knew he had created a bridge of commonality between the Unionist and himself.

"Aye, indeed, but that's the same message I get from Agnes about yer Margaret. It seems they are both staunch advocates of the women's vote despite their religious and political differences. Perhaps we

Part IV: May 1918–December 1921

should look to their example and venture upon our own pasture together as wolf and lamb?"

Pickering and he chuckled together. The ship seemed to settle. Billie had carefully tacked his sloop to win over Pickering's confidence and comfort. Over the next two hours and a few pints, Pickering began to share some major Unionist Alliance's strategies. Unbeknownst to Pickering, Billie would remember them all and share them with Erin upon his return to Dublin.

For the moment, the banshees were silent. They just listened.

CHAPTER 14

An Exchange—February 5, 1919

Upon arriving at Holyhead, the two men took a carriage together to Liverpool where Maurice Pickering and Billie parted ways. Pickering headed straight to London, Billie to Camden Town just north of the grand city.

Billie had been successful in convincing Maurice that Billie's ailing, great-aunt, Molly McGregor who lived in Camden Town, warranted a stopover before arriving in London.

"Mother would be ashamed of me if I didn't visit her 102-year-old aunt to offer our family greetings. Or should I say *blessings,* as we doubt very much that any of us will see her again. As you see," he said, taking a large tin labeled Lemon's Confectioner's Hall out of his satchel, "the Irvines are patrons of the Lemon's products, particularly the mint humbug and yellow man rock. I must deliver this to her quickly or I'll devour these delicacies myself. What shame that would bring on our family."

Maurice laughed. "Ach, that's actually yer wee lass speaking, young man, not your ma. I hear my Margaret saying the same, but only after she has lectured me on Lemon's employment of so many women! Nonetheless, ye wouldn't have just one of those humbugs free to send me on my way?" asked Maurice, descending from the carriage before hailing a cab to catch the morning's ten o'clock Liverpool train to London.

"I should be so generous, good sir. But, they are wrapped with such care I can't even open the lid myself. When next we are in Dublin, we'll have tea with our fair ones and delight in both humbugs and yellow man rocks. Until then, I wish ye farewell and will await our next discourse on the floor of Parliament." With that, Billie waved Maurice good-bye and tucked the tin back into his satchel.

Part IV: May 1918–December 1921

"That was a close call," he murmured to himself, for Billie had no intention of leaving the tin with his great-aunt in Camden Town. No humbugs nor rock candy were inside it. Instead, a large barley cake of more than just sweet sugar rested within. Billie would have tea with his great-aunt but keep the tin for his visit to Holloway prison just outside Camden Town. There, he would meet with Countess Markievicz, interred within after the November 1916 arrests of Sinn Féin leaders.

Billie nodded off to sleep during the overnight journey from Liverpool, comforted by the rotating wheels of the Camden Town train and by the fond memory of Agnes' parting kiss as she had handed him the tin.

Unlike de Valera who was sent to Lincoln Prison, or Griffith to Gloucester, the Countess (along with Maud Gonne and Kathleen Clarke) went to the most famous English prison for women, Holloway. Seven years before, the suffragette leaders Emmeline Pankhurst and Emily Davison had held their hunger strikes amidst its squalid cells.

Billie had presently been tasked by Michael Collins to deliver messages from various Sinn Féin leaders—among whom now was his own dear wife, Agnes. On small notes, she had written coded messages about the progress of IRA actions and had delicately rolled them into the spongy cake.

After a sumptuous lunch the next day with his great-aunt and her housekeeper, Billie was physically prepared for the day when he entered the stone-floored reception room of Holloway prison. He was, however, not emotionally prepared. Dusk had enveloped the building's entrance behind him, making it seem as ominous as its reputation. The façade of the stately stone structure had reminded Billie of a besieged Elizabethan castle with its multiple, three-storied turrets juxtaposed at cross-angles to each other. A formidable and imposing site, it was purposefully impenetrable. Billie had shivered at the sight of it, wondering how anyone could ever escape from this place.

As he now sat on the wooden bench facing the registration desk, he could imagine the desperation one felt entering as an inmate, fearing what ultimately lay deeper inside. He could hear the cries of those fated never to leave. That will not be the case for the Countess, he thought to himself, as a stout, middle-aged woman approached him.

"Mr. Irvine?" asked the prison's governor with a Scottish brogue that surprised Billie. He stood and took the extended hand she offered.

"Aye, 'tis I," he responded.

"It's good to meet ye," the woman said as she lifted the straw-backed chair behind the registration desk and placed it gently in front, right next to his. "Please, be seated."

Billie was taken aback by the gracious demeanor of this person. There was something quite paradoxical in her presence, in contrast to the cold walls surrounding them. Hanging from under her white matron's cap, he noticed speckles of gray amidst a background of red curls, which mocked her furrowed brow. Her ruddish cheeks and crystal blue eyes hinted at a perspective that problems needed to be solved, not caused. The silver cross resting upon her linen blouse suggested a view of life more as a blessing than a curse.

"I know ye are here to see the Countess. Is that not right?" she queried in a quiet tone as she crossed her hands upon her skirt as though in prayer.

"Aye, again," he offered, his anxiety beginning to quiet by her presence.

"The Countess is one of our most admired inmates, ye know, although I really should not be saying that. We've had many accomplished rebels stay with us. They have always comforted our indigent women to find their worth, regardless of sorrowful fates. The Countess has been one of those leaders. She has encouraged, rather than diminished, our ladies." The governor leaned back in her chair and looked away from Billie. "I will be sorry to see her go."

Part IV: May 1918–December 1921

Billie was astounded at this last informed remark. How could she know that just two days before de Valera had escaped from Lincoln and that Griffith would soon be released by government fiat from Glouchester?

"Ye look surprised at that comment," she noted, returning her gaze toward Billie. "It will not be long before the Brits realize you cannot pacify the voice of people through internment, nor does punishment resolve a grievance. I predict she will be back on Irish soil by the end of winter. And, I can see by your reaction that ye assume the same."

Billie's shoulders had relaxed as he returned the matron's gaze with his own. "Aye, I must say for the third time. Ye have strangely sensed my hope."

"Indeed, it is the hope of all of us who come from lands with a history unseemly to the civilized world." She paused, looking away from him again.

"May I ask from where ye come?" Billie ventured.

"From Paisley in Scotland." She frowned, cocking her head to the left and unclasping her hands. "Why do ye ask?"

"Ye speak with the lilt of my maternal grandmother who came across the channel from Paisley in 1820."

"Ach, now did she? My great-uncle might have known her, for his family lived just five miles from the Greenock jail. Did your gran ever tell you about the rebellion there?"

"Aye, we heard about it quite often," offered Billie. He leaned forward anticipating how this conversation would be among those he would share in detail upon returning to Dublin.

She continued, "My great-uncle Edward McCarthy was hanged in 1820 along with a man called Angus McGregor. They were caught smuggling pistols into the Greenock jail so that interred rebels could escape." Her face softened. The furrows on her brow faded.

Billie sat frozen, incredulous that here before him was the descendant of his own grandmother Bella's Scottish fiancé, Edward—

the man for whom she had broken Angus McGregor's heart. This prison governor was someone who shared the history of his own mother's heritage.

"I believe, governor, that our visit today has been prescribed by the gods. Let me tell you how I know of Edward McCarthy and Angus McGregor." Billie quickly, despite much emotion exchanged between the conversants, related details of his two grandmothers—Bella McKnight Irvine and Kate McGregor—during their youth in Scotland. The governor, then having given him her proper name, Fanny McCarthy, listened intently and interjected various facts—and myths—about her family and the Scottish rebellion of 1820.

"We have much in common, Mr. Irvine." Fanny rose from her chair and, again, extended her hand. Billie took it, and in totally uncharacteristic style, brought it to his lips and kissed it. "This is from my mum. I know she would want you to know she is with you."

"Thank you, dear sir. Please tell her I am with her as well."

The two walked through the opened door at the back of reception area and entered the prison's inner hallway. They would meet the Countess together before the governor would allow this prisoner and visitor the privacy she so rarely allowed others.

Billie held his satchel close to his heart, the tin of sweet cake still emitting a comforting smell of barley sugar.

In addition, he heard the whisper of a strange presence and felt a slight brush on his forehead—like a tender kiss.

PART IV: MAY 1918–DECEMBER 1921

CHAPTER 15

Confessional—February 12, 1919

Eamon tucked the two messages into his vest pocket. He could feel the weight of their content on both his chest and mind. During his convalescence at Craigmaddie Hospital in Scotland, he had sat through numerous therapeutic sessions with Dr. Chadwick. From those, Eamon learned that his physical and emotional states were inextricably linked. Now, he had to consider a third state: moral obligations. Like his philosophy students, he, too, pondered the question, *What are the ethics of a just life?* These notes would force the answer.

After the Queen's University class three weeks ago, which Michael Collins had attended to scout out potential IRA agents, Eamon had decided not to bother Mick regarding the threatening note he had received at the beginning of the class. He reasoned that there were probably hundreds of threats sent to Republicans every day, and that Mick did not need to concern himself with each and every one.

Nonetheless, Eamon had saved the note, which he placed inside his diary on the bedside stand, beside the current book he was reading to ease evening anxieties, *The Source and Aim of Human Progress: A Study in Social Psychology and Social Pathology* by Boris Sidis.

Eamon drew comfort from Sidis' view of war as a social disease and his discussion of how people behaved in mobs, specifically when exhibiting religious mania. Eamon had been moved by Sidis' opinions, enough so to consider going to Collins for a discussion of this view. Might it inform how the IRA could address the growing antipathy by each side of the political divide?

But, it wasn't until Kat shared that she, too, had received a threatening note, that Eamon's consideration transformed into action. He knew he had to talk to Collins. And their conversation would be about more than Sidis.

Eamon reasoned to himself, "If I can only understand the psychological, not just the political rationale, behind these threats to my family, perhaps I can take some action to protect my Shamrock and our children. Collins is an expert judge of men, not just a commander of soldiers. I know he will guide me in being the ethical man I must be."

So, Eamon arranged to meet Mick. To avoid any detection, Collins had recommended they meet in the confessional booth of St. Peter's Cathedral off Albert Street in West Belfast. Collins had been known to dress as a priest to foil any suspecting Black and Tans on the streets. He often flummoxed them by offering various blessings in Latin.

On this night, Eamon—despite being an acknowledged Church of Ireland congregant—entered St. Peter's nave, turned right, and looked for the confessional cabinet. Tucked along the side aisle, the wooden structure with two doors facing the pews invited the obedient, or the guilty, to confess their sins and seek forgiveness. Tonight, Eamon wanted only to share the threats proffered against his family and seek the advice of the impersonator cleric. Forgiveness and blessings depended upon the counsel offered and if Eamon would act upon it.

Eamon opened the door on the left side of the confessional. He entered the six by three darkened space, turned around and shut the door. Sitting upon the oak bench, he leaned forward. He waited for the window to his left to slide open and shed light on his predicament. Soon, he heard footsteps on the stone flooring outside the booth. The right door opened. There was a pause. Then, it shut. As Eamon questioned himself as to whether they had been betrayed, his heart began to pulse louder than his fears.

"Be not afraid," came the sonorous voice of his confidant, followed by a chuckle. Eamon relaxed as the screen between the two

Part IV: May 1918–December 1921

opposing compartments opened, revealing a latticed separation. He noticed the profile of his friend Michael nestled above a friar's robe that enveloped the sturdy shoulders and torso of the IRA commander. The two men began their ritual of priest and penitent, never mentioning the other's name nor exact details. Even in the sacred confessional, one never knew who, besides God, was listening.

Collins began the confessional instructions.

"Sir, tell me what grieves you?" came the first instruction from Collins.

"Ach, good Father, I have received these messages from a miscreant. I am uncertain what I should do to redress them." Eamon passed the two slips of paper through a slot in the latticed screen that separated the faces of the two men.

Silence followed.

"Humph," came the priest's response. "Don't bother yourself with this. I'll ask for forgiveness of the author in due time."

Eamon sat back on his bench and considered what that meant. He knew the IRA's Invisible Army was escalating its attacks on the Black and Tans as well as on Irish collaborators within the Royal Irish Constabulary (RIC). Less than one month prior, on the same day the Dáil sat for the first time, two RIC policemen had been shot by Volunteers in Solohedbeg. This attack was being marked by the public as the first day in the War of Independence. Eamon knew more violence about which he was extremely conflicted would follow. Little did he know as the Anglican that he was, that like a good Catholic in the moment of confession, he was also examining his conscience.

The priest continued his instructions. "I absolve you from your sins, in the name of the Father and of the Son and of the Holy Spirit. Just say three Hail Marys and ye need not worry. God has taken charge." Again, Eamon heard a chuckle.

A second silence followed. Eamon sensed Michael leaning closer to the intervening screen. Sitting forward, Eamon also leaned nearer. He could barely hear the next instruction Michael made.

"Ye have a relative in New York City married to yer brother's widow, don't ye?" came a question.

Eamon was shocked that Collins would know about the marriage of Robbie's widow Margaret to the New York City banker Francis McKenzie.

"Aye," Eamon responded.

Slipping a folded piece of paper through another slot in the screen, Collins directed, "In addition to the Hail Marys, do as I say. Send this coded message to her via telegram. She'll know what it asks and will answer you directly."

Eamon was stunned. Were Margaret and her husband involved in the American Irish diaspora that was supporting the rebellion? How ignorant was Eamon, reclining in his academic tower, of the vagaries of political intrigue going on around him at home and overseas among his relatives? He would have to question Kat tonight. Why hadn't she told him about this connection? Eamon sighed in exasperated resignation.

"Now, don't ye go blamin' yer sweet missus about not knowing what's behind this request. She's a lass living a just life. I'll take care of the threats against both ye and her. Ye take care of her and the weeins by playing whatever role ye can in yer own just life. Eamon, I would trust ye with my own. Until that may be necessary, trust me."

Michael paused. He could hear Eamon's breath settle. Giving a final chuckle, he offered, "Now, don't ye think we should pray together?"

PART IV: MAY 1918–DECEMBER 1921

CHAPTER 16

Transatlantic Plans—February, 1919

Thursday, February 13

Eamon had memorized the message Mick gave him the previous day in the confessional. Entering the Belfast Queen's University Street Post Office this morning, he had transcribed it, paid the transatlantic fee, and tucked a copy of the telegram inside his vest pocket. As innocuous as the words were, he felt a chilling suspicion that someone was watching him commit an act of espionage. The threats against Kat and him lingered uncomfortably before and, then, behind him—like the dark spirit of an evil puca goblin, changing shapes and positions at will. He was startled when a black cat almost tripped him as he exited the post office door and stepped into the street.

"Ach," he mused, "Collins will take care of the person who has intimidated us. Be it a cat or lion, man or woman, Mick will protect us."

Eamon took out the copy of the telegram from his pocket, and reread it:

TO {Margaret Smiley McKenzie, 20 Park Avenue and 34th Street, New York City, New York

Baby boy due March. Family of five with baby will arrive June. Can you accommodate? Love, Kat

He then placed the telegram inside the book he would be discussing in today's philosophy class, *Utilitarianism* by John Stuart Mill.

How smart Collins had been to portray, in code, the arrival of de Valera and other Sinn Féin members in New York as the Smiley family's visit after the pending birth of their third child. Collins must have been particularly pleased in labeling de Valera as a "baby boy."

Eamon knew there was a conflict among the Sinn Féin party leaders and IRA commanders, rumored as occurring specifically between Collins and de Valera themselves. The current point of contention was whether de Valera should leave Ireland for America during this new phase in the War of Independence. Yet in hiding from the RIC and British Army, de Valera had come from Liverpool to Dublin just last week and was in refuge at a whiskey distillery near the Archbishop's grounds in Drumcondra. Discussions on his next steps were ongoing, and heated.

It appeared that Collins and several other IRA and Sinn Féin leaders did not think that de Valera should leave Ireland. After all, he would soon be voted in as the first President of the Dáil. However, "de'V" wanted to go to America—his nation of birth. He believed he needed to convince Woodrow Wilson that Ireland was worthy of membership as an independent state in the U.S. President's newly promoted League of Nations. As such, Ireland's status would be recognized internationally and embarrass the British government. In addition, the movement needed the wealth of Irish Americans to support their homeland battles. The War of Independence would soon be in dire straits once the British emasculated the new Dáil through trade and legal constraints.

Eamon knew of these conflicts. He did not, however, want to participate in any of their resolutions using violence. He wanted to avoid unnecessary bloodshed among friends, families, and foes instigated by those who had yet, in his mind, determined the characteristics of a just life.

For now, on this morning, he had at least sidestepped a black cat.

Part IV: May 1918–December 1921

Thursday, February 20

Kat read the Western Union telegram to Eamon:

FROM $\begin{cases} \text{Margaret McKenzie, 20 Park Avenue and} \\ \text{34th Street, New York City, New York} \end{cases}$

Family and baby accommodations secured. Await update on arrival. Am missing you all. Boys loved their Christmas sweaters and books.

Seated across from each other before the living room fireplace, Kat had just tucked a bulky, lap rug around Eamon's legs. Now, around her own shoulders, she wrapped the Paisley shawl her brother Billie had delivered with a note from the governor of the Holloway prison. According to Billie, Fanny McCarthy had literally taken the shawl off her own shoulders and insisted Billie give it—plus a long letter—to his mother, Lizzie. Kat wore the shawl tonight as she waited for her mother's arrival from Dublin.

"How amazing that Governor McCarthy knows our family history as well as we do and can add so much to it," Kat said as she began the knit-purl row of a yellow, baby blanket already one foot long and wide.

"And now we hear from Margaret in New York City regarding the pending visit of de Valera to America. So much is happening these days that I honestly cannot untangle the interweaving threads of family and political connections within one cloth. My head seems to spin from one warp—parallel or perpendicular—to an opposing woof."

Eamon smiled at his life partner's literary acumen. She had been through so much literal intrigue with him in the past seven years: his brother Robbie's criminal behavior, emigration and death in Ypres; the marriage of Robbie's widow to a wealthy New York City banker; Eamon's own struggle with the physical and mental vestiges of war; the passing of her parliamentarian father, Will Irvine; the angst of fear for her brother Billie and sister BB during the Easter Rising in Dublin. All these events had tainted her normally jovial attitude. And yet, she kept imagining the best in life—the pattern of a finely woven linen cloth.

He saw both of them rapidly aging. Or was it maturing? Besides dedicating themselves to their two sons and the new child on the way, they were secretly trying to undermine the Unionist partition plans of Ulster from the newly declared Republic. Eamon, Kat, and Eamon's sister-in-law, Margaret McKenzie in New York City, were the transatlantic cables of communication between the IRA and Irish Americans supporting the Republic. If somehow that communication could hasten a resolution to the conflict between Unionists and Republicans, they could rest.

Kat was sure of that; Eamon, not so.

The knock on their front door brought them out of their contemplative reveries.

"That must be Mum," Kat asserted as she set down her knitting needles, put aside the blanket, and rose. She folded the governor's shawl on the back of the sofa. "She'll bring us much reassurance from Dublin."

Eamon looked at Kat's departing back.

"We can only hope," he whispered. He feared another cat was prowling nearby.

Chapter 17

More Black Cats—February 20, 1919

Lizzie arrived at the 7 Parkview Street home of Eamon and Kat in Bangor around eight o'clock in the evening, physically weary from a day at the women's clinic sponsored by the National Aid and Volunteers Dependants' Fund, The Irish Women Worker's Union, and the newly founded Cumann na Teachtaire (The League of Women Delegates). Emotionally, she had been tossed by the arguments among the women in each group regarding their roles in this now formally declared War of Independence. Like the men in the movement, some wanted to leave Ulster Protestants behind; others wanted to force them to align with the Republic as a whole. Some preached forgiveness; others preached revenge. Lizzie wondered how women ever became labeled as "the gentler sex."

As she reached the door of her daughter and son-in-law's home, she was in deep thought, remembering the volatile argument Christine O'Leary voiced before all of the women—leaders and patients alike—attending the clinic. Lizzie was worried about the revenge they might endure by the RIC and British patrols due to the impassioned rants of Christine. She wished the Countess Markievicz was back home to reign in Christine.

Lizzie could feel her heart pound in an increasingly uncomfortable way as she rang the doorbell. She prayed for a quick response both within her heart and from her daughter. "I'm getting too old for this," she sighed.

Fortunately, Kat had been awaiting her mum's knock, so rose quickly from her knitting and opened the front door in time to see her mum frown.

"Mum, you look exhausted," exclaimed Kat, grabbing her mother's medical satchel and briefcase—supposedly full of patient records, but actually containing coded documents of IRA communiques.

"Aye, I am a tad fatigued tonight, my dear," responded Lizzie as she pulled the pins from her navy blue, beaver hat that secured her finely braided bun. She longed for an equally secure way to slow her rapid pulse. Loose wisps of gray framed her flushed cheeks as Kat helped her mother out of her winter jacket. Both women would ignore the presence of mortality in the entrance way—the mother out of concern for her child; the daughter out of denial.

"Come sit and have some tea before dinner, Mum. Ye need to rest and tell us all that has transpired this afternoon. We also have much to share with ye about Billie's visit last night."

Kat escorted her mother into the salon. Eamon rose and kissed both of his mother-in-law's cheeks. She, in turn, kissed his forehead.

Lizzie settled into the chair Kat had vacated next to the fireplace and picked up the yellow baby blanket—not to continue knitting it, but rather to hold it close on her lap for both warmth and inner comfort. She would cling to whatever earthly time she had left to cherish.

Lizzie raised her concerns quickly. "Ach, I'm glad Billie was here. I had thought he would visit me before departing to the Dáil in Dublin but understand he had to rush. What did he tell ye about the visit with the Countess in Holloway?"

Kat noticed another type of rush in her mother's voice. Calmly, Kat placed her mum's favorite, Belleek china teacup and special raisin scones on a plate before Lizzie. They sat next to a fresh pot of steaming tea.

Lizzie smiled at her oldest daughter. "Ah, me darling. Ye know exactly how to please your mum after a long day at work. I see your da is reminding ye. How your face is like to his, always smiling and showing such gentility. Ye are surely yer father's daughter."

Kat blushed. "Mum, let's talk as da would want us to do about the tasks before us."

Part IV: May 1918–December 1921

Lizzie nodded, wondering why she was becoming so sentimental these days. She shook her head, placed two lumps of sugar in the teacup before her, a few drops of milk, and sighed as Kat poured the steaming nectar.

Slowly stirring her spoon within the cup, Lizzie could feel her heart's rapid pace slow. "Thank you, my dear. Now, tell me what Billie related."

Eamon pulled his chair closer to the fire as Kat brought one of the children's stools next to her mum and sat upon it. She leaned toward her mother.

For the next hour, Eamon and Kat told the news of Billie having met with the Countess. They handed Lizzie the letter of instructions from Maud Gonne, Kathleen Clarke, and the Countess. Lizzie would convey those instructions to the local Cumann na mBan leadership.

The letter read like a short story, describing the prison conditions that were the plight of so many Scottish and Irish women, and the haunting sounds of suffragettes who had been imprisoned earlier in the decade. Coded instructions were offered. Finally, the Countess alluded to a collaborator in the prison using the words, "We hear the sweet trill of a lark in the grassy courtyard at the prison's entrance from time to time. She brings us great comfort."

"We know who the lark is, Mum. Ye will be surprised." At that, Kat gave her mother the letter from the prison governor, which had been concealed in an inner pocket within the shawl that Kat now took off her own shoulders and placed around her mother's. Lizzie took the letter and read it silently.

Soon, her tears began to flow. How long she had pondered the memory of her own mother Kate's flight from Scotland and that of her mother-in-law Bella's. Those memories had been couched in such mystery. Now, both women's stories were expanded and corroborated by the words this new family historian had shared. In addition, Governor Fanny McCarthy had presented herself in code as the lark singing to the Countess and the other women imprisoned as fighters for freedom from the British.

"Mother, are ye truly all right?" Kat asked, rising from her stool and putting her arms around the person whom she thought was impenetrable from pain and suffering.

Lizzie immediately regained her composure and faced her daughter directly. The red cheeks flushed again, the hands trembled a bit, but the voice was as strong as that of all the Irvine-Gallagher-McKnight women who had proceeded her on this journey of independence—Bella, Kate, and Sister Bridgette. Fanny McCarthy now accompanied them.

"Aye, I'm fine. Let's have our dinner, and I'll tell you what the Countess and Governor McCarthy are asking of us."

"Excellent, Mum" replied Kat. "Eamon and I will also tell ye what we heard from Margaret in New York City as well. Her telegram just arrived today."

The three rose and proceeded to the kitchen where together they enjoyed a fine evening supper, leftovers from the formal five o'clock dinner Kat had prepared for their two boys, Devin and Neil. Animated conversations continued with keen insights, hope, and much laughter about the newest Smiley yet to arrive.

Little did they know, however, that several black cats were watching them from the dark recesses of the backyard—none of whom were laughing.

Part IV: May 1918–December 1921

Chapter 18

The Skunk and the Cat—February 20, 1919

"Ain't they havin' a grand time in there?" came the raspy brogue of a young Derry boy, scraping the barrel bottom of envy.

"Ach, the devil is in that house breeding evil. No grand time is that," came the embittered response from an older youth of Orange extraction.

The two laughed—or was it a cackle?—as they poised for action in the backyard of 7 Parkview Street.

A third voice caught the two upright. "Boys, stop yer yawing. Words won't bring sense back to this country. Only what we do tonight will." Samuel Acheson knew what he was talking about. He had years of experience in open and covert warfare that tempered the hubris of novitiate combatants and transformed them into seasoned warriors. He knew how to lead.

The three had been assigned to inflict retribution on the Smiley family for its rumored collaboration with the Irish Republican Army's Flying Squads. Within the last month, the Collins guerrilla army had bombed a number of Belfast shops owned by Ulster patriots. In one incident on Adelaide Street, four patrons had been killed, including a three-year-old girl. Samuel and his boys were out for revenge.

"Do ye have any idea of why we are here?" Samuel questioned the two, sputtering his disgust at their vapid bravado.

"Of course, we do," replied the Orangeboy. "Me mum told me the Black and Tan are our saviors and that we need to do away with the sinful Catholics. She volunteers at the Bushwick Presby workhouse kitchen every Friday and sees their women with four or five weeins in tow for free fish and porridge. She says the gals give it over to their hubbies who sell it for whiskey money. Ach, the stories she tells me and my brother Sam. And the warnings she gives my older sister, Sarah, to never flirt with a son of Mary."

Samuel sensed the Orangeboy's disgust, despite the darkness of the night, and swore under his breath. By the end of their talk, he would set the youth straight about the true reasons for their action and focus the youth's antipathy into a potent strike.

"And ye, laddie?" Samuel turned to the second youth. "What is yer idea?"

"Nay, I have no clue. I just know that I'll get 10 p from you to give to me mum to buy milk for my little sis. Mum tells me her Catholic neighbors ain't so bad. She says they just want to live their lives as they want without being told they're ignorant or dirty. They don't want to move away from us into those crowded tenements along Falls Road." His voice faded at the end of this rendition which, for him, was a repetition of the sermon he had heard from Pastor Edmundson of the Quaker Meeting for Worship he and his family attended.

Samuel considered both responses, and thought to himself, "Where do the Irish National Volunteers get these supposed soldiers? They're far from the 36th Ulster Division boys I led into battle at Somme where we lost over 5,000 brave lads. Now those lads were dedicated to the cause—victory for the British Empire and defeat for Germany. Today, this street by street battle with these untested boys has no set compass like the Great War just ended." Samuel knew he had little time and no fallow ground waiting to be seeded by his intentions for these novitiates tonight. But, he would try nonetheless.

"Let me tell ye a very brief story. There was a cat stalking mice in Drumcairne Forest one evening. Upon reaching a stream bank, there was heard a rustle in the ferns behind the feline. A skunk was slinking out from under the brush, watching the cat with its beady eyes. The cat, being quite old and wise about the tactics of these smelly creatures, slowly turned, let out a guttural moan and bared its claws. The skunk reversed itself, lifted up its bushy tail and expelled such a stream of pungent stench. They circled each other. Which one do you think walked away and left the other dead?"

Samuel could hear the two minds spinning their singular synapses.

The oldest youth spoke first. "After using its claws in attack, the cat scratched up the skunk and left it lifeless."

"Nay," replied the Derry boy. "The skunk sprayed the cat breathless."

Samuel chortled to himself. "Ye're both wrong. Neither died. For sure, the skunk sprayed the cat, and the cat clawed the skunk. But, they backed off, each catering more to its own wounds than finishing the other off. They sulked away—away from any victory over the other. Sure they survived, but they lived in fear and hatred of the other for the rest of their wandering lives in the forest. Anyone who entered the forest could smell the skunk's stench and hear the cat's hiss, but no one ever saw the two re-meet and claim a victory.

"Now, listen to me straight and square. Life isn't worth living through only smells and sounds or bragging and blustering. You must take a smart action against what you fear and hate. And we Ulster men fear the takeover of our homeland by the Republicans. We hate those Catholics and their advocates who want to separate us from our mother Britain."

Samuel continued in a controlled yet ardent voice. "So, why we are here tonight is to be neither skunk nor cat. We are here as soldiers for our Ireland to be part of Great Britain's victory—a victory by the grandest nation in the world. Now, let's get on with our task."

Samuel took out three bottles of kerosene from his Paisley satchel. "Here, each of you take one and listen well to my instructions."

CHAPTER 19

Righteous Justice—February 20, 1919

The three did not hear the click of a pistol nor sense the presence of adversaries until the voice of Christine O'Leary alerted them.

"And what are ye devils up to?" came the question. Dressed in trousers, her slim yet muscular legs were well hidden. A dark, woolen coat covered any semblance of womanhood. The tam enveloping her length of red, twisted hair and the tattered scarf across her chin completed the disguise.

Samuel and the two youth froze; the three whiskey bottles filled with kerosene were clutched tightly—one in each respective fist. Samuel rose to his full stature and considered whether to lunge or speak. He wondered what the hell this tramp was doing here tonight, and surmised from the smell of him, that he was just a wanderer looking for the next drink. Samuel could not see the gun Christine held behind her back.

Speaking harshly, Samuel growled, "What does it look like? Get out of our way and be gone. We have our business here tonight, and ye have yours. Leave us and find yer next swig." The leader turned to the boys beside him. "Let's get on with it, boys."

"I fear ye won't," replied Christine, pulling the gun forward into sight and aiming it straight at Samuel.

A second figure appeared behind her, then took a stand to her left. At fifteen, Ian McNulty's bulk was square, not vertical, wrapped also in dark clothing. Heavy textured farm pants, boots covered with dried manure, a low-browed black hat, and bulky sleeved jacket added to his disguise. He looked like a formidable foe. No gun had he, but his demeanor assumed he was ready to fight.

"Take your trash and go before us," Christine growled, pointing the gun at Samuel's head. "Yer deed is done here and so are ye."

Part IV: May 1918–December 1921

Samuel quickly considered his options. He could hesitate and attack this heathen when opportunity and time allowed a best advantage. Or, he could lunge now and take his chances. But what about the gunman's accomplice, standing so ready? Would Samuel's second—the Orange youth or Derry boy—take that person down? Samuel's years of tested judgment briefed his decision. He could not trust these novitiates. He needed time to think before acting.

"Boys, pick up the satchel and do as these blokes order." Turning to his two accomplices, he saw their faces confirm the decision not to act immediately. The Orangeboy was full of fury, tense as the string of a crossbow stretched to its longest length, but wobbling, not yet steady enough to directly hit its target. Samuel hoped the boy's anger would serve the three later, once it was under control.

The Derry boy was the opposite. Samuel could tell from the sight and smell of the drippage along the inside of the boy's pants that the lad had released his fear in the most natural way. Samuel had to either protect this lad or let him reach his own destiny.

Taking the boys' bottles and placing them back into the satchel, Samuel faced Christine and waited. His face had turned an inflamed red, eyes stoked with anger and lips pursed in disgust. Christine could feel his hatred. Her lower-trebled brogue rasped as she spit out the instructions.

"Walk ahead of me, out through the backyard gate, and down to the shed at the alley's end. Your fate will be there."

Her gun focused on Samuel as the five left the backyard and turned right onto the alley's pathway. Ian strode next to Christine behind the three. His pace was measured, one foot before the other. But, he could feel his heart triple-pace in anxiety, as he thought, "What have I gotten myself into? I thought I was only accompanying Miss O'Leary to Belfast to get information about the threats to the Smiley family. What would Liam McCormick tell me to do if he were here? What would me da tell me?"

The caravan of five slowly walked the lane's uneven ruts, four minds as unsteady as their grounding. Only one was perfectly clear. The three prisoners and two guards approached the shed in silence. On her way just an hour before, Christine had seen it as a perfect site for her mission's purpose. The wooden structure, obviously worn in time and covered by nature's brambles, abutted the rear entrance to an abandoned house at number 10 Parkview Street.

In passing it just minutes before, she had asked Ian to clear away the debris before its debilitated wall facing the alley. He wondered why but had followed her instructions. It took him a few minutes to complete the task during which he remembered Rachel's warning to him two days before in Dublin: "Be careful of her words, Ian. Nanna Lizzie and I know them to be duplicitous, if not outright lies." As he caught up with Christine in the backyard of 7 Parkview Street, he had begun to sweat.

Having witnessed her gun, heard her bitterness, and now watching the three prisoners in line before him, he realized that all was not true about her motives. Ian continued to sweat but also began to plan his own actions. "Father, guide me!" he prayed.

Arriving at the shed, Christine ordered the three to enter it. "Turn around and face your maker," she demanded, speaking now in her feminine voice.

"Ach," said Samuel. "Ye're the witch O'Leary. I know all about ye." His care for the boys immediately fled his mind as he knew it was time for his own survival.

She pointed the gun directly at his heart. "Who are ye to call me a witch? Did ye think of the children whose fathers ye have killed in the last decade—those who wished only to live in a country free from evil men like you? You led them into battles they thought would secure that freedom while ye knew yer Home Rule would only put them and their families back home to servitude and poverty! Get on your knees. All of ye."

Part IV: May 1918–December 1921

Samuel yelled out a banshee howl and lunged at her. A piercing shot from the pistol sounded as it flew into Samuel's chest. His face took on an anguished expression of pain and, perhaps, one last flash of anger as he fell to the cluttered floor of the shed. The remaining lads—Samuel's two accomplices, as well as Ian—stood in shock.

"Take the bombs and light them, Ian," Christine commanded, but Ian could not move.

"I said, take the bombs and light them!" As she turned to face Ian, the Orange youth leapt at her. Turning quickly to face his assault, she shot him directly in the forehead. He fell under a curtain of blood, closing out his life's play.

"Light the bottles, Ian. I'll deal with this remaining culprit. We'll leave their bodies here to burn in hell, and no one will be the better for their disappearance except us. This is your initiation into the Flying Squads. Do it quickly, and I'll meet you tomorrow where we planned. Go, tell your family that all is well with their safety now. No more threats."

She stepped forward to aim her gun at the remaining boy, kneeling before her, head tucked down into his trembling neck, arms embracing his sobbing body.

"Nay," said Ian, garnering all his wit and bravery into a semblance of confidence. "Let me deal with this boy. For sure, I'll do what ye are about to do to prove my loyalty to the cause. You leave and travel on. I can quickly finish with him and the burning."

Christine chortled, "Ach, ye're finally making up for yer father's frailties. He should have taken on those soldiers at the post office barricade back in '16 instead of trying to negotiate with them. I know what happened, and ye're ready to be the rebel he wasn't. Here, take the gun and keep it until we meet again. Do the job." Christine handed him the arm, cuffed him on the shoulder, and exited the shed turning left into the late-night mist now crawling through the alley.

Ian bent down to the boy. He saw in the lad's frantic eyes that same fear Ian was certain he himself had shown in the last minutes of his father's life. The final words from his beloved da had haunted him to this day, more so to this minute: "Run, dear son. Do not be a lesser person than these men as they take my life. Run yer own race for righteous justice."

"Come, get up," said Ian. "Turn right out the shed away from her, not left. Forget what ye have seen and heard tonight. May ye only remember what I say to ye now: 'Run, dear boy. Do not be a lesser person than those whom ye have seen kill tonight. Run yer own race for righteous justice.'"

The boy looked up at Ian, incredulous. His face smeared from tears, he sputtered, "I only wanted to gain 10 p for me mum to have milk for me sister." His shoulders shook as Ian raised him to a standing position.

Ian reached into his pants pocket. "Here, take this pound and give it to yer mum."

The boy grabbed the note and ran out of the shed. He turned right. Ian poured the kerosene upon the two remaining bodies, placed the gun in Samuel's hand, and lit the matches. He backed out of the shed, turned left in the alley, and walked quickly to the Smiley home at number 7.

Chapter 20

Wordless—February 20, 1919

The kitchen door of 7 Parkview Street was opening just as Ian entered its backyard. Already the bells of the Bangor Fire Brigade had begun to ring and cries of "Fire!" were resounding in the alley. Eamon, cautiously descending the back steps, suddenly saw a figure stealthily approach him across the yard. He recognized the face of Ian, miraculously illuminated by a finger of light. The full moon had momentarily revealed itself between darkened clouds.

"Hurry, lad," Eamon called in a muted whisper, reaching the bottom of the staircase and grasping Ian's outstretched hand. The clouds again covered the moon. The finger disappeared.

Eamon steadied the bowed boy and guided him up the wooden structure. They entered the kitchen to face an astonished Kat. Immediately, she assessed the situation—both before her and outside in the alley.

She hurriedly drew Ian away from the windows and into the salon. From the velvet settee, she grabbed the same blanket that she had used to calm her beloved Eamon, and threw it around the shaking shoulders of the lad. She drew the curtains tight, extinguished the reading lamp on the side table, and lit a small candle on the stand next to the smoldering fireplace. The darker the room the better, so they could not be seen from the side or back of the house.

Eamon's winter-white companion dog, Sceolang, had been on alert near the kitchen door. He followed the three into the salon. Born of warrior stock, the hound, too, sensed the danger.

Clutching the blanket around him, Ian collapsed into a wooden rocker at the right of the fireplace. Eamon and Sceo stood at attention to his left.

"I'll get ye some hot," said Kat returning into the kitchen to prepare the traditional, yet conservative, brew of comfort. She was not going to offer the more anesthetizing whiskey to a fifteen-year-old lad, although she was sure Eamon would have suggested it.

Eamon looked at Ian's face, quickly recognizing the anguish of battle and death. He waited for Ian to speak. But nothing came. The smell of smoke on Ian's jacket filled the room with musty silence. Beads of sweat, emanating from under the black hat, streaked lines down the youth's sooted cheeks. His hands twisted round and around the tassels at the edge of the woolen blanket, now repositioned over his waist to legs. Eamon waited for that spiraling to subside. He knew to honor time and thought as he had done himself in Craigmaddie Hospital.

Kat returned with a steaming pot of tea and several biscuits poised on a porcelain plate. Placing both before Ian, she offered him an empty cup. He stared at it. She hesitated, then placed it on the table, poured the tea herself, and handed it back to him.

He stopped twirling the tassels, looked up at her and took it in both hands, steadier now that the trembling was subsiding. He took one sip, followed by a gulp, before placing it back on the table.

The three kept vigilance of their emotions. No one spoke. Only Sceo displayed his by settling next to Ian's chair and placing a paw on the blanket covering the youth's lap. Ian stroked the dog's head. One wave after another of tension transferred to the beckoning body of the canine and, then, into the air.

"Ye can tell me whatever ye want or need to say," solicited Eamon gently.

"Nay," replied Ian. "There is nothing. And yet, there is too much." Eamon nodded, frowning at Kat whom he knew wanted to ask multiple questions and offer protracted, sympathetic advice. Kat saw Eamon's caution and held back.

Ian took several more sips of tea. He felt his heart's quickening pace quiet down and began to think. He knew the less Eamon and Kat heard about this tragic night the better for them. The Black and Tan would soon be invading every house to query whatever the residents had heard or seen . . . and then some.

Part IV: May 1918–December 1921

Although he was fairly sure Nanna Lizzie had alerted the Smileys of his pending arrival, he was also certain the elder had no idea of Christine's ultimate intentions, least of all regarding his role in them. He also knew that Michael Collins had alerted Eamon that the threats against him would soon be addressed. But like Eamon, Ian was sure that no one surrounding him in the house had any knowledge of how this would happen.

Had he only been familiar with Christine's duplicitous history with the various Smiley and Irvine members—her attempted recruitment of Eamon at the hospital in Scotland, her vehement dismissal of Patrick McCann at St. Stephen's Park, her manipulative behavior with Rachel at Linen Hall—he would have known the evil this woman, tonight called a witch, carried forth. But he didn't. Again, he queried himself, "Why didn't I listen to Rachel? Tonight might never have happened."

But, alas, it had, and he was going to live with it forever. Someday, perhaps, he would speak at length about it.

Tonight, though, he would not. When he returned to Dublin, he would share some words with Liam McCormick, his father confidant. With Bigger, he would shed the tears.

"Come," said Kat. "Upstairs to the bath. Ye must immediately rid yerself of the stench of smoke on ye. Eamon will take yer clothes and burn them in the fireplace. We'll put ye to bed in the knitting room. Mother is sleeping with the boys so won't hear ye. If the Black and Tan come round in the next hours, we'll say ye're our nephew studying at Queen's who has been quarantined for the past week with influenza. When neighborhood suspicions and gossip subside, ye and I will return ye home to Dublin saying we're visiting my sister and her new baby. Move quickly now."

Ian followed Kat up the stairs. Eamon stoked the fireplace embers into flames. He turned to Sceo, whose ears now waited for a command.

"Aye, go with them, dear companion. He needs ye more tonight than I."

Chapter 21

The Master Trio—April 27, 1919

Una's Interlude . . .

Never believe that I alone have the power to see my ancestors and their descendants. Nor am I alone in guiding them through the best of times and the worst of times. As another spirit, who sometimes walks with me, has so eloquently written:

> "It was the best of times, it was the worst of times, it was the age of wisdom, it was the age of foolishness, it was the epoch of belief, it was the epoch of incredulity, it was the season of light, it was the season of darkness, it was the spring of hope, it was the winter of despair."

While Master Dickens and I have had many a discussion about the similarities among Ireland, England, and France during their respective ages of wisdom and foolishness, we have recently reflected on who can best sense and resolve the root causes of these paradoxes. Who can create belief out of incredulity, light out of darkness? Just last week, during one of our sojourns around Lough Leane, we contemplated how the human species might not be the best equipped to accomplish such a feat. Rather, perhaps, members of another species are—members who have often survived and thrived more effectively than *Homo sapiens*.

We were discussing, of course, the *Canidae* family—or, better known as the canid family. These warm-blooded creatures seem to have refined their unique senses and skills over centuries to survive all kinds of environmental and human interferences during the best of times and the worst of times. Haven't wolves exploited crevices of mountainsides to escape the arrows and bullets of hunters? Haven't coyotes used bramble and bush to spy on their predators as they pass by in futile pursuit? And haven't many a fox outfoxed the hunter by remembering their hidden holes in the ground?

During our ramblings, though, Charles and I focused on one particular species in this family: dogs. Yes, dogs. For they are unique in their victories during the worst of times. They seem to have employed their senses and skills not just to escape environmental or human obstructions, but rather to exploit such dangers to their own advantage.

Assumed to be servants domesticated by men, dogs have actually turned that hierarchical order upside down to become loyal companions—beloved and honored. Often, as in the days of pharaohs and ancient kings, they are buried alongside their masters when earthly lives have ended. True, many canines have been used by those same masters as labor: guardians of hearth and manor, shepherds of flocks and herds, spies during battle. But more often than not—no matter what the demand of the human—dogs have become masters of their masters.

Charles and I laugh when seeing so many couples here in this afterworld—and by couples I mean a dog and his master—gaily pass us on our walks. Men saunter with their hounds rather than with their deceased wives or mistresses. Is this because more family secrets have been shared with a loyal canine companion than with a human confidant? Might dogs possess a unique wisdom and fortitude to lift humans out of their winters of despair into their springs of hope?

Just the other day, taking a pause in our meanderings, Charles and I looked earthward and listened in on a conversation among three, fine members of the *Canidae* family during a picnic of the Irvine-Smiley-McCormick family. Lying luxuriously in the shade of a palm tree on the green at Queen's College Belfast, were Boru, Sceo, and Bigger, the respective dogs of Billie Irvine, Eamon Smiley, and Ian McNulty.

Here is what we heard:

> **Boru:** Ye'll be happy to know that Billie has finally made up his mind on the role he shall play in this War of Independence. It was a struggle for him, but, after many a walk with me around the streets of Rathmines, he lingered last Saturday on a bench just outside the house of Countess Markievicz. In his hand was a copy of the speech Pádraig Pearse delivered at the 1915 burial of Fenian hero O'Donovan Rossa[9]. Dozing on the bench, Billie let the paper slip onto the ground beside him. I retrieved it and set it upon his lap. My teeth pierced the following paragraph in the speech:
>
> 'Splendid and holy causes are served by men who are themselves splendid and holy. O'Donovan Rossa was splendid in the proud manhood of him, splendid in the heroic grace of him, splendid in the Gaelic strength and clarity and truth of him. All that splendor and pride and strength was compatible with a humility and a simplicity of devotion to Ireland, to all that was olden and beautiful and Gaelic in Ireland, the holiness and simplicity of patriotism of a Michael O'Cleary or of an Eoghan O'Growney. The clear true eyes of this man almost alone in his day visioned Ireland as we of today would surely have her: not free merely, but Gaelic as well; not Gaelic merely, but free as well.'
>
> I nudged my master awake.
>
> "Boru," said my Billie, after he shook his head clear and cleaned my spittle off the page. He read the marked words. Then, he patted my head.
>
> "How brilliant ye are in pointing out exactly what I need to do. I will take my stand in the Dáil, continuing to speak out on behalf of the whole island of Ireland being free and

Part IV: May 1918–December 1921

Gaelic. No Ulster split for me. And if it means I must take up arms, I shall. But God forbid, I won't have to. I pray my words in both English and Gaelic will be enough that the Republic's Dáil and British Parliament come together for a unified Ireland through humility, devotion, holiness, and patriotism."

Sceo: Your master sounds determined in speech, but still a tad hesitant to actually take up arms. Let me share how my own master made his decision about the role he is taking, coming to it with my help, of course.

We were both sleeping by the fireplace late one evening after the February visit of Ian McNulty—the visit about which I'm sure ye know from whispered conversations in our own kitchens. Eamon awoke with a start from a nightmare about a Somme battle. Boru, I need not tell ye about what he had been dreaming. And Bigger, ye too, need no elaboration given your tumultuous Easter week of '16.

"Fetch me my gun," cried out Eamon. He rose from his seat, staggered, and grabbed at my leash. I didn't move. Instead, I looked him straight in the eyes and started to whine.

Eamon was startled. He fully woke, looked into my eyes and saw back his soul as a pacifist. He was amazed and abruptly sat back down.

"What am I doing, Sceo? What am I thinking of? I cannot raise a gun again, no matter how I feel the Ulster Unionists are wrong-headed. Ye're right. As ye have shown me my soul, let me look into theirs at church and in my classes. I will share in words what I believe is just and ethical. In that way, hopefully, I can move the minds and hearts of men to stop their fighting."

Bigger: Ach, ye two have masters full of ideas and words. My Master Ian is the opposite. He was never taught those ephemeral theories and strategies. His young life experienced only sacrifice and death from Coalisland to Dublin and now to Rathmines. I fear it is too late for me to influence him about the value of politics and religion. He has seen all too clearly how such venues are undermined by corrupt individuals. But . . . because he has slept with my own heart beating next to his, he knows the power of unconditional affection and healing. He will not continue as an IRA agent. Rather, he will soon prepare for his medical studies with the tutelage of our beloved Doctor Lizzie and Nurse BB. He will learn to save, not end, lives. Only when needed to protect the innocents—those on either side—will he garner the gun. And, if he must, I will be there to protect him.

When they finished their conversation, Charles and I watched them linger under the tree: Boru, the master of persuasion; Sceo, the master of passivism; and Bigger, the master of healing. The three returned to their watchful stances.

Across the green, we heard their human masters call them. Each dog rose. Boru and Sceo lumbered a bit toward the family; Bigger raced. Surely, this beloved triumvirate had influenced their companions' decisions on how to act during the best of times—and the worst—to differentiate between wisdom and foolishness, and to model belief instead of incredulity.

Now, the master trio would continue to lead their companions out of the winter of despair and into the spring of hope.

Part IV: May 1918–December 1921

Chapter 22

Ashes, no coffin. Ale, no whiskey. Laughter, no tears.
—April 27, 1919

While the three dogs—Boru, Sceo, and Bigger—sat alongside their respective masters, the women began to arrange the afternoon's china and tasties on two iron benches abutting the path to the Tropical Ravine House. Several plaid blankets had been arranged upon the grassy lawn on this southwestern edge of the Botanic Gardens. The family preferred this section of the grand park for Sunday outings, since it was sequestered away from strollers who favored the Palm House on the northeast side. Predominantly middle-class to upper-middle-class Protestants avoided the Ravine for reasons of prejudice—it had become a haven for Catholics and their Protestant friends. As Lizzie set a brass urn upon the third bench, she knew it was especially important today to distance.

So often, BB would remark, in an uncharacteristically critical way, "I wonder if those who parade before the Palm House know it is predominately Catholics who dirty their hands plantin' and nurturin' the delicate flowers and stately palms inside. Do such people realize whose sweat and beleaguered fingers cultivate such attractions, while earning only a shillin' a day?" BB was grateful that her brother, Billie, in his MP role, was supportive of the recent labor strikes by both Catholic and Protestant workers to secure better wages and hours. Belfast, Dublin, Cork, and Limerick had witnessed these efforts. Out of deference to BB's sentiment and for other reasons, the entire family—whether individually or collectively—would always walk away from the Palm House and gather in the tranquil environs outside the Ravine House.

Today was no exception. Not one family member was missing under the tropical ferns towering over reflection pools dotted with white-blossomed lily pads. Among the men and boys were elder John Gallagher (Lizzie's brother); Eamon, and his boys, Devin and Neil; Billie and his adopted sons, Jon and Thon; and Liam McCormick and Ian McNulty. The women and girls included Lizzie, Kat, BB and baby Maggie, Agnes, Rachel, and Morna. Both groups and, of course, their canine companions, had much to consider about what wove them together—this growing family, now numbering sixteen. This spot was the spinning wheel that fabricated the family cloth.

Most of the family knew that it was here, before any benches had been secured, that in 1843 William Irvine had knelt to propose marriage to Bella McKnight. However, none knew that it was also here, three years later, that Bella's tears flowed after his passing from typhoid—and what she would learn later was actually an assassination. She had placed a handful of dirt from his grave upon the path.

They also all knew that in 1880, inside the Ravine House, the marriage proposal by William and Bella's son, Will Irvine, had been accepted by Dr. Lizzie Gallagher. Unlike his father, Will had not knelt, for he knew Lizzie was a strident egalitarian. To prove that stance, she had to be asked twice. And on their tenth anniversary, the two had returned to plant a magnolia bush behind the third bench in honor of Bella's introducing them to each other.

Here, too, in 1912 at Mrs. Quilon's Tea Shop, Kat, Billie, and Agnes had confirmed that Eamon was not his criminal brother Robbie, but rather his twin.

And it was also here that four years later, in 1916, Patrick McCann encountered what he thought was the ghost of Robbie Smiley. Patrick's fear that he had killed Liam McCormick's brother, Ryan, was calmed by Lizzie as they sat on the second bench. Weeks later, Patrick learned that the apparition was actually Eamon, Robbie's twin brother and husband to Kat.

Finally, in 1918, Eamon came to the Ravine House and threw his British-awarded medal of honor into the sunken wetland along with his brother's death certificate from Ypres. The water and wind carried both he knew not where, nor did he care.

Part IV: May 1918–December 1921

On this Sunday in 1919, another occasion would prove the site's significance to this family. The sixteen born and extended members would honor their oldest patriarch, Anthony Gallagher, Lizzie and John's brother and mentor to Eamon in the philosophy department of Queen's College.

Anthony's seventy-five years had come to an end the week before in the college's Lanyon Hall. He was giving a lecture on Kant's work, *Religion within Bounds of Bare Reason*. About to explain what bare reason meant to Kant, Anthony frowned, placed a hand on his chest, and then collapsed. Observing the session, Eamon raced to Anthony's side and heard his last earthly words: "Believe only what ye know." Whether that was Anthony's interpretation of Kant's work or a message to Eamon, Eamon did not know—at least, not yet.

What was known, nonetheless, was the intention behind Anthony's earthly farewell. Ever the prescient and contemplative philosopher—and devoted agnostic—Anthony had written simple instructions for his brother John, not a priest, to know and follow: "Ashes, no coffin. Ale, no whiskey. Laughter, no tears. My ashes will surely ride on the wind from city to lough; ale will certainly suffice to assuage my soul's thirst and that of my colleagues; and laughter will comfort my loved ones with joyful memories, not sorrowful regrets."

Lizzie took the urn off the bench and passed it with a teaspoon to John.

He began, "To Borrum, the god of the winds, I offer the blessed breath of my dearest brother and friend." He flung a spoonful of ashes into the air and returned the urn and utensil to Lizzie.

"To Canta," she said, "the god of healing, I offer the blessed heart of my dearest confident." She gently scattered a small dusting onto the pebbled path.

In turn, each adult member took the urn and spoon, retrieving a portion of the embers and releasing it while offering a blessing.

The children watched in awe. John gestured them to line up along the path beside their respective parents. Starting with Billie and Agnes and ending with Liam and BB, each couple gently placed a powdered thumbprint on a child's cheek after he or she had spoken a blessing. Then they kissed the forehead. BB gave the last blessing on behalf of tiny Maggie who giggled when her mother's soft touch left a dusty blush. The entire family laughed as well. The ale was brought out and mirthful tales of Anthony Gallagher filled the air.

As for those before them, the Tropical Ravine House had become a magical place for this growing family. Each current member knew that this spot—this place of joy and sorrow, questions and answers, doubt and certainty—had provided the unbreakable threads of a loving family.

And for the generations to come, Anthony Gallagher would join their ancestors to make sure those ties would strengthen—defying the bounds of bare reason.

Part IV: May 1918–December 1921

Chapter 23

The Gift of Memory—June 30, 1919

The Henry Street Clinic was barely visible from York Street in Belfast's "Linenoplis" section. All the workers, however, knew exactly where the entrance was—just a few turns left from their employer's front gates. The York Street Flax Spinning Company—one of the most prolific producers of Northern Ireland linen—took up an entire city block. Throughout the day, its four-story walls extended physical and social shadows over its employees inside and their families outside. Blocks away, the Harland and Wolff dockyards spread the same.

Tucked off an alley on Henry Street was the clinic. Open from 5:00 a.m. to 10:00 p.m. every weekday, the volunteer staff—doctors, nurses, and caregivers—offered diagnoses, treatments, and, more often than not, distressing prognoses. Most mill patients came after a hard day of labor, suffering persistent coughs, bodily wounds, or the "mill fever" of nausea, headache, and chills. Others came from the dockyards pained by black lungs and injuries from constructing ships or loading and unloading cargo. Their family members, affected by malnutrition, accidents, or infections, traveled miles to the small clinic from the outskirts of Belfast on Saturdays or after their Sunday worship—Catholic or Protestant—for the additional hours from 3:00 p.m. to 10:00 p.m.

Dr. Lizzie, BB, and Rachel were busier than ever this Monday in June. Ian had accompanied them, as his interest in medicine had been well noted by Liam and BB. Now, Lizzie and Rachel recognized it as well. Only Liam—and Bigger—knew its true motivation, which grew out of a commitment to never, ever kill anyone.

But, the three Dubliners had arrived in Belfast not only to attend to the physical needs of the city's beleaguered. They had been asked, in addition, by none other than Michael Collins to come to the northern city on an IRA mission regarding the factories' laborers. The War of Independence required a continuous effort to mobilize strikes that would financially injure Unionist managers and British owners. Diminishing their wealth garnered from bent backs and dark lungs of Free-State-leaning laborers was a strategic, offensive tactic of Republicans Collins and de Valera. In addition to attacks on the Black and Tan and RIC, the two leaders knew mistreatment of workers had to be addressed by the new government in Dublin. Strikes were needed to improve working conditions and gain the votes of the common citizenry. If laborers could see the benefits of union organizing to their own livelihood and welfare, they might even take up arms within the independence movement.

"Help me lift this woman onto the table, Ian," asked Lizzie in a tiny examination room. "And, Rachel, fetch some apples and carrots from the storeroom down the hallway."

Ian leaned over a small woman, bent in a wicker chair like the head of a shepherd's crock. She was about thirty-five, yet looked fifty, her hair greying under a soiled cap. Her chapped fingers were gnarled. Her face was an ashen color, like the mist hovering over the peat bogs on a damp winter night. Lizzie and Ian heard the woman groan as Ian lifted her to the table. Fortunately, its surface was covered by a clean, linen sheet over a soft, lamb's wool blanket. The woman's sigh upon being carefully positioned on her side was almost inaudible; yet, her two attendants clearly heard it.

"Tell me, dear. What be yer name and what ails ye?" queried Lizzie, already assuming the answer. Taking out her stethoscope and readying it to place on the patient's back, she leaned her ear toward the woman's lips.

"My name is Alma O'Malley, and I can't breathe properly, me lady." She wheezed once, was silent, and wheezed again. Lizzie and Ian waited for an ease in Alma's struggle. "I can't stand up at the loom for more than an hour," she whispered. "Help me, I beg. I can't lose me job."

Part IV: May 1918–December 1921

Lizzie placed her hand on Alma's head. "Calm thyself, dear. I'll just listen to yer lungs and see what we can do." As Lizzie held the instruments to the woman's back, she frowned at Ian and shook her head.

Pushing back the white hair falling from her own cap, Lizzie straightened her back, walked around to the other side of the table, and rolled the woman onto her back. Alma kept her eyes on Lizzie's face.

"Let me now hear yer heart." The doctor avoided Alma's eyes. After a seemingly endless minute, Lizzie raised the woman to a seated position on the side of the table and faced her directly.

"I can't be sure, but I fear ye may have consumption." Alma started to weep and, then, coughed. Lizzie did not want to turn her own head away from the distraught figure's face but knew she must, as consumption was highly contagious.

She motioned to Ian to leave the room. "Ian, can you see what's holding Rachel up?" He understood the real intent of Lizzie's instructions and hesitated. She repeated her request. "Please Ian, find Rachel." He turned away and left the room.

Outside in the crowded hallway, Ian saw Rachel, a basket of fruit and vegetables in hand. She was talking intently with a young lad who seemed familiar to Ian. He couldn't quite place from where.

Rachel gestured Ian to join them. "Ian, meet Shawn O'Malley. His mum is in with Dr. Lizzie now."

The young lad gazed at Ian. His mouth opened, but no words emerged. Ian's memory sought the familiarity of the expression, the red cheeks, and the furrowed brow.

"Are ye from Coalisland?" asked Ian.

"Nay, " the youth replied. "I'm from Falls Road."

"Have ye been to Bangor recently?" pursued Ian, now beginning to place the face with a voice.

The youth looked down, then up, water beginning to tide over his eyes but not flow onto the cheeks below.

"Aye," came a mumbled response.

Ian reached for the stooping shoulders of the lad. "Ah. I know who ye are and ye need not worry about how I do. Ye're here now, and we're all together trying to help your mum. She'll need more than a British pound for milk, Shawn. My friend Rachel has some fruit and vegetables for ye. That will help."

Ian could not bring himself to tell this young lad that he recognized him—the lad whom he had rescued from death in the shed next to the alley near the Smiley home just four months prior. Nor, could he tell Shawn about his mother's fatal condition.

"Come, let's talk to the doctor." Rachel watched as the two strode side-by-side to the examination room, Ian's arm around the trembling shoulder of the youth.

"Ach," she thought. "There's something more between these two than I know. Ian will have to tell me."

PART IV: MAY 1918–DECEMBER 1921

CHAPTER 24

Circling Around the Carpet—July 10, 1919

"This enigma is too much to bear, Agnes." Billie put down the day's edition of the *Irish Bulletin*, took off his spectacles, and looked toward the three, beveled windows of their Rathmines salon. No night breeze entering through the opened panels could cool his angst.

The late hour had offered the two a respite from their respective, daily activities of Dáil negotiations and IRA meetings, as well as from the common household chores of caring for their two energetic McCormick adoptees—Thon, now age eleven, and Jon, now age ten.

"Tell me what ye're fearing, my dear," asked Agnes, resting a lace handkerchief and its crochet needle on her billowing lap. Happily, they were finally awaiting their own child. Thus, Agnes' bulbous torso was the resting place for her evening handiwork. As yet, she had not finished even one blanket for the new arrival. All her finger work, instead, was focused on producing items for sale by the Dublin section of Cumann na mBan in support of *the Cause*.

"'Tis the Irish question at the Paris Peace Conference," responded Billie. "After the November armistice, various surrender and compensation treaties are being formulated among the victors—France, England, Italy, and Japan—and conquered Germany plus its allies of Austria, Bulgaria, and Turkey. The *Bulletin* has a recent article by J. C. Walsh, a correspondent of the U.S. publication *America*, who is currently attending the conference. He says Ireland may be identified in some of the treaties as a free nation, independent from Great Britain. But that will only happen if our Irish-American brothers and de Valera can convince President Wilson to include it as such in the initial Treaty of Versailles."

"Is that possible, Billie?" Agnes stood to stretch her stiff legs. She placed her delicate, lace piece on the side table and stepped awkwardly across the worn Donegall carpet. The family heirloom, given to Billie and Agnes by Mother Lizzie upon their marriage, comforted her swollen feet and spousal concern. The yellow and blue phoenixes embedded within the floral design were fading due to all of the foot and finger trafficking it had endured over the decades. Irvine, Smiley, McCann, and McCormick fathers and uncles had sat patiently on the carpet alongside curious and often rambunctious sons. Together, they had read newspapers and escorted wooden carts and miniature trains along the lined wings and blossoms of the figures. Daughters and nieces had also played and read their books upon that same intriguing surface—competing, at times, with their male peers for the attention of their elders and a favorite section of the rug. Both sets of children had settled into its woolen façade to listen to the adults seated around them.

Agnes smiled as she looked down upon the indentations in the old carpet and anticipated the new member of their family who would soon benefit from the rug's history. "May ye keep comforting us with yer enduring foundation," she said to herself as she began to walk around its parameter.

"De Valera has opened up Pandora's box in his relations with opposing factions of the Irish-American community," Billie continued. "Since his June arrival in New York, de'V has alienated the New York branch of the Friends of Irish Freedom led by the elder Judge Daniel Cohalan and John Devoy[10] by taking the side of an opposing Philadelphia branch headed by the younger Joseph McGarrity[11]. The New Yorkers support self-determination by the Irish people whereas McGarrity advocates for a Republic of Ireland. de'V wants nothing to do with self-determination if it precludes Ulster remaining in the Republic. In addition, it seems that most Irish-Americans don't like anything about the League of Nations since it assumes British sovereignty over Ireland. It's not suitable by them to revise the Paris Peace Treaty; they want it totally abolished. Finally, de'V doesn't understand that ye can't tell Americans what to think or do, even if they are Irish-Americans. Cohalan bristles at de'V's assumption that de'V thinks he controls the Irish-American community. In either ignorance or arrogance, de'V is willing to set Irish-American against Irish-American—as well as Irish against Irish—to attain the final goal of a unified Ireland.

"Ach, Agnes" sighed Billie, as he continued, "And there is another component to the enigma. Although in 1918 President Wilson pledged before the American Congress that 'National aspirations must be respected; peoples may now be dominated and governed only by their own consent', he is quick to remember betrayals. He considers both Irish-American factions as treasonous since several of their leaders supported Germany during the Easter Rising and the war itself. You may remember that Cohalan and Devoy funded Roger Casement's purchase of arms from the Germans for the first days of the Rising. This disloyalty to America, coupled with the fact that a majority of pro-Democrat Irish-Americans voted against Wilson in 1912, have convinced the president that we do not deserve representation at the Peace Conference."

Billie stood up as Agnes made her third circle around the carpet's parameter. He took her arm and joined her slowing pace. They were silent walkers for a few minutes.

Agnes spoke first. "I read Mum's article last week in *Our Ireland* where she said Wilson had declared all colonies' claims be adjusted to honor self-determination. In the proposed 14 Points he wants included in the Versailles Treaty, Wilson has vowed that colonies, like us, have equal weight with colonizers in determining our nationhood. What has changed his applying this to Ireland?"

Billie sighed. "Ach, 'tis true. He did state that, but he still resents Friends of Irish Freedom's attitude toward Germany, and the lack of Irish-American votes during his presidential election. He also feels allowing Ireland to be identified in any treaty as an independent nation will alienate Great Britain in supporting his dream of a League of Nations. Great Britain will never accept a self-determined

Irish Republic in actuality, let alone in writing within any peace treaty document. I fear de Valera has taken a step too far in America and didn't heed Collins' warnings against alienating our brothers and sisters there."

"What does the journalist Walsh say may happen next?" Agnes queried. The two had stopped their circular walk and stood in front of the open, middle panel of the salon's windows. They watched convoluted clouds swiftly darken a full moon. Billie placed his arm around Agnes' shoulder.

"Like those clouds, Agnes, there will be ever changing shadows over the next months covering the light of our future." He turned and picked up another newspaper, the *Irish Independent*. "Let me read you Walsh's concluding paragraph.

> "'It came to me that the new map of Europe has been drawn in terms of nationality. There are no Continental Empires left, no subject peoples. Every state is a nationality, every nationality has been erected into a state. From the Dniester to the English Channel there is no exception to the rule. Ireland's case, which ante dates all the others, is alone excluded from the reckoning. Does the exception prove the rule, or will the rule preclude the exception? As Mr. Wilson has both formulated the rule and applied it, I suppose he must expect to be asked this question.'"

Billie paused, then said, "I fear de Valera may not like the answer, nor will our Dáil. We are headed for a continued war of independence without international support." Billie looked at Agnes who sought the eyes that usually shined hope.

She held his hand tightly. "Let us not be dismayed, my darling," she said. "Mother Lizzie is coming from Belfast tomorrow. For certain, she will carry news more current and more private than this article. I know she has been in correspondence with our Margaret McKenzie in New York as well as Countess Markievicz. Ye know us women. We have ears much wider than our smiles to know what surrounds us. Calm yerself."

Agnes bent Billie's head down and kissed him on the forehead. She looked down at the carpet once more. She remembered her times visiting the Irvines as a child and listening to all those around her on the carpet. Its grounding would continue to comfort the men and women, lads and lassies, in her family, and, for certain, the next generation already being nurtured within her.

CHAPTER 25

Train of Thought—July 11, 1919

Lizzie gazed out the window of the Great Northern Railway Ireland express. "Me darlin', darlin', Will," she murmured, thinking to herself. "How can I tell them what lies ahead?"

Her unsettled thoughts were as blurred as her vision, loosing focus on the white and yellow figures dotting the vibrant green hillsides between Belfast and Dublin passing rapidly alongside the train. Predictable summer shearing of molting sheep and careful gathering of thorny gorse were as illusive to Lizzie's eyes as were her thoughts. No easy diagnoses and treatments were clear to her. "Ach, Will. Ye would know the best words to say."

Too much was on Lizzie's mind and in her heart. She and Countess Markievicz had met for dinner two evenings before in one of the finest hotels in Belfast, the Grand Central on Royal Street. Despite being released on amnesty from Holloway prison in 1917, the Countess was still considered a person of import by the Belfast Royal Irish Constabulary. In the election of December 1918, she had won a seat representing Dublin St. Patrick's, becoming the first female elected as a Minister of Parliament in the House of Commons. Like her colleagues in Sinn Féin, however, she had refused to take that seat in London. Instead, in January 1919, she swore to the newly formed Republic of Ireland in the Dublin-based Dáil Éireann. Four months later, she was appointed as the Republic's first Minister of Labour—the second woman to serve in any European nation as a government minister. That night, as she and Lizzie had taken their dinner seats, they hoped the Countess would not be recognized. Fortunately, despite her beauty and notoriety, only a few eyes had turned in surprise upon seeing the pair.

Part IV: May 1918–December 1921

As the landscape passed more rapidly with the speed of the train, Lizzie's memory also sped through the conversation she and the Countess had held. Their table had been tucked into a back corner of the massive dining hall, away from the entrance and raised platform upon which an ebony, Steinway Model M grand piano was quietly playing Gershwin's newly published "Swanee" . . .

"I don't understand why, instead of these American songs, we can't hear a few Irish jigs and just throw ourselves into the dance," mused Constance to Lizzie. "I guess we must feign an English decorum and allegiance to anything American, mustn't we, to serve the cause? God forbid our actions would reverse the disparaging remarks I assume Unionists in this room are sharing against de'V and us. How they are like scavenger gulls gobbling up the detritus of cod and haddock along the docks."

The Countess tossed her head back and straightened her spine. The pheasant feather decorating her gray, felt, cloche hat bounced with her defiance. "I'd love to get on that dance floor and show them all our splendid Gaelic culture. But alas, not tonight; for you and I have much to discuss."

Lizzie leaned in to hear the Countess' whispered message that Lizzie was to convey to Billie and Agnes in Dublin. Eamon's sister-in-law, Margaret McKenzie's, recent letter to Lizzie confirmed the content. Margaret's banker husband had secured American funds for Sinn Féin. They would soon arrive in Billie's bank account as a gift for the family to purchase land. After all, hadn't Billie openly stated in *The Irish Times* last month his intentions to open up an academy for both Catholic and Protestant youth? The Countess congratulated Lizzie on her son's brilliant strategy to camouflage the transfer's actual intent. Lizzie agreed but was not totally sure the strategy would work.

. . . Now, as she sat back on a worn seat within a GNRI's third-class cabin, she fully recognized the danger her family was facing.

And yet, she also knew its commitment and courage—traits transcendent from genetic fragments of so many ancestors. Her medical acumen was convinced of that.

At the same time, however, she realized that physical and personality characteristics could not ensure longevity within a person. After all, humans evolved along complex lines, influenced—or perhaps even determined—by political interpretations as well. Were not her current family members evolving in different ways? Billie and BB had disavowed violence; Kat had not. Eamon had also rejected violence. Perhaps Thon and Jon would as well, or would they follow Kat? Would Agnes' passion, inherited from Wolfe Tone, flow into the life growing within her? And what about the extended family members—Rachel, Ian, Morna, Devin, and Neil? How would their lives evolve due to the influence of their adopted parents?

Lizzie closed her eyes and called upon Will again. "What shall I say to our children, me darlin'?"

She heard him say, "The truth, me love. The truth, and then—"

She suddenly raised her handkerchief and coughed into it. Pale pink colored its white lace shamrock design.

"Aye. I will tell them the truth and, then, I'll come to ye."

Chapter 26

The Falcon and the Dove—July 11, 1919

At 11:00 p.m., while Lizzie's train was entering Bangor Street Station, the Hawk Tavern in the northern town of Coalisland was closing its doors to the general public. The three McLoughlin daughters had gathered the empty jugs of poitín strewn upon tables randomly set in the common area. During the evening's earlier ceilidh, chairs had been anchored, raised, and dropped again as the tides of conversations and song rose and ebbed. The girls' hands were red from washing out the dried foam of jugs and glasses covered, all too often, with the spit of drunken customers who mistook the containers as their personal spittoon. Worse yet, some used them as the repository of another bodily waste, the color of amber.

"Ach, how I hate those feckin' eejits who think we're their personal maids on their grand estates. Someday, I'll find me revenge by handin' them a new jug ripe with their own remains," joked the eldest daughter Meghan. Her two sisters, Becca and Ruth, laughed aloud.

"'Tis old Eve McNulty speaking through ye, Meghan," remarked Becca, referring to the spirit of that mystical grandmother who, during her wake in this very same pub December of last year, had invoked the death of a conspirator who had betrayed Meghan and Becca's husbands. No love was lost nor regained by the daughters when considering the Orangemen in Coalisland. That was why they were cleaning up the tavern for tonight's meeting.

As branch members of the Irish Land and Labour Association (ILLA), the attendees—both rural farmers and nationalist town merchants—would focus on the disappointing impact of agricultural reforms in the North. Due to twenty years of Irish Parliamentarian pressure, boycotts, cattle drives, and outright murders of landowners

—particularly English royalty residing in Ireland or directing estate managers from London—numerous Land Acts between 1883 and 1906 had actually been passed by the British Parliament. These acts had enabled some Irish (Catholic and Protestant) tenants to reduce their monthly rents or, better yet, to purchase outright the land they had worked upon for generations. Regretfully, these acts had been compromised eventually by diminishing agricultural prices, resistant landowners, and very bad weather. Each had been exacerbated, in the North particularly, by the actions of local paramilitary Ulster Volunteers. Tonight, Coalisland citizens wanted to plan to confront their human adversaries. Curtains had been drawn and lamps lowered.

"We have to utilize our strengths and diminish our differences, good folks," said Stuart McCormick, at the beginning of the meeting. He was Liam's younger brother by six years and Rachel's older by sixteen. Like his two siblings, Stuart had escaped their alcoholic mother at a young age and, unlike them, had taken up farming with a relative of the McCann family outside the southern town of Macroom. Through Thomas and Maud McCann, Stuart had become an organizer for the tenant rights movement in County Cork, much like Bella's brother Aiden fifty years before. Soon, Stuart was noticed by the McCann ally James John O'Shee[12], the nationalist, labor advocate and solicitor who co-founded the ILLA. Stuart was now O'Shee's law apprentice and ILLA spokesperson in the North.

A confronting voice was heard from the back of the room. "It's fair game for ye to say that, laddie, but me land needs to come back to me. I can't stand workin' in the mines. It's no replacement for the smell and feel of the soil in me hands and below me feet and the song of me cows bayin' at milkin' time. And me dear Becca needs to feel safe at night walkin' back from the shop. We've boycotted, driven our cattle into the streets and still the Orange Ulster buggers threaten us. Just last week, Paddy here was shot in the leg by one and can't work his fields no more. We need to take up arms and fight back. What do ye say to that?"

Part IV: May 1918–December 1921

Crackles of agreement flowed toward Stuart like an incoming tide over rough-hewn shale and gurgling rockweed. He thought quickly.

"I understand yer grievances. I understand yer fears. But I know what has worked in other towns feeling the same offenses ye have. How might it be if we talk tonight about what they have done and, then, what ye want to do? I just beg ye to be honest and just Irishmen like those we honor before us, from Wolfe Tone to Parnell to Pádraig Pearse."

Seated by a front table nearest Stuart, a young man stood up with the help of an oaken staff. He turned to the crowd of mumbling men and women. They went quiet. Paddy McNulty began to speak.

"Ye know I am not an educated sort, nor have I a priestly tongue. Like ye all, I'm just a man tryin' me hardest to care for me family and me land. But tonight I hear this young lad remind us how we need to care for our greater family, our greater land, and our Ireland with honor in mind and heart. Ye see me leg here? It's destroyed. No longer can I easily walk the paths to Lough Neagh, nor carry me weeins on me back."

Several women bowed their heads, reached into their pockets for a soiled piece of cloth. Eyes were rubbed regardless.

Paddy noticed their movements. He hesitated, then continued.

"But—and this is a grand *but*—I have me mind and I have me voice. And I have me love of ye all and this place we call home. Those are deep and lastin' powers that can never be made lame, no matter what other physical harm may strike me."

Now, the men seemed to listen.

"Hear this lad out," Paddy continued. "He's right about our needin' to be the just people our ancestors have been. We can't keep goin' on only by arms taking out legs like mine. He's telling us that our neighboring communities are beginnin' to wear down those who act against us. Like them, perhaps we can win this war against the Brits and Unionists by expanding our actions, not restricting them only to violence. Let us continue the merchant boycotts, keep the cattle blockin' the roads, and exchange our goods among ourselves at fair prices. Let's go ahead with this lad and form our own courts, man our own police and vote for those who support us here at home and in London."

Paddy paused, looked back at Stuart, then, at the crowd.

"Ye all knew my gran Eve. She never went to school nor could she read. But she loved the songs of poetry, especially those which were short and easily remembered."

The crowd murmured a soft laugh. Paddy continued, "Here's what I think she would say tonight, one that she especially liked from the poet, John O'Reilly . . .

'The red rose whispers of passion,
And the white rose breathes of love;
Oh, the red rose is a falcon,
And the white rose is a dove.
But I send you a cream-white rosebud,
With a flush on its petal tips;
For the love that is the purest and sweetest
Has a kiss of desire on the lips.' "

Paddy looked again at Stuart. "What do ye want us to do, young man? What can be our cream-white rose bud that desires freedom?"

PART IV: MAY 1918–DECEMBER 1921

CHAPTER 27

Silent Listening—July 12, 1919

Stuart traveled the next day to Belfast to report on his meetings in the various towns and villages around Coalisland. His time with Paddy and the McLoughlin women had been particularly enlightening. The compass guiding the War of Independence had perhaps been magnetized too strongly toward its political pole, abandoning the economic, social, and religious directions.

"We can't forget that our brothers and sisters survive on daily wages and bartering, not on protests or strikes," warned Stuart as he pulled up a chair to the Smiley's kitchen table in Bangor. James John O'Shee and Liam McCormick were already seated with Eamon and Ian after savoring Kat's fine evening meal of mutton and cabbage. Lizzie had claimed weariness from her previous day's travels and had retired to her special bedroom off of the boys' room. Kat and Rachel were washing up the simple pottery plates and Bella's fine silverware—the last vestige of her Scottish inheritance.

Now, the McKnight-Irvine-Smiley family was solidly invested in being Irish, either native or Scots-Irish; Protestant or Catholic; politician, teacher, or writer. They were all activists fighting in their own, unique ways for a new nation.

"The shoulder-pulling and back-aching work most men suffer in the mines is now being replaced by burns of molten metal in foundries producing car and cycle parts along with kitchen utensils of kettles, pots, and spoon," said Stuart.

The womens' backs—but not ears—had been turned away from the conversing men. Rachel shrugged at Stuart's description and muttered, "How much better can aluminum pots—or alania, or alunior, whatever the term is—be than our good old stone ones?"

"Ach, Rachel," laughed James John. "Ye must become part of the future, not live in the past. Ye'll be drivin' a motor car soon, just watch ye."

"Not on yer life, Mr. O'Shee," the youth responded. "All that coin for what? Gettin' to church a bit faster? Or beepin' those silly horns at the cattle moseyin' up the roads? Just you watch. For sure, their milk will come out sour in the market soon as both they and we are scared to death by those troublemakers!" For a thirteen-year-old, she sounded like an eighteenth century matriarch.

O'Shee laughed. "Ye sound just like Grace O'Malley must have before the Queen defending her son!"

As an aside, Ian nudged Liam. "She's a fine lass, isn't she? Stubborn as the moon breaking through on a cloudy night."

Liam whispered back. "Ye need to live with her a while as I did while she was a weein. Then, we'll see what ye think of her." Ian blushed.

"Rachel is right in one way," continued Stuart, "but the death isn't by noise. It's by the poor workin' conditions and duplicitous manipulation of our men. Gas and electrical companies are rivaling for our men who need and want better payin' jobs. Once hired, none have any interest in joining unions that are perceived as threatening such employment. Regardless of the hours—which are from six in the mornin' to nine at night, with little breaks and littler compensation—the workers are desperate to be hired. Worse yet, the company managers are turnin' Protestants against Catholics by encouraging Protestants to lie about the quality of Catholic work. The situation is fertile for turnin' our independence movement into a labor struggle amongst our own people."

"Aye, it's a dicey situation," acknowledged John James. "We have to turn this tide and prove our movement honors any worker, regardless of religion or employment—be it on farms, mines or mills, on the sea or on docks, in the foundries or shops, or even in the garda."

Part IV: May 1918–December 1921

He turned to Rachel and Kat as well as to the men around the table. "What thoughts have ye?"

For the next hours—well into the lighting of the oil lamps, as no electricity could yet be afforded by the philosophy professor of Queen's University—the seven deliberated. A plan was formed to which even the stubborn Rachel agreed.

As the lamps were being extinguished, Liam could not help but chuckle at Rachel's good-night blessing to Sceo as she patted his head, "Bless ye, fine friend, for being so loyal and patient without knowin' what our words tonight have meant and what tomorrow will bring."

Sceo gave a whimpered retort but muttered to himself. "Ah, missy. It is in silent listening that wisdom is heard. Ye would be wise to practice that as I do."

Chapter 28

Farewells—July 12, 1919

In her room, Lizzie set down her pen on the worn desk upon which, for forty years, she, as Ms. Inde Pen, had written editorials for *Our Ireland*. The piece she had just finished would not be published. She wanted it read by her family only.

As she exhaled with some difficulty, she felt a gentle breeze upon the back of her neck. A soothing warmth began to surround her. Raising her head, she asked, "Is it time?"

"Aye," came the reply. "And so it is."

A tender touch brushed Lizzie's cheek as a mystical shape began to form in front of her.

"Are ye an angel?" Lizzie asked.

"Of sorts," murmured the shape, emerging from the yellow glow of an oil lamp positioned on the desk between the two. Lizzie could make out a woman's figure, shimmering while seemingly floating. Veiled in a gossamer nightgown and draped in a filigreed-like shawl, her body appeared youthful. There were no distinct features on the face to interpret an expression of intent, yet there was a semblance of grace and peace in her presence. White hair was gathered into a body-length braid that hung over her left shoulder. A ribbon of fingers hovering in the air reached forward. To Lizzie, the image was miraculous.

"Am I dead?" asked Lizzie.

"Not yet, my dear. But soon." The figure whispered with a Scottish lilt, flowing like ripples across stepping-stone pebbles in a country stream leading to the River Clyde.

Lizzie recognized the cadence from her childhood when, during evening baths, her own Scots mother would sing the nursery rhyme "Wee Willie Winkie." When the coolness of eventide would abate

Part IV: May 1918–December 1921

hot summer days, Lizzie sang it herself to her three weeins as they bathed in Bangor streams leading to the lough.

"Ach, why am I reminiscing so?" She shook her head to return to the present, wondering what the present actually was.

"I am just finishing a letter to the family. Do I have time to do so?" Lizzie asked.

"Aye," whispered the figure.

"Shall I read it to ye?"

"Aye."

Lizzie began.

"My darlings. I have perhaps been remiss in not informing ye sooner of my imminent and inevitable departure. Forgive me, please, if ye are offended. As ye well know, death is not something I fear. Nor is it something about which I have pondered in regard to myself. My work in the Lying-In, mill, and city clinics has prepared me for this moment. I don't know if it—nor I—have prepared ye. Let me try in these few words.

"Yer father—whom I will soon join— and I are most proud of each of ye.

"Billie, me darling. Yer fortitude, keeping bright the light of our movement in London's Parliament and in now Dublin, is more than admirable. Ye're the true grandson of yer grand-da William, the son of yer father Will and, for certain, a model of integrity, diplomacy, and negotiation for yer Jon and Thon. Dare I add, Rachel? Indeed, I must. But ye may need to work a bit harder understanding her. Exploit her stubbornness, don't criticize it. Never dismiss her as a possible Minister of Labor for the Dáil once the Countess retires.

"Kat, my dear, yer gran-mum Bella's voice is in every word ye write and speak. I will be forever grateful for the lessons ye have given me to talk with women in our movement—to not just address their social needs, but to listen to their daily trials. Ye have helped me hear their voices, not just my own, and to find the best words to speak on their behalf. Devin, Neil, and yer new one are blessed by yer gifts. They, too, will lead our nation forward by listening to and speaking up for all.

"And BB, my precious. I look forward to being with Sister Bridgette and hearing how much she has loved watchin' ye choose yer own path of conscience. The lives ye have saved physically equal those ye have saved spiritually. Through the Grand War and, now, our War of Independence ye have lived by the cross. Never have ye put it down when asked to do something that compromised yer faith in God and in humankind. Ian and Morna will take it up for ye, I know.

"As for the loves of my children, I have nothing but praise and admiration. Eamon, Agnes and Liam, ye have chosen and been chosen well. May ye grow from the nurturance of Irvine roots and they from yours, add layers and layers of strong bark upon yer already noble trunks, and bask in the crown of yer collective branches. Together with Billie, Kat and BB, ye are family and with the children now, ye are all that matters in forming our nation."

Lizzie stopped reading.

Her eyes closed; she tried to inhale; her head folded into her shoulder; a final breath was taken.

The oil lamp flickered and went out. In its place was a radiant light that glowed around the two figures—the spirit and Lizzie. Both were now translucent.

"Have I passed?" Lizzie said, opening her eyes.

The figure embraced her.

"Aye."

Part IV: May 1918–December 1921

Una's Epilogue to Part IV

Passages—December 1921

These past months have been full of paradoxes for our family and dear Ireland. Like the rainbow that appears after a horrific storm, the sight of land after a traumatic sea journey, or the first cry of a babe after a mother's anguished labor, great joy has accompanied great sorrow. Let me explain.

Since August 1919, two Irvine-Gallagher members have joined me and Will on our walks: Lizzie and her brother John. Their passings provoked great sorrow in the families, but great joy for Will. Older brother Anthony, who preceded his siblings here, often strolls with us; but, he seems to be more interested in Sarah McCracken (Agnes' sister) who just made her transition during Bloody Sunday of November 1920. While the presence of these family members has given me great comfort, we often weep over the loss of so many others in just one year—1920, the Year of Terror during Ireland's War of Independence.

At the same time as we mourned, however, we celebrated the birth of several new family members whom, you might say, have replaced Lizzie and John. Our Kate Tone Irvine was born at the end of 1918. The boys Wolfe McCracken-Irvine and Kieran Irvine-McCormick were born nine months apart on August 7, 1919 and May 7, 1920, respectively. A wee lass, Maggie McCormick, came in April 1919. Her cousin Elizabeth (Liza) Irvine-Smiley, was born on Christmas Eve, 1919. Billie and Agnes almost lost Wolfe to consumption when he was just a month old. But, by the grace of the gods, he survived. Lizzie blames herself for his illness contracted from her before she passed. John, Anthony, and I have had to comfort and contradict her mightily. We label Wolfe the "Fightin' Irishman," named for Agnes' great, great granduncle Wolfe Tone. Like him, baby Wolfe heroically garnered his strength to live, as the disease would have killed any other infant. Besides this fortitude, we foresee much insight emerging from him. After all, he has his father's, grandfather's, and great-grandfather's piercing blue, Irvine eyes.

What can we about Maggie Margaret McGregor-McCormick born say with a full head of red tufts, some curly and some sticking up like furze on a hilltop? Liam swears she has the voice of Michael, having listened to his stories in BB's womb. Ach, she will be the storyteller for sure.

As for Kieran, he is his mother BB's joy and his father Liam's pride. If one is seeking an exemplar of the "spoiled child," just ask Rachel, Ian, and Morna the question of who among them loves Kieran the most. The three siblings—albeit non-biological—have focused their daily arguments over who gets to care for the infant more. From afar, Lizzie roots for Ian as he practices his medical knowledge on the child. John praises Rachel's interactions with Kieran for her Irish Gaelic fluency. And, Morna—well, Morna is my beloved. She is the peacemaker, calming Kieran when he frets, and negotiating between Ian and Rachel when they argue about no matter what. Morna lives within her own thoughts, yet often speaks up when reminding her peers—as well as her adoptive parents—to resolve conflict amicably. How bravely she has coped with the loss of her own parents in Coalisland, and abides, like her brother Ian, by her father's message: "Do not be a lesser person than those who want to take yer life. Run yer own race for righteous justice."

And Liza, the newest female to our family. In her first year, she has captured everyone's admiration and love. Like her great-gran Bella, her gran Lizzie, and her mum Kat, her bubbling smiles accentuate her sparkling hazel eyes that follow everyone who engages her—and with whom she engages. She delights herself and others whenever awake and the fairies when asleep. What a future she will have as she explores her world and contributes to it.

These new offspring are the seeds for a bountiful harvest cultivated upon our rich Irish landscape. We elders are so proud.

As for the members of the collective Irish family, we are not so pleased. There has been too much deception and bloodshed over the past two years. I can't bear to mention their examples, but I must. As for deception, de Valera spent most of the last eighteen months in America confusing, alienating, or turning Irish-Americans against each other. None wanted him to dictate what they should be thinking or voting upon. Sorrow number one for us is de'V's alienation of the Irish-American community.

Equally disappointing was the fact that the Dáil had sent $1.5 million to de Valera to secure a U.S. Congressional declaration of the Republic of Ireland independent from Great Britain. That declaration never came. The House of Representatives, instead, recognized the split between de Valera and the Irish-American representatives and vetoed, not only the declaration, but Wilson's entire League of Nations proposal. Sorrow number two for us is de'V's alienation of the U.S. government.

In addition to these two sorrows, de'V secured $5.1 million in Republic of Ireland bonds bought by our working American brothers and sisters. However, $3 million has remained in America since his return this past December. We worry that it will never see the sun of an Irish day. This sorrow number three for us is de Valera's undermining the trust of many Republicans here in Ireland, including some of its leaders.

Thus, de'V's trip is not considered a success. He has split the Irish-American community's support of Ireland, did not succeed in the inclusion of Irish independence in either the Paris Peace Treaty or a League of Nations, and is increasingly criticized for mishandling the Irish-American bond funds. We three cannot dismiss the rumors about his lavish dinners, expensive hotel stays at the Waldorf Astoria in New York City, and a supposed extramarital affair with his secretary Kathleen O'Connell. Shame, shame, shame.

The greater sham, however, is the months of bloodshed he avoided by being in the U.S. and not at home. We wonder what his conscience said to him when he heard Arthur Griffith report last month to the Dáil about the terrible losses among our Republicans. And, despite our loyalty to them, we also grieve the losses on the Unionist side.

It is within this context of bloodshed that the dear life of Agnes' sister, Sarah, was lost. On Sunday, November 21st of last year, "Collins' Squad" attacked the Dublin-based Cairo Gang, a ferocious British intelligence group of former WWI British soldiers intended to undermine IRA rebels. Sixteen Cairo Gang members were killed. In retaliation that very afternoon, the RIC entered a Gaelic Athletic Association football match in Dublin's Croke Park and indiscriminately shot into the watching crowd, killing fourteen civilians and wounding sixty-five others. Sarah was in the stands with her primary school students from Protestant and Catholic families. She died shielding two of them from RIC bullets.

That day, known as Bloody Sunday, has turned the tide of the Irish majority against the British. More and more common folk have rejected the Black and Tan and their own neighbors who support Great Britain. Mill and mine strikes have galvanized the labor unions and, aligning with local farmers, have sorely damaged our economy. Shop owners haven't allowed Unionists to shop in their stores; judges have refused to try IRA members captured by the RIC; and RIC police have resigned and joined the IRA in droves. This change of Irish hearts and minds has led both the UK Government and the IRA into peace talks. Tomorrow—yes, we know it will be tomorrow—a truce will be declared and peace talks will begin between de Valera and UK Prime Minister Lloyd George.

Thank the gods, in de'V's absence, Collins was acting here at home as the true leader of the movement. Without him, this truce could never have happened. He is the consummate diplomat, never criticizing the vagaries of de Valera's actions, nor the man himself. Collins always presents them in the best light of rationalization. He is a genius performing multiple roles. He has successfully led the military wing of the IRA in their guerrilla tactics, carefully assessing each assault and retaliation on traitors. He has aptly managed the Dáil's finances and calmed the concerns of IRA and Dáil members about de Valera's conflicting positions. Collins' conscience must be clear as peace approaches.

May the gods protect him and all those who contribute to this peace. And may those who counteract it, never walk with us here.

PART V:
JULY 1921–APRIL 1922
ANGLO-IRISH TREATY
DELIBERATIONS

PART V: JULY 1921–APRIL 1922

CHAPTER 29

Façades—August 1921

The lobby of the Grand Central Hotel on Royal Street in Belfast was festooned with crystal chandeliers and magnificent Mandarin vases full of silk roses and gardenias. Despite the exterior vestiges of war and poverty outside the hotel, the interior presence of glitter and wealth displayed a British veneer of calm. As Winston Churchill, Britain's Minister of War, had recently stated, "We have always found the Irish a bit odd. They refuse to be English." Such vanity rationalized the oppressive Black and Tan colonialism Churchill had fostered in 1920. The lobby glowed and glowered with it.

Four people greeting each other amidst the hotel's hubris exemplified the Irish capacity to outwit—and more surreptitiously exploit—the British label of "odd." Kat embraced Margaret Smiley McKenzie while Eamon shook hands with her husband Francis. The two Irish-Americans had arrived the day before. They looked rested after their transatlantic voyage from New York to Liverpool, and then a ferry ride to Belfast aboard the *Patriotic*. A good night's sleep had bolstered their energy, spirit, and their determination to counter an oppressor's assumptions.

"It's grand to finally meet you both," began Francis, a second-generation son of Ireland with both entrepreneurial and linguistic roots in County Cook parentage. His diminutive height of five feet, six inches belied his formidable stature of experience and determination that had earned him the vice presidency of the prestigious, New York-based bank J.P. Morgan & Co.

"Our visit will certainly bring our two families closer as we get to know you both and your little ones," he continued. Eamon nodded, understanding the subtle message behind these words. The term "families" was an IRA pseudonym used by de Valera during his U.S. visit to represent the ties between Irish-American emigrants and their ancestral clans. Now, in Belfast to negotiate the expansion of the bank's offices, Francis had a perfect cover to outfox the British military and deliver funds to the IRA "family."

"Let's find our way to yer homecoming dinner," nodded Eamon, placing his hand on the shoulder of Francis and guiding him to the dining salon.

Kat and Margaret followed, already engrossed in conversation. It had been nine years since Kat had watched the image of Margaret, alongside her then-husband Robbie—Eamon's twin—and their two little ones fade into the evening fog aboard the ocean liner. As part of the Irvine's escape plan for Robbie, the four Smileys had sailed from Belfast Harbor on the *St. Paul* to Liverpool and then on to New York. Letters between the two women and various newspaper articles had kept each other abreast of family and national news. They knew there was much more now to share.

And share they would over the month ahead. Like their respective husbands, they were members of sister IRA networks—albeit miles apart. Margaret had joined the American Women's Pickets and had been arrested during the August 1920 protest at the New York City Chelsea Piers. That action had galvanized the Irish-American as well as the African-American longshoremen to strike against British-owned ships. Regretfully, while in America, de Valera had seen this women's action—as with Devoy and Cohalan—as a threat to his own power. He had exploited the chasm growing between American women leaders in order to stifle their collaboration and increasing impact.

While thrilled to reunite with her sister-in-law Kat, Margaret was also in Belfast on behalf of her colleagues to meet with Countess Markievicz of Cumann na mBan and address de Valera's disruptive efforts. Kat knew about de Valera's nefarious ability to exploit internal conflict—both overseas and now at home. She would accompany Margaret to meetings with the Countess. But planning those could wait.

Part V: July 1921–April 1922

"You must tell me all about your cherubs, Devin, Liza, and Neil," exclaimed Margaret, encircling her arm around Kat's waist as they entered the dining hall.

"And ye about yer four—David, Edwin, Rose, and Arthur—or is it five with Francis' adopted son?" replied an equally exuberant Kat.

The statuesque women gave no notice to the turned heads of other guests seated around the linen-covered tables that were adorned with silverware and gold-rimmed china bearing the royal crests of George V. The hotel accoutrements were evidence of its loyalties to the Union cause; not all of the clientele were. The room was full of oddities.

This was apparent as the foursome reached a table where two others were already seated. In an Anglican, clerical frock coat and pectoral cross sat Erin McCann. Across from him, in a modest, cotton chambray nursing uniform—minus the apron and cap—sat the Countess Markievicz[13]. The small Red Cross insignia above her left breast indicated her supposed allegiance. Around them were several tables where various dapperly dressed male and female members of the IRA underground and Flying Squad were also seated, assigned to protect the two leaders and their dinner guests.

"May God bless ye, Francis," came an accent more London, high-browed than that of the current King George. "I bring you blessings and greetings from Canterbury," offered Erin.

"Et vous, aussi," came the French greeting of "And you, also" to Margaret from the Countess, displaying her early French training.

Francis chuckled as did Margaret, both quick to recognize the subterfuge. Eamon and Kat smiled, having witnessed these two characters in similar performance numerous times before.

"May God bless you as well, Reverend Charles. I have looked forward to meeting Your Grace. And you, Madam—or is it Mademoiselle?" asked Francis, turning to the Countess.

"It's actually just Rose, good sir," speaking in English with a Liverpoolian Cockney to round out the disguise. "The same as your daughter," replied the Countess, winking at the banker.

The repartee continued throughout the dinner, concealing and, then, revealing the month-long schedule of the McKenzie's visit. The accompanying Squad members, while diligent, relaxed over the free meal they appreciated on this assignment. Someone in the kitchen had prepared a traditional Irish meal of shepherd's pie with its potato-topped minced lamb, accompanied by cabbage and turnips. The multiple glasses of Allman's Pure Pot Still Whiskey that seemed to surprisingly appear—at the bequest and benevolence of Francis, freed from U.S. prohibition constraints—brought the evening gathering to a jovial and successful close.

Those who waited on and surrounded the six had been vetted by none other than Michael Collins, so there was no chance of information being shared by them with any Unionist groups. Or, at least, that was what the six, their waiters, and the accompanying Squad members believed.

While every Republican in the dining hall that night was a person of integrity, not everyone in the kitchen was.

Chapter 30

A Just Decision—Early September 1921

"Thank ye for meeting with me, good sir." The standing figure handed a pint to his seated companion before pulling out a wooden-backed chair around the timeworn table.

Since 1720, Kelly's Cellars on Bank Street in Belfast had witnessed many a whispered or rousing craic about Irish politics, culture, and history. Tonight, it would be a whispered one between two friends: Michael Collins and Eamon Smiley.

"Ach, Mick. It's I who needs to thank ye. For too long I have wondered and worried about ye. I know ye have been receiving my messages over the last months and dearly appreciate the risks ye have taken in responding."

Collins smiled an endearing grin, humor twinkling from his hazel eyes. "Now, ye know me well, Eamon. The fact that each of your reports arrives in the bodice of yer young student Kitty must give you some assurance that I first reach for it, and, then in good time, read it. Along with our bliss, Kitty keeps me well content with your philosophy class assignments which, ye may be surprised, we dutifully ponder together. Meeting her at Queen's in January 1919 was the greatest benefit I have ever gained from an academic setting and, may I say, an IRA recruitment. She's quite a debater, ye know, and a formidable strategic companion. I'd be lost without her."

He paused. His eyes began to mist over. When Collins quickly raised his pint to his lips, Eamon noticed a slight tremble in his friend's hand.

"Aye, Mick. I'm happy for ye in finding such a comfort in her. It sounds like ye need all ye can get. Tell me what's in yer mind, not just yer heart," queried Eamon, drawing his chair closer to Collins and lowering his voice.

Collins took a long swig, swallowed, and placed the glass before him. He took out a linen handkerchief, embroidered with a K monogram, to wipe the foam from his lips. His smile became a straight line below a furrowed brow. "There's a choice I must make for which I seek yer guidance. Ye remember the assignment ye gave that fortuitous class two years ago?"

Eamon frowned. Then, he chuckled. "By God, Mick. Ye're either a financial wizard, a military genius, or a brilliant historian. I have always believed you are all three. Yer keen memory proves that. Yes, I do remember the assignment, but only because I offer it each year. Do you mean writing a response to the question 'How do ye define a just life?'"

Michael nodded. "Aye, that it is."

Eamon was baffled. "Aren't ye too occupied with securing the future of our nation to consider spending time on such a task? Tell me, why are ye reconsidering it now?"

Eamon angled his chair towards Michael, moving his own pint glass to his right and settling in to listen. Eamon sensed the following discussion would be one for which he had to garner all his sensitivities from the war and years afterward of physical, emotional, and mental recovery. To date, he himself had not resolved the many conflicting facets of a *just life*, especially living as a Protestant in the North, during the last months of this War of Independence.

"De Valera and the Dáil Council may soon ask me to go to London with our delegation negotiating a formal treaty with Prime Minister Lloyd George, Colonial Secretary Winston Churchill, and Lord High Chancellor F. E. Smith. Griffith and others will be on our delegation, but they are all politicians. I am only a soldier."

Michael looked directly at Eamon. "What if we must compromise our desire for a unified Irish Republic? Ye know yerself that in the recent May elections, we lost six of the Ulster counties to the Ulster Unionist Party. Already, they now have formed their own Parliament of Northern Ireland. This war has kept us fightin' for unification with the North when their citizen votes aren't with us. And, too many lives are being lost on both sides."

Michael paused and lowered his voice to a murmur. "The truce of last month came just in time as our supplies were decreasing at a terrible rate, not to mention the lives of our brave men and women. And so it was for the Black and Tans. Both sides are at a point where we must stop and reach an agreement. I fear, though, that to ensure the peace, our delegation will have to make more accommodations than the Republicans among us are willing to accept."

Michael paused, took a deep breath, and asked the primary question he had wanted answered. "Having just led so many men and women to their deaths on behalf of an island-wide Republic, am I a *just* man knowing that I will have to give in to the Brits on their demands and sacrifice our dream of unity?"

Eamon reached for Michael's hand. Now, Eamon's own was trembling. "Good friend. I cannot give you an answer. But I will share some thoughts."

He stared directly into Michael's eyes. "Many philosophers, kings, farmers, and even women have asked this question over, not only years, but centuries: Does the end justify the means? Ye'll have to answer that question for yerself, Mick, on behalf of our mother island. What is our end, and what must be done to reach it? And what if you never see that end?"

Michael bowed his head, obviously pondering the questions. He raised his eyes and looked above Eamon's focused look. There on the venerable wall was a portrait of the mythological King of Ireland, Eochaid mac Eirc. Contemplating the white-bearded face, Michael thought to himself, "Ye were the first King who brought justice to our land. What did justice mean to ye? Although it is told that no rain fell in your reign, dew did and the harvest was plentiful each year. Was that because of yer belief that if ye couldn't have full rain, dew was just as fruitful?"

Collins returned Eamon's stare, thinking, "While I may want rain, perhaps I should be satisfied with dew as long as the harvest provides."

Speaking out loud, he mused. "I believe I have just been visited by your philosophers and farmers, and our King Eochaid." Eamon turned around and looked at the portrait. He felt his shoulders ease along with his anxious mind.

Returning to the military genius before him, Eamon knew Collins was inviting himself to be a politician after all. What Eamon heard confirmed that Michael was a military leader and budding politician grounded in philosophy.

Collins quietly reflected, saying, "If we keep fighting, island-wide independence from Great Britain won't come this year. If we make peace today, it can in the near future. Perhaps—just perhaps—that end will justify whatever a treaty requires. I can seed and water the field now for that eventual harvest."

Michael rose. The upturned smile returned. Taking his empty glass in hand and making the sign of the cross in the other, he said, "Bless you, St. Eamon. Ye may yet make this ignorant fool a student of philosophy. But first, how about another wee pint before we return to the comforting lassies we love?"

Part V: July 1921–April 1922

Chapter 31

Below the Surface—Late September 1921

"Auntie, Auntie. Look! There are mermaids in the sea!"

Morna grabbed BB's hand and pulled her toward the pebbled shoreline of the beach.

"Aye, me luv," said BB, as they glimpsed two seals breaching together just yards before them in the tidal pool of Killiney Bay. "It seems that they are with us today."

The October afternoon sun captured the frolicking shapes and the sea's glistening foam as the two pinnipeds dipped under the unsettled water. BB and Morna watched in silence, their own positions changing from hands held to arms around waists.

"Do ye believe in mermaids, Auntie BB?" asked Morna, looking out at the now tranquil shallow.

"Aye, I do." BB's arm moved from Morna's waist to her shoulder. "Ye know the tale of Thady Rua O'Dowd?" asked BB.

Morna frowned. "I think I do, but remind me, Auntie."

"Well, according to my grandmother—yer great-aunt Bella Irvine—Thady was searching for a wife. Walking one day along a beach near his home, he found a selkie combing her hair. Immediately, he fell in love with her. He stole her cloak—which actually was her fishtail—without which she couldn't go back to the sea. Reluctantly, she married him, had seven children and, while eventually loving him, always longed to return to her original home, the sea. The story is that one of their children found the cloak hidden away and told his mum. She retrieved her tail and, able to carry only two of the children, she and they slipped away under the waves, never to return to Thady. The remaining five children she turned into stone next to the shore."

BB felt Morna's sigh more than she heard it.

"I wonder if those two seals are descendants of Thady and his wife?" Morna pondered aloud. She turned away from the shoreline and looked back to the beach. "Do ye ever wonder if our family is made up of selkies and humans?"

"Ha!" exclaimed BB. "Ye are our most imaginative member, dearest Morna," turning her own face around to look at the large gathering that had become Morna's family—Uncle Billie and Aunt Agnes plus Thon, Jon, Katie, and Wolfe; Uncle Liam, Ian, Rachel, Maggie, and Kieran; and Cousin Erin as well.

The family members were enjoying a Sunday outing in Killiney just a short train ride south from Dublin. They were lounging on blankets, savoring the various delicate and hearty pastries prepared the day before, and carrying on with their usual heated discussions. The infants Katie, Wolfe, Kieran, and Maggie were scooping up sand for their own afternoon delights, much to the reprimands of any adult or youth supposedly watching the weeins but distracted by the conversational hubbub. Erin had brought news from Collins about the negotiations in London as well as about the rumors of dissension within the Dáil.

BB and Morna laughed at the raised voices directed at the toddlers before them but did not move. A number of seconds passed as both reflected instead on Morna's statement.

"I believe ye're right," BB said, breaking the contemplation. She was incredulous that this twelve-year-old lass was so insightful. "But, why do ye say that?"

Morna turned to face BB. "Some days I think my brother Ian is a selkie, exploring all that is unknown to us under the sea. He is so open to saving the lives of those he assists at the clinic—no matter what their backgrounds and loyalties to the Republic. He truly doesn't care what he knows about them above the surface. He only cares about what lies below that he can explore to heal them. Then, I hear Rachel argue with him because she thinks we should only consider what we see and hear. She sees so much hatred on the surface

Part V: July 1921–April 1922

of Unionists and doesn't care about what lies below their actions, let alone their beliefs. Without considering their thoughts, she thinks they deserve the Cumann na mBan's attacks and IRA killings. I wish she were more selkie than human."

BB held her breath to take in what Morna had just said. How had BB missed Rachel's enmity described by Morna? As a new member of Cumann na mBan, was Rachel involved in the exploits of Countess Markievicz or those of Christine O'Leary? If the former, BB could exhale, for they would be tempered by the Countess' common sense and understanding; if the latter, BB could not, for those would be fed by the sheer hatred and bigotry of Christine. Only to continue this immediate conversation did BB exhale. What was turning Rachel into a rebel without recognizing the consequences of such hatred or, more so, without considering how the future of Ireland depended upon compromise and reconciliation?

"I must talk to Liam about this," she decided. "And soon."

"My luv. Ye are such a gift to our family." BB took Morna by the shoulders. "And how brilliant ye are. Indeed, our family is a mixture of selkies and humans—and, sometimes each of us is both. I think it depends on . . . depends on . . ." BB could not finish her sentence.

Morna did. "It depends on if you want to see under the surface. If ye're not curious, ye won't look. If ye are curious, ye will. I know Rachel can be curious, but only when she's ready to consider ideas contrary to her own. And that depends on who states those ideas. She doesn't listen to me, as she thinks I'm too sensitive. She will listen to Ian despite their arguing. There's something between them that lets her trust his thoughts more than mine." Morna looked out at the sea again.

"No matter," she said, scanning the water. "And look, there are the selkies again. They are still together, although now one is following the other." BB also looked at the two figures dancing along the surface.

"Maybe, someday," said Morna, "that will be Rachel following Ian."

Chapter 32

On the Surface—Late September 1921

As the sun was setting on the shoreline of Killiney Bay, shadows reached across the family members, including Erin McCann. They had moved their blankets up against the dunes for protection from the incoming tide and its concurrent winds. Luncheon pastries were finished, tea catties closed, and napkins placed back in empty wicker baskets.

Their accommodation for nature's predictability would not, however, shelter them from the flurry of emotion about to wave over them.

"Calm down, Erin," voiced Billie, offering a silver flask full of whiskey to his former St. Enda student and now leader of Collins' County Cork IRA Volunteers. "Ye need to consider the facts and not the rumors that abound."

"Ach, ye sound more like the politician ye are than a Republican," came Erin's response. "I'm going to tell ye the facts that substantiate the rumors!"

Erin, at age twenty-five, had progressed from student to messenger to guerrilla tactician—all roles, it seemed, he had practiced since birth. Despite his physical deformity, no limp had ever constrained his capabilities to plan and act—overtly or covertly. He was a budding playwright as well, having written two popular plays and several books of poetry over the last five years. The first play, *Resurrection*, about the legacy of Pádraig Pearse after his execution in 1916, had been well received in Belfast.

The second, *Who Is The Just Man?*, recently performed at the Abbey Theater, was receiving mixed reviews. As a writer and actor, Erin's IRA roles had been effectively camouflaged, but his political leanings had not escaped assumptions. Resident Unionists were crit-

Part V: July 1921–April 1922

ical of the play and, as owners of many Dublin-based businesses, they were convincing their peers and Catholic employees not to act in it nor attend the free performances on Sunday afternoons.

This Sunday evening, however, no censorship or caution were warranted. The truth would be told without costume, make-up, or ghostly whispers. Erin had rushed to Killiney on the late afternoon train from Dublin to inform his extended family members immediately of an impending blow.

Liam could sense Erin's angst and set the stage for his expected monologue. "Rachel and Morna, can ye take the weeins down by the shoreline?" pointing to the youngest. Smiling at Billie's two boys, he detoured their evident curiosity about what Erin was going to say.

"I hear there are some selkies below those waves. Can ye find them for me?" The boys, Katie, and Maggie scampered away as Morna reached for Wolfe. Liam gave Kieran to Rachel. She frowned at her brother, obviously wanting to stay and hear Erin's news. When she started to complain, Liam cut her off.

"Rachel, please. Do as I ask ye. I promise to share all I can on our way home." Reluctantly, Rachel took Kieran from Liam's arms and sauntered slowly down the beach after the others, kicking the sand as she went.

The family members positioned themselves in a semicircle around a worn plaid blanket. The women—Agnes and BB—seated themselves upon it, their backs to the dunes rising behind them. The men—Liam, Billie, Ian, and Erin—stood around its three, remaining parameters. The family was assembling itself for whatever danger would be foretold.

Erin passed the whiskey casque back to Billie who handed it to Agnes. She filled five small glasses with the remaining amount and passed one glass at a time to each adult, keeping one for herself. She knew BB would not imbibe, being the consummate religious among them. BB gave an appreciative smile.

Erin took a full swig from his glass and began to speak.

"Ye know that there have been terrible losses among our IRA Volunteers and followers over the past two years of this war. Over 4,500 of our folks have been interned and 2,000 more are in prison. While I deeply regret this, we had to hold accountable over 250 collaborators. Our conflict has been horrific to victims on all sides—both Republican and Unionist. Lest my passion for the Republic be too cruel, we have also killed many a RIC and British youth who had no idea why they had to shoot those with whom they had fought side-by-side in France."

The five listened intently. An uneasy air surrounded them as the shadows of dusk began to extend over their thoughts. Agnes pulled her shawl tightly around her. BB clutched the silver cross on the necklace Liam had given her on their wedding day. Billie coughed in discomfort.

Only Liam and Ian stared knowingly at Erin.

Liam spoke first. "We are aware of these figures, Erin. Please, we need no introduction to your message. Get to the point of how these numbers warrant your visit to us today. How do they relate to us?"

"It's Rachel who may be the next number." Erin looked at each of the five adults and saw the same expressions he had scripted for the faces of characters in his recent play—shock, confusion, anger, dismay, and resolve.

"What do you mean?" blurted out Billie. "It can't be true."

"There must be some mistake," stated BB incredulously. Immediately, though, she recalled the conversation with Morna just an hour before.

"Who dares threaten her?" sputtered Agnes, her usual pink cheeks reddening.

Ian and Liam looked at the other. They had feared with dismay that this probability was now inevitable. After all, both knew that, two-and-a-half years before, Ian had not fulfilled Christine O'Leary's demand that Ian kill the last culprit who had threatened Eamon's family in Bangor. They also knew Christine bore grudges like the

Part V: July 1921–April 1922

permanent tattoos on her right arm. Thus, the rumors that she had finally found out about Ian's failure were not rumors at all, but true. It was only time before she would punish Ian somehow—and Rachel was the means to that end.

Ian wondered if Christine would actually put Rachel in danger of losing her life. Was Christine that evil?

Erin corroborated only the truth of the rumor. Christine's complicity in punishing Ian was palpable. If it included Rachel's death, Erin could not predict.

"It seems that Rachel has been recruited by Christine O'Leary to spy on the British quarters in Rathmines. Our young lass has been cozying up to a Black and Tan commander. Last night, I learned from one of my actors that, two nights ago when leaving the barracks, she was followed by the commander's second. Rachel went directly to Murphy's Pub where he saw her talking to Christine. I fear there will be a quick and quiet retaliation against Rachel when she returns again to the barracks.

"Damn," whispered Liam under his breath. Ian heard the curse and repeated it in his own head.

The two had much to do.

Chapter 33

Rising Mists—Late September 1921

It was at dawn when Rachel and Ian arrived on the outskirts of Macroom, just west of Cork city. Mists over the peat fields were rising, lending mystical auras to the emerging horizon before the couple. Nothing was clear to Rachel; everything was to Ian.

"Ye can't go back to Rathmines, Rachel," insisted Ian. "I don't know how many ways I can explain the danger ye are in."

"I don't care about the danger. I don't care what happens to me. There is a mission I must accomplish, and I'll do it no matter what." Rachel turned her flustered face away from Ian and looked out the sooted, back seat window of the Benz Velo automobile. Its driver was none other than Finbar McCann, a wealthy, Killiney hotel and estate owner who seconded as an IRA brigade leader. He was more than happy to accommodate his brother Erin McCann's request for Rachel's "speedy escape" with Ian.

The vehicle usually traveled back and forth from Dublin under the auspices of procuring hotel supplies. Sometimes it transported resort staff before and after their seasonal employment from and to their villages. Authorities didn't realize that many of those supplies were actually arms and the staff were the worker members of Collins' Flying Squad.

Since October was the end of this year's tourist season, Rachel and Ian would easily be disguised as laborers whom the hotel owner was returning home to Macroom. If Black and Tan or RIC constabularies stopped the car, Finbar would offer an official letter, forged by the IRA, that documented permission for travel during curfew hours. Tonight, Rachel was now maid-servant Liza McCann and Ian was chief-waiter Seamus, Liza's brother.

Part V: July 1921–April 1922

Only the McCann brothers knew that the vehicle was also delivering arms to the IRA volunteers of the 3rd Cork Brigade for actions against the IRC's Cork Auxiliary Division. So, sitting in the front seat, the brigade commander and playwright quietly discussed the political vagaries of de Valera and the war tactics of Collins. Sitting in the back seat, Rachel and Ian engaged in what one could hardly label a political discussion. The glass window between the front and back seats was closed allowing both sets of occupants to speak openly, yet secretively.

"Please, Rachel. Just pretend who you are for the next hour until we reach the McCann family home. Then, you can complain at the highest decibel once we are safe." Ian took her hand, which she abruptly pulled away.

Rachel had fumed throughout the trip to Macroom, occasionally blurting out her anger. "Why must I go into hiding? Wasn't I doing what Christine wanted me to do? I am not afraid of facing that bastard commander and sharing all I can of his company's tactics."

After hours of rebutting Ian's arguments with her own, Rachel's emotions had finally exploded, turning embers into full flames. Knowing he had to calm her, Ian quickly rethought how to extinguish them.

"I beg ye to listen to me just one more time." He must now tell her the truth behind their flight; he did not wait for her next barrage.

"I have not told ye all about why ye must leave the Dublin area. Yes, ye have been exposed as a Cumann na mBan spy. Yes, ye will be arrested the minute ye return to Rathmines. But, Rachel, listen to this that I have not wanted ye to know. Ye have been misused by Christine as a tool for revenge against Erin's brother Patrick McCann and, as I and your family have just learned from Erin, against me."

Rachel was stunned into silence. Her face turned toward him, displaying an intensity Ian was grateful to view. She frowned, and he knew he had captured her curiosity, not her anger.

"What do ye mean, revenge against Patrick and ye?" she asked.

Ian quickly—but with much detail—related the betrayal Christine had felt from Erin's brother, Patrick McCann, during the Easter Rising when, despite being her lover, he planned to leave for America instead of fighting in the resistance. Ian also told Rachel—now for the first time—how, in Bangor, he had witnessed Christine shoot two men at point blank. They had intended to kill Uncle Eamon. Ian described how Christine had demanded he kill a young boy who had accompanied the two assailants and left him to complete the task on his own. Ian, instead, had allowed the youth to run away. That was why in the Henry Street Clinic, he had questioned young Shawn O'Malley, the boy he had refused to kill behind Eamon's house in 1919. Christine never knew about Ian's inaction until recently and, according to Erin, now considered Ian to be a traitor.

Rachel's face turned bright red; her brows angled; her lips pressed shut.

Ian saw her emotion and gave his final argument. "Christine is a deluded woman, Rachel, the worst of our IRA members. Her soul has been consumed by an unnatural and inhumane hatred for the British and anyone aligned with them. She is using our cause to make amends for her own grievances. I can assure ye she would not credit ye for any of the information ye have collected. Once ye were arrested by the RIC, she wouldn't tell Mick ye were acting as her spy. Instead, she would say ye colluded with the enemy and that ye should be banished, if not killed as a traitor . . . unless the RIC acted first. Ye would not want to be part of her contrivance, would ye?"

Ian lowered his voice to a plea. "Do ye want to become like Uncle Eamon's brother Robbie who killed yer brother Ryan? Do ye want to be like the man who killed my father? Rachel, think. Put yer emotions behind ye and be the virtuous person I know ye are. Do ye want to become like Christine and lose yer soul? I don't believe ye do."

Part V: July 1921–April 1922

The mist over the Macroom fields was gone as Rachel turned away from him and looked out the car's window. She saw the clear-cut outlines of peat mounds undulating across the horizon. Ian could feel her move from emotion to thought, then saw her recognition. Not only was the horizon coming to view before her, but also the need for an Ireland that was just. She returned her gaze to Ian and took his hand.

"I love ye, Ian McNulty. God knows I always have, and now I know you love me—and the Ireland we long for. I will stay in Macroom as ye request. But I must continue to serve the movement. I will act here as a person of honor to the cause until I can return home to ye."

She placed her hand upon his cheek. He lifted it to his lips.

"Aye, dear lass. I'll be waiting for ye in our home—our new Ireland."

CHAPTER 34

From the Bench—First Week of October 1921

The Hungry Tree bench, tucked into the stubborn and sturdy London Plane oak, was the perfect Dublin place for the three men to meet. In the past, each had experienced the fortitude and comfort of this setting when making decisions. Liam McCormick had recognized the blessings of BB as they first touched hands here five years before. Eamon had outlined his first philosophy book three years ago while visiting the McCormicks and watching his two sons play with Kat and Sceo in the grassy park before him. Michael Collins had sat alone on the bench, catching his breath, after fleeing the British on that last day of the Easter Rising. Now, the three men would again benefit from the tree, its roots grounding their lessons from the past, its branches protecting them in the present, and its leaves whispering their future amidst the wind. As BB had previously asked when seated here with Liam, "What is it about nature that enables this tree to endure the passage of time, survive, and actually thrive after ravages of storms?" Today, all three men sought the answer.

Collins began. "Thank ye for meeting with me on such short notice. Tomorrow, I venture to London for the most onerous yet necessary task. The circumstances around it are coming to light—yet they darken my mind. As ye two have done so many times for me, I want to hear yer voices. What do ye know and what do ye think?"

He was pacing in front of his two companions as they sat on the bench. Eamon frowned, lowered his chin, and pulled the collar of his topcoat closer about his neck. He shivered, not just from the brisk October wind, but from the quickening pace of his heart. Knowing Mick's mind well from hours of philosophical bantering, Eamon knew the conversation would be circuitous, perhaps spiraling down, then up.

Part V: July 1921–April 1922

In contrast, Liam McCormick's eyes did not lower, nor did he shiver. He followed Collins' angular body from left to right, counting the paces between. How long he had admired this IRA commander who had trusted McCormick with the most secretive of messages. He knew the conversation would be direct and, most probably, conclusive.

Both Eamon and Liam considered Mick as a brother, a member of the ancient, Gaelic Irish clan in which all three were blessed by the same roots, despite their different branches. Together, they were the protectors of Ireland's future. It was the uncontrollable gusts blowing through those branches that they now needed to pacify.

Collins stopped before Eamon. "Eamon, tell me what ye know. I understand that ye have met many of our Ulster colleagues while travelin' with Francis McKenzie. What did they share with ye?"

"Aye, Francis has a way with him. He asks the most discerning questions and listens well to our folks' responses. His financial acumen has certainly enabled him to carefully query the needs of both common and wealthy, bank clients. That skill contributed to a surprisin' openness in our own people who shared their stories with him. The issue of Ulster having its own Parliament and the South having its own is no longer a top priority for them. If the North stays within the United Kingdom and the South steps away as a dominion like Canada and India, so be it. It's peace and jobs they want. Once both become real, our separate communities believe they can plan a unified Ireland for the future."

"Hmm. Thank ye, and quite interesting, good sir." Collins winked at Eamon and turned to Liam. "Now, brother Liam. What say ye?"

Liam stood up, his six-foot stance grounding, yet elevating, his thoughts. "Honestly speaking, Mick, our comrades here in the South are splintered between ye and de'V. Some favor an island-wide Republic over a Dominion. Some want self-determination whereby we vote now on our relationship with Britain rather than in the future. Some want the war to continue and regret the July truce; but, like our Ulster companions, some just want the fighting to stop. Sadly, many don't trust either you, 'the Big Fellow,' or de'V, 'the Long Fellow.' Worse yet, some trust de'V more than ye, or ye more than de'V."

Collins chuckled. "Ach, that last group sounds more like Lloyd George and Churchill waiting for me in London than any Irishmen I know."

For more than two hours, the two answered more of Collins' questions. Together, they bantered various ways by which Collins—during the forthcoming treaty negotiations—could best represent the sentiments of the South, as well as the partitioned counties of Ulster.

From Eamon's perspective shared later with Kat, Collins gained insight by being a leader with integrity—a just man. From Liam's perspective shared with BB, Collins embellished that insight by being a leader with wisdom—an equally just man.

By the end of their time together, despite their enhanced understandings, none knew exactly what would face Collins nor how he would respond.

Only the Hungry Tree knew. The wind had whispered that future to its branches and down its trunk. The roots vibrated underground.

PART V: JULY 1921–APRIL 1922   143

CHAPTER 35

Righteous Revenge?—First Week of October 1921

The two youth had much in common, but they didn't know that. As a matter of fact, they didn't even know who the other was.

Sitting across on the Rathfarnum and Drumcondra tram from Dublin, they barely looked at each other as they approached Rathmines. One was intensely focused on a page in a worn, cloth-covered book. The other gazed out one of the car's windows reflecting the wobbling street lights blurred by a sudden downpour. His hands anxiously twisted around a woolen tam upon his lap. Despite their differing behaviors, each youth had the same mission and the same resolve. Each wanted to confront Christine O'Leary's sins.

The first youth was Shawn O'Malley whose life, just two years before in February 1919, had been spared by Ian McNulty when Shawn and two other Orangemen had attempted to bomb Eamon Smiley's home in Bangor.

The second youth was none other than Chester Acheson, nephew of Samuel Acheson who had been shot dead by Christine that very same night. The past two years had led each boy upon opposing trajectories. Soon, those would cross.

Shawn had been taken under the tutelage of Ian and Rachel after their meeting in June of 1919 at Belfast's Henry Street Clinic. Shawn's mother, having been diagnosed with consumption by Dr. Lizzie and comforted by Ian, had sadly passed away four months later. Left alone to care for his two younger siblings, Shawn had been befriended by Rachel and Ian along with the entire Smiley family. He had pledged to honor his mother's last prayer to become a "good Irishman." Because of this, Kat and Rachel had introduced him to the Countess Markievicz and other members of the Belfast section of Cumann na mBan's youth group, Na Fianna Eireann. Miraculously, a childless Quaker couple, who championed Home Rule and were dear friends of the Countess, had opened their home and hearts to Shawn O'Malley and his two sisters.

Shawn had thrived due to this couple's compassion and faith-based empathy—plus their encouragement of his education. Despite the Countess' disappointment, but her understanding, he eventually rejected the covert, paramilitary activities of Na Fianna Eireann and, instead, immersed himself into the larger Quaker community—reading poetry, fables, and plays by Irish pacifists.

Now, at sixteen, he had just gained a seat in the Belfast Royal Academy. Tonight, he was reading a current writing of the Quaker pacifist John Rowntree. Only two nights ago in Bangor, Eamon Smiley had given his own version of *The Society of Friends: Its Faith and Practice* to Shawn.

That reading calmed Shawn's nerves as he was about to confront O'Leary in the presence of the Countess about O'Leary's betrayal of Rachel. He had promised Ian he would do that after hearing Ian's angst shared with Eamon and himself. Shawn had convinced Ian that the Countess who, despite her disappointment in Shawn's pacifism, had encouraged his literary interests and sponsored his Academy attendance. "Indeed," Shawn had said to Ian. "the Countess would be the best agent to hold Christine accountable." Eamon and Ian agreed.

Chester Acheson, on the other hand, had never really known sympathy nor compassion in his short fifteen years. Although his mother had been loving to him as a child, her death when he was five confused him at first. Then, it embittered him as he endured his father's anger at her "abandonment"—his father's term during many a drunken stupor. When Uncle Samuel was killed, two years ago, the father and son's paired bitterness doubled. Chester dropped out of school and joined the Ulster Volunteer Force (UVF). He took a job in the kitchen of Belfast's Grand Central Hotel as a cover for his assignments with the militant group. He had shared informa-

Part V: July 1921–April 1922

tion with his UVF allies about the McKenzie's August dinner with the Smileys, but not much had warranted retaliation. UVF members continued to school him, however, in British loyalty, the art of spying and street fighting. His father schooled him in hatred.

Chester's father would take Chester to the newly reconstructed St. Anne's Cathedral, a Church of Ireland stronghold located on Donegall Street in Belfast. They would attend services only when Sir Edward Carson, the first signatory of the Ulster Covenant, was giving the sermon, followed by a UVF meeting. Chester would remember Carson's words of disdain for Catholics and Republicans. They enflamed his own desire for revenge and bravery.

During Carson's tirades, Chester's eyes would fixate on the stained glass window in memory of the choir men lost in the war. He would ignore the window depicting the Good Samaritan. Sometimes, he would gaze at the painting of the Virgin Mary embracing the fallen Christ or the window dedicated to the Virgin's mother Anne, after whom the church was named. But those reminders of his own mother would offer fleeting moments of regret—regret for who should have comforted him through his many losses but was gone. Regret would turn quickly to enmity.

Tonight, he focused on the instructions given the night before by the commander of his UVF unit: "Go to Dublin. O'Leary will be meeting with the Countess Markievicz at her Leinster Road home in Rathmines. Do what you must for the sake of the Covenant."

The two young men got off the tram at the corner of Rathmines Road Lower and Leinster Road. With the rain turning to mist and darkness surrounding them, neither noticed the other walking on the opposite side of Leinster. The Markievicz home at 49B was on the right, set back from the street by a grassy lawn and path from the gate to the front door. Chester took that side; Shawn the other.

As the two approached their common destination, Shawn finally noticed the figure opposite him. "Strange it is," remarked Shawn to himself," to be accompanied by a youth like myself. I wonder what his purpose is on this bleak night." Shawn crossed the road and trailed the figure, now ten paces before him. The figure did not seem to notice his follower. When Chester stopped in front of 49B, so did Shawn, now more concerned than curious. He queried himself, "Who is this person? Why is he stopping here?"

There was little time to answer those questions. The Countess and Christine appeared on the stone path leading from the front door to the gate abutting the street. They were holding an intense conversation so did not notice the raised hand of a youth as they reached for the iron latch. Nor did they comprehend the impact of the shot until Christine fell to the ground. Only when Shawn grabbed Chester from the back and the gun fell to the ground did the Countess grasp the intent and result.

"My God!" shouted the Countess. Responding to the shot and cry, two men and a woman, watching from the open front door, raced down the path. Billie Irvine, Liam McCormick, and BB quickly assessed the situation. The men joined Shawn in restraining Chester. BB cradled Christine.

Looking up at the Countess, BB quietly confirmed, "She's gone. God have mercy on her soul."

As the three men raised Chester from the ground, he muttered only, "Thank God, she's gone."

Chapter 36

*Enlightened Perspectives—
Second Week of October 1921*

Erin delivered the message about Christine's murder to Collins on the evening of the second day of treaty negotiations. London's 15 Cadogan Gardens, where the two were staying, was a solid brick row house, three stories high with a large vestibule at its entrance. Facing the street, floor-to-ceiling windows spanned the first-floor salon on one side of the vestibule. Half windows spanned the dining room on the other side. All windows were covered by traditional Irish lace, framed by plush but fading, velvet curtains. A sense of simple, yet worn, elegance had struck Michael upon entering through the heavy, wooden framed, brass-handled front door. Its beveled glass was etched with a heron balancing on one foot in a shallow pond embellished by tall ferns rising to spread-winged swallows flying freely above. He chuckled to himself that he felt more like the heron than the swallows.

The central vestibule led him quickly to a set of oak stairs leading to the second floor and, then, in the opposite direction down a hallway was a comparable staircase rising to the third floor. He gripped the thick, wooden banisters abutting those stairs and stepped up into a hallway that led to doors that opened into a plainly, yet tastefully, decorated room.

Usually the lodging welcomed dignitaries from Commonwealth countries, hoping to persuade British government leaders and businessmen to invest in profitable ventures and policies. This second week of October, however, all rooms had been reserved for the intelligence and security members of Southern Ireland's representatives seeking an investment in their country's future—peace.

As he surveyed his sleeping quarters, Michael could tell that he had been relegated to a subservient position by de Valera. The delegates assigned to lead the full team—Arthur Griffith, Robert Barton, Eamon Duggan, and Erskine Childers—were staying at the posh 22 Hans Place in Knightsbridge. In contrast, the former elegance of 15 Cadogen Gardens' lace, velvet, and oak accentuated the slight Michael felt. But he would not complain. That was not his nature.

Instead, he had joked to his roommate Erin, "Blimey, negotiating with the Brits may have some temporary benefits after all, despite the challenges ahead. Enjoy, at least, the hot water and bright lights, laddie. Times certainly have changed for this Irishman since '06 when working in London as a bank assistant. Then, I bunked with four other chums in my sister Hannie's cold-water flat. Her lace was only in the doilies she brought from home and upon which she placed yer McCann family picture, illuminated by candlelight. I remember laughing at it—ye and Patrick in yer white, soccer shorts.

"But now ye bring me this news about yer brother's nemesis, Christine O'Leary—as though I have no other lives about whom to worry or to mourn." Collins sighed.

Erin stood before Michael in their shared bedroom. On the walls, a newly installed electric light nestled within a flowered globe reflected the shadow of the men's frames standing a fair distance away from the windows. Despite the curtains being drawn, Michael knew his enemies could act at any time. Information on his location was now well shared within the London-based compatriots of Ulster Volunteers who had followed him across the Channel. Already he had received a postcard with a blatant threat. Both he and Erin felt the tension for, not only their location, but their purpose and lives.

"Why in God's name did Christine put Rachel in such a frightful position? And why didn't I know about Christine killing Samuel Acheson?" Collins queried.

"I had asked her only to deter Acheson, not finish him off. Now, two years later, I learn the truth?" Collins' voice began to rise.

Part V: July 1921–April 1922

"Why didn't ye or Liam tell me what happened that night?"

"Mick," implored Erin. "Listen to me. Ye had then and have today so much more to consider than an event that started further back than on St. Stephen's Green in '16. Who knows what Christine felt as an orphaned novitiate in Rathmines or as a nurse in Ypres. Her distrust of others was exacerbated by what she considered Patrick's betrayal when he decided to leave for America. Not only did she not trust the church and the British government, but also my good Irish brother who tried to befriend and love her. Like many abandoned lassies, she was bitter—bitter about her religion, bitter about the war in France, bitter about Patrick, and bitter about the executions of Pearse and our martyred brothers. Perhaps she was also bitter about her role—subservient to others' commands. There was no way ye could have changed her mind nor heart. However she could reap the seeds of her revenge, she would do so." Erin paused to see if Collins had absorbed all just said.

Collins sat down on one of the twin beds. He held his head in his hands. "I know what love is when it is sweetly reciprocated, Erin. I have yet to feel the grief or anger when such love is retracted. I can only imagine it. But I do know the grief of losing friends and family members during our struggles. Sadly, there are too many of us who cannot distinguish between love of country and hatred of an individual. So many of us—on both sides—have lost that ability since '16 and the fields of Flanders in '18, not to forget the past two years throughout the North and South. More souls, I fear, will die if we don't transform our perspectives and attain a peaceful reconciliation this week."

Raising his head to Erin, Mick changed his focus. "But let's deal with this Acheson problem first. After that, we can discuss tomorrow's strategy for dealing with Lloyd George and Churchill. What say ye that we do with Chester Acheson? The message says he is being held by our IRA colleagues in Coalisland. That does not bode well for his life."

Erin sat down next to Mick. "Christine was a good soldier, Mick, despite the anger blurring her vision of justice. We cannot let her death go unpunished, but, at the same time, we could make it serve as our vision of peace with those Ulstermen and Southern Unionists who despise us. Could we keep Chester imprisoned while the Treaty is bein' decided? As part of our negotiation strategy, we could then offer an exchange of him and their other prisoners for our boys yet to be hanged by the IRC?"

"Ach," said Collins. "That's a grand idea. Let's send that message tonight to Liam in Dublin, to forward on to Coalisland. Now, let's move on to tomorrow."

Erin and he moved over to the sofas near the windows. "We'll take our chances lounging in these old plush chairs by the windows. Another benefit. Just turn off the lights."

At the exact time that Erin dimmed the lights, miles across the Channel, the lights of Chester Acheson's life expired. Michael's message would arrive in Coalisland too late—another soul lost to revenge.

Part V: July 1921–April 1922

Chapter 37

Ploughing the Mind—Third Week of October 1921

The briny swells of the Belfast Lough shimmered under a sun that kissed their arrival upon the rocky shoreline of Bangor Bay. Kat and Eamon followed that shoreline past wooden piers lined with small rowing boats and forty-foot yachts. The couple took the pebbled path at Wilson's Point that led to Helen's Bay, a village just two miles to their south west. Over the past five years, they had walked there every Sunday after church with their children Devin, Maggie, Neil, Liza and, of course, their dog Sceo, off leash. They would share the afternoon with the McCann family—Maud and Thomas, now in their fifties, and son Erin if he were back from London. Not widely known, the McCanns managed a small inn called the Beastie King as a safe house for IRA travelers in Northern Ireland.

Today, they would share in a robust discussion on the current Anglo-Irish Treaty negotiations, primarily conveyed by Erin's secret letters from Cadogen Gardens to his da. Since Francis and Margaret McKenzie were staying with the McCanns, much would also be offered about their visits to Republicans confirming Irish-American support. To round out the informants, Ian McNulty and Rachel had arrived the night before from Macroom via Dublin. Undoubtedly, they would bring news about Southern opinions for—or against— the negotiations.

That each of these sources would detail one unified perspective was doubtful. But, as Thomas McCann would caution, "You'll never plough a field by turning it over in your mind." While all of the extended family members wanted the field ploughed, they agreed that, first, one had to consider the best method. Belaboring wasted labor.

Eamon was particularly anxious to learn how Collins was handling the various conflicts within and outside his immediate circle of negotiators. Kat wanted to know the details of every proposal in order to compose her column in *Our Ireland* newspaper. Like her mother and gran who wrote anonymously for the daily, Kat continued their commitment to speak as the third Ms. Inde Pen for the women of Ireland. She knew their voices represented the needs of Ireland's children. She feared the men's voices were founded on their need to have their own way.

As the family reached Helen's Bay and turned off the shore path toward Church Road, Eamon and Kat were still debating the rumored stipulations posed by Prime Minister Lloyd George and Churchill as requirements for the formation of an Irish Free State. The two British leaders were insisting that the South become a dominion of the British Empire, like Canada, with executive authority vested in the king through a governor general. In exchange, the 1800 Acts of Union—whereby Ireland was made part of the United Kingdom of Great Britain and The Kingdom of Ireland—would be revoked. The king's executive authority would be exercised by the newly formed Dáil Éireann as a "lower house" of the British Parliament. The difference between vested and exercised had been the focus of Eamon and Kat's debate.

"If the free state remains under the authority of the king through vestiture, then he could easily repeal any exercising legislation we proffer," exclaimed Kat, stopping while breathless—not just from the elevating level of the path they were walking, but from the numerous points she was rapidly elucidating to Eamon. Kat never conserved her energy by refraining from uninterrupted speech; Eamon always did by pausing for thoughtful clarity before speaking.

"Aye, ye're correct, Kat," Eamon replied, halting his trek up the road to face her and changing the tiny Liza from one shoulder to the other. "But, remember, George needs all the votes he can secure to retain his post as prime minister. He must appease those in both

Part V: July 1921–April 1922

his Liberal and opposition Conservative parties who want the Irish issue resolved and unburdening the British economic progress after the devastating war. In addition, George doesn't want to alienate the Northern Unionists who already believe they secured a permanent separation from the South just last May.

"Churchill, on the other hand, wants the Black and Tans withdrawn and wouldn't mind leaving the Irish to forever fight among themselves. As long as there are no more English lads' lives lost on this island, both men will be happy. Vestiture or exercise doesn't matter to them. I'm sure they have more stipulations they will demand than labels such as these. We'll have to see what the McCanns and McKenzies know," he concluded.

"And, from our own side, we'll need to hear from Ian and Rachel. After all, they are listening to the people on the farms and in the factories in the South. Alas, Francis is only meeting with the 'big and tall' folks who have trade and money in mind, not the hearts of our people. Margaret is trying to provide him with that perspective, but he's definitely a successful banker." Kat stopped and turned toward Eamon.

"How can we serve everyone, Professor Eamon?" she asked. "What do your philosophers say to ye?"

Eamon looked ahead at their two sons racing before them, Sceo in the lead. "I believe that Kant would instruct us to ask three questions: What can I know? What ought I to do? And what may I hope?

"Once we can answer those, as our own philosopher Thomas McCann always cautions us, then we'll plough the field."

CHAPTER 38

The Beastie King—Third Week of October 1921

The 1750 Beastie King Inn was festive this Sunday night. Locals had gathered to hear the magical tones and words of master fiddler Colum McGregor and, of course, to imbibe in the tavern's golden pints of poitin and boxty fare. Such an evening could refresh not just the body of a traveler, but the soul. A spirit reverberated from McGregor's voice to the ears of all and back again as they joined in his refrains. At age eighty-four, the poet-musician knew everyone's yearnings and woes, victories and joys. He sang with a resonance generations young and old, and in between, cherished.

The Beastie King was the Helen's Bay refuge Thomas and Maud McCann managed covertly on behalf of roving IRA members. The inn's name itself a subtle, yet understood, slight to former British royalty and the current King George V, convinced the couple to secure it. And so this evening, the group of enthralled children seated on the floor before Colum's tapping right foot included Neil, Devin, and Liza tucked into Neil's lap.

Their parents sat with the adults of their extended family around a small table separated from the performance area by a frosted, glass window framed by solid oak borders. Kat and Eamon sat catty-corner from Rachel and Ian with the McKenzie's at each end—Margaret next to Kat, Francis next to Ian. As the "mother" waitress, Maud occasionally stopped by while Thomas tended the bar. The intimacy of the family's space paralleled the intimacy of their conversation, often tempered by the timbre of McGregor's voice and sentiment of his sung words. He had just finished a fine rendition of the song "A Little Bit of Heaven." Not an eye was dry in the house.

Part V: July 1921–April 1922

"'Tis fine the words of that last song, don't you think?" asked Francis. "Ireland surely is 'a bit of heaven that fell from out the sky.' And wouldn't you know that song was written by two Americans?"

"Aye," said Kat. "But we count on our Irish-American brothers and sisters to offer us more than just words in a song, Francis. Tell us what ye have been able to learn in your travels that will help ye secure more support for us upon yer return to New York."

Francis did not relish a contrary change of topic nor sentiment when pontificating. Kat's insistence upon talking about the challenges ahead—not the romanticized version of the emerald isle—irked Francis, particularly when posed by a woman. He was used to having his way in both professional and personal actions or opinions. Fortunately, Margaret caught his eye and frowned, letting him know—as she always did—to count to five or more before making an indelicate remark.

Margaret followed her look with her own response—woman to woman. "We've had great success with the Dublin businessmen in promising to partner with our Irish-American whiskey and linen buyers in exchange for whatever they can provide politically and materially in America once the Republic is secured, if not before. To a person, they have understood the need for American support to the Cause, but their commitment, as well, to restore Britain after the war's devastation. Friendships are complex, aren't they?"

A silence fell over the group. Each contemplated the value of what Margaret had just said about friendships dependent upon national alliances.

Eamon spoke first. "Aye, but loyalties should dictate friendships. We can establish the ties between America and our new nation based on understanding each other's economic needs for the future. However, I agree with my dear Kat that the goal now is not really aimed at that far, far future, but at the present desire for a free and unified Ireland. The cross-seas ties forged now will certainly determine our ties in years to come, but they first must honor the ties amongst ourselves here at home. For sure, we can 'sprinkle the land with stardust to make the shamrocks grow,' but all must benefit from those shamrocks, and that depends on this forthcoming Treaty. It could tear us apart right here at home."

Just as Eamon said that, Maud approached the table. She put her arms around the shoulder of Margaret and leaned in, whispering, "My loved ones. I have heard from Erin, and it does not look good for us to have the united Ireland nor the Republic we desire. He says that Lloyd George has threatened a return of the war unless we agree to certain stipulations." She pulled a chair from behind the glass frame, sat down around their table while opening Erin's message. Quietly, she read from it.

> "My darling mum. I fear Mick and I are in terrible straits. We are torn between not just two opposing sides. Here is what is being asked of us by the Brits: a self-governing dominion status for an Irish Free State—not a recognized Republic; a mandatory option for the partitioned counties of Ulster in the North to withdraw from any Irish Free State by plebiscite majority; an oath of faith by us in the Free State to the king; the continued control of several Southern ports by the British navy; and crown forces withdrawn from the entire island. These terms require compromise among our own delegation members and within the Dáil. Griffith and Collins are not happy, and they are trying their best to appease everyone on both sides of the sea while securing no more lives are lost."

Folding it into a small packet she placed in her bodice, Maud continued her own thoughts, "Erin says there is fighting back and forth between de'V and the Dáil, between Mick and de'V, plus amongst the negotiators themselves. 'Tis a sad state. Where are the angels to bless us now?"

Part V: July 1921–April 1922

Again, the table went silent. The men had nothing more to add. Rachel felt Ian's hand clasp hers under the table. Kat reached for Eamon's. Margaret caught Francis' eyes as Maud turned away. It was Neil and Devin who broke the table's contemplation when they ran up to it.

"Mum! Mum! Isn't Master McGregor grand? Can I learn to play the fiddle? Please? Please?" begged Neil. "Then I can sing about the fairies and the wishing well, the stardust, and the lakes and dells."

Kat could feel the tears come to her eyes. "Aye, my sweetheart. We'll see what we can do about getting ye yer own fiddle. It would be our country's joy to have you carry on that blessing."

She paused. "Ach, but where in Heaven's name have ye left yer sister Liza?"

Chapter 39

Irish Wine—Early November 1921

There was not enough stardust nor silver to make the negotiations in Hans Place fill the wishing wells needed within the Irish delegation, nor between its members and the British. Recognizing the discord among the delegates—and de Valera's chameleon role in setting them each against the other—Collins and Griffith were at a standstill.

de'V's three allies on the delegation—Childers, Duffy, and Barton—were following de'V's unstated, yet assumed, commitment to a unified Republic of Ireland with no oath of allegiance to the king.

Collins and Griffith, on the other hand, were following de'V's equally vague instructions to negotiate an "external association" that might still require an oath. Despite being designated by the Dáil as "plenipotentiaries" who could negotiate freely, Collins and Griffith had been forced to form into a sub-team for daily talks with the British without the constraints of de'V's three allies. The British had agreed. Collins and Griffith would represent the Irish. Lloyd George and Austen Chamberlain would speak for London.

"How are we going to manage this chaos of intentions and directions, Mick?" asked Griffith. The two were seated around a mosaic-tiled, coffee table in the smoking salon of Brown's Hotel in Mayfair. The dark, wood-paneled walls and their comfortably cushioned highchairs provided a perfect cover for their intimate conversations. No Irish nor British man would ever expect two Sinn Féin leaders to walk into, let alone enjoy a smoke in, such an elegant and prestigious setting.

"Do you mean paying for our drinks and smoke, Arthur, or succeeding in tomorrow's negotiations?" quipped Collins.

Arthur chuckled. "Ach, ye're quite the joker, Mick."

Part V: July 1921–April 1922

"Well, let me tell ye a wee secret," began Collins. "It seems that Churchill has enjoyed my bantering in our meetings such that he gave me his card to flaunt here. He says it will allow us to pay for anything we want in several hotels, this one included. Of course, we don't want to exploit his generosity . . . and I'm not even sure it's his sincere largesse or just a calculated ploy for intelligence. But, ye know, I never look at the teeth of a stallion before riding it a short distance. If the hoofs are sound and it takes me at least a mile, that's fine with me."

Arthur Griffith grinned. "Spoken like our true Minister of Finance, Mick. Come. Let's order some Guinness and see what the waiters think of us."

Collins turned and called over a lean, ruddish-faced youth waiting at the parlor's door. He was dressed in a white shirt and bib with pressed black pants.

Reaching their table, the youth bowed and questioned forcefully, "What do you want?" He fidgeted with the napkin folded upon his bent arm.

Both Griffith and Collins stared at him, recognizing the cocky insecurity they were accustomed to in young IRA recruits and teenaged IRC adversaries.

"That sounds like a Cork accent covering up a British one, young man," said Collins, rising from his seat.

The youth looked up at the six-foot figure hovering before him and blushed. "Ach, ye're right," he said, coughing into the napkin and moving closer to Collins.

"Laddie," tutted Collins, "if ye're new to a post, ye better learn yer job better. Feigning to be a British waiter in such a place as this, ye need to cover up yer accent more carefully. And, besides, ye never initiate a conversation with a guest, nor do ye dare cough into a napkin he might use. Good God, where were ye trained?"

The lad's face now turned a brilliant red spreading around deep frowns and pursed lips.

"I'm sorry." He took a deep breath, exhaled, and paused. His shoulders relaxed. "I hid away in steerage two months ago. Me mum needs the money for my sister's weeins, and I'm not skilled in anything but shearing the sheep. On the boat, I got talkin' with someone and asked him if he knew where I could get a job. He sent me to meet with an uncle who works here. This is my first day as a waiter, Mr. Collins, and I apologize for being so clumsy." The lad stumbled over his next words. "I . . . I . . . I . . ."

Griffith and Collins looked at each other. The Big One put his right hand into his trousers' pocket. By which side did this young man abide—Republican or Unionist? What was his purpose in approaching the two negotiators?

"How did ye know me name, lad?" Mick whispered brusquely.

Just as the boy was about to answer, Griffith saw another waiter approach them, an older man. Collins stiffened until he noted the man's stride. It harkened back to military exercises before the Dublin Castle in '16 and those in Frongoch internment camp.

"Is there a problem here?" came a Cork accent, lowered so no one else could hear.

"Dear Lord," replied Collins, staring at the man. "'Tis Danny O'Rourke, isn't it?"

The older man bowed, playing the role of deferential waiter while re-enacting that of deferential soldier.

"Commander Collins," the man spoke softly. "I don't use that name anymore. But ye're right. I'm Danny."

Collins and Griffith immediately understood the circumstances of this encounter—the allegiance and reason behind it.

"I thank ye for your service and training this young man," Collins quietly responded. "I know ye both will take care of whatever we two need and what the movement needs."

Returning to the comfort of his mind and secured chair, he spoke in tone. "For now, let's have two Guinnesses and two cigars plus matches."

Part V: July 1921–April 1922

O'Rourke winked, straightened his posture, and offered loudly in an obviously well-rehearsed, Devon accent. "May I suggest the 1920 Baron du Pichon-Loncueville Bordeaux instead? I understand you are Lord Churchill's guests this afternoon?"

"Aye, ye're right. And that suggestion sounds grand." Collins nodded at the elder waiter.

"Come lad," said O'Rourke. "That's the way to serve our customers." The two waiters retreated, shoulders bowed.

Reclining back into the armchair's plush velvet cushion, Collins winked at Griffiths. "I think we know exactly what our strategy will be tomorrow, Arthur. Let's play the British cards, not our Irish, and see what response we get. We may end up with an Irish wine."

Griffith laughed. "And shall we call it 1922 Countess Gore-Booth du Lissendell and nickname it Connie?"

CHAPTER 40

Dancing with the Devil—December 8, 1921

On December 6, at 2:20 a.m., the Anglo-Irish Treaty (formally known as the Articles of Agreement for a Treaty Between Great Britain and Ireland)[14] was signed by seven representatives from Great Britain and by five from Ireland.

Just before the final hour of December 5, Collins had indicated to Lloyd George that the Irish delegation could not sign the agreement without ratification by the Dáil Cabinet. Lloyd George balked at the delay and turned on Griffith for not keeping his previous words that had accepted the transcribed terms. Griffith responded vehemently saying, "I have never let a man down in my whole life and I never will." He immediately signed the agreement.

George then laid down a heavier gauntlet requiring all of the Irish delegates to sign. If they did not, he threatened to send Unionist leader Sir James Craig in Belfast a letter that very night saying that the Sinn Féin representatives refused to sign. It would include the phrase, ". . . it is war and war within three days." Lloyd gave the remaining Irish delegates only two hours to join Griffith. Exactly two hours and twenty minutes into December 6, they reluctantly did—for the sake of peace.

A copy was in the hands of de Valera and the Dáil Cabinet by 7:30 p.m. on December 7. Upon also receiving it, the newspapers in great Britain and the island of Ireland went wild. The presses of *The Irish Times* ran twenty-four hours straight during the following days, providing details of the agreement and its deliberations in Dublin and Belfast, as well as in London. Editorials and letters offered predictions—more accurately, speculations—on the consequences for the Irish isle.

Part V: July 1921–April 1922

December 8 was a blustery winter day. By early evening, Eamon and Kat sat in worn, winged armchairs facing each other next to a glowing fireplace in their Bangor salon. Sceo was sleeping on the floor next to Eamon. A full copy of the Agreement had been secretly sent to the two Smileys by Erin McCann. Already, de Valera was objecting to it and aligning his followers to oppose ratification. Erin was sure conflict would erupt within the newly proposed Free State and, as well, within Northern Ireland. He wanted the Smiley family to be prepared.

Having read it over and over since its arrival that morning, Eamon was poised to share the highlights with Kat, who had been hearing rumors all day long at the women's Lying-In Hospital where she had taken over her mother's Board Chairman role. Eamon knew Kat would carefully parse each word of the document herself later in the evening before writing tomorrow's Ms. Inde Pen column:

"Here ye are, Kat. Seven major points." He leaned back into a needlepoint pillow behind him, prodded his bifocals closer to far-sighted eyes and, then, patted Sceo who had just risen, stretched, and placed his head on Eamon's shawled-covered knees. Like the philosophy professor he was, Eamon raised the document and began a well-organized, synoptic lecture.

> "Point 1: Ireland shall have the same constitutional status in the Community of Nations known as the British Empire as the Dominion of Canada . . . and shall be styled and known as the Irish Free State.
>
> "Point 2: The oath to be taken by Members of the Parliament of the Irish Free State shall be in the following form: I . . . do solemnly swear true faith and allegiance to the Constitution of the Irish Free State as by law established and that I will be faithful to H.M. King George V, his heirs and successors by law, in virtue of the common citizenship of Ireland with Great

Britain and her adherence to and membership of the group of nations forming the British Commonwealth of Nations.

"Point 3: Until an arrangement has been made between the British and Irish Governments whereby the Irish Free State undertakes her own coastal defense, the defense by sea of Great Britain and Ireland shall be undertaken by His Majesty's Imperial Forces.

"Point 4: The Irish Free State shall assume liability for . . . the payment of war pension . . . to any just claims on the part of Ireland . . .

"Point 5: With a view to securing the observance of the principle of international limitation of armaments, if the Government of the Irish Free State establishes and maintains a military defense force, the establishments thereof shall not exceed in size such proportion of the military establishments maintained in Great Britain.

"Point 6: Until the expiration of one month from the passing of the Act of Parliament for the ratification of this instrument, the powers of the Parliament and the Government of the Irish Free State shall not be exercisable as respects Northern Ireland and the provisions of the Government of Ireland Act, 1920, shall so far as they relate to Northern Ireland remain of full force and effect . . .

"Point 7: By way of provisional arrangement for the administration of Southern Ireland during the interval which must elapse between the date hereof and the constitution of a Parliament and Government of the Irish Free State . . . the British Government shall take the steps necessary to transfer to such provisional government the powers and machinery requisite for the discharge of its duties . . .

Part V: July 1921– April 1922   165

"Ah, Kat," sighed Eamon, setting the Agreement down upon his lap. He took off his glasses. "On behalf of all Irishmen and women, Collins and Griffith have chosen the goal of peace over the goal of a Republic. The end has justified their means. This Agreement is a step toward that end—an eventual Republic. However, that step requires a pledge of allegiance to the king in order to be a self-governing Irish Free State. Republicans will detest this. Ulster will reject being governed by the Dáil. By the end of next week, they'll clearly veto the Agreement within their current Parliament. Partition will be set in stone. I know our friends have chosen the most justifiable means for a righteous end, but it is going to divide family against family, friend against friend."

"Indeed, my darling, I pray their decision is considered worthy of praise despite the compromises made. All of us must remember that, above all other disappointments, peace is what our citizens want now. They are jubilant," replied Kat opening up *The Irish Times* to page one. "Listen to today's editorial.

"Today, Ireland's future is in her own hands. She knows what she wants and, if she chooses to insist, she will get what she wants. The country has welcomed the Peace Treaty as men welcome water in the desert. The people, their Churches, their newspapers, have lifted a single voice of thanksgiving and joy. They hail the end of a long and bitter conflict, the prospect of happiness and progress, the sure and certain hope of unity in their own land. Already, they are girding their loins for the noble task of nation-building. They know that Mr. Griffith speaks truly when he says that the Treaty 'will lay the foundation of peace and friendship' between Ireland and the rest of the British Empire. It is being laid at this moment; for the Commonwealth of Australia has flashed a greeting to Ireland as 'our new sister Dominion.' Sinn Féin has dared and suffered much, and its methods, however we may detest many of them, have been effective. Now the country is completely satisfied of two things: that it has won an almost unprecedented measure of freedom as the result of a wholly unprecedented act of imperial magnanimity, and that rejection of this boon must mean ruin. If civil warfare is renewed, it will be renewed by an infinitely weaker Ireland and by an infinitely stronger England. The Roman Catholic Bishop of Killaloe declares that the moral effect of the Treaty 'will be worth half a navy to England.'

"By this agreement, England surrenders much of her secular authority over Ireland for the sake of peace with Ireland. Mr. Griffith and his fellow delegates, as we admit freely, have sacrificed a measure of their idealism for the sake of peace with England. They have done rightly, and the mass of the nation supports, and will support, them in that sacrifice. Ulster is asked to abandon deep-rooted convictions for the sake of Irish unity, and we hope and believe that, under the beneficent influence of new conditions, she will find the abandonment not merely possible, but easy. The Southern loyalists, perhaps, are surrendering most of all. They have watched the passage, in mournful procession, of the host of laws, institutions, traditions, and ideals that bound them to Great Britain.

"They have embarked—not gladly, yet not afraid—on uncharted seas. They are entrusting themselves to the goodwill of a majority from which, politically, they have suffered much, and with which in the past they have had little in common save the love of Ireland. The Southern loyalists accept the Treaty because the country accepts it and invites their aid in making it a success."

Part V: July 1921–April 1922

The two looked at each other but did not speak. In their silence, embers sputtered from behind the hearth's brass grate.

Finally, pointing to the fire, Kat said "For many this peace comes at too high a cost. Do ye not hear in our fire the exasperated gasps of hundreds of Irishmen and women tonight who will detest these compromises? They will never, ever take an oath to the king. Because their ultimate dreams of an island-wide Republic have been doused by British threats, their bellows will spark another revolution. The fire might go underground, but I assure you its flames will eventually rise up and consume us again. What were Collins and Griffith thinking?"

"Kat, Kat. Calm thyself," cautioned Eamon. "We must wait to see how the Dáil votes on ratification and what de'V's next actions will be thereafter. I refuse to believe that our friends didn't do the best they could to gain the least onerous concessions from the British. Consider these: First and foremost, we'll be able in the South at least to govern ourselves in a Dáil recognized around the world. We will have rid ourselves of the Black and Tans and can form our own police and defense forces. We will have the power to determine our children's education that will honor our Irish culture and manage our own economy and social affairs. We'll be an Irish Free State."

Kat rose from her seat, stepped over Sceo, and knelt next to her husband. She took his hands.

"How I wish I had yer calm, trusting heart, Eamon Smiley. But, I don't. Those rights will only pertain to the South, not to us in Bangor nor to our six Ulster counties. My own heart trembles with fear for us here. Oh, my love. The devil has been awakened, and he is one of us."

Chapter 41

A True Friend and Patriot—December 20, 1921

"He's trying to sabotage the Treaty, Liam. There's no doubt about it. If he succeeds, we'll be at war again."

Collins was pacing back and forth before the Hungry Tree bench in Dublin. Liam was seated on it, watching the Big One stride from one argument to another, not looking from left to right but straight ahead, head bent down, breathing heavily between words.

"Our delegation has been back from London for two weeks and every day there has been a continued debate—first within the Cabinet and now within the Dáil. Lest I misrepresent our discussions as debate, they've actually been like a soccer match with the ball being kicked around the field farther and farther away from the goal. Sometimes the opposing team has the ball, kicking it into the air above us; sometimes, the ball isn't even on the field. It's a buggered mess, Liam. A buggered mess."

"Ach, Mick. Ye're a good captain of yer team. And the team will follow you anywhere. Look at yer success so far. Ye had Griffith, Barton, and Cosgrove support our Southern Cabinet vote on the 8th to remove the Cabinet's power to ratify the Treaty and, instead, move the decision to the Dáil. The Army GHQ has already voted to ratify it. More and more county councils in the South are passing pro-Treaty resolutions."

Liam rose and stopped Collins in full step. "More importantly, most of our IRA brothers and the Irish people are behind you. All want peace."

Collins looked directly at Liam. "Ah, but does de'V? And remember, he has his devotees—within the Dáil and within the Southern IRA."

Part V: July 1921–April 1922

Both men turned their backs to the tree and sat again on the bench. Their long legs stretched out in front of their lean torsos, hardened by years of military training in and out of peat bogs, alley ways, and prison courtyards.

"What is the Tall One up to now?" queried Liam.

"I fear his ego has got the better of his mind. And yet, I'm grateful that others are now experiencing his vagaries. Just last week, he said that no one in the Dáil should comment on his alternative to the Treaty—his 'Document 2'—which had already been vetoed by the Cabinet. And then, what does he do? He brings it up in the Dáil."

Collins continued, "He continues to negate the Treaty by promoting this vague 'external association' relationship with the Empire whereby Ireland is not a Dominion within the Empire but, rather, an entity associated and outside the empire. Thus, the Treaty's current oath of allegiance would have to be revised to pledge to an Association of Dominion States and the Free State's Constitution, not to the king. He knew all along that the Brits would never accept that, but keeps going back again and again to it."

Collins paused and shook his head. "I swear, the man is either completely mental or completely malicious in his duplicity. I don't know whether to laugh or cry."

Collins continued, "Hear the second evidence of my confusion: He says that Northern partition is unacceptable, yet he pledges to support however the citizens of Ulster vote on being governed by the Dáil. We—and he—already know Craig, Carson, and the majority of Protestant advocates in Belfast will reject such a position. To what end is de'V making these arguments and, then, changing his mind? He should know better."

Liam placed his hand on Collins' arm. "Good friend. Ye know that he is fiercely jealous of ye. He thinks ye have turned against him by signing the Treaty without his approval, even though the Dáil declared ye, Griffith, and the other delegates as 'plenipotentiaries' who could decide the final words. He's furious at ye for not sending the Treaty to him before signing it. "

Collins frowned and raised his voice, declaring, "But he, himself, refused to go to London in December and negotiate his terms! He left us to be the scapegoats for what he knew the British would not allow. By God, he knew all along that we would be signing a treaty that would not permit a Republic. How could he not know the choice was between war and peace?" Michael pounded his left fist into the open palm of his right hand, his cheeks flushed with frustration and anger.

Liam let the emotion and color subside. "Mick, he's a Machiavellian character out of *The Prince*. He feels he is losing power. His greatest fear is that yer followers will want ye—not him—as the President of our Free State and Republic when it comes. I have heard more than enough rumors about him plotting against ye if the Treaty is passed by the Dáil. Sadly, Agnes has been warned by the Countess that we McCormicks—as well as Irvines and Smileys—should turn ourselves away from ye and openly state our objections to the Treaty."

Collins stared at Liam. "And…?" asked the Big One.

Liam rose and stood in front of his leader.

"Never, never, ever question our loyalty to ye and this nation as ye foresee it. We know our ancestors have waited more than six centuries to finalize the journey. We can wait a few years more."

Collins rose as well. He embraced Liam.

"Ye're a true friend and patriot, Liam McCormick. Ye make me proud." Tears glistened in Collins' eyes.

Liam saluted. "I pledge my life to ye, Commander."

Part V: July 1921–April 1922

Chapter 42

The Unraveling—Sunday, January 15, 1922

The morning mass at Mary Immaculate Refuge of Sinners on Rathmines Road, Dublin 6 was supposed to provide peace and unity for local parishioners in attendance this frigid Sunday. Father Sullivan usually followed the required liturgy when greeting congregants. Today, however, he revised his welcome due to the extraordinary circumstances of the preceding weeks. There was much guidance to seek from the Almighty.

Total confusion reigned among the public regarding the status of the Anglo-Irish Treaty. On December 8, against de Valera's wishes, the Dáil Cabinet had deferred its ratification to the full membership of the Dáil. In response, from December 22 to January 3 during the Dáil's holiday recess, de Valera had been on a full-blown campaign to convince the general public to not support the Anglo-Irish Treaty. Demonstrating his contradictory behavior, his initial commitment to respect the Dáil's vote was abrogated when he and his followers, including the Countess Markievicz, walked out of the Dáil after members voted on January 7 by a majority (64 versus 57) to support the Treaty. Committed to undermine its validity and value to the Irish people, Eamon De Valera had chosen the goal of a Republic over peace—his own ego versus that of war-worn citizens.

Two days later, de'V returned to the Dáil and resigned as President of the Republic of Ireland that he had always labeled as the sovereign Republic. He refused to acknowledge that the Treaty existed, attempted to revise the already implemented ratification procedures, and waited for members of his newly founded political party, Cumann na Poblachta, to re-elect him as president. If reinstated, he promised to fire all the pro-Treaty Cabinet members and submit his own version of a revised treaty. All of these undermining attempts by de'V failed in the Dáil.

On January 9, Griffith—not de Valera—was voted in as president by the Dáil, which according to the Treaty's stipulations, would be condoned by the British as the Southern Parliament while a separate Northern Parliament in Belfast would be welcomed by London.

On January 14, Griffith called the first meeting of the new Southern Parliament retaining all of the "first" Dáil members—at least all who had not walked out on January 7 with de Valera. The Southern Parliament became, in sequence, the "second" Dáil and again, as such, approved the Treaty. In accordance with the Treaty, an eight-man Provisional Government of Ireland was appointed by the Dáil. Collins was elected as the chair. Together, on January 14, he and Griffith "received the surrender of the Dublin castle" (the former seat of British rule in Ireland) and began the art of governing a divided people. The British no longer would play that role.

Now, on January 15, Billie and Agnes Irvine sat next to Liam and BB McCormick waiting for Father Sullivan to speak. Along with their youngest children and wards, they occupied the full width of the third pew facing the aging priest and the rose window above him. Rachel had promised to meet them but, as usual, was late having attended a meeting of Cumann na mBan the night before with the Countess. Thon and Jon, teenagers now, were at a soccer match with their school chums. They had been given papal—or was it mater?—dispensation from Agnes, ". . . as long as ye attend this evening's vespers," she had required. The two youth agreed before winking at their adoptive father, Billie, who of course, winked back.

Four-year-old Katie sat next to Billie, cradling her favorite doll and quietly telling her a story about a rabbit and fox. Agnes settled three-year-old Wolfe on her lap, before opening the pages of his favorite picture book. She hoped that would occupy him through what she knew would be a very somber service. Morna McNulty sat next to BB, ready to entertain two-year-old Kieran. Instead of a picture book, Morna held a fuzzy ball of Irish wool which she had originally knitted into a tiny rabbit. Its bushy tail and floppy ears

Part V: July 1921–April 1922

had already been chewed upon by Kieran into an unrecognizable mass of threads. BB and Morna believed he was just kissing the tiny toy, not devouring it. Of the remaining offspring among the McCormicks and Irvines, three-year-old Maggie had already evidenced her attention to the Catholic faith, and was fast asleep in her mother BB's arms; as was three-year-old Kieran, thumb in mouth, over Liam's shoulder.

The five adults looked up at Father Sullivan.

"Let us pray," the priest beckoned, raising his arms above the altar and looking out at his congregants. Silence followed, except for some shuffling of feet and coughs. Not all attendees were focused on the request. And Father Sullivan knew that.

He closed his eyes and prayed to himself that, by the grace of God, he could bring the peace and unity his parishioners so desperately needed to face the challenges around and ahead of them.

"Dear, Father Almighty. Please grant me the wisdom during this hour to bring yer solace from Heaven to this earthly place. May yer presence lighten the souls before me. May yer words enlighten their minds. May yer forgiveness offer alternatives to anger. May the unity of ye, yer Son, and the Holy Spirit imbue in everyone's hearts the harmony of love."

He felt a sense of grace and opened his eyes. He knew what to say.

"My brothers and sisters, God has heard yer prayers. I collect them for ye and the Almighty, reminding us that as ye seek Him, He will seek ye. He will never leave ye. As He never left his Son, Jesus Christ, despite the pain that Son experienced, He is beside and within ye—in yer minds and yer hearts. He's always guiding ye as to how to face the days ahead, how ye can set yer feet on the path of righteousness, and how ye can love each other, particularly when some of ye disagree with the decisions of the past weeks and others of ye are grateful."

The shuffling feet stopped, as did the coughing. All eyes were directed toward this man of God. Father Sullivan had guided each one of them like a shepherd through their individual sorrows of poverty, illness, marital betrayal, and death. He had rejoiced with them in their happiness of prosperity, healing, loving marriages, and births. Now, he spoke to them as a shepherd of sheep.

"Let me invite ye to the Lord's table where ye can put yer troubles down, lay yer differences aside, fill yer bodies and minds with the light of God, and be led by the Holy Spirit to follow the path of peace and unity. We have been through too much in the last four years to go back to war, especially among ourselves. I know many of ye have heard this prayer of St. Francis of Assisi before, particularly ye women during yer meetings. God begs ye all to take it to heart. Please open yer missals and let us now recite it together.

"Lord, make me an instrument of your peace.
Where there is hatred, let me sow love;
    where there is injury, pardon;
    where there is doubt, faith;
    where there is despair, hope:
    where there is darkness, light;
    where there is sadness, joy.
O Divine Master, grant that I may not so much seek
    to be consoled as to console;
    to be understood as to understand;
    to be loved as to love.
For it is in giving that we receive;
    it is in pardoning that we are pardoned;
    and it is in dying that we are born to eternal life."

There was a resounding "Amen" from the front of the church. Father Sullivan knew it might be the last time the miracle of common words being spoken among his congregants would happen. He noticed several parishioners, with disgruntled faces, quietly leaving the back pews. He was not surprised to see Rachel McCormick among them.

Chapter 43

Choosing Sides—Monday, January 16, 1922

"Ye must choose sides, Rachel. Ye can't be wavering like the tide at Killiney Bay."

Countess Markievicz was sitting at the formidable kitchen table of her 49B Rathmines Road house. Rachel was standing by the new cast-iron gas stove, fingers around the handle of a tea kettle reaching its boil. Her back to the Countess, Rachel was frowning, watching the steam rise from the kettle's spout and feeling her own fiery angst rise with it.

Rachel's mind was racing with questions, as she thought to herself, "Why are Liam and Ian on the side of the Treaty? During the Rising, didn't they both fight for our Republic? Didn't they hear the words of Pearse on that Monday morning in '16? Together, our family has read his Declaration every Easter since. At school, we pledge it each morning. How I cherish the phrase, 'We declare the right of the people of Ireland to the ownership of Ireland, and to the unfettered control of Irish destinies, to be sovereign and indefensible.' How can my family allow the British to refute that declaration? Worse yet, they agree to the vow of allegiance to a king who will never understand nor free us? Oh, how angry I am!"

"Bring the tea and sit thee down, Rachel," came a mellifluous voice behind her. The Countess was rehearsing her new role as lead campaigner for de Valera's anti-Treaty efforts. Now that he—and she—had publicly declared their resistance by walking out of the Dáil, they were actively galvanizing Republican stalwarts against any who supported what they termed "The Betrayal."

"We have much to discuss," the Countess said.

Rachel poured the hot tea into two china teacups settled beside scones and brown bread slices on cream-colored, porcelain Belleek dishes. In protest, a jar of Chivers' Old English Marmalade had been repurposed to hold a bouquet of Irish shepherd's purse flowers—beautiful to see but poisonous to taste.

It was Monday morning after a long night of meetings among members of the anti-Treaty movement de'V was growing against Collins, Griffith, and their newly formed Provisional Government of Ireland—one of the Treaty's stipulations.

On just the previous Friday, the sides had been set. The Dáil Éireann was recognized by de'V as the alternate governing body of the Republic, declared by the Easter Rising martyrs. Its parallel body, the Parliament of Southern Ireland, had been recognized by Collins and Griffith and the British as the legitimate governing body of the Treaty's Irish Free State. The two opposing parties were identical twins for they included the same structure. They did not, however, share the same titles nor intent. The members of the Dáil Éireann bore Pearse's, and now de Valera's, outer garment of armor, completely unattached from any British ties. Members of the Treaty's Southern Ireland Parliament had woven Collins and Griffith's fine, linen thread into the undergarment of a free future.

The Countess needed Rachel as one of her scissors to snip the thread.

"Remind me of how ye grew up, Rachel," asked the Countess when Rachel sat down.

Over the next half-hour, Rachel described her youth, living in poverty on Dublin's Henrietta Street. Her tenement was next to the Encumbered Estates Court house where she witnessed beleaguered men, women, and children forced legally into insolvency by wealthy ascendants. She related how her brother Ryan was killed by a Protestant terrorist in Belfast and how Ian's father was shot by an Ulster Volunteer during the Rising. She described the Kelly sisters who lived next door and had told her stories of Irish heroes—Cuchalain, Wolfe Tone, Daniel O'Connor, and Nano Nagle. Rachel kept silent about her mother's alcoholism and cruelty to herself and her siblings. By the time she finished these renderings, she was depleted.

Part V: July 1921–April 1922

But, she had one more recollection to share.

"I have many heroes now in my life—my brother Liam and my laddie Ian. I also loved my special nanna, Dr. Lizzie, who just passed." Rachel paused, feeling her heart expand. Never prone to tears, she instead felt an inner stubbornness begin to surround it.

The Countess reached forward, placing one hand on Rachel's arm. "Aye, there are many a hero you name. They are all admirable figures. It's time, however, for you to ask yourself why you admire them. For what did they live? And for what did they die? It seems to me that each wanted Ireland to be free—free from any outside tyrant that cursed our homeland with poverty, prejudice, and persecution. Ask yourself, Rachel: Whom would you follow today among your heroes and why? Once you find that answer, then choose which side you will take in this fight for Ireland's freedom."

The Countess' eyes searched Rachel's. Rachel looked away, saying to herself, "I need to talk to Ian."

Chapter 44

*The Hungry Tree Revisited—
Wednesday, January 18, 1922*

The Hungry Tree bench was not accustomed to young people sitting upon it. Usually, only the elderly or political captains of the time pondered the essence of life and liberty while resting upon the cast-iron structure, now embedded in the trunk of its century-old Plantanus Acerifolia. If any youth did recline on the bench, it was for the occasional—and always furtive—intimate groping that parental and public opinion did not condone.

Tonight, that was not the intent of Rachel and Ian.

"What are ye thinkin', Rachel?" exclaimed Ian, in as gentle a tone as he could muster despite his frustration. "Why have ye left Macroom to put yerself in danger here in Dublin? Ye know that the commander of the British quarters here in Rathmines—even though he'll soon have to retreat based on the Treaty's stipulations—can still punish IRA informants like ye. He knows ye, Rachel, and ye could be his last target—just to be vengeful."

"Ach, Ian. Never ye mind that possibility. It won't happen. The Countess and her Cumann na mBan are protecting me. And, by the way, there are more important reasons that I have come to Dublin. The one tonight concerns ye, not me. I want to know what ye have been thinkin'. How in God's and the Republic's name can ye support the Treaty?" Rachel turned a flushed face toward Ian's, shadowed by an evening growth of facial hair.

Ian was taken aback. He did not know about Rachel's resolute departure from the Sunday mass at Mary Immaculate Refuge of Sinners. Liam and BB had only said she had not appeared, as promised, at the service. Since they had not heard from Rachel in the last month, they were worried about her activities in Macroom, partic-

Part V: July 1921–April 1922

ularly given Republican unrest against the Treaty and Rachel's relationship with one of its leaders—the Countess. Her guardians were unsure if Rachel's allegiance would fall on the side of her brother or on the side her mentor. Liam had asked Ian to check on Rachel and, if she were leaning away from the Treaty advocates, to convince her otherwise.

Talking to Liam last night, Ian had been sure he could. Now, he was reminded of Rachel's stubbornness. Like a sailboat's skipper facing a change of wind, he grabbed the boom and tacked. He would have to change course from cajoling to addressing her passions first, then her logic. Given her dismissive attitude toward the physical threat of a vindictive British commander, Ian knew her passion clouded a true compass reading.

"Ye are mad to support the Treaty, Ian. Just mad," she blustered.

"Rachel. Rachel. Rachel. Calm thyself and tell me why I can't," he implored, quieting his voice to lower the atmospheric pressure.

"Don't ye condescend to me, laddie. Ye know all about me past and what I have done in our war for independence. How many messages did I carry between Macroom and Dublin and between Dublin and Belfast over the last four years? How many times have I played the role of—well, ye need not hear—in order to gain information from that Commander and others for the sake of our raids? Ye have no idea, do ye, of the children I have seen made orphans by Belfast thugs converted by our supposed countrymen as conspirators with the devil himself. I hate the British and those who now have given in to their lies. They will never let us be fully free, never. Why can't ye see what I see?"

Rachel's voice rose as she left the bench and paced madly in front of Ian. The pounding of her legs could have unearthed the roots capturing the bench's legs and release them from the tree's trunk. Only nature's century-old ties deterred that.

Ian's voice rose as well. "Rachel! The Treaty will eventually bring us freedom. Ye must believe that. If Collins and Griffith had not signed it, we'd still be seeing those children orphaned. And God forbid, ye still would have been—let me not say it. Can't ye see that de'V is only playing a game to increase his power? He knew back last spring that the British would never allow us to be a republic. By God, Rachel, Lloyd George told him that London would keep on fighting to crush our total independence. But, its Parliament didn't want to lose any more British sons so it needed a face-saving way to stop the bloodshed. de'V just didn't want to be seen as the one supporting a compromise such as the stepping stone Griffith and Collins proposed. de'V's a manipulator, Rachel. Just ye watch. Give him less than five years and he'll say the Treaty was his own idea, leading eventually to an independent Republic." Ian stopped abruptly as Rachel turned her back on him.

Calling over her shoulder, she said, "Nay, Ian, de'V won't. The Countess won't. The people of Ireland won't. We never will accept that Treaty."

She marched away from Ian, now blustering loudly, "Goodbye, Ian. Goodbye to yer ideas. Goodbye to yer loyalties. Ye're not the Irishman I knew and loved. Goodbye."

Ian watched Rachel's figure disappear into the darkness. He fell back onto the bench, breathing heavily, arms crossed upon his chest. He started to weep. Tears, like those when his father died in '16, flowed down his cheeks and onto his shirt collar. A breeze fluttered the leaves on the Hungry Tree's branches above him. He heard voices among them. He calmed himself and listened.

"Have faith, me lad," said one. "Be brave, me lad," said another. "Be strong and bide ye time," said a third.

He looked up and noticed a fine, white linen handkerchief swinging from the lowest limb. Reaching up, he plucked it off and dried his eyes. Then, he read the initials on it: U. B. L.

PART V: JULY 1921–APRIL 1922

CHAPTER 45

Jumping into Puddles—Friday 3, February 1922

Erin McCann and Billie Irvine stood outside the main door of the Abbey Theater in Dublin at the corner of Lower Abbey and Marlborough streets. Along with his role as aide to Collins, Erin had continued acting and writing throughout the war. Tonight, he had performed as the character Hugh in the theater's production of *The Revolutionist*, a play by Terrance MacSwiney. Billie had attended to see his former student and to learn about Collins' next steps in negotiating the Treaty with its opponents. The play and their discussion afterward provided more than just an evening's entertainment.

A sudden rainstorm had forced the two men to halt their heated conversation on the curb and seek shelter under the theater's metal entrance canopy abutting Lower Abbey. Pellets of rain, pounding the top of its gabled arch, were like bullets ricocheting above them, consonant with the short bursts of their words. Neither man was pleased with the other's news.

"Can't be true," sputtered Billie.

"'Tis," retorted Erin.

"How do ye know?" Billie challenged.

"Mick told me." Erin asserted.

"She's mad." Billie shouted.

"Aye. Literally, Billie, but not mentally."

Rachel's reaction to the Treaty, her alliance with de'V and the Countess, and her rejection of Ian had shocked the McCormick family. For over two weeks, she had not communicated with anyone among her relatives, either birth or adoptive. It was only after Ian had shared the Hungry Tree conversation with BB and Liam that they understood her disappearance. Ian had not yet told Billie and Agnes of what was then considered Rachel's betrayal.

Erin had just told Billie.

"She's too ignorant to take such a stand," accused Billie.

"Ach, watch yer assumptions, Minister Irvine, of our new Southern Parliament," warned Erin. "She's experienced more abuse from the Brits than ye can ever imagine."

"Mum warned me to never underestimate Rachel." Billie's voice lowered, along with the pellets now turning to drizzle. "I have, haven't I?"

"Perhaps ye have. We're all learning what our countrymen and women believe about the steps we have taken. Some are willing to join us in waitin' for the destination; others are not."

Erin pointed to the puddles forming before him on the street.

"Look at these, Billie," Erin continued. "Laborers cover cracks and holes in the street that have been here for months, maybe even years. They are filled with dirt, pebbles, tar, straw, or whatever. No matter what is thrown into them, a new rain comes, seeps through the straw or dirt and the pools appear again. Then the sun shines, the water recedes, and the hole remains the hole. Rachel will always be Rachel, no matter what ye try to do to fix her. Ye must accept that."

"Ye were always the gifted dramatist, Erin." Billie grinned to himself, remembering Erin as the brilliant St. Enda student seated before him during the years leading to the uprising. "Ye still are."

"I hope I am." Erin sighed. "But reality has taken imagination away from me. Now, I only see actual scenes and characters around me. I'm not sure of their words or plot. Rachel is one of many we must acknowledge in the next months. We cannot write them out of our scripts." Erin shivered as the rain stopped. A cold mist rose before the two men.

"Ye know from tonight's performance that MacSwiney is sending us a message. Remember what my character Hugh said: 'Ireland is in small danger from traitors, but in grievous danger from fools.' We cannot be the fools who ignore folks like Rachel."

Part V: July 1921–April 1922

Billie folded his arms, tucking his bare hands inside his tweed jacket. Warming himself with a chuckle, he commented on Erin's reflections.

"Indeed, Erin. MacSwiney also wrote in the play's preface, 'Intellect without imagination is dull; imagination without intellect is foolish.' For example, we can step away, into, or over this puddle. To decide our course, we must combine our intellect with our imagination."

"Ach," Erin laughed. "Ye are still the consummate teacher, MP Irvine. Let intellect and imagination guide our learnings when jumping into our country's puddle—huge as it is. But first, let's beg some wellies from Churchill. We'll need them!"

CHAPTER 46

Louisa and Lester—Friday, February 10, 1922

"Tell us a story, Uncle Mick!" asked the two older boys, Thon and Jon, sitting impatiently after dinner in the living room of the three-up, three-down Irvine row house in Dublin proper. Lizzie's will had provided enough for her children to substantially enter the growing, middle class. Billie and Agnes had left Rathmines behind and purchased a home that let them expand their number of rooms and their work. Tonight, they were welcoming their families to the new home with a sumptuous dinner and festive evening of folklore.

"And what would ye like to hear?" responded the amicable "Uncle" Mick, the title of endearment and respect given to this illustrious, yet humble, Michael Collins by the younger generations of Irvine, McCormick, and Smiley offspring. Billie and Liam had decided the newly elected chairman of the Provisional Government and minister of finance for the Dáil needed a respite from the daily challenges and threats, which were increasing in number and intensity—a £10,000 bounty had been posted for his corpse. A festive meal, jovial craic, and a story calling on imagination were required.

Wolfe Irvine, just three years old, Maggie and Liza, also three, and Kieran McCormick, just two, were seated on a woven, hook rug before the fading, red velvet sofa which had comforted family members over more than a century of stories—imaginary and real. The attention span of the youngest was limited, but their eyes were still transfixed upon the figure asking them the question.

The Smiley brothers' attention was far from limited. Devin, age nine, and Neil, age eight, raised their hands as they had been taught in school.

"Louisa," blurted out Devin.

Part V: July 1921–April 1922

"No! No! Lester," retorted his equally adamant brother, Neil. They started to shove each other to gain a place closest to their favorite uncle.

"Boys, boys!" exclaimed Kat. "Stop yer fighting, right now!"

Morna McNulty, age twelve, moved quietly between the rivaling boys, taking one hand of each and sitting them down beside her. She reached for Wolfe and Maggie, then nestled them both on her lap. Kieran sat on his father's knees. The semi-circle was formed: eight youth representing the future of their surrounding families. Their parents settled, too, behind on wicker chairs. They faced the storyteller, knowing he would share more than just a tale. The meaning of his words would capture them all.

"Ah, the story of Louisa and Lester it shall be. Now, who can tell me who Louisa is?" asked Collins.

"A dog!" shouted Devin.

"Nay," said Neil. "She's a lamb, ye knucklehead."

"Now, now. We'll not be calling anyone by disparaging names. There are no knuckleheads here, nor anywhere in our dear Ireland," cautioned Uncle Mick.

"Okay," mumbled Neil. "But I bet he doesn't know who Lester is! I do."

"And who is Lester, pray tell?" asked the smiling uncle.

"Lester is a lion!" insisted Neil.

"Aye, he is. And where did he hail from?"

"He came from across the sea, from Scotland," stated Neil, puffing out his chest.

"Indeed, he did," replied Uncle Mick. "And tonight, I'll tell ye a little tale about how he met Louisa the lamb just near us on the beach at Killiney Bay."

The adults and children listened intently—all except two. Morna rocked Kieran who was already asleep, as was Maggie. Wolfe was not, nor was Liza. They and the others were mesmerized, not only by the story, but by the melodic rhythm of Collins' voice. It resonated with the magical lilt and pace of Irish Gaelic, cultured by centuries of craic and ceilidh.

Collins leaned toward the children, folding his six-foot figure at the waist. He lowered his voice to almost a whisper.

"Many moons ago, on a star-lit night when the sea was shimmering like silver woven into a magical carpet, a lion swam from the far shore to the Irish coast. He arrived at a tidal pool off Killiney. A tad tired, he decided to doze on a sand spit before continuing his mission that night. Ye see, he was a messenger sent by the Goddess Morrigan to bring peace among the various animal clans. They had been arguing for decades over who owned the lakes, streams, and mountains of our island."

"Why were the animals fighting?" asked Jon.

"Very good question," replied Collins. "There isn't a proper answer, for, at the beginning of time, the Goddess Morrigan had provided much land for each of the animals. They lived well and peacefully shared the space with each other. As time passed, however, they became greedy. They started to steal from each other. The wolf took chicks from the hen; the fox grabbed fledglings from the nests; the eagles swooped down upon the mice."

Devin frowned. "That wasn't nice of any of them, was it?"

"Nay, it wasn't. That's why the Goddess Morrigan sent Lester across the sea to bring peace among the animals." Mick winked at the adults.

"But how can a lion swim across a sea? There are no seas in the deserts of Africa where the lion lives. How did he learn?" queried Thon.

"Ach, another good question, me lad. Lester was a special lion —a magical lion. He had such strong legs and brilliant mind that both enabled him to navigate all the way from Africa to Scotland on the far shore. He already knew how to swim right when he jumped into the sea toward Killiney," responded Collins.

Part V: July 1921–April 1922

"Oh, he's just like me da, then, who swims every day in the Bangor harbor." Neil turned to smile at his father Eamon, who nodded his head and rubbed his wounded leg. Eamon had not realized how his son had noticed the early morning, rehabilitation routine.

"Aye, Lester," said Collins. "He's just like yer da." Neil faced Uncle Mick again, and Kat took Eamon's hand in hers. "Now, let me continue."

"Strolling along the beach that night was a beautiful figure, bulbous like a balloon with a tiny tail at one end and a short nozzle at the other. Completely covered by an ivory-colored coat of the finest wool, only two black eyes and a shiny black nose emerged from the bundle of white. The figure wasn't very careful and stumbled over the body of the lion.

"'Oh, dear. Oh my. Who are you?' the bundle exclaimed as the Lion rose, stretched, and towered above her. A gaping mouth yawned wide. The lamb pulled back and cowered as a flash of moonlight exposed two rows of needlelike teeth. 'Oh, dear! Oh, my!', she cried again."

Neil jumped up and interjected. "That's the lamb, Louisa. But, how can any lamb speak? All I've heard lambs do is bleat and go BAAAAAA!" Neil frowned.

"True, me lad," responded Uncle Mick. "Ye must listen closely to that sound the next time ye're at a farm. She might be calling ye to feed her or, better yet, she might be singing a song."

"Oh," said Neil. "Maybe she's like Aunt BB when she prays. I hear her singing something like a BAAAA in the morning. It's quite pretty."

"Yes, just like your aunt, some lambs have lovely calls that seem like prayers. I bet Louisa in our story was praying too, for she was deathly afraid of the lion. Let's see what happens next.

"'I'm Lester, the lion,' continued Uncle Mick, lowering his voice into a growl. "Lester saw the fear in the lamb's black-dotted eyes and quickly closed his mouth. 'I've been sent by the Goddess Morrigan to make peace among your neighbors. Who are ye?'

"'I'm Louisa, the lamb. I have tried so hard to help my neighbors get along. You are most welcome to succeed where I have failed.' Louisa started to bleat and tears ran down her woolly jowls.

"'Stop crying, my little friend. Let's join together and see what we can do. I am a foreigner here and ye know everyone. Can ye call a meeting of yer neighbors? We can then see what they might say about the solution I bring from the Goddess.'

"'Oh, that would be grand, Lester. May I call ye that?' Louisa bowed her head and, if white wool could have turned red, she would have been seen to blush.

"Soon Louisa had contacted all her neighbors and just before the full moon reached the top of the night sky, all the animals had taken their places at a round table. Louisa's heart pounded as she introduced Lester. 'Here is Lester, a representative of the Goddess. He will bring peace among us.'

"There was a collective drawing in of breath and expulsion immediately afterwards." Collins asked the boys to mimic the two sounds with him before continuing. The adults and Morna were amused and joined in as well.

"'How can we all get along?' howled the wolf." Collins, of course, let out a long howl.

"'Why should we all get along?' fluttered the eagle." Collins flapped his arms.

"'Who could I ever get along with?' cackled the hen." Collins raised his hands in a questioning gesture.

"'And who would ever want to be my friend?' squeaked the mouse." Collins wiped his handkerchief across his eyes, feigning tears.

Both the children and the adults chuckled as Collins enacted the sounds and movements. When the laughter stopped, he regained his own composure and speech.

"Now, Lester rose up from his seat around the table. 'Just listen to ye all. Hear each other out in answering those very questions. Let

Part V: July 1921–April 1922

us make up some rules we can all live by that give us the reasons and ways we can get along.'

"'Like what?' asked the mouse?

"'Well . . . what rule would you like?' responded Lester.

"'I want to be able to sniff wherever I want,' replied the mouse, squiggling his nose. The other animals giggled while crunching up their own noses.

"'And you, eagle, what rule would you like?' Lester pointed to the large bird.

"'I want to be able to spread my wings as wide as I can.' He extended his wings and wrapped them around the animals seated beside him. They snuggled into his feathers.

"'And you, wolf?'

"'I want to howl at the moon be it half, quarter, or new!' All the animals that slept during the night moaned. The nocturnal ones clapped.

"Much discussion followed. A cacophony of sounds rose and rose. The lion and lamb looked at each other.

"Lester began to quietly sing. Louisa joined him. Their harmonic duet silenced the crowd. Their tune and words resonated with each of the round table members. It was the song of Ireland's creation centuries before.

"Soon all the animals were singing it along with the duo, in pairs with each other: the wolf as tenor with the mouse as soprano; the fox as baritone with the eagle as alto. Multiple pairs joined in. The animal chorus was formed.

"And to this day, whenever there is a conflict among them, the chorus is convened. Members come together, voice their different parts, and create a new symphony. Then, they part, knowing that as the moon sets and the sun rises, they can and will continue to live together peacefully. Their voices are as strong as the lion's muscles and as prayerful as the lamb's. Ye can hear them whenever ye make a wish."

"I like that story," said Devin.

"I do, too," said Neil.

"Ach," said Uncle Mick. "Finally, me lads agree on something. Good boys. If ye can find a way to sing in harmony with each other and yer neighbors, ye're going to be great leaders of our nation. Remember tonight's tale."

Not completely understanding Collins' last words, the boys, nonetheless, kissed him and their family goodnight, all on their bowed heads. They made their way to bed, Morna carrying the sleeping Wolfe, and BB carrying Kieran. Thon carried Maggie; Jon carried Liza.

"Thank ye for the lesson to us all, Mick." said Liam, after the children had left.

Collins pulled out his handkerchief to wipe his eyes again. He paused for a long minute before adding, "Ach, but who else will hear it?"

Part V: July 1921–April 1922

Chapter 47

Cows and Clover—Friday, February 17, 1922

Kat and BB rested on a wooden bench in the lobby of the former National Aid and Volunteers Dependants' Fund (NAVDF) clinic on Falls Road in Belfast. After Bloody Sunday on July 10, 1921, when more than seventeen people were killed, at least one hundred wounded, and around one thousand Catholics deemed homeless after their houses were burned, the Fund had expanded its services to Catholics and Protestants, employed or unemployed, Loyalists or Republicans. Those espousing pro-Treaty or anti-Treaty allegiances were welcomed as well. Collins, who had once directed the Fund after the Easter Rising of 1916, required that inclusivity.

Helping Belfast women and their families, regardless of their affiliations, had also been written into the will of Dr. Lizzie Gallagher-Irvine. Her two daughters now dedicated their time to ensuring the Fund held true to their mother's munificence and wishes. Due to both, its budget had doubled in the past year. The original storefront clinic behind the linen factories in Belfast's dock quarter had relocated to a spacious three floor, row house in the middle of the city. Renamed the Gallagher Women's Center, it was open to all—a haven for women of any background, need, or hope.

Kat and BB spent every Monday and Friday at the Center. Between times, they traveled around the six Ulster counties that, as predicted by Eamon and due to the Government of Ireland Act of 1920, had separated from Southern Ireland to remain within Great Britain. That separation had been constituted in the May '21 vote by the Northern Parliament of Belfast when it formally rejected the Anglo-Irish Treaty. The Center's newly inaugurated, rural clinics were scattered among the Northern Ireland Ulster counties of Antrim, Down, Armagh, Londonderry, Tyrone, and Fermanagh.

Kat and BB covered over 360 square miles each week such that by Fridays, the two women were exhausted by all they were doing and hearing.

"What a trying week," said Kat. "I feel like a rag that's been paddled through our mum's washboard and stretched out on a rock atop Black Mountain to be dried by the winter sun."

"True 'tis," replied BB. "There was nothing better this week than feelin' me legs land on terra firma in Coalisland after bouncing up and down over its cow paths. I now know how Liam feels when he moans about his morning "wobblies" after an evening with Eamon at Robinson's Pub."

The sisters shared a quiet laugh.

"Ach, we mustn't complain," reminded BB. "We know all too well the women we see each week suffer much more than we. There's as much for them to fear these days from walkin' the streets as there is from illness. Poor Annie McCarthy's boy was shot last Monday in a cross-fire between the IRA and RUC. Sad to say he was just comin' home from getting a loaf of bread at his gran's. And only a month ago, Annie lost her wee, little girl to the influenza. Such a shame that man and nature are colluding against the young."

BB's shoulders rounded down.

"Aye, 'tis cruel," responded Kat. "And just as tragic is the news about Rachel. I was able to talk with one of the midwives in Belleek who had seen our young one just the week before. It appears that Rachel has taken up the gun alongside a young man whose uncle is none other than Rory O'Connor. Did ye know that O'Connor has gone ahead and turned half of the IRA against Mick and the Treaty?"

BB nodded her head. "That will not bode well. O'Connor is out to get Collins even though they were brothers in the war. Already the anti-Treaty supporters are mobilizing arms to attack the Provisional Government army. Our Rachel will surely be held accountable once this turmoil ends if she stays with that nephew. And it will, indeed, end when de'V and O'Connor are defeated by Mick. God pray she is not killed beforehand." BB crossed her hands upon her lap.

Part V: July 1921–April 1922

"Ah, that poor, poor girl," Kat said, shaking her head and vigorously twisting the strings of her apron's ties bowed before her.

"Calm thyself, Kat." BB placed her hand on the ties forming a ball upon Kat's lap. The twisting stopped. "I'm going to be meeting with the Countess tomorrow and will beg her to return Rachel to us. We can only hope for the best."

They sat in the quiet of contemplation. A moment of tranquility embraced them.

"Do ye remember the song our gran Bella sang to us when we were frustrated and angry, unable to think clearly?" asked BB.

"Ye mean the one about the cow and the clover?" replied Kat.

"For sure," BB smiled and turned toward her sister. "Didn't she remind us then of our loyalties to family and this good land?" Quietly, she began to sing.

"I love to wander by the brook
That winds among the trees,
And watch the birds flit to and fro
Among the Autumn leaves;
'Tis my delight from morn till night
To ramble on the shore;
But when I do, my mother's voice
Comes from the kitchen door."

Kat hummed along with BB's ethereal tone in the refrain.

"Maggie! Maggie!
The cows are in the clover,
They've trampled it since morn,
Go and drive them, Maggie,
To the old red barn."

She continued.

"I'm not allowed to have a beau
Except upon the sly,

So yesterday he came and took me
Walking thro' the rye;
We strolled along so lovingly,
It seemed just like a dream,
When just from out the kitchen door
Came that familiar scream.

"Maggie! Maggie!
The cows are in the clover,
They've trampled it since morn,
Go and drive them, Maggie,
To the old red barn."

Kat joined BB in singing the words.

"He took me to the county fair,
We went up in a balloon;
Says he to me we'll go and see
The man up in the moon;
We drifted over towards the farm,
Perhaps a mile or more,
When suddenly I heard that voice
Come from the kitchen door.

"Maggie! Maggie!
The cows are in the clover,
They've trampled it since morn,
Go and drive them, Maggie,
To the old red barn."

The two fell silent. Each knew the task before BB would be difficult. But, perhaps, just perhaps, both the Countess and Rachel would listen to the voices of the past and the call of their homeland.

Perhaps, just perhaps, Rachel would "drive the cows home to the old red barn."

Part V: July 1921–April 1922

Chapter 48

St. Jude's Prayer—Friday, February 24, 1922

BB held her breath, pulled her shoulders back, and said a quick prayer to St. Jude, the patron saint of lost causes and desperate situations, but also of hope.

"Dear St. Jude Thaddeus, friend of Jesus Christ, give me strength in this endeavor to bring a lost lamb back into the fold. Help me understand her grievances and enable me to convince her of your holy will to honor all life. By your grace of faith, bless me with compassion and strength."

Feeling at peace—albeit, she knew, only temporarily—she knocked at the door of 49B Rathmines Road, the home of Countess Markievicz. It opened slowly to reveal a young woman whom BB did not recognize; nor did she recognize the accent nor the clothing.

"What do you want?" came the abrupt demand. The reddish face was obviously Irish in complexion and form, but not in attitude. An arrogance was portrayed—a certainty without gentility, foreign to the Gaelic people.

BB was confused, as the Markievicz home had always hosted the most considerate of souls, despite their social or political leanings. This young woman was a foreigner in more ways than appearance and demeanor.

BB heard a bustling behind the "guard apparent," then silence.

"I'm a friend of the Countess here to pay a call. Is she here?"

The woman did not move. She frowned, asking, "What kind of call are you making?"

BB could feel her own back stiffen. She inhaled slowly and exhaled just as slowly, repeating part of her solicitation to St. Jude: ". . . . give me strength, give me strength."

"I believe the Countess will know why I have come. Can ye just let her know that BB McCormick wants to see her? That is, if she is here."

The woman's eyes narrowed at the name. "Are you Liam McCormick's wife?"

The bustling resumed. A stately figure quickly appeared behind the disgruntled woman.

"Molly, please let her in. Names only carry the histories of men in this country, nothing else. We don't turn any woman away until we hear her words." The Countess placed her hands upon the guard's rigid shoulders, moved her to the left, and gracefully sidestepped to face BB.

"Ye must forgive our newest suffragette right off the boat from America. Molly knows quite a bit about our men but not our women. She also has yet to understand the courtesies of our Irish culture. Soon she'll know all about us, won't ye, Molly?"

Molly pulled her head back, lowered her shoulders, and expelled a loud "Humph."

The Countess reached out to escort BB through the doorway.

"Can ye please get us some tea, Molly? We'll set it up in the parlor. Come BB sit there with me and let's chat."

Through the hallway door that led into the kitchen, Molly left the two. A cold wind seemed to follow her. The Countess led BB into the parlor where, in contrast, a glowing hearth greeted the two.

BB sat upon the ladder-backed, straight chair. She was grateful for the soft, green cushion that covered its hard seat. She needed all of the physical, as well as spiritual, support she could garner. The Countess reclined on her paisley-pattered sofa. The two women faced each other. A mahogany, tea table stood between them, but each knew more than that physical stand was separating them.

"I have a good idea why ye are here, BB," began the Countess.

"Aye, ye probably do," replied BB.

Part V: July 1921–April 1922

"There is nothing I can do to return Rachel to ye and yer kin, just as I doubt there is anything I can do to bring ye and the family to our side. Ye have chosen to support Collins and the Treaty. de'V, O'Connor, and I cannot."

BB saw the eyes of the Countess darken. Again, BB reflected on her prayer to St. Jude: "Help me understand her grievances." She could not understand this woman sitting before her who, with Pádraig Pearse's mother just six years prior, had recruited BB to the Cumann na mBan. They had promised that BB would not have to take anyone's life. Now, the Countess was condoning BB's sister-in-law Rachel to do just that.

"I know what ye are thinking, BB. Ye fear Rachel will take up the gun and use it. I think she will. Know that I mourn that. But times have changed. We no longer have the Black and Tans to fight against for our freedom. We have our own delusional people. It's not a free state we are fighting for. It's a Republic—a republic for all of Ireland, not just the South. The sooner we can agree on that, the sooner violence will cease. Then, and only then, will Rachel come home to ye."

The Countess' face lightened a bit. "I'm sorry to see ye so worried, BB. Please believe me."

Despite the façade of sympathy the Countess was portraying, BB felt her pulse race. It was time to air her own grievances.

"Me lady," she began. "We both know ye are taking a lead role with de Valera in his new party, the Cumann na Poblachta. Whatever he says, ye condone. I invite ye, however, to consider him as the actor he is, for ye are quite familiar with that thespian world. Was he present fighting in the bog during our War of Independence? Nay, he had escaped to America under the ruse of raising funds for the cause. Instead, he disrupted our alliances with Irish-American brothers while supposedly gallivanting with his mistress in fancy hotels. Was he at the table in London negotiating the Treaty? Nay, he was home sending conflicting directions to Mick and Griffith in order not to be seen as compromising with Lloyd George."

BB noticed the Countess stiffening in her chair. That did not inhibit BB from continuing.

"In other words, he was playing a role, speaking from a fictional playbook he knew didn't reflect the real world. Yes, I and most of Ireland know the Tall One likes his stage better than our streets. How can ye accept the script he is now following when ye know he'll eventually rewrite it and make himself, not Ireland, the star actor?"

She had heard the Countess' grievances and knew there was nothing she could say to alter nor accept them. But she had also made her peace with what she believed was the truth. The distance between them was too wide to continue the conversation, let alone their relationship.

Now BB would have the last word.

She faced her former mentor and current adversary. "My dear Constance. We both know the trials ahead of us. The IRA split is too much to bear—O'Connor turning against Mick, his life-long comrade, and de'V sitting on the side just watching their conflict simmer. The boiling point has been reached, and the kettle is whistling."

The Countess' face turned a burning red as Molly entered the parlor through the kitchen door, tea tray in hands. BB rose.

"I will take my leave, asking you only two questions. What is better: A people at peace free to plan for the future, or a people at war locked in the past? A republic will eventually come, but at what cost if ye and your anti-Treaty followers kill our brothers and sisters and they, in turn, kill ye?"

The Countess did not rise. She turned her face away from BB.

"I will pray for us all," finished BB. She skirted Molly who was setting the tray down. "I will see myself out."

As BB crossed the hallway and approached the front door, she paused, remembered the final section of St. Jude's prayer, ". . . bless me with compassion," and whispered aloud, "Rachel. I know ye're here. I will pray for ye, too."

The slightly open kitchen door off the hallway closed with a muted thump.

Part V: July 1921–April 1922

Chapter 49

The Souring—Friday, February 24, 1922

Rachel backed away from the kitchen door after she heard BB's words and the front door close. She felt as though she were also slipping back into her youth, remembering how BB had held her closely, ten years before on Henrietta Street. Then, BB had come to let Liam know his brother Ryan was in trouble in Belfast for having planned the assassination of Thomas Clarke. BB and Liam had walked away from the house at number 7 so Mrs. McCormick could not hear their conversation. Rachel, in BB's arms, did hear it and kept it alive in her mind and heart. The last words she had heard BB speak that day stayed with Rachel forever: "But what about the milk for yer mother?"

To Rachel, BB had always supplied sustenance to her—material, emotional, and spiritual. Today, however, that sustenance had soured, like aged milk.

"Come away from the hallway door, Rachel," said the Countess upon entering the kitchen with Molly in tow. "I know you have heard what BB said. Sit and listen to me once again. I'll tell you what you must do."

The Countess pulled a kitchen stool over to Rachel and motioned her to it. Molly placed the tea tray on the long and wide center counter, then turned to the iron sink and began to wash potatoes for peeling—one eye to the task, one ear to the words.

The Countess began, "Both of us heard our leader's speech last Wednesday at the Sinn Féin Ard Fheis annual conference. You heard de'V say that no one among the 3,000 representatives from all over Ireland, including the six counties in the North, should 'give a British Monarch a democratic title in Ireland.' Each must forswear taking the oath of allegiance and must vote against the Treaty. It's as simple as that."

"'Tis true what ye say," said Rachel, positioning herself to listen and assess. Two eyes to the task and two ears to the words. "We must not ever let a crown be placed upon the head of any Irishman or woman. Only the cap or cloche must be worn."

The Countess smiled at Rachel's metaphorical reference. Upon meeting Rachel at St. Stephen's Green six years before during the Easter Rising, the Countess had sensed the young girl's intelligence and imagination. In her own acting career, the Countess had known many a thespian who possessed one or the other, but not both. Before her now was a young woman not to be underestimated. Rachel would have to be carefully directed.

Rachel lowered her hands and straightened her posture. She held tight to the edges of the circular seat of the stool. She, too, recognized the woman in front of her was a formidable presence, combining both intelligence and imagination. The Countess had been fired in the kiln of experience during three decades of action and several prison terms. She could become a powerful adversary to Rachel's plans, rather than supporter, if Rachel were not careful.

Rachel would keep her next steps to herself without consultation. "I'll put on a grand performance for this actor. One she will never discern until the end of my play."

"Ye need not worry about me, Countess Markievicz. I'm off to Macroom tomorrow and will stay with the Cork Number 3 Brigade. Its members will be my guide."

"And what shall you do there, my dear?" asked the Countess, assuming Rachel would expose her plans.

"Not sure yet, but, indeed, they are supportive of the Republic. Whatever role they want me to take, I will." Rachel slid off the stool, straightened her dress and turned to Molly. "Here, Molly, let me show ye the best way to peel a spud." Her back to the Countess, Rachel stood next to Molly, took a knife and began to scrape.

Part V: July 1921–April 1922

The Countess knew the current act was over. She was taken aback by the young rebel, but the curtain had only fallen for an intermission. Unabated at having lost the immediate direction of her production, she vowed to control the next scene.

Thus, after dinner that night when Rachel had retreated to her room, the Countess gave Molly a new role. "Tomorrow, I want you to follow Rachel wherever she goes. Send me a message every day regarding her actions."

Molly smiled. It was a sour smirk. "It would be my pleasure, Countess."

Chapter 50

The Warning—Saturday, February 25, 1922

Rachel approached the 6:15 a.m. "Slow and Easy" train to Cork. The Dublin and Southeastern Railway station platform was crowded with young men and women, single or children in tow. Some men wore the Nationalist Army uniform, indicating an assignment to either protect the railway system or mitigate the increasing attacks in Southern counties by anti-Treaty guerrillas.

A young man, around the age of twenty, in a tattered tweed jacket, pleated trousers, and worn work boots opened a carriage door and escorted her in. She nodded a silent acknowledgment.

Now, sitting across from her, he took off his tam, placed it on his lap, and directed his gaze and voice at her.

"Where are you off to?" he asked Rachel.

"Just off," she replied.

He quickly recognized the sullen rejection of a potential travel companion or, as he had perhaps hoped, a cuddle doll. He lowered his head, opening the morning edition of *The Irish Times*. His eyes focused on the front-page headline announcing the British turnover of the Beggar's Bush Barracks to Collins. "Sad day for our country," exclaimed the youth, looking up at Rachel.

She quickly recognized that he was not a Republican supporter. Perhaps he was even a Unionist, although his accent was neither Irish nor British. He sounded like Molly. Turning her head away and gazing out the cabin window, she drew her shawl about her shoulders and expressed an obvious and dismissive sigh.

The sound of the wheels picking up speed as the train left the station did not hide her disgruntled demeanor. He knew she was definitely not interested in his overtures. Little did he know her true opinion of him nor, for now, did he really care. Feigning disappoint-

Part V: July 1921– April 1922

ment, he returned to the newspaper. Time and opportunity were on his side.

Rachel's mind wandered away from him to the Countess' efforts to determine Rachel's reason for traveling to Macroom. She thought, "I'm glad my stubbornness held her powers at bay. Once, I respected her so much and still do, but, now I'm unsure of trusting anyone—her, Ian, Liam, BB . . . "

Again, Rachel's mind wandered. Soon, the side-to-side rocking of the train and continuous hum of the wheels lulled her into a deep sleep.

She began to dream . . .

"Rachel, my child," came a soothing voice. A woman's figure appeared wearing a sheer, fine-linen, ankle-length shift. Over her shoulder and nestled on her breast was a braid of amber hair, shimmering with silver threads. Emerging from a mist surrounding the bodice, an ivory-colored neck rose to a rounded chin and two slim lips. The nose was well centered between salmon colored cheeks. What caught Rachel's dream-state attention, however, were the long black lashes surrounding glistening blue eyes. They stared directly at her.

"Who are ye?" Rachel asked, reaching out—but strangely through—the figure. She pulled her hand back.

"Ah, my child. Ye need not know exactly who I am. All I can say is that I am what ye want me to be. I can see ye are troubled about who ye are today. Am I correct?"

Rachel shivered in her sleep. The figure faded out of view, leaving remnants only of a voice and smile from moving lips.

"Aye," replied Rachel. "I have left behind those I thought I loved more than life itself and now have chosen to betray them."

"Ah," the figure reappeared. "And what has caused ye to take such a turn?"

"I have always wanted . . . always wanted . . ." Rachel struggled to form her words. She opened her mouth, but nothing came out.

. . . A sudden screech of the train brakes jostled her awake. Wide-eyed, she saw the rejected youth staring at her. He leaned forward, dropping *The Irish Times* onto the aisle between them.

"Are you all right, miss?" he queried. "You just yelled something out."

Shaken by the dream more than the abruptness of the train's motion or the young man's question, Rachel frowned.

"Of course, I am. Ye need not ask." She lowered her head, shivered and wrapped the ends of her shawl around her fidgeting fingers.

What did this dream mean? Who was that figure? She looked so familiar—the eyes of Dr. Lizzie, the lips of Auntie Kat, the dress like that in one of the photos of Grandma Bella. And yet, she was different—older, much older.

Rachel looked at the newspaper, now resting next to her foot. There on the folded, front page facing her was a graphic drawing commemorating the 1641–42 Irish Rebellion by Catholics against the British and Irish Loyalists. Rachel squinted to see the figure of a finely dressed woman, hair braided over her shoulder, walking up the steps of a gallows platform. The headline read "History Warns: Hanging Rebels Begs No Discrimination."

Rachel shivered again.

Part V: July 1921–April 1922

Chapter 51

The Oasis—Sunday, March 5, 1922

Despite the rain, an expectant crowd filled the Dublin streets between Trinity College and the old House of Lords. Michael Collins was about to speak.

So much had hardened between the signing of the Anglo-Irish Treaty by Griffith and Collins in December, followed by its ratification in the Dáil in January. Southern Ireland would take on the title of an independent Free State and the status of a commonwealth nation within Great Britain. Northern Ireland had voted to withdraw from the Treaty and retain its dependent union with Great Britain. Opposing sides had formed—pro-Treatyites versus anti-Treatyites. Even within the IRA, members opposed each other—some supporting Collins and others supporting de Valera. The dream of a united Ireland—North and South under one Irish constitution and one governing body—had turned into a nightmare.

Partisan attacks were now taking victims on both sides, primarily in the partitioned counties of Ulster. Despite Collins' efforts to negotiate with the newly elected Prime Minister of Northern Ireland's Parliament (Stormont), Sir James Craig, tensions had risen among both Catholics and Protestants within Northern Ireland. Catholics did not believe Craig's promises for their safety nor for their economic equality. Protestants were angry at the loss of three of the nine Ulster counties to the Free State as well as an ongoing embargo by Catholics and pro-Treaty Nationalists—including Protestants—of their businesses.

Specifically, in January and February, Northern Ireland's Royal Ulster Constabulary (RUC) police had arrested members of the Monaghan Gaelic football team on its way to a match. The police suspected correctly that several were local, IRA insurgents traveling north to free comrades sentenced to death in the Derry Gaol. Only a few weeks later in retaliation, IRA captured more than fifty Special Constabularies and Loyalists at the Clones, NI railway station, killing four. The tit for tat escalated with thirty people killed by Loyalists in Belfast just three days later. Six West Belfast Catholic children were killed in a bombing by Loyalist paramilitaries. Collins and de Valera, while espousing the need for peace, were actually flaming the fires by their private and public political rhetoric.

This afternoon, Mick hoped to tamp down, not fan, the flames in advance of the upcoming national referendum that would approve of the agreement and institute the Free State's constitution.

"Mick, ye have to reassure the crowd that the Treaty will benefit them in both the short and long run," Erin McCann advised. He stood behind Collins at the foot of the steps leading to the speaker's podium facing Westmoreland Street.

"Aye, Erin. Ye're on the mark there. So will ye edit my speech such that it conveys that?" Mick chuckled, knowing all too well—as did Erin—that the two pages in Collins' top-right, breast pocket written solely by himself would need no such editing.

Erin smiled back. "I'd be more arrogant than Sir James Craig if I offered that service. And I'd be a mule's arse to boot!"

"Well, I'm glad at least one person in this crowd has a proper respect for me," retorted Collins, "even if I want him to be as stubborn as a mule. Keep those big ears of yers open while I keep my big mouth going. I need to know what the crowd is thinking."

Mick took the steps two by two and reached the top of the platform. As he heard the crowd shouting his name, he knew their thoughts exactly.

He waited for the reverberating thunder to subside. Then, in his booming Cork brogue, he welcomed them in Irish: "Failte a chur roimh mo dhearthaireacha agus dierfiuracha saor in aisce. Welcome my free brothers and sisters."

The crowd roared its praise.

For the next hour, the Big Fellow spoke the message of patience and peace. He used the words of his opponent, de Valera, who had

Part V: July 1921–April 1922

spoken just a week before in Limerick to a similarly enthusiastic crowd. de'V had likened pro-Treatyites to travelers across a desert—content to stop and rest at an oasis, but never continue on to their ultimate destination.

Mick exploited that image.

"Yes, we had come by means of the Treaty to a green oasis, the last in a long weary desert over which the Irish nation has been traveling. Oases are resting places in the desert, and unless the traveler finds them and replenishes himself, he never reaches the ultimate destination.

"The position in Northeast Ulster is not ideal. If the Irish Free State is formally established, however, Irish unity would eventually be a certainty. Destroy the Irish Free State now and you destroy more even than the hope, the certainty of union . . . You destroy our hopes of national freedom, all realization in our generation of the democratic right of the people of Ireland to rule themselves without interference from any outside power."

The crowd cheered Collins on, particularly when he described the Commonwealth status as a certainty against British interference in the Free State's governance. Such an intrusion, he reminded them, would threaten the status of other dominion countries, such as Canada and South Africa. Surely they and other members of the Commonwealth would defend Irish self-governance as they would their own.

Just as Collins finished his speech, the rain ceased. Sun began to peer between the clouds. Mick smiled. The crowd roared in approval. He descended the steps to the street below. A mass of youth surrounded him, cheering still. Erin had to push many away, but Mick made every effort to shake hands with each one.

"Keep up the spirits, me lads. Ye see the sun is shining. Never doubt its return after a storm!"

Only one youth held back and watched Collins intensely, observing every feature of the Big Fellow's face and torso.

Erin noticed and took note. He would share his fear of covert spies with Mick later that night. But, for now, Erin McCann would bask in the light of his mentor and hero. The Civil War was beginning.

CHAPTER 52

Playing an Innocent—Friday, March 10, 1922

Rachel held her knitting sack close under her arm as she entered the thicket behind O'Sullivan's farm. She had been given instructions to find an abandoned shed just beyond the tangled branches and at the end of a tow path that crossed an open field. Pulling the limbs away from her face and forging ahead, she felt as though the anti-Treaty IRA Brigade commander was testing her mind, strength, and determination by sending her on this circuitous route.

"Take the road beside St. Mary's church in Macroom and walk about three miles. Look for the Eagle Tavern on your right, go behind it and follow a dirt path next to Fisher's Pond. Then . . ." Eoin O'Duffy had added at least five more twists and turns for Rachel to memorize. No written guide—nor lamp—was to be found on her if she were caught by pro-Treaty supporters.

"Ach," she muttered to herself. "It's a good thing I was taught poetry by Mother Margaret Pearse at St. Ita's. Her making us recite Pádraig's poems by heart gave me the gift of memorization I use tonight. I just wish the moon would be more forceful in pushing the clouds away, at least for a few minutes. I'm walkin' blind."

Gratefully, she emerged from the woods, alighted onto the tow path, and quickened her pace. The large field had obviously fed a number of cows that very day, for the smell of their droppings and its squishy remains forced her to steady her mind. "Good sense and balance is what I need right now," she mused.

As she gripped the bag closer to her chest, the angled shape of a small revolver inside comforted her. "No matter what and who I meet tonight, I am ready."

She was not ready, however, for what greeted her at the shed. Despite its appearance of abandonment, it was alive with the noise of

Part V: July 1921–April 1922

a very active group of inhabitants, human not bovine. When Rachel walked around a collapsed eve, angled in back, she saw a doorway with two burley-looking men in front. They, too, held satchels close, but Rachel saw the glint of two rifles in hand.

The men faced her and asked, "What's a young gal like ye doing here tonight? Picking up the mornin' milk?"

Rachel responded, "Aye, I hope it hasn't curdled." The milk and curdle dialogue was code for each party to secure the identity and purpose of the other. They let her pass through the door.

As her eyes grew accustomed to the inner light and features, she saw thirty men and ten women gathered away from the door in the rear of the structure. Gray wooden pillars secured roof to floor, creating a three-sided framework alongside a back wall of canvas. Before the cloth, a small platform, upon which hay had previously been stacked, served as the focal point to which the crowd was facing. On it were none other than de Valera and the Countess. Alongside were the two anti-Treaty leaders: Brigade Commanders Rory O'Connor and Eoin O'Duffy.[15]

"Welcome my brothers and sisters," began de'V. "Tonight, we gather to launch our collective efforts to confirm the Republic of Ireland that has been suppressed by an alliance with the Crown. Ye see before ye the true alliance—that of our brothers O'Connor and O'Duffy. Together, we form a new political party, Cumann na Poblachta. And we will fight to support it and our homeland."

Most of the crowd clapped. Others, however, did not, for they knew that O'Connor did not trust de Valera and was forming a paramilitary army behind the Tall One's back. O'Connor saw the world as black and white—pro-Treaty or anti-Treaty. de'V saw it as gray. According to the militarist O'Connor, the politician de'V was vacillating in order to secure a leadership role in whatever government survived the current conflict.

O'Connor's eyes rolled when de'V closed his welcome with the words, "If you don't fight today, you will have to fight tomorrow;

and I say, when you're in a good fighting position, then fight on . . ."
O'Connor did not believe the Tall One or his words.

Rachel watched as O'Connor then spoke, inviting the men and women before him to take up arms and join the various Specials who would, in pairs and in small teams, attack various Provisional Government troops and supporters. The tactics would be clandestine in the form of bombing bridges, burning pro-Treaty stores, and assassinating so-called collaborators. At the end of his speech, O'Connor's colleagues distributed arms and assigned actions to designated pairs.

Eoin O'Duffy came to Rachel. "Ach, ye succeeded in finding us and without a scratch. Good girl." She frowned at his description of her as a "girl" and was about to confront him when she noticed who was behind him. "I want ye to meet yer partner."

There, smiling a grin as large as Lough Corrib, was the youth from the Dublin to Cork train who had initiated what Rachel had considered an unwanted conversation. Eoin moved aside so the lad faced Rachel directly. "I'll leave ye to it, then." He chortled and quickly walked away.

Rachel was shocked, but she knew she could not show it. For a few moments, though, her guard was down. The youth noticed the redness of her cheeks along with the stiffening of her posture.

"So, I have surprised you, Miss McCormick?" he asked, a twinkle in his eyes that displayed no mockery, just pleasure.

Rachel immediately regained her composure and control. "Who do ye think ye are? How dare ye play me on the train as . . . as . . ." she could not retrieve the correct descriptor.

"As an innocent?" he offered. "That's exactly what you were at the time. How could I tell you my name and the purpose of traveling with you in front of whoever might have been listening? Wouldn't that have been a bit daft?"

Rachel's face turned a brighter red, not from disdain but from embarrassment in knowing he was right. She was speechless, but not for long.

Part V: July 1921–April 1922 211

"Who are ye?" she asked, reverting to her reasoning rather than emotional wits. "I won't partner with anyone whom I don't trust, especially someone who is not from Ireland. And ye are not, are ye?"

"No, I am not. But I am of Irish blood. My name is Robert Smiley. I grew up in Canada and America."

Rachel was shocked for a second time in just an hour. "Smiley?" she queried. "Who was yer father?"

CHAPTER 53

The Magic of Fairies—Friday, March 31, 1922

Robert had not yet answered Rachel's question about his paternity. Before he could at the end of the O'Sullivan farm meeting, she had hesitated and turned away. Despite now being together for three weeks, he was learning that she could definitely hold an indefinite grudge. Their personal relationship was icy, if not frozen. They communicated only about orders given to them as members of the anti-Treaty IRA, Mid-Limerick Brigade.

Those orders came from ardent Republicans Eoin O'Duffy and Rory O'Connor who had just conducted a political coup against Collins' National Army of the Provisional Government. The two anti-Treaty men claimed Collins' troops were pledging to the Irish Free State and Britain, not to the Republic. On March 26, O'Connor had called a Convention of the IRA in defiance of the Dáil and Provisional Government. That Convention declared its own military force—the Army of the Republic—in direct opposition to the Provisional Government's National Army under Collins' G.H.Q. (General Headquarters) command. The two armies and their respective guerrilla arms began organizing to fight each other, overtly and covertly.

Tonight, Rachel and Robert had been ordered to position themselves behind the rocks and low bushes of the Grange Stone Circle, just west of Lough Gar in County Limerick. Collins' newly formed Civic Guards, specialized pro-Treaty IRA fighters within the National Army, were reported to be transporting arms and supplies along the Limerick-Kilmallock Road that abutted the Circle. Rachel and Robert were to watch for any such movement along the road.

Part V: July 1921–April 1922

Heads directed toward the road, they had not spoken a word to each other for the past three hours when, all of a sudden, the midnight moon emerged around the clouds and sent its rays across the Circle.

"It's very beautiful here, isn't Miss McCormick?" initiated Robert.

Rachel did not alter her gaze directed at the road. She tightened her woolen shawl around her, emitting only a "humph." After a few minutes, however, she begrudgingly said, "Aye. The moon is helping the fairies peer around the rocks and choose the softest grass upon which to begin their barefooted dance."

Robert grinned to himself. Was the ice melting?

He spoke, eyes also focused on the road. "My mother would recite tales about Oona, the High Queen of the fairies—of her beauty, wisdom, and magical dancing in the woods. I learned about her power to change the heart of—who was the giant she conquered?"

Rachel immediately informed him: "Benadonner."

Robert continued. "Yes, that was his name. Wasn't he going to harm Oona's husband Fin?"

"Aye, she used her beauty and wisdom to patiently change Benadonner's mind," offered Rachel, redirecting her eyes momentarily to Robert.

"What a grand Queen she was," mused Robert. "Whenever I imagine Queen Oona, I see my mum. She, too, was beautiful, wise and patient."

Rachel continued to look at Robert, slightly turning her torso toward him. "Are ye ever going to tell me who yer parents are and why ye are here?"

"I think you mean who my parents *were*. Neither is alive today." Robert lowered his head.

"Well, what happened to them?" Rachel asked brusquely.

"You're a funny girl, Rachel." Robert said, raising his face to look at hers. "I've not met many girls who are so direct."

"Then ye haven't yet met the best women," she retorted, staring again at the road and dismissing his label of her as a girl. "That's the only way women, not *girls*, should be."

Robert laughed. "I certainly see that's the way *you* are."

"Good. Now that we agree on that, are you going to tell me about yer parents or not?" she persisted.

"It's a sad story, Rachel, one that has been told by many an Irish family over the centuries. In '98, my mother met my father, Robbie Smiley, in Belfast. She was Catholic. He was Protestant. Despite my father's hatred of Catholics, he could not resist her beauty. When she became pregnant with me out of wedlock, he abandoned her, and her parents sent her away to live in Canada."

Rachel was engrossed in Robert's tale. She began to frown, again, bewildered by his reference to the family name, Smiley.

"Before I came to Belfast last month, I learned who my father was. You see, Robbie Smiley was a Unionist who in 1912, taking his British loyalty to the extreme, tried to assassinate Thomas Clark. Somehow, his brother and friends smuggled him out of the country. I know nothing else other than he died at Ypres during the war."

Rachel could feel her heart race. She began to look at him both incredulously and sympathetically.

"Robert, did you know the name of your father's brother?"

He noticed the look of amazement on her face.

"Yes. It's Eamon Smiley. Supposedly, he still lives in Belfast."

Robert lowered his voice to a whisper. "I hope my uncle—if ever I meet him—is a kind man, loyal to his family and to Ireland. I need to know that I'm different from the Unionist, pro-British terrorist I had as a father. That's why I'm here."

Part V: July 1921–April 1922

Rachel was uncharacteristically silent. Moments passed. The clouds covered the moon again, but she had already seen light in Robert's background. In her imagination, the fairies had started to dance in the Circle.

"Ach," she stated adamantly. "Ye have no need to fear. Ye are just like your uncle, not yer father."

Now, it was Robert's turn to frown. Before he could question her certainty, there was a rumble on the road.

The two ducked behind one of the large rocks within the Grange Stone Circle. The moon's rays began to illuminate a caravan of National Army soldiers. Rachel and Rob started counting.

Chapter 54

A Tapestry of Family Threads—Friday, March 31, 1922

At the same time Robert was sharing his father's history, BB was reading about it in a letter just received from America. Her hand trembled as she placed it before her on the writing table she used to create her Inde Pen Articles for *Our Ireland*.

She and Kat alternated their weekly editorials—one reflecting news from Belfast, alongside one from Dublin. The two perspectives were necessary to offer a balanced view of the political conflict now emerging into a military one. Like their mother Lizzie and gran Bella, the two sisters always wrote about peaceful resolutions to conflict. Tonight, BB recognized that finding commonalities, not differences, was more difficult than she ever imagined, especially when the differences were inherent within her own family.

She picked up the letter and read it again.

March 3, 1922
New York City

My dearest BB,

Thank you for your long and detailed letter about the news from Dublin. While Francis tells me quite a bit about the political battles between de'V and Mick, I feel he protects me from the fearful truth that those battles may soon erupt in disastrous ways, causing a terrible loss of life. I pray you, Liam, and the children will be protected from any harm.

This note, however, comes to share my concern for another member of your family—and interestingly—a new member of mine. Please bear with me as I unravel a very complicated story.

Part V: July 1921–April 1922 217

You know all too well that my first husband was Robbie Smiley. By the grace of God, your family helped us and our children to flee to America. After his failed attempt to shape the destiny of Ireland by assassinating Thomas Clarke, how often I have thanked you for shaping the destiny of my children and me.

What I have never told you is that Robbie had a relationship with another woman at the turn of the century, before he and I were married. She was Catholic. He was Protestant. You know that, as today, any mingling of the two faiths was not approved. This woman was so beautiful; Robbie could not resist her. When she became pregnant out of wedlock, he abandoned her. Her parents sent her away to live with family in Canada. When she died in 1906, her five-year-old son Robert was legally adopted by her sister, Anne, and her husband, Francis, a kind and responsible soul.

Yes, you are reading well, BB. That Francis is my own, dear husband of today.

A year later in 1907, Anne died. Francis was so grieved, he left Canada with their adopted son and moved to New York City, taking on the position of Vice President at J.P. Morgan & Co. At one of the bank's first staff picnics in Central Park, Francis was there with Robert. I was in attendance, too, having just been hired as a teller. I kept staring at the boy. He had the same sculptured face and curly red hair as Robbie. I just shook my head when Francis introduced himself and the boy as Robert McKenzie. I thought it was our Irish fairies weaving a magical tapestry in my mind of an imagined resemblance.

Throughout Francis' and my courtship, I kept noticing certain expressions and quirks in the boy that reminded me so much of Robbie. I never questioned Francis about the boy's parentage, but he fit in so well with my own sons by

Robbie—Edwin and David. They were like three leaves on a clover with their similar square chins and unruly curls. By the time Francis and I were married in 1915, Robert was fourteen and had become a "big brother" to them. I still didn't say anything to Francis about my wonderment.

It was only when Robert turned twenty-one, two years ago, that I finally asked Francis right out about Robert's background. I was shocked to hear his response.

Here is the double rub. First, Robert is, indeed, the son of Robbie Smiley by the woman Robbie abandoned in Belfast at the turn of the century. She was the sister of Francis' first wife, Anne. And, secondly, Robert now knows that, too.

Just a few months ago, he began to query Francis about the history and politics of Ireland. I'll never forget the night he sat in our library and asked us to join him for a family chat. Books were strewn across a large mahogany table—books from his studies at Princeton University where he had just graduated with a degree in philosophy. One book was propped up before him, opened to a map of Ireland in 1845 on one page and a graphic of an impoverished family from the South on the opposite. Robert asked us both to tell what we knew of that period. We did. He became so quiet and pensive.

I knew what his next question would be. He asked, "And what did your family do during that period?" Francis shared that his family fled the famine by immigrating to Canada. I said that my family left the plantation from which we were ejected by the owner's manager. We moved to Belfast and secured work in its linen mills.

His next question struck me to the core. "Did any of your family members fight back against the British or their landowners? Did any of mine?" I honestly didn't know what to say. Francis, God bless him, answered as sensitively

Part V: July 1921–April 1922

and objectively as he could. He knew Robert had read considerably about the history of Irish/British conflicts. It was of no use to conceal Robert's own Irish background by speaking in the abstract. It was time to tell him the truth about his birth family.

And so Francis described the affair of Robbie Smiley and Robert's mother, Robbie's abandonment of her in Belfast, and her banishment to Canada. Acknowledging Francis' gentle request for me to speak, I then explained who Robbie Smiley was in relation to me and the boys. As accurately and sensitively as possible, I detailed Robbie's involvement with a Protestant, pro-Unionist group in 1912, and his attempted assassination of Thomas Clarke, an Irish Republican Brotherhood member. I mentioned Robbie's brother, Eamon, and your family's influence in helping us and Robbie—who was then on an IRB death list—flee to New York.

Dear BB, I couldn't continue the story that night. Francis did, though, telling how Robbie had left us in New York to join the Canadian Army in the war and had died in Ypres. I'll never forget the look on Robert's face when Francis finished. It was exactly like that on statues of Christian martyrs—their chiseled faces expressing such anguish and sorrow.

Robert left us that night as a changed person, one whom I now implore you to find.

You see, he has journeyed to Ireland to join the anti-Treaty IRA. He told us he must purge his family lineage of his father's alliance with the British and the Protestants. I fear he may cross the line from philosopher to militant and never know the way to a united Ireland through peaceful negotiations. He must meet you and his uncle Eamon. Only you two—through your respective spirituality and philosophy—can bring him back to us here as the thoughtful and compassionate person I know he is.

We have heard he is attached to the Mid-Limerick Brigade outside Macroom. If there is any chance you, Eamon, or members of your dear family can reach out to him, I beg you.

Forgive the length of this letter and its selfish focus, dearest BB. Please know I am always thinking and praying for you all in both Belfast and Dublin and all of Ireland.

All my love, and hope,
Your devoted Margaret

Post-script: By the way, we have heard that Francis' estranged niece, Molly, has also arrived in Dublin. We aren't sure you may encounter her in your work. I will share our concerns with you about her in another letter.

BB again placed the letter down before her. "I must tell Liam. Then, Eamon and Kat." As she rose from her chair, she noticed to her right a small photo of the McKenzie family—Robert's face aglow. Next to the photo was one of her own McCormick loved ones—Rachel's face aglow.

"I wonder if Robert has met Rachel in Limerick—two pilgrims seeking their High Cross of St. Tola and their life's purpose."

BB sighed. "Dear God, protect them."

Chapter 55

*The Philosopher and the Activist—
Saturday, April 8, 1922*

"I'm not sure what to do," said Eamon, looking across the kitchen table at his dear Kat. Their sons Devin and Neil and little Liza had been sent on a day of exploration at Cave Hill with their Aunt BB, Morna, Maggie, and their two-year-old cousin, Kieran. BB had arrived in Bangor the night before, guarding Margaret's recent letter in the family's overnight catch. The three adults had agreed to Saturday's outing so that Eamon and Kat could discuss at length what they should do about Robert Smiley. They had to come to a mutual agreement.

In the past, when they were faced with difficult decisions, such as helping Robbie and Margaret flee Ireland, becoming actively involved in the Republican movement, or choosing a church that would accept them as an ecumenical couple, they collaborated well. Eamon would philosophize; Kat would act. At this time, however, their roles had reversed.

"Wait until Robert is ready to see you, my darling. He's supporting the anti-Treaty folks now," exclaimed Kat, "and, perhaps, he'll be just as foolish and irrational as yer brother following his emotions, rather than sensibilities. Ye mustn't go to him."

"Now, Kat, be kind," Eamon replied, placing his hand on the open missive before him. "We have read in Margaret's letter how Robert wants to purge his father's lineage of any alliance with the British and Protestants. I can't begin to imagine his exact state of mind until I find him and listen to him. Only then, can I know his intentions and be prepared to support him, or . . ." Eamon paused, "or deter him."

Kat rose from the table, turned away from Eamon to the kitchen window overlooking the back courtyard, and whispered, but loud enough for Eamon to hear, her words, "I am so afraid of what may happen to you in Macroom, my dear. I almost lost ye once and can't bear that possibility again. I am haunted, too, by the fate that my grandfather William Irvine faced there—shot by that nefarious Dickson, agent of the landowner Earl. Ye'll be among people whose minds have been soured in one direction over another and who would die before listening to 'the other.' This is not the time to act, Eamon. Can't ye just wait?"

Eamon stood up from the table and approached Kat, whose back was turned to him. He tucked his arms around her waist and held her, his face buried in the crook of her neck where wisps of her curly hair kissed his nose.

"I will never leave ye, Kat. I almost did once, but look at how the fates brought me back to ye. They'll never abandon ye or me until they have set us on the tide, and we cross the bar together. And that won't be for a long, long time."

They retrieved their inherent roles and faced each other.

Kat went into action. "I'll fix yer bag and go to the station with ye. The afternoon train to Cork leaves at two o'clock."

"Grand," replied Eamon. "I'll just leave the boys another reading assignment—perhaps from Plato's *The Republic*. I just finished editing the young person's version. What beneficial advice it offers." He looked at her and smiled.

"And what is that, my professor?" grinning with inquisitive delight.

"This: '. . . That when a man has led a just and holy life, sweet Hope cheering his heart, the nurse of age, is his companion—Hope, who more that aught else, governs the wavering mind of mortal men.'"

Eamon started to pull away from her but not before he bowed his head. Kat kissed him gently on his forehead.

Part V: July 1921–April 1922

"Ye are that just and holy man," she said.

Raising his head, he held her gaze. "And ye're the hope that governs my wavering and mortal mind."

On the train to Macroom, he would think deeply about her words. In Bangor, Kat would distract herself by writing the next *Our Ireland* editorial with BB.

Chapter 56

The Macroom Spirits—Sunday, April 9, 1922

Eamon was unsettled by the tension he felt disembarking from the Dublin and Southeastern train in Macroom. The late evening rain, punctuated by needles of ice crystals, set a stage of duplicity. Was this a night of fog or would there be a massive blizzard? And why in April would such a climatic phenomenon occur? As a philosopher, Eamon considered the relationship of the visual scene to the personal tension he felt. Was there a message in the fog or was it in the ice crystals? Had nature infiltrated the character of the humans around him? If so, what was its message?

He shook his head to stop the questions as he reached for the grip Kat had packed for him. Grasping the handles tightly and releasing them several times stabilized him. Connecting with whatever she touched had always comforted him. During his recuperation in Craigmaddie Hospital in Scotland, he and Kat had learned this calming technique and used it during times of stress. This was one of those times.

On the train, he had reflected on her words of fear. The Irvine family had certainly experienced the impact of conflicts within Ireland's last century—plantation and factory exploitation, famine and catastrophic pandemics, religious antipathy, civil and world conflict, and continuous political struggles within and outside the Isle.

The Smiley family had also experienced these events, but through a different lens. The "curse" of the Irish in the form of alcoholism had permeated numerous Smiley generations and tainted their reactions. Eamon had considered Robbie's attraction to the darker side of the Unionist movement as predestined genetically and deluded by the "drink." Eamon now worried about his nephew's

Part V: July 1921–April 1922

capacity to face conflict soberly. By the Macroom stop, Eamon's head had been spinning, and he knew it had to stop.

"Ye're here safely, professor." A voice came out of the fog, followed by a figure limping toward him.

"I saw yer dear Mrs. at the Belfast station just as I boarded this train myself. She told me ye were traveling here and asked that I meet up with ye." Erin McCann reached for Eamon's satchel.

"Come. Mick and I have a place just outside town where ye can stay. It's a cozy farmhouse, originally lived in by my grands back in the '40s. I believe yer grandfather-in-law, William Irvine, stayed there as did my saintly Aunt Bridgette and her less holy beau, Aiden McKnight. We'll feel their spirits there for sure!"

Eamon could sense his tension dissipate into the air, clearing his mind. The ice pellets stopped. The fog rose. He was grateful for the handclasp now reaching out to him from a known friend.

When they arrived at the McCann farmhouse around eleven o'clock, the interior was aglow with golden light sending rays of welcome onto the path leading to the front door. It opened to the code of Erin's triple knock, followed by two and, then, three more.

"Well, bless me soul, the seeker is finally here!" The boisterous greeting was followed by laughter. "I thought ye had been captured by the local banshees, and I'd have to pay a heavy ransom in gold coins for ye!" The Big Fellow grabbed Erin by the shoulders and pulled him into a muscular, hurler's embrace. Over Erin's shoulder, Mick saw Eamon.

"And, by the blessed Virgin Mother herself! Is this not our Professor accompanying ye? Ach, for sure, we're in for a long craic this night. Come, come. Let's sit by the fireplace, have a good pint and solve the Isle's problems." Mick led the two back into the tiny kitchen area where a blazing fire in the stone hearth warmed the air. The smell of burning peat permeated Eamon's olfactory senses. He knew he was now safe and stable.

A large table, taking up two-thirds of the kitchen, was scattered with plates of half-consumed meats, cabbage, and bread. Two women stopped cleaning it off, looked up at the new visitors, and quickly reversed their plans. Replenishment, not clearance, was required.

In addition to the two women, three men rose from their seats around the table. They, too, hugged Erin and looked at the man whom they had heard Mick call "the Professor." They had never met him before. What they did know about Eamon was that he had been a significant source of information about Belfast Unionists and IRA recruits during the War of Independence. His current role in this civil war was unknown to them. Trusting Mick and Erin, however, each man enthusiastically shook his hand. The women nodded their acknowledgment.

Shortly, the six men and two women settled around the table. The fire had been freshly laid and stoked with additional turf pods and the table with pints, soup, and chunks of soda bread. The conversation started with a question from Mick.

"Good Professor, I didn't expect ye here in the South. Tell us what brings the Lanyon Hall lecturer of Ireland's brightest men—and women—to the fields of Ireland's pigs and sheep? Obviously, ye're not here to transform a sow's ear into a silk purse?" The group tittered.

Eamon was hesitant to share his task at hand. He looked at the men, then the women. He recognized Mick's fiancée Kitty Kiernan, a friend to both Kat and BB. She would be sympathetic. The other woman looked familiar, but Eamon could not place her. She noticed Eamon staring at her.

"Professor Smiley," she offered. "I'm Shelley McCormick, Liam's sister. You taught me at Trinity in the class Mr. Collins attended back in 1919. It was the philosophy class in which you asked the question about the lenses through which we define a just life. I answered economics. Not sure why that made Mr. Collins think I was a perfect recruit for the movement, but, nonetheless, he did and here I am four years later."

Part V: July 1921–April 1922

Eamon smiled. "Ach, now I remember ye, but more so from the wedding of Liam to my sister-in-law BB. Ye played the piano so beautifully while yer younger sister, Rachel, sang that lovely song by Olcott—"My Wild Irish Rose." Am I recollecting correctly?"

"Aye, so ye are. Interesting, though, that ye remember my piano prowess more than my academic." Shelley frowned as the others in the group chuckled. Eamon immediately saw and heard Rachel in her sister.

"Now, now, Miss Shelley. The Professor has more on his mind right now than memories and the suffragette mission. Tell us the reason for coming all the way here tonight?" Mick turned toward Eamon and placed a hand on his arm. "Trust us, my friend."

And trust Eamon did, telling them all about his brother Robbie, his nephew Robert, and the letter from Margaret McKenzie. Surprisingly, each man and Kitty knew the history of Robbie Smiley and Tom Clarke, plus the role Margaret's husband Francis played in funding the War of Independence. The news of Robert being in Ireland intrigued them, particularly Shelley.

She listened to the end of Eamon's tale and, when the room fell silent, raised her voice. "There are spirits among us tonight weaving an extraordinary web of connections." The men and Kitty looked at her.

"I am here to find my sister Rachel because of my brother Liam. Ye are here to find Robert because of your deceased brother Robbie. Just yesterday, I heard from one of our Special Guard members that he saw both of them outside Lough Gar. It seems they have been paired by Eoin O'Duffy to work for the anti-Treatyites." She waited for a response.

Mick nodded his head. "Ach, me lads and lassies. It seems we have an opportunity here."

The fire flared up. The peat crackled. Sparks flew against the stone wall behind the flames. All heads turned toward the fireplace.

Erin chuckled. "I believe we just heard that Grandfather William, Sister Bridgette, and Uncle Aiden agree."

Outside, the moon appeared. Reflected against it, the three spirits and Una nodded their heads.

PART V: JULY 1921–APRIL 1922 229

CHAPTER 57

Naming a Better Ireland—Monday, April 10, 1922

Billie and Liam sat at the table farthest from the front door of the Flying Pig pub off Leinster Square in Rathmines. After 6:00 p.m., the usual crowd of Dublin factory workers was lined up, shoulder by shoulder at the bar, foot by foot on the brass rail below them. Others sat around the wooden tables scattered across the open floor or in partitioned off "snugs." Billie and Liam had chosen a table for their private conversation, not a snug. The latter would obviously be too secretive to the multiple eyes they knew were watching.

"It's a good thing our lassies are anonymous in their Inde Pen editorials," Billie said, leaning toward Liam while wiping a small wisp of beer froth from his beard. The gesture muted his words.

"Ach," replied Liam, meeting Billie halfway. "I fear the editors at *The Times* know exactly who the two ladies are and will not be as professionally confidential as we trust pressmen would be. Remember, the Countess has her eyes and ears in every nook of Dublin and Belfast. That includes print shops, alleyways, and kitchens. I bet she's fuming about their latest piece."

"Indeed, she probably is," sighed Billie. "I keep warning my sisters to be careful, but it's like calling the sheep home to their pens when the clover over the hill calls more appealingly."

Liam chortled. "Neither of us is as quick-witted as a skilled border collie in quartering them. We're more like Bigger, Boru, and Sceo —mere lap dogs. Our lassies just pat us on the head and say 'good boy' when we speak. Then, we obey their commands."

Billie laughed aloud. "'Tis true. 'Tis true." He and Liam both took another swig of their drink.

"I have to say, though, that their recent work was brilliant," Liam continued. "The fact that they joined together to write just one piece, rather than their usual two from the different perspectives of Dublin and Belfast, was perfect for this period."

Billie patted his breast pocket. "I cut it out of the paper to read in the Dáil this week. We can't acquiesce to de'V's vitriolic statement about Irish brothers spilling Irish blood instead of British to create an immediate Republic. We must come together to convince the British to withdraw their troops rather than see them remain to quell a civil war."

"Aye, I agree Billie," Liam replied, placing his hands tightly around his glass mug. "The problem is that there are too many opposing sides among us. The Brits cherish that. Not only is the IRA split between pro- and anti-Treatyites, but the farmers and factory workers are as well. Last week I met with James Connolly's son, Roddy, of the Communist party who is adamantly Republican, against the Treaty, and pro-labor. Two days later, I was talking with union leaders whose laborers support the Treaty. And then, we have the farmers of the South who are demanding land rights along with the expulsion of plantation managers and landowners. None of these opposing sides will accept the other's view. I truly fear an explosion of contrary minds and arms is on the horizon."

Billie nodded. "Ye're right, good Liam. Unfortunately, the dynamite has already been purchased and tested. The recent killing of thirteen Protestants in Cork in retribution for a murdered IRA member is indicative of what we may be facing in the future: quid-pro-quo retaliations. God forbid the innocents who will be caught in the cross-fire of our own people killing our own."

The two men sat silently. Then, quietly, they began to share their knowledge of what Collins had told each in separate conversations. He was trying to unite members from opposing IRA segments along with recruits from laborers and farmers to organize together in an all-out assault on Unionists in Belfast. Unify us and conquer them

Part V: July 1921–April 1922

was Collins' mantra. However, he also had shared that Rory O'Connor was adamant that the anti-Treaty IRA members, now under O'Connor's command in the South, would never support the Treaty. Divide us and conquer them was Rory's mantra.

"I can't imagine how Mick can appease so many disparate groups around a common goal. I fear it is impossible, and I fear for his life." Liam bowed his head. Billie sensed an emotion on Liam's face that he had never seen before: pure anguish.

"What can we do, good sir?" Billie asked, quietly moving his chair closer to Liam's.

Liam raised his head. "I don't know. I don't know."

Una's Epilogue to Part V

A Call for a Better Ireland—April 8, 1922

Well, I Una, do—and so do BB and Kat. They have proposed what all Irish men, women, and children must do. And, lest I dismiss their wisdom, let me repeat here what they wrote in their first collaborative piece for *Our Ireland*.

Saturday, April 8, 1922

Editorial by the Inde Pens: A Call For A Better Ireland

Dear Readers,

You will note that this week's Inde Pen editorial is not written in its usual two-part format—one representing Dublin's sentiments, the other Belfast's. Instead, we two authors are writing together as Inde Pens. We pray that you, the reader, will understand the sentiments and principles upon which our new approach is based. We will label it "A Call for a Better Ireland."

To begin, we are all Irish—be we Protestant or Catholic, Scots-Irish or Gaelic, landowner or farmer, factory manager or factory worker, pro- or anti-Treaty. The blood of Cuchulain flows through each of us by birth or marriage. The words of Johnathan Swift grace each of our mantels. We step dance, eat thick mutton and potato stew, and raise our whiskey glasses to honor our dead. We sing the "Fields of Athenry" and recite the poetry of Mary Barber. We play with our children, comfort them when sick, teach them to be truthful and righteous. This is who we are—Irish.

Each of us wants a peaceful and productive life—one in which we can believe what we want to believe, dream what we want to dream, and act according to our values. We want to learn, to work, to worship, to love. This is what we want to do as Irish.

Why can we not come together around what we hold in common rather than what we fear separates us? Certainly, the former is grander than the latter. Certainly, the former is possible.

We implore, we beg, we pray that you will hold your children close to you tonight and consider what they have in common with other children. What might the future of those children look like if they played together, learned together, laughed together? Would it be one of peace or war, understanding or prejudice, acceptance or resistance? We all know what is better for Ireland.

Thomas Moore reminds us of that in his poem "Oh, Call It By Some Better Name." Let us have the courage and compassion to name it.

> Oh, call it by some better name,
>   For Friendship sounds too cold,
> While Love is now a worldly flame,
>   Whose shrine must be of gold:
> And Passion, like the sun at noon,
>   That burns o'er all he sees,
> Awhile as warm will set as soon--
>   Then call it none of these.
> Imagine something purer far,
>   More free from stain of clay
> Than Friendship, Love, or Passion are,
>   Yet human, still as they:
> And if thy lip, for love like this,
>   No mortal word can frame,
> Go, ask of angels what it is,
>   And call it by that name!

PART VI: 1922
THE CIVIL WAR

CHAPTER 58

Serving Two Masters—Saturday, April 15, 1922

Rachel sat in the third pew from the front while Robert sat in the third to the back. This evening's Vigil Mass at St. Coleman's Roman Catholic Church on Chapel Hill in Macroom was sparsely populated. Only a few dozen attendees were scattered among the pews. Rumors had spread rapidly that a Republican IRA observance was going to give sight to an action. That had not stopped Rachel nor Robert from entering the church and taking their places. In actuality, that had been part of their overall plan, albeit known only by one of them.

The church had been built in 1841 and remodeled in 1893. Its Gothic, gabled façade housed a new chapel and convent that was attached to the original church's five-bay nave and three-story, bell tower. Overlooking a slate courtyard linking the contiguous structures was a circular clock at the top of the tower. The time read exactly 5:30 p.m., which is when the welcoming—or were they reminder—bells rang out. A stillness followed their echoes.

Inside, Rachel considered what was to happen. She placed her right hand over the satchel placed close to her hip. She could feel the outline of a pistol through the bag's rough tweed pattern. On her lap, her left hand rested on the Bible that Rory O'Connor had given her as a cover. She laughed to herself as she remembered his words.

"I know ye're not a Catholic by practice, but shame if ye don't remember a bit of the ritual. After all, isn't your brother's wife a former nun?"

Rachel had reddened and then, in her inevitably argumentative style, responded, "I practice my faith, sir, unlike others who just blabber it away in fancy phrases and baseless judgments."

O'Connor merely shrugged his shoulders, and had said, "There's only one true faith and that's in our Ireland. Use your beliefs as ye wish, but I'll tell ye how to use your actions." He took Robert aside to give him, not Rachel, the evening's instructions. Rachel had a growing distaste of the male IRA leaders she was meeting in Cork.

"How I wish they were more like Uncle Mick and Liam," she had thought then and now, again, as the priest before her began to speak.

"I welcome you this evening to St. Coleman's Vigil Mass. Whatever hangs heavy on your mind, whatever burdens you in your heart, ye are invited to lay it at this altar and renew your spirit and soul. In the name of Jesus Christ, our one and only Saviour. Amen." A muffled chorus of amens followed.

Rachel knew this priest only by name and reputation. Father O'Hare was in his 80s. Probably, his appearance would have mimicked his own surname by comporting a full head of white hair if he had not gone completely bald at age 30. Some said he had been a hero in the 1916 Rising; some said he had been a traitor. No confessional—nor drunken exposé—had confirmed either. Over the years, his presence reflected this conflicting aura of hero and traitor—a banshee's actions written into history as fact. For Rachel and the Republican IRA, he was deemed a collaborator due to his current peacemaking behaviors with Collins. Today, he needed to be taught a lesson that would resound in the church and its community classroom as well.

"Let us read together today's scripture," the priest beckoned, and then continued, "This is Romans 16, verses 3, 4, and 16.

"'Greet Prisca and Aquila, my fellow workers in Christ Jesus, who risked their necks for my life, to whom not only I but all the churches of the Gentiles give thanks . . . Greet one another with a holy kiss. All the churches of Christ greet you.'"

Rachel sensed he was giving a message to someone in the congregation. But to whom? And what was it? She would listen more intently and hoped Robert would as well. He, being a philosopher, could read more into these writings than she.

Part VI: 1922 | The Civil War

Next came the Gospel reading. Father O'Hare continued.

"Now, let us turn to our Gospel of the evening: Luke 16, 13.

"'No servant can serve two masters; for either he will hate the one and love the other, or he will be devoted to the one and despise the other. You cannot serve God and mammon.'"

"Aha," Rachel thought to herself. "Father O'Hare is telling his flock—or one within it—to choose between God and mammon, meaning to choose between the church and wealth. But who among these poor attendees has that choice . . . unless . . . unless . . . someone here is being offered a bribe to turn on Father O'Hare and he knows it. I wouldn't put it past this old fox to already have identified the person. Ach, how can I tell who it is?"

Father O'Hare raised his head and arms before the congregation. "My brothers and sisters, let us pray."

As Rachel considered her next steps, she felt a hand upon her shoulder. The smell of lavender wafted toward her and a voice she quickly recognized whispered a warning, "Rachel, do not proceed in whatever action ye were planning. I beg ye. Trust me that I know more than ye about what may take place. Kneel down quickly and pray."

Rachel knew her sister Shelley's voice and—albeit resentfully—obeyed, taking on a prayerful posture and closing her eyes.

As she did, a shot rang out. Heavy boots reverberated in the back of the nave. An elderly woman screamed. The sparrows that had nested in the bell tower flew out of the shutters in a flurry.

When Rachel looked up, Father O'Hare was lying prostrate across the altar steps. Blood was flowing from his head. It was not holy blood from a communion chalice. She shivered in the sudden realization that Father O'Hare was dead, and she knew who the assailant was. She prayed, this time for real. "Dear God, what has Robert done?"

Chapter 59

The Surprise Reunion—Saturday, April 15, 1922

"Dear God, what has Rachel done?" Robert cringed when he heard the shot. Over the heads of congregants seated before him, he saw Father O'Hare collapse. Frozen in place, Robert's thoughts and actions were likewise. Only when he felt the grasp of a hand on his arm did he return to the present.

"Follow me," came a quiet command. "Don't ask any questions and don't look down the aisle." Robert was stupefied, glancing at the back of the man now guiding him out of the pew. The two merged with the meager congregation, stunned yet instinctively exiting the nave. Only one man raced in the opposite direction toward the altar. Quickly and in silence, the rest of the attendees moved toward the massive oak doors, now being opened to the courtyard. As though a final blessing had been offered, they were dismissed.

The light of the narthex candles illuminated the steps upon which they exited. Robert could finally examine the man leading him. Robert was surprised that the figure appeared quite confident, despite a rounded back and slight limp. He could hear heavy breathing as the man increased his pace down the steps and across the stone squares. Catching up to glance at the side of his companion's face, Robert noted a russet and yellow plaid tam atop a moon-shaped visage. Bushy, graying sideburns reached toward wire-rimmed glasses skewed upon a broad nose. The two men, now paired, rapidly moved to the right side of the courtyard and through a trellised overhang into a tree-lined graveyard.

Only when they reached the farthest, southwest corner of the cemetery, did the older man stop. He quickly turned toward Robert who, still in a daze from the incident, stumbled into the man's awaiting chest. Robert immediately spoke his fears.

"Who are you?" he asked his captor, for Robert truly believed he had just been taken hostage.

"It is a long story, Robert, but rest assured I am a friend of yer stepmother and stepfather, the McKenzies. Ye're safe. But, we need to leave this place as quickly as possible to ensure that. Leave anything ye brought to the church that might incriminate ye and take all with ye that might identify you."

Just as Robert was going to ask another question, two female figures rushed toward them.

"Robert, what have ye done?" exclaimed one. Rachel stopped abruptly upon noticing the older man.

"And Uncle Eamon. What are ye doing here?" The habitually verbose lass was uncharacteristically stymied.

Her companion, Shelley, responded impatiently, "Rachel, don't query anything right now. We must depart as quickly as we can. Eamon and I are taking ye both to a safe house just outside of town. There, we can answer all of yer questions. For now, be silent and just follow us. Leave any incriminating evidence ye have here and keep everything else that identifies you in that satchel. Come. Quickly. We must go."

Robert and Rachel emptied their bags. Rachel left the gun in hers.

Without another word, the four left the cemetery by the rear gate and followed an ambling path along the Macroom Canal. Soon, they approached the back of a darkened tavern that abutted the waterway. Its rear door was slightly ajar. Opening it, they entered a narrow hallway leading to a tiny kitchen. On the left, they found the wooden door of an enclosed staircase. Climbing the worn stairs, each felt a sense of relief mixed with some trepidation.

Shelley worried that they had been followed. Eamon silently recited the imminent conversation that would place him in Robert's history and present. Robert could not make sense of anything except Rachel's probable guilt. Rachel fumed believing her role in the Republican cause had been foiled. None was at peace.

At the top of the stairs, numerous oil lamps hanging from the room's ceiling led to an oaken table. Only one person sat at its head—Michael Collins.

"Well, bless me heart. If it isn't at least four of the infamous Smiley-McCormick clan. I hear ye've had quite an adventure this evening." Collins rose from his chair and approached the four. First embracing Shelley, he whispered, "Ye did well, Commander McCormick."

Turning to the man who had just taken off his tam, Collins said, "And Professor Smiley. How does it feel living a just life outside of the classroom?" Mick gave Eamon a chest-to-chest hug. Eamon nodded his response.

"And to this young lass, I will leave my words to later." He turned his side to Rachel and faced the young man behind her.

"This must be Robert Smiley. How I have heard you praised by your American family. And to know there's a second philosopher in the family. The blessings of St. Thomas Aquinas have fallen on ye and yer uncle here."

Robert's face flushed as he turned his gaze of amazement away from the Big One to the shorter figure behind Collins. Rachel and Shelley took appropriate steps to move away from the men.

Eamon stepped forward and looked squarely at Robert's shocked expression. "Aye, as Commander Collins has said, I am yer uncle Eamon Smiley, the twin brother of yer father Robbie." A moment of incredulity accompanied the intensity of unspoken assumptions between nephew and uncle. Collins, like Rachel and Shelley, also retreated to the table and pursued a fiercely animated, yet whispered, conversation with the women.

Eamon broke the tension of expectation. He calmly parsed out the initial thoughts he wanted to share with his nephew. As the words flowed, he held back on the details until what he hoped would be another more intimate setting—one in which Kat would assuage the emotions of each man.

Part VI: 1922 | The Civil War

Eamon shared how, in 1912, he and the Irvines had become aware of Robbie's attempted assassination of Thomas Clarke and had helped the errant Smiley escape imprisonment and, worse, fatal retribution by the local Irish Republican Brotherhood. It was only recently that the Irish side of the family had learned, through the McKenzies, of Robert's existence. Eamon assured Robert that they were not part of any Unionist loyalty to Great Britain, rather advocates of the future Republic of Ireland.

Robert listened carefully. He recognized that the man before him looked just like his father in pictures his birth mother had shared. But this Smiley's aura appeared to be quite different. Robert felt his body relax. His mind began to untangle the threads of a paisley rug his birth mother had put over him in his crib. He felt the warp of the horizontal threads of fate woof with the vertical ones of choice. The philosopher in him calmed his troubled soul. Robert looked squarely at Eamon, leaned forward, and embraced him. Eamon responded by tightly holding onto the lad.

Distracting them from their reflections on the past and present, both heard an argument arising between Shelley and Rachel.

Chapter 60

A Tangled Web—Saturday, April 15, 1922

"Ye must calm down, Rachel, and listen to Uncle Mick." Shelley grabbed the shoulders of her younger sister. Reminiscent of decades of sibling rivalries between the two, Shelley felt her frustration rise beyond the boundaries of familial tolerance and public civility. In the past when Rachel was in the heat of a temper tantrum and their mother was in the ashes of a drunken stupor, Shelley had been able to restrain the dervish twirling of the young child by holding Rachel close and caressing her tear-streaked cheeks. Rachel would collapse in quiet sobs and cling to Shelley who would sing the soothing lyrics of "Too-Ra-Loo-Ra-Loo Ral . . . hush now, don't you cry . . ."

Now, the sisters were ten years past that time. Their mother was long dead. Younger brothers had been scattered among compassionate relatives. Older brothers had joined various national or secular armies. Shelley had graduated from Queen's College into Collins' National Army as a special agent. Rachel, at age 16, had not yet secured her place in any overt—or covert—group. She was still seeking where to harness her resentments that linked logic with action. Like the injured and temperamental child of her youth, anger enflamed her thoughts and words, particularly tonight.

"I will not calm down," she interrupted Shelley. "And why should I listen to a man who doesn't fight anymore against our greatest enemy? Instead, he turns against his Irish brothers and befriends those damn Brits." Her face had turned a fiery red and the tangled, auburn curls about her shoulders were bobbing up and down like untethered sea buoys in a storm.

"Don't say that, Rachel. Ye have no idea what Uncle Mick has done to ensure that all of us, de'V's followers included, can live in peace."

Shelley let go of Rachel's arm and backed away as Eamon and Robert approached the two. Collins rose from his seat at the head of the table, having watched and listened to the two sisters "go at it." The elongating of his stature before the four foreshadowed an expectant resolve. Even Robert, who had only heard about this mythological Collins, could feel a powerful spirit about to address the group.

"Ah, Rachel McCormick, I hear your words. Though they sting like a bee's venom piercing my arm, I know ye are capable of seeking the sweet nectar of the gods. Right now, sit thee down and let me tell ye what ye don't yet know. Once ye hear me out, if ye want to sting me again, I'll gladly bear my other arm."

His compassionate eyes and cheek-to-cheek smile caught Rachel off-guard as they enveloped her in a web of memories. She knew he was a kind and honorable man whom she had dearly loved before this time of turmoil that she labeled betrayal. She glowered, clutched her satchel to her chest and glared at her sister. But not at Mick. She would listen to him despite her antagonism.

She could not look directly him, however. Feeling totally exasperated by the situation from which she had no planned escape, the small enclosed pistol reassured her that she had at least one tactic —and time—in place. Begrudgingly, she pulled out one of the table's chairs, three seats down from Collins, and sat down hard in it.

The Big Fellow sighed, approached Rachel, and folded his height into the chair next to her.

"Rachel, I have known ye since ye were born. What I am about to tell ye is said out of the love I have for ye, yer brother, and Ireland itself. Ye know these are difficult times to trust in what's best for us all. Like ye, I have been presented with many a strategy to satisfy all of the possibilities. Believe me when I say, I have considered them all. But, I cannot support them all. Thus, I had to choose a course that I believed would lead our people to live in a Republic where they can practice the ethics of a just life.

Eamon and Shelley nodded their heads, recollecting Eamon's philosophy class just two years prior in which Eamon had asked his students, including Mick in the back row, to describe such a life.

Rachel was not interested in hearing Collins rationalize his pro-Treaty stance. Nor did she know about Eamon's philosophy lecture. She continued to look askance at Mick.

Having negotiated his views with such luminaries as Lloyd George and Winston Churchill, he was not deterred by Rachel's stubbornness—at least, that's what he thought. He proceeded, not to convince her of any political or philosophical theory. Instead, he was trying to save her life. He would try a new tactic to warn her of the danger she was in. He would tell her the truth.

"There are groups within groups within groups among our opposing parties, Rachel. And, sadly, within those groups are individuals exploiting allegiances to wage their own personal wars against old and current enemies. We know one person who holds a grudge against yer family. We now know that ye, too, have alienated that person with yer, may I say, bullheadedness. Ye don't know that ye have been followed over the last month by that person's accomplice, a lass called Molly. And tonight, that accomplice has implicated ye as the murderer of Father O'Hare for which—if ye are caught—ye will surely hang." Mick took a deep breath, but before he could continue, Rachel had risen from her seat and turned belligerently toward him.

"Nay! Nay! Ye are full of lies. The Countess would never do such a thing to me." Rachel's face turned vividly red.

"Rachel, please. Listen to Uncle Mick." Shelley moved toward her sister. "I fear he is telling you the truth. I met a friend of Molly's at the Woman's Clinic In Rathmines. She warned me about just this. The Countess assigned Molly to follow ye when ye left Dublin last month. Molly was to relate back to the Countess what ye were doing for O'Connor or independently on yer own. Molly told the Countess that ye were partnered with Robert Smiley. Right then and there, the Countess knew you were compromised because of Robert's father.

We don't know exactly what the Countess told Molly to do, but, we do know that Molly, not ye, killed Father O'Hare."

Rachel stared at her sister. "Why would I be compromised by associating with Robert and how can I be blamed for Father O'Hare's death?"

Eamon now stepped up. "Rachel, dear. Sometimes ye are so naïve about what motivates individuals to act as they do. The Countess is supporting de'V's new party, Cumann na Poblachta[16], in order to secure a Republic and earn a seat in his new government when it is formed. She must eliminate any chance others could question her loyalty to de'V. Having recruited ye—a member of our McCormick, Smiley, and Irvine families who support the Treaty—would definitely throw doubt upon her own fealty to the Republican view. Yer partnership with Robert, the son of a Unionist who tried to assassinate Thomas Clarke, has certainly been reported by Molly to her. The Countess had to find a way to discredit ye in the eyes of the IRA."

Rachel looked aghast. "But why would I kill Father O'Hare? Robert, tell them! We had been tasked with warning him about a possible attack by Free Staters, not by IRA members. His defiance of Pope Pius' decree to deny communion to anti-Treaty parishioners would put Father O'Hare in the line of fire by them, not us. We were to alert him to that after tonight's service."

Mick stepped in again. "Aye, Rachel. We knew that ye were to warn him. And Shelley was there to ensure ye were safe enough from the Countess' revenge to do so. But, alas, the tangled threads of a spider web have caught ye and Robert in it. In killing the Father, ye will be seen as betraying the IRA and aligning with the Free Staters. And it will not be just ye. The entire McCormick family will be placed on O'Connor's IRA revenge list. Ye must leave Macroom quickly and return, not to Dublin, but to Belfast with your uncle Eamon. Robert must also return with ye."

Rachel's hands began to shake as she pointed to Shelley.

"Nay. Nay. It doesn't make sense. The Countess could not be that cruel. And, I didn't do anything that could link me with the shooting. I was just sitting there praying."

"True, it looked as though ye were, Rachel," said Shelley, before continuing, "but what ye didn't notice 'twas Molly McKenzie sitting in the aisle directly behind ye. When I heard the shot, I turned around and saw her throw her pistol directly onto yer pew. It was she who killed Father O'Hare. While he was falling, she hurried into the side aisle and left by the south transept door. Several stunned parishioners looked straight at ye and the gun next to ye. I swear they'll tell all that ye were the culprit. That's why we left so quickly."

"And where is the gun, now?" asked Rachel.

"I threw it into the canal as we hurried here," said Shelley. "No one will find it, but that doesn't matter. Molly will tell O'Connor what ye did and spread the rumor of yer guilt. Ye will be a marked person by his circle, and the Countess."

Rachel paused for only a minute before she turned on the four individuals before her. She opened her satchel and pulled out her own pistol.

"I won't leave Macroom until I hear the truth from Molly herself." She pointed the gun at the group and backed toward the staircase.

"Don't follow me or I'll shoot ye all. I swear I will."

Chapter 61

The Spirit of Truth—Monday, April 17, 1922

Rachel had spent the last two days in a physical and emotional frenzy. Her understanding of the political intrigues running rampant within and across the IRA and Free Staters had shaken her beliefs. Now, they were assumptions tainted by fears and doubt.

She kept questioning herself, "Are others' words and actions no longer valid? Is my loyalty to the Countess and, thus, the Republic, no longer warranted? If the answers to these questions were *nay*, in what can I now believe? And how can I act on my hatred of the British and my passion for a free Ireland? After all, aren't these the very reasons for my existence?"

As she hurried toward the Ox and Bow Tavern outside Kilkenny, her mind swirled. It had been a challenging journey, physically and emotionally, to the "Marble City" where she and Robert had been told to meet on Monday after their assignment to warn Father O'Hare. They had been told by O'Connor to lay low for 48 hours—separately. Robert was to take the southwest Ballycallan Road from Macroom to Kilkenny; Rachel, the southeast Bennetsbridge Road. The genesis of a civil war between local IRA anti-Treaty members and Free Staters had been conceived in Kilkenny just months before, so the town was vying as home to many factions. Their number was evident along Rachel's route.

She had kept the north-south Waterford and Kilkenny Railway tracks in view to guide her, sleeping on Sunday night in a garage behind the Bennetsbridge train station. Just before midnight, she had seen whom she assumed were three IRA members planting explosives along the well-worn tracks. Within minutes, however, the three were detected and captured by a group of local men. Fortunately, for the men, women, and children returning late from Easter holidays, no lives were lost. This incident added to Rachel's confusion. "Who would intentionally kill innocent children for their own cause?" she pondered.

She thought of Molly's motives. "Why would she strike out at me, whom she barely knows? What had the Countess told her to do?" On her travels this day, Rachel had heard that Molly was lodging at the Ox and Bow, so questions would be answered. Then, Molly's actions could be avenged, if required. "But how can I take another person's life?"

Rachel slowed her approach to the tavern and shook her head, realizing she had too many unanswered questions flying around her. Seeing the lights of the establishment ahead of her, Rachel stopped along its mudded cow path, and said to herself, "Let me do as BB has done to slow my mind and heart ever since she held me in her arms as a child."

Rachel set her satchel down and repeated a short prayer three times. "Lord, give me ears to listen to yer words, eyes to see yer visions, and love to feel yer heart beat with mine. Grant me thy understanding and peace."

After the third repetition, there was suddenly a warmth that rose up below her from the damp and chilly hoof marks. She could feel it swirling around her legs and, then, her waist, reaching like a woolen blanket over her shoulders. "What is this feeling? What is embracing me?"

"Rachel. Dear Rachel."

She heard a melodic Ulster-Scottish lilt calling her.

"Calm thyself, dear lass. Ye need not be afraid of yer thoughts."

"Who are ye?" Rachel whispered, raising her satchel and pressing the gun inside closer to her.

"Ye need not know exactly who I am. Just close yer eyes and imagine I am those who understand the tangles in yer mind. There have

Part VI: 1922 | The Civil War 249

been many a soul before ye who also had to choose a right path for their beliefs and actions. Like ye, they had to determine loyalties based on what they deemed as true and just."

The warmth now swept around Rachel's head and settled around her ears. She began to listen intently.

"I don't know how to find that truth. How can I?" Rachel asked, no longer voicing a whisper but rather an impassioned plea.

"Rachel. Dear Rachel. Look for times ye felt loved."

Rachel obeyed the melodious voice, closing her eyes and envisioning a time. At first, there were too many disturbing ones before she was able to refocus her thoughts on a comforting one. She alighted on a night three months before when she was sitting at the McCormick dining room table in Rathmines . . .

Liam and BB were smiling at each other. Morna and Ian were playing with Bigger and young Maggie, while baby Kieran was sleeping in his bassinet. There was laughter and song.

The front door opened and in walked Uncle Mick and Shelley. The conversation turned quickly to the Treaty—its detractors and supporters. Rachel remembered Uncle Mick's words: "We need to save the lives of our Irish brothers and sisters and those who will benefit most—the next generation like Maggie and Kieran here. A Republic will certainly come, but we must first stop the killings among our own so that such a time is secured. Let's take the stepping stone approach to rid us of the Brits forever and, then, we can love our brothers and sisters again."

. . . The recollection of that night shimmered before Rachel's eyes, now opening to a white mist swirling before her. She was sure she recognized the shape of a stately lady within it before the outline began to fade. "Are ye the same lady from my dream, from on the train to Macroom?"

Rachel saw a faint smile and heard these words before they, too, faded away.

"Listen to and see where love lies. It will reconcile yer doubts. Then, ye shall know the path to truth."

Rachel shivered as the warmth receded, descending from her head to her shoulders to her feet upon the rutted path.

She bent over and took the gun from her satchel.

She felt one last sense of warmth upon her bowed head. She swore it was a kiss.

Standing up, she threw the gun far over the thicket next to her—away, away, away.

Chapter 62

*Understanding by Inference—
Wednesday, April 19, 1922*

BB opened the door to find a rain-drenched figure before her. This Wednesday evening, the beveled-glass, kerosene lamp sat upon the top step of the backyard staircase leading up to the kitchen. Since Liam had told BB about Shelley's search for Rachel and Eamon's quest for Robert, the lantern had been placed there at dusk each night in hopes that Rachel would come home. Its golden light now illuminated her outline. Long curls, soaked by the wet, streaked down around an oval face that looked like a wizened spud discarded from a late-evening market cart. Her entire body seemed wrapped in a muslin shroud for the dead.

"Rachel, my love. Thank God ye are here. Come quickly out of the rain and let's warm ye." Despite her shock at the appearance of the usually vibrant youth, BB embraced Rachel's drooping shoulders and hurriedly led her into the kitchen.

"Good heavens," thought BB, "what has this lass been through?" Recognizing quickly the immediate need for restoration, BB knew the questions she longed to ask—and the answers she feared to hear—would have to wait. A hot fire and bath, clean slip dress, and warm soup were current necessities.

Within an hour, the two hands of the dining room clock had coupled north in a straight line. The conversation below them, however, was anything but coupled nor straight. BB and Rachel sat opposite each other—BB on the plush red sofa, Rachel on the wooden chair next to the fireplace.

Between them was Bigger, rump nestled at Rachel's feet but head looking across at BB. Even he knew that the words exchanged between the two above him might be circuitous in nature and evasive in content. The observant Bigger thought, "Why can't my loved ones just listen to each other and be honest like Sceo, Boru, and I? Life would be so much easier and pleasant." Bigger lowered his head upon his extended paws, closed his eyes, and pretended to sleep, as he mused, "There will be quite a play of words between these two tonight."

BB was the first to speak. "I won't pry, Rachel, so whatever ye want to tell me, please do." Rachel did not move, her eyes looking directly into the fire beside her. Her curls, washed and drying, seemed to tighten up around her ears, perhaps symbolically closing them off or warming them up. BB was not sure which. Trying to open them, BB continued, "Know I will keep whatever ye say to me'self. Remember, after loving our family and ye, my greatest devotion is to my church's tenants of confession and forgiveness. We must be honest in our actions, trusting that whatever we do will be forgiven."

The silence that followed was full of anguish challenging hope and hope challenging back. Rachel shuffled her feet around Bigger's tail and slowly turned toward BB.

"Ye may think that confessed honesty is worthy of forgiveness, BB, but I don't." Her gaze returned to the fire. A longer silence accentuated the crackling of flames on split bark and the clock's hands marked each minute until the quarter-hour chime.

When the chime's last note sounded, BB continued, "Don't concern yerself with forgiveness. Please, dear Rachel. Tell me what ye can."

Rachel kept staring into the fire. The clock kept ticking until the half-hour chime.

BB sighed. "Let me start, then, with what I know; if that comforts ye, Rachel. I know about the plan by Molly to implicate ye in the murder of Father O'Hare. I have a feeling ye think that plan was initiated by the Countess and, thus, ye may have planned some sort of revenge." BB let these two assumptions circle around Rachel.

BB would not directly ask Rachel to confirm them. Like decades of Irvines before, the McCormicks and Smileys were exquisitely versed in the subtle style of "understanding by inference." Assumed meanings behind words were more telling than their exact definitions. Everything was dependent upon context. BB hoped to draw Rachel out by offering what she could deny. Rachel, instead, was unable as she wasn't really sure herself what had actually transpired in the last two days, or why.

She knew she had arrived on Monday night at the Ox and Bow Tavern. It had been crowded with men of all walks from the Kilkenny patronage—some in National Army uniform, some in newly tailored business suits, some in worn farming gear. The boots of each had revealed the tasks accomplished that day. Mud had covered those of the soldiers, lacquered floor wax the business men, and dried manure the farmers. While their attire clearly had indicated professional differences, their conversations did not indicate their political allegiances, for double agents and the undecided were rampant within each group. Only by catching key words in their muffled conversations could one tell whom they supported politically—Michael Collins or Eamon de Valera. Rachel had not been sure whom she could ask in order to find Molly. She had only been certain that she needed to listen for the name of Rory O'Connor.

Soon, she had heard it whispered by a young farmer near her. He had been directing the eyes of his companion to a couple approaching a door behind the bar. Rachel had seen O'Connor open it and sneak furtively up a staircase to the second floor. She also had caught sight of the back of Molly following him. Rachel had felt a shiver of hatred. "I must calm myself." Surprising her, the hatred quickly had turned to resolve. After a few moments of hesitation for quick planning, she had walked to the bar, skirted around it, and followed them up the stairs.

Returning her gaze now to the fire before her, she hesitated, thinking, "Should I tell BB what happened? Will she understand or judge what I did next?"

Rachel pondered until she felt Bigger rise up, shake his tiny torso and, turn toward her, resting his chin on her lap. Their eyes met. For some strange reason, Rachel saw in him the spirit she had encountered on the path to the Ox and Bow. Bigger gave a soft groan, or perhaps a whimper. Rachel heard the meaning behind the sound, as Bigger thought, "Tell the truth, Rachel. That is your path."

And so she told BB how she had confronted O'Connor and Molly in one of the guest rooms, how she had threatened to tell the National Army members in the bar below of Molly's crime and betrayal of Rachel, and how she was going to tell Collins all she knew the next time she saw him. She described to BB how Molly's face had turned a vivid red and how she had called Rachel a liar. O'Connor had called her a traitor.

"I was so fussed up that I regretted throwing away my gun earlier in the evening. But I also couldn't stop thinking of the children who might have been killed in the bombing at the Bennetsbridge train station. I didn't want to be a murderer. My mind was in such a dizzying state."

Rachel paused and stroked one of Bigger's ears, twisting its shaggy locks in her hand. He nudged her gently knowing his role, silently urging, "Keep going, lassie. Keep going."

BB raised her voice, asking, "Rachel. How could ye think they would let ye go free after having accused them like that?"

Rachel lowered her head. "Ach. I was foolish, I know, BB. When I saw two men with pistols come out from behind O'Connor and the drawn curtains, I realized I was doomed. If it were not for shouts and pounding on the room's door and the flurry of O'Connor, Molly, and the two men rushing out onto the window's porch and leaping to God knows where, I would surely have been shot dead. Two National Army soldiers and a farmer saved me—on the orders, they said later,

Part VI: 1922 | The Civil War

of Uncle Mick. The farmer took me by cart to his house and, then, this morning to the Army's transport train which arrived in Rathmines this evening. My mind still feels like an uprooted thicket of furze after a terrible tempest."

BB stood, approached Rachel, and knelt beside Bigger before her. "My dearest, sister Rachel. Ye are one of the bravest women I know. What you intended to do and what you did were both courageous and just." Her arms pulled Rachel toward her. Rachel could feel BB's heartbeat again—matching her own.

The clock stuck the hour of one. Hands, arms—and paws—were coupled and straight. BB could now offer her last words of the night. "Perhaps this will calm your mind. The Countess has given me a note for you. Do you want it now?"

The meaning behind BB's words of "sister" and "woman" gave Rachel the assurance she needed to speak her last words. "Yes. May we read it together?"

Rachel would still have to determine the meaning behind "brave" and "forgiveness," but that could wait. For now, the two women sat next to each other on the sofa. Rachel opened the letter.

Bigger began to snore.

Chapter 63

The Assumptions—Wednesday, April 19, 1922

Rachel read aloud the lines before her as the master clock continued its journey toward the next, quarter-hour chime.

> Surrey House
> Leinster Road, Rathmines
> April 18, 1922
>
> My dear Rachel,
>
> It has just been brought to my attention that you have been caught in a complex web of misguided interpretation and duplicitous intent. While I am unable to explain in detail how I have come to learn this, I want you to know that I have always honored you and your family's dedication to our beloved island.
>
> Whatever you may be thinking of our new party's commitment to a free and independent Republic, you should not be influenced by your experience during the last few days. Often in a storm, winds rush across the moors with little consideration for whom or what they fell. Sometimes the furze is torn from its roots and catches on the horns of a ram who can't shake it off. Sometimes, the bogs water up and capture the fox who can't wiggle free. The wren harboring on the branch of the oak may be blown off balance, and the swallow unable to take flight. The nature of man facing a comparable force may be incapable of deciding which direction is the most expeditious.

Part VI: 1922 | The Civil War

Perhaps you feel like the ram and fox caught in the grip of this tumultuous time. Perhaps you are like the wren, now off balance. Worse, I fear you are like the swallow, unable to take flight and continue your journey to support the Republican cause. However you feel, please know I remain dedicated to guiding you.

If you would like to have tea with me this weekend, I welcome you to Surrey House at four o'clock on Saturday. I will await your confirmation of this visit.

C.G.M.

Rachel placed the letter on her lap. BB waited for the response she knew was coming.

"If she thinks I am ever going to enter her house again, she's hee-hawing like a castrated donkey stupidly searching for a willing jenny!"

Chapter 64

Coming Home—Friday, April 21, 1922

From his rocker, Eamon watched the ebb and flow of his nephew's breathing as the youth reclined on the family's green velvet, chaise lounge. The young man's unbuttoned vest and unclasped collar moved fitfully up and down in a staccato reminding Eamon of his post-war convalescence at the Craigmaddie Hospital in Scotland. While physical wounds like Eamon's were not evidenced in his nephew Robert, Eamon could tell that the psychological were.

The two men had just spent the last days together traveling from Macroom to Bangor and then venturing out to Belfast. They had talked, as much as they felt comfortable, about Eamon's twin brother and Robert's father—the one and same Robbie Smiley.

In Macroom, Robert was preoccupied with the murder of Father O'Hare and Rachel's safety, unable to hear Eamon's statements about Robbie.

Upon meeting Michael Collins and Shelley McCormick at the safe house, Robert was again distracted. He was confronted by forces contrary to his own beliefs regarding independence from Britain.

While on route to Belfast, in the back of the McGregor grocery truck, he was hidden with Eamon behind cages of chickens and stacks of recently sheered lamb skins. Robert had too many sensory inputs to access his usually stable mental and emotional capacities.

Now, after meeting Kat and hearing her relate his father's history, he was exhausted. Even a graduate of one of the most prestigious colleges in America could not take in the complexity of information flooding over him and waving him off-balance. No philosophical theory could center him.

This was particularly true after today's expeditions through Belfast. Guided by his uncle, Robert had first visited Robbie's home where he had planned the assassination of Thomas Clarke in 1912. In the late morning, the two had walked on to Corporation Street where Robbie and Ryan McCormick had encountered Eamon and Rachel's brother, Liam, and where Ryan had been shot dead.

Finally, in the afternoon, Robert had leaned against a barrier wall along the Prince Albert quay and heard how Robbie and his former wife Margaret—now Robert's adoptive mother—departed to America. It was too much for Robert to consider let alone understand. The dinner Kat had prepared for the family this evening was left cold on his plate.

"We have exposed him too quickly to his past," Kat cautioned, watching the sleeping youth. She knew this comment was quite contrary to her hasty and reactive nature.

"Nay," replied Eamon. " 'Tis best to offer him the facts and give him time to consider them. I remember Dr. Crawford at Craigmaddie telling me to visualize the trenches and smell the smoke, then talk about both with him and ye. That gave me the courage to accept what had happened and to acknowledge my fears. Only after realizing them could I move ahead and know there was a new and safe life before me. Robert will fare well being with us."

Eamon's hand reached down to stroke Sceo's head. "And with ye, dear boy," he said to the dog.

Kat sat on the far end of the chaise lounge and watched Robert's face contort and, then, relax. She said, "I can't imagine what he must be thinkin'—or dreamin'—after this past week. Poor lad."

"Nay, again, dear Kat." Eamon leaned toward her. "Throughout these past days with him, I have experienced a brave and thoughtful young man. When he saw all the places we visited, he would pause, look about him, and reflect on God knows what. When we had tea at Quinlon's, he asked many questions—some perfunctory, some profound. He has a brilliant, analytical brain nestled within a sensitive mind. It may take time for him to decide on his purpose and role here, but I am well assured it will serve our land well. He appears to be the exact opposite of his father."

Kat faced Eamon, raised her hand to touch his face. "He is like ye, then, my darling. Just like ye."

Eamon smiled as Robert's eyelids fluttered and his breathing settled into a rhythm of serenity.

CHAPTER 65

Stepping Backward and Forward—May, 1922

Eamon's office in Lanyon Hall at Queen's College was dark, except for a pair of kerosene lamps illuminating the three men. The heavy, paisley curtains had been drawn to cover the three-quarter windows, out of which Eamon often gazed for lecture inspirations—a habit he was now routinely exhibiting.

Motivating his first-year philosophy students in this time of turmoil was challenging. Like the myth of Sisyphus, he felt that each step forward to engage them resulted in two steps backward, as he saw them doze off or whisper among themselves. Several had dropped out of the university to join one of the IRA factions or the opposing Irish Royal Constabulary (IRC). Some had withdrawn to seek safety in the South. Allegiance to education had been trumped by political loyalties and survival.

Tonight's gathering would be different, though—more indicative, in Eamon's view, of Aristotle's advice: "Be a free thinker and don't accept everything you hear as truth. Be critical and evaluate what you believe in." Eamon kept that saying close in mind and heart as he conversed with two of his most respected allies, Liam McCormick and Michael Collins. Eamon labeled them his "PPs"—his practical philosophers. This evening, they would consider the question: Was Ireland going two steps backward for every step forward, or two steps backward followed by two more and two more?

An obvious yet confounding pattern in the tapestry of negotiations between Southern Ireland's IRA members around the Treaty camouflaged any design resembling peace. A challenging thread within the pattern—both in the South and North—was the partition of Ulster's six counties from the South. Implementing the 1920 Government of Ireland Act in which the North could vote to remain in or leave Great Britain, the Parliament of Northern Ireland in January of '22 had rejected the Anglo-Irish Treaty full stop. Thus, six of Ulster's counties were now jointly governed by the Northern Ireland Parliament and Great Britain. Catholics living there were being ostracized—socially and economically—if not physically injured or killed.

While Collins was negotiating the partition's geographic and commercial boundaries with Northern Ireland's Prime Minister Sir James Craig, Collins was also promoting a covert military action in the North that would abrogate the partition and protect Catholic communities. He believed that would placate both Southern pro-Treaty and anti-Treaty IRA members and unite them around a common mission—the unification of North and South. Managing these two "fronts"—one between Southern-based IRA members and the other between Catholics and Protestants in Northern Ireland—was too much for one thinker.

Several actions had already proven that this two-pronged strategy might work. But to what extent were the facts of such actions accurate and would such a strategy lead to a sustainable peace? The three friends had been debating the circumstances behind various incidents that had baffled one or the other of them.

Liam questioned incidents that entailed hostages. On January 14, a football team, representing Free State Monaghan County, had been arrested in N.I. on its way to a match in Derry. The IRC believed that team members were actually on an IRA covert mission to free three comrades imprisoned in Derry and sentenced to hang on February 9. In retaliation, on February 11, at the Clones Train Station in Monaghan County, the Southern IRA confronted a number of Ulster Special Constabularies (USC) organized by the Unionist government to keep peace in N.I. Three USC were killed, eight wounded, and five taken as hostages. Tit for tat was in play for a hostage exchange.

Eamon queried incidents where women and children were killed. Two days after the Clones Train Station attack, six Catholic children at a school on Weaver Street in Belfast were killed by a bomb explosion. Between February 6 and 25, twenty-seven Catholics and sixteen Protestants were killed in Belfast alone. Tit for tat was in play for revenge.

Liam was adamant. "This pattern of one for two, and two for one must cease. We either accept partition or begin a full-scale battle against it."

Michael frowned. "Ach, Liam. The snake is out of the bag, I fear, but I am safely grabbing its neck. Look at what happened earlier this month. Our IRA lads took forty-three Unionists from border counties and held them hostage so our Derry boys will no longer face hangin'. I'm working diligently with Craig to have them be part of a prisoner exchange. He and I are also working on ceasing our trade boycott of Belfast businesses if Craig can promise to keep our Catholic brothers and sisters employed."

Eamon countered. "But, Mick. I read ye have distanced yerself from those IRA who took the forty-three and that Craig is reneging on his promises. Do ye trust Craig more than yer old comrades? Look at the facts there."

The Big One smiled. "Aye, Eamon. Ye're right. I have distanced myself from several of our IRA brothers. But it is for a greater good. If I can keep the press reporting on my negotiations with Craig—and with Churchill—we'll have time to get to the national election and referendum date settled for June. Then, we'll have the entire South supporting the Treaty and, as a formal government, we can convince the North that we are with them economically. That, more than anything, will protect the Catholics who remain there to work and live peacefully. And, God willing, it can stop the murder of any individual—man, woman, or child; Catholic or Protestant. Two steps forward and no steps back."

Eamon and Liam were silenced as they considered Mick's comments.

"How can ye keep yerself straight, Mick?" Liam asked. "On the one hand, ye're dealing with the devil in Churchill and Satan in Craig. On the other, ye're dealing with the devil in O'Connor and Satan in de'V. Man, how can ye live like that?"

Eamon stepped in. "Ach, Liam. Ye must take my class, *The Ethics of a Just Life*. Let me quote the seventeenth century philosopher Baltasar Gracian, 'A wise man gets more wisdom from his enemies than a fool from his friends.'"

"Partially true, dear Eamon," replied Collins. "But tonight, I am with those friends who will give me more wisdom than my enemies. Come, tell me what ye think I must do next. I have a meeting tomorrow with Griffith and de'V on the date for the election, during which Free Staters approve or reject the Treaty. We'll also be discussing O'Connor's anti-Treaty IRA takeover last week of the Four Courts in Dublin and how to respond."

As a true diplomat, Collins changed the subject. "If ye believe I have a difficult time keeping meself straight, consider de'V himself. I feel consoled by his being sidelined by O'Connor to not know about the Four Court action beforehand."

Both Liam and Eamon laughed. "Best to know yer enemy is more challenged than ye," said Liam.

"Aye," said Eamon. "Four steps backward for him, and four steps forward for ye."

Collins was not so sure of that; but, tonight with his friends, he would try to believe it.

Chapter 66

Opening the Gates—June 26, 1922

"I don't think we should let them go," said Liam.

"Ach. I don't think we have a choice," replied Billie. "Ye know I have dealt with many a difficult British and Irish parliamentarian. I swear on my gran Bella's grave, there are no two spirits more stubborn and less willing to listen to our logic, than my Aggie and yer BB. Actually, there's a third. That's my other sister, Kat."

Liam chuckled but inhaled a deep breath as he placed his hand on the latch of the gate outside Billie's Dublin home. Looking at the backs of the two women hurrying down the street behind him, he paused and circled his fingers around one of the gate's scrolled spikes. He was determining whether to open the gate or chase after the two.

Billie made the decision for them both. "Liam. Ye and I are plagued and blessed by the choice we made to love their brilliant minds and munificent souls. We know it's best to let them have their ways."

Liam turned toward Billie and smiled. "Well spoken, Billie, as the lawyer and diplomat ye are. I just hope in this circumstance, our trust in them wins out over our mistrust of those whom they will soon encounter. O'Connor's IRA boys at Four Courts are becoming more and more suspect in their intentions. Anyone, even our two fine women, who comes on behalf of the free press to report on the words of the IRA, are confounded by those warriors. It's been over two months since O'Connor and his cadre took over the building. No one, not even Mick, knows their minds. No matter how he tries to placate them, they become more and more resistant and more and more devious."

"'Tis true, Liam," said Billie. "My last conversation with Mick was not hopeful about any amicable resolution. Did he tell ye about the last meeting he had with Rory?"

"Nay," sighed Liam. "When we were about to talk about it last month, he was called away by Griffith to Belfast. In retaliation for the April Special Powers Act of Northern Ireland[17], the IRA had just assassinated Unionist MP Twaddell. Mick was sent to negotiate with Craig about the retaliatory internments of so many IRA members —including Cahir Healy. Worse yet, innocent Catholics who, having just spoken in favor of the Free State, have been arrested and don't even have the right to trial. Ach, that 'Flogging Act' has been the curse of this decade on our people in Ulster. I haven't seen Mick since then, but I know Dublin's Four Courts appeared to be the least of his challenges—until now."

"Again, ye speak the truth, Liam." Billie unlatched the gate and entered the path leading up to the front door, now opened with two children rushing down the steps.

Billie continued, "Let me tell ye now what Mick related me last night and the next steps we hope to take in the Dáil and with London's Parliament. Thank God the people of Southern Ireland approved the Treaty last week. That gives our Free State a clear and even path to deal at home with O'Connor and his anti-Treaty folks. I must admit, however, that I feel like an agent of both the North and South as I sit among our brothers in the Dáil and across the sea among the British, Welsh, and Scottish MPs. Listening to de'V in Dublin and Lloyd George and Churchill days later in London makes me ill, but I must keep speaking up for a future, unified Ireland." Billie opened wide the gate and turned toward his home. "Come, let me give ye news of Mick's next steps."

Liam followed his brother-in-law who was holding out his arms to capture the rush of his three-year-old son, Wolfe Irvine, and two-year-old nephew, Kieran McCormick. Both boys were stumbling

Part VI: 1922 | The Civil War

toward their fathers. Their laughter made the men smile and forget, for a few minutes, the possible danger their wives were about to face.

That danger, however, was not just possible—it was definite. By the time Agnes and BB arrived at the gates of the Four Courts, the smell of smoke and gunpowder was overwhelming. The brilliant minds and souls of these two women were about to be severely tested.

Chapter 67

Behind the Gates—June 26, 1922

BB and Agnes approached Inns Quay and Four Courts from the south of the River Liffey. As they passed Christ Church Cathedral, they could already smell gunpowder and see wafts of smoke coming toward them over the Richmond Bridge. Knowing they would soon traverse that bridge, BB crossed herself before the cathedral and mumbled a prayer. She did not discriminate between God's houses as either Catholic or Protestant. Prayer was prayer was prayer. God was God was God. This Protestant Church would serve her Catholic soul.

She silently recited the traditional prayer for peace, honored by both religions and many an agnostic, "Lord, make me an instrument of your peace; where there is hatred, let me sow love; where there is injury, pardon—"

Before BB could finish her prayer, Agnes interrupted with, "We will have to have our questions ready before we meet O'Connor and his men. Ye know that they will want to control the information we hear so that their propaganda is spread. Now that the general population in the South has voted to support the Treaty, we'll only hear lies about votes being bought by the Free Staters or, worse yet, coerced by armed threats. I doubt we will gain any rational reasons for their current resistance."

BB paused, finished her prayer, ". . . Where there is darkness, light." She turned to face Agnes.

"Dear Agnes, I welcome anything said by those we encounter today. Remember, we are entering the Four Courts not just as journalists at the behest of Mick and Rory, but also as nurses to treat the wounded. Yer role as the ears for Cumann na mBan was superb in sharpening yer listenin' skills. Now, being the ears for the new Dáil

Part VI: 1922 | The Civil War

and Billie in London, may I suggest ye just listen keenly to what the Four Courts' leaders and wounded feel free to say? We need not plan any questions in advance, for I feel opinions will flow willingly and freely."

Agnes looked bewildered. She was usually overly organized and prepared for any task bestowed upon her by the pro-Treaty IRA circle to which she still belonged. To be asked to be flexible—and worse yet, silent—was not in her McCracken family genes. After all, it was her father Bruce, as a leader in the Irish Republican Brotherhood, who had taught her in Macroom to load a gun in three seconds and fire in two. Listening had only been a strategy to hear the target in the night—animal or human—not to hold back on striking it.

However, she recognized that today's assignment was to glean O'Connor's plans. Her complicity with BB required Agnes to serve as both a nurse's assistant and informant. Thus, she would follow BB's advice and listen—until her own third role was summoned.

The two turned right onto Wine Tavern Street and approached the south side of Richmond Bridge. A blockade of the Free State Army stopped them.

"And what the heavens are ye two lassies doing here?" came a sturdy, yet amicable, Cork lilt. An elderly man placed his hand on the pistol holder hanging to the left of his belt. He was dressed in an untidy and unbuttoned woolen jacket, obviously worn out from when he was in the 36th (Ulster) Division during the war. BB noted that the garment's clasps were unable to meet their respective opposites across his bugling stomach. She also noticed that there was no pistol in the holder.

BB laughed, whispering to Agnes, "Ah. How many granddas are supporting the Free State by bravado alone. It's a miracle they can even walk, let alone stand for hours at these key posts."

"Good sir," said BB softly. "Here is a note of passage written by no less than our great leader, Commander Collins. I am a nurse and this is my assistant. We are here to serve the wounded. Commander

Collins and President Griffith have already negotiated our presence today with Mr. O'Connor. They all hope to show a mutual concern for any Irish brother who has been afflicted." BB opened her medical bag and showed the man its contents.

His queries ceased. "Ye're a right good pair," he replied, moving the debris of disassembled chairs and broken whiskey barrels to open a path for the two women. "God bless ye."

"And ye as well," said BB, expelling a long breath of accumulated tension. She grabbed Agnes' hand as the two proceeded north over the cobblestoned bridge above the Liffey.

At the end of the bridge, they turned left onto Inns Quay. Just ten feet before them, they were confronted alongside the Four Courts gates by more barricades of barrels, these covered by smoldered tar and linen sacks. Behind the fabricated defense walls, a row of men and boys stood shouldering Lee-Enfield rifles or holding shotguns and revolvers. Unlike the previous guard, nothing they wore hinted of uniformity. Instead, tweed coats, ragged corduroy trousers, and soiled linen shirts were the attire of defense. Not even their caps conveyed a trace of military consistency, only age and social identity. The older men wore woolen tams, the middle-aged donned caps, and the boys wore nothing but their naturally created mops of uncut and shaggy hair.

The eldest man came from behind the barricade, holding up a blackened hand.

"And what the heck do ye think ye two gals are doing here?" sounded another Cork accent, this one loud and gruff.

BB and Agnes looked at each other, holding the other's hand more tightly. They knew they were about to have the same conversation as conducted on the other side of the bridge. This one, however, was bound to be more argumentative. "Good heavens," thought Agnes, "What is it about these two groups fighting each other? Why are their concerns about their womenfolk the same but totally different about their fellow men? Don't they see they should care for all people—young or old, male or female? We're all Irish! Why are they blinded by stubbornness?" She shook her head.

BB again showed a note of passage, but not the one she had previously shared. This one was written by O'Connor. The guard read it, although BB noticed he held the note upside down. She explained Agnes' and her roles as nurses.

He demanded she open her bag. Frustrated that he found only medical supplies, he hesitated and looked closely at her face. "Ye look very familiar. Are ye Liam McCormick's gal?"

BB thought quickly. "Yes, I am his wife. But that has nothing to do with the role I and my assistant are to play here today. I know ye have wounded who have received no medical help. If we don't treat them soon, they will die."

The man glared at BB. "And why should I believe ye don't have other reasons for being here?"

Agnes knew this was her opportunity to act, for she had already planned what to say if such resistance occurred. She stepped up to the man's side and softly warned, "Good sir, I know ye don't want any man to die because ye denied him help. What would ye tell his wife and children? And . . . what would yer missus and children think of ye?"

The man's cheeks turned red below two bushy, gray eyebrows angled toward each other like swords crossed on a family crest. He knew he was foiled. He thrust the note into his vest pocket.

"Let me check with Rory first. Stand here." Turning his back to them, he pushed over a barrel to his right and hurried behind the barricade. The women saw him pass through the main gate that opened onto the Four Courts' cobbled yard.

Within minutes, he returned with a totally different demeanor on his face and in his posture. Next to him was Rory O'Connor.

"Mrs. McCormick, welcome and bless you for the help you will give our wounded. Please follow me with your assistant." As he turned to Agnes, Rory asked, "And what is your name, may I ask?"

Agnes smiled and replied, "Beatrice McDonald." BB looked confused but kept silent.

Agnes had definitely planned in advance, but it was not to offer solace to the wounded, nor to remember facts for a report back to an IRA circle, Collins, or even Billie.

As the three passed through the barriers and gate into the foyer of the courthouse, Agnes acknowledged her thoughts. "Now, I will have my revenge."

She clutched her sack close to her chest.

Part VI: 1922 | The Civil War

Chapter 68

Natural Revenge—June 26, 1922

Agnes knew exactly whom she was seeking as she entered the staircase off the Four Courts lobby. Her IRA circle had been assigned numerous retaliatory acts over the years during the War of Independence and now the conflict between pro-Treaty and anti-Treaty factions. Willingly, the night before, she had volunteered for this particular commission. After all, she had heard about this individual throughout her youth and young adult years.

The first time she remembered was one freezing, winter eve in 1890 when her father, Bruce McCracken, and she were visiting her grandfather Seamus McCracken in his Macroom cottage. She was wrapped in a woolen blanket at his feet next to a blazing fireplace. He, an already aging forty-eight; she, a growing six. As he spoke to her, his lungs bore the brunt of peat smoke and printers ink. As he repositioned himself in the wicker rocker, his bones also evidenced the burden of damp nights spent in sheds and cellars of safe houses. Besides being a union leader for the printers at *The Nation* in Dublin, much of his adult life had been spent carrying messages undercover for his hero, IRA leader and writer David Davitt. Only he and Bruce knew the impact of these factors on his physical stamina and the short time left he would have with the family. He had been blessed with another ten years since Sister Bridgette and Doctor Lizzie had foreseen his death in 1879 when he had delivered the message for them to attend to a wounded man in Cave Hill. Time, sadly, was not his current doctor.

Tonight, he would give Agnes her first—and his last—message.

"Do ye know the story about the elk, the wolf, and the fox, me Aggie?" He placed his hand upon her head which was leaning against his leg.

"Nay," she said. "Tell me, Granddah."

Agnes' father Bruce frowned. He had wanted to protect Agnes from his father's accelerating need to speak of Irish battles with the British. Bruce was torn between respecting his father's last days and protecting Agnes' first. Having taken up his father's place as a popular union leader, Bruce had won a seat in the London House of Commons representing John Redmond's Irish Parliamentary Party and the hope of peaceful reconciliation with Great Britain. Bruce wanted Agnes to grow up knowing there were numerous roles she could play in the new Ireland if Home Rule passed. On this night, however, he would let his father have his way.

"There was a lovely valley nestled within the Mourne Mountain range that welcomed the lads and lassies of our fellow creatures from the natural world," Seamus began. "Birds would rest on the antlers of elks; fish would spring up in the rivulets and gurgle along with the wolves who howled like bagpipes; moles would crawl over the tummies of fox to warm themselves in the night. All the animals lived in peace for centuries.

"One winter, alas, was so frigid and snow laden, that it was impossible for the birds to fly out of their nests, the salmon to break the ice above their heads, or the moles to leave their underground tunnels. The elk and wolves and fox were dismayed. They individually roamed throughout the winter over the barren and cold moors to find their friends. Becoming more desperate, three of them met in a very unconventional confabulation and decided to join together in their hunt. They waited until the last April snow fell and began to search. The elk took the highlands range, the wolf the midlands, and the fox the lower valley. They were to meet again in June to share their findings.

"Now, the elk was a tall animal, able to see wide and long. He quickly saw evidence of various holes in a patch of snow cover—mole tunnels. The fox was a wise fellow and sniffed out gaps in the ice to find one in which several salmon were sleeping. And the wolf

Part VI: 1922 | The Civil War

was an athletic gal, able to jump in the air on her strong back legs. She quickly noted several birds' nests within a furze bush. Each waited for the first of June to report back to the others.

"Now, the fox had also been very hungry during this winter period, before and during his search. He began to think about his own needs and how he could feed himself. Recognizing that a lush dinner of sleeping salmon was right in front of him, he decided to indulge himself. Within minutes, all the sleeping salmon—friends of the wolf—were in the fox's stomach.

"Now, when I say the fox was smart, I don't mean he was wise. He was smart about the laws of nature and needs within his own clan, but not very wise about working collaboratively with other clans, such as those of the elk and wolf. So when he joined them in June, they had already learned of his betrayal of the wolf. The birds had awakened in mid-May, alighted on the elk's branched antlers and told of the fox's actions. Then, the elk had told the wolf. Both were shocked and angry. Revenge was planned, not only by the two but by the birds and the moles as well.

"I need not tell you what happened to the fox as he merrily came before the elk and wolf. Let it rest that revenge was taken."

Agnes raised her head from her granddah's knees. "'Tis a sad tale," she said.

"Aye, me lass. 'Tis. But it's also a lesson on what to do if ye are—what shall I say—making peace with others. Always, be sure of how full their stomachs are before ye trust them." The senior McCracken laughed.

Now, thirty-years later, as Agnes walked up the staircase in Four Courts, she remembered that laugh. "Tonight, I will take down the fox," she said to herself, repositioning her sack over her shoulder. "Granddah would be proud of me."

Chapter 69

Catching the Fox—June 26, 1922

Agnes immediately recognized the fox as she reached the second-floor level of the spiraling staircase. She paused, held her breath and slowly turned the corner to face him—from a distance of space and time. He had aged from when her father Bruce had pointed out the elder on the streets of Macroom those thirty years before. Agnes had been eight at the time. Tonight, at age thirty-four, she blinked and refocused on a face two generations later. Here was the Dickson grandson.

Before her, the thirty-year-old Nathan Dickson was holding court in an alcove just left of the windows that offered the Four Court occupiers a perfect view of the Inns Quay below and approaching Free State Army militias. Nathan was definitely a "bull calf off the old steer," bragging loudly before three young recruits about his family's exploits in the South.

"Like my grandda, I've taken down a number of traitors with our trusty rifle here," brandishing his Lee-Enfield and chortling. "They're all yellow like the striped underbelly of a dying tortoise, slow to run and quick to be toppled. Trust me. Tomorrow will be an easy victory for us with Rory." The three youth stood enraptured before this storyteller.

Agnes watched for a few moments. She approached the quartet. Nathan looked askance at her. Ignoring her, he resumed his oratorio.

"Let me tell ye about my success just a month ago. I was in Kilkenny at the Ox and Bow Inn with Rory. There we took no one less than a traitor to our cause—the woman who killed Father O'Hare in Macroom. She put up a feisty fit, but it was easy to humble her. She certainly won't be a bother anymore. Why Collins is putting women in such roles I can only guess. I bet he's running out of brave men like me and knows the gals can serve as distracting and disposable fodder in the real battles." His chortle became a full laugh, embellished by that of his audience.

Agnes could feel her temper rise, her cheeks redden and her hands fidget around the sack she held close. She stepped toward the group.

"Good evening, young men," she said in a voice more hesitant than her natural tone. She would play the part of an innocent. "I wonder if ye can tell me where I can find Commander O'Connor?"

Nathan squinted his eyes; his nose lifted up by the push of scowling lips. "Why do ye want to know, lassie? What business do ye have with him?"

Agnes considered how to respond. She could lower her guard and expose her secret or she could continue the charade behind it. She chose the latter, like the wolf tracking the fox.

"I cannot tell ye, sir." She stared directly at Nathan's eyes. They began to narrow.

He hesitated. "Ye look familiar. Do I know ye?" He moved closer to her.

Agnes moved closer to him. "Maybe so; maybe not."

Nathan reached out for her sack. She pulled it away.

"Give me that sack," he demanded. The three recruits backed away. They sensed that this would be a test of Nathan's prowess as real or not. One chuckled in anticipation.

"What are ye laughing at, laddie?" Nathan roared, turning away from Agnes to the culprit, then back to her.

"I *do* know ye," Nathan said. "Ye're the sister of that girl. What was her name? Ha! What a lass she was. Too bad she was up the pole."

Agnes ceased her charade. "'Tis finally time. Grandfather and Martha, know I am with ye. Aye. I'm Martha's sister."

Her family's hatred of the Dickson's exploded. She turned to the three youth. She began her revenge, quietly raising its volume word by word until, she was shouting. Her message resounded throughout the second-floor hallways. A crowd of other IRA members who had heard the ruckus gathered around them.

"Did ye know that this *hero* of yours, beat my sister Martha throughout her pregnancy and left her to die in a field one night? Did ye also know this *hero* did not capture the woman who killed Father O'Hare. Rather, he colluded with the woman who did? Did ye also know that this man before ye has switched allegiances so many times it would make yer caps fly off? Tonight, he actually is an agent in the RIC assigned to the Four Courts. Right now, he is sending messages back, not just to the Free State Army outside, but to the British battalion here in the Royal Barracks and to London itself."

Nathan lunged at Agnes. Two members in the crowd grabbed him and held him back. His saliva sputtered onto Agnes' sack.

"What is happening here!" came the voice of Rory O'Connor emerging behind the crowd. Miss McDonald, what are ye doing to this man?"

Agnes thrust the sack at O'Connor.

"It is not a case of what am I doing to this man, but what is he doing to ye. Look inside this sack and ye will find his latest communications with and from the British about yer actions here in Four Courts and throughout the South. He is no IRA hero."

O'Connor opened the bag, took out one missive and read it silently. The crowd, Nathan, and Agnes went quiet and waited.

"Take him away," came Rory's response. He looked at Agnes, and said, "Ye're a true Irish woman, Miss McDonald." He reached to shake her hand, but she quickly tucked it under her shawl.

"Nay," she said calmly. "I just know a fox when I see one."

Chapter 70

Riddles—June 27, 1922

BB and Agnes left Four Courts in the early morning of June 27. Each had accomplished her mission assigned by another—one by Michael Collins for intelligence, and one by Grandfather McCracken for revenge.

BB had cared for several, severely wounded men, listening carefully to and for any IRA anti-Treaty tales of recruitment, instructions, or battle plans.

A middle-aged man had grimaced when BB moved him to a make-shift bed in the Courts' appropriated repository of Irish national records and archives. "I was with me chums," he had said "when we kidnapped that traitor J. J. Ginger O'Connell, the so-called Provisional Deputy Chief of State for this new Ireland. Got me'self shot by those Free Staters. But, all in all, 'twas worth it. The bloody hooligan is here now, and we can use him in an exchange for our own Leo Henderson. Thank ye, miss, for takin' care of me leg."

Under whiskey, he had gabbed more than he would later recall, let alone admit. He had waxed excessively about the plans O'Connor and his second, Ernie O'Malley[18], were considering for the next day's actions. BB found them easy to remember.

Agnes had also cared for the wounded, but only those slightly injured. They were located in an anti-chamber next to the office of O'Connor. As she had served them cold tea and soda bread, she had easily overheard arguments between O'Connor and O'Malley. Neither felt adequately prepared to defend the Four Courts nor to coordinate with other anti-Treaty units located around Dublin proper.

"We can't fire the first shots tomorrow," said O'Malley. "The public needs to know the Provisional Army, Collins, and Griffith started this civil war."

"Ach," grunted O'Connor. "How can the public believe our motives, regardless of who strikes first? We have yet to believe in them ourselves. The June election on the Treaty says our people want peace; but here we are, choosing between two paths to purgatory for a unified Ireland. One is fighting the British again. Two is fighting our own. I fear too many fists have been bared already and too many shots fired to reach an amicable agreement between kin walking on the same path. No doubt, stubbornness has set our backs to each other with no one willing to turn around, face the other, and talk sensibly.

"Tomorrow is the crucible. If we refuse to release O'Connell to Collins by the time he has set, we'll be blasted into the Liffey. If we do release Ginger, we'll still be blasted, but in an execution line at the Kilmainham Goal. Don't ye see the gun carriages lining up before our gates? Mick is serious about making us choose either of our paths. We can only hope that, if we are captured, he and God—in that order—will have mercy on us."

O'Malley grunted. Throughout the three-month occupation of Four Courts, he had tried to reason with O'Connor and other leaders of the Republican IRA. Agnes heard him try again during the night, offering tactical strategies to fight, retreat, or surrender in response to the imminent crisis.

As dawn approached, awakening her from a terrifying nightmare, Agnes knew their snores were the only resolute sounds between them. She would not retain their arguing. Like BB, Agnes would only remember their detailed plans of defense. She wanted to forget their indecisiveness, rationalizing that it is easier to hate those whom you want to hate if you can't sympathize with them.

By the early evening of June 27, the Irvines and McCormicks had gathered at the McCormick home outside Dublin. After hearing their wives' reports, the husbands were certain that the next day, June 28, would be a day of reckoning in city. Both families had agreed that the Irvine children would be safer away from the inevitable chaos that would soon engulf it.

Part VI: 1922 | The Civil War

After-dinner conversations had been subdued except for the chatter of the youngest cousins—two-year-old Kieran McCormick, three-year-old Wolfe Irvine, and four-year-old Maggie McCormick—with their older McCormick cousins—thirteen-year-old Jon and his fourteen-year-old brother Thon. All five were sitting on the rug before the fireplace playing with the two family dogs, Boru and Bigger.

A knock on the back door announced the visit for which the adults were awaiting.

"Time for bed," exclaimed Rachel, quickly reaching for Kieran while Morna lifted up Wolfe. Maggie scampered behind them.

"Ye stay," Rachel directed Thon and Jon. "It's time ye meet Commander Collins." Billie looked askance at Agnes. How relieved he was to have decided four years ago that Rachel would be better raised by her brother Liam and Billie's saintly sister BB. Billie knew he could never keep up with two women suffragettes in his home, let alone one. Agnes shrugged her shoulders and smiled.

Liam opened the door and led Collins into the kitchen.

"I can't stay long, me friends. I just need to hear the news from me best gals here." The Big One leaned against the standing, dry-food cabinet while the members of his favorite clan lined up around him: Liam and BB, Billie and Agnes, Rachel and Morna, and the young McCormick-Irvine boys, Thon and Jon.

"Ah, I see our wandering lamb has returned to the flock," Collins remarked, gazing at Rachel.

Her cheeks flared red, blushing from anger, or was it shame? Her response strongly indicated the former. "I am not a lamb. Call me a ram instead who knows the better field to graze."

"I shall, indeed," Collins retorted, "as ye have definitely angered the Countess which, in turn, makes me rejoice in yer choice of fields. Brave lass ye are, despite yer stubbornness, Rachel."

Billie again looked at Agnes. She, in turn, ignored her husband.

Now, Rachel did blush, not from anger nor shame but embarrassment at being praised.

Quickly, the elder women related what they had heard during their time in the Four Courts complex. Michael listened intently, as did the others. From the oldest Liam to the youngest Jon, each knew the pending impact on the entire island of whatever their leader gleaned from this information.

"'Tis a shame that Rory O'Connor and Ernie O'Malley have turned against us, regardless of their doubts and equivocations. I love them both as brothers. Thank ye, BB and Agnes, for what ye have shared. I'll now consult on next actions with Griffith and the Provisional Government leaders."

He turned toward the back door but not before offering his final warning. "Best ye all stay home tomorrow and over the next few days as well."

Liam accompanied Mick out the door. When Liam returned, the kitchen went silent at his noticeable frown.

"Come!" he said, turning the frown into a broad grin. "Where are Boru and Bigger?" he asked. "Let's sit in the salon and play a game of jovial riddles? Thon, will ye start us off?"

All knew he wanted to ease tonight's tensions by a semblance of gaiety.

All knew the gloom of reality's riddles lay ahead of them.

Chapter 71

The Muddles—June 28–July 3, 1922

At 3:40 a.m. on Wednesday, June 28, anti-Treaty Republicans Rory O'Connor and Ernie O'Malley received a message from the Free State's National Army commander, Tom Ennis. In short, it demanded their surrender by 4:00 a.m. By 4:07 a.m., there was no surrender —only the blast of two British Army QF 18-pounders sending shells through the Courts' western facade. Collins' threat had been real.

For three days, the defenders of the Four Courts complex had stood their ground, but to no avail. On June 29, the buildings and morale at Four Courts had been severely damaged by the increasing accuracy of opposition shelling and targeted infantry assaults.

By Friday, June 30, the anti-Treaty sod had sunk into a quagmire of mud. That morning, a huge explosion blackened the Dublin sky. Its fire spread to the main Public Records Office (PRO) and spewed records of divorce, probate, and land tenures throughout the city. Despite National troops clearing as many explosives as possible from the surrounding buildings the day before, fires ignited the additional repository of records in the PRO's basement. There it was that invaluable records of births and marriages, dating back to the Norman conquest, went up in flames and out of Ireland's history.

Many members of both sides resisted killing their own. The Free State barrage had actually intended not to injure rebels but, more so, to intimidate them into surrender. At the end, however, it was fires that caused the latter—plus an order from Oscar Traynor, the anti-Treaty commander for all of Dublin. His brigade of 500 men had been checked by 4,000 National Army fighters and was, thus, unable to assist O'Connor and O'Malley in their Four Courts defense. At 3:30 p.m. on June 30, O'Malley surrendered. Three National Army soldiers and three Republicans had been killed, fourteen National

Army wounded, and thirty-three Republicans taken prisoner. Rory O'Connor was one of those captured; Ernie O'Malley had escaped.

The Civil War had formally begun.

Having learned via the Sunday Belfast newspapers and Erin McCann's evening telegram that a civil war raged in the South, Eamon, Kat, and Robert had discussed the causes of the war and its impact on those in the North. Kat noted Eamon's words with his nephew—and his nephew's rejoinders. Their exchange, typical of philosophers, revolved around the topic of making decisions. Do men actually make their own decisions or does an external force dictate them? Eamon decided he would ask his Monday philosophy class that seminal question: "Is there an intersection between free will and destiny?" Eamon asked Robert if he wanted to observe the class. Robert was more than willing.

At his uncle's suggestion, Robert had just finished reading Terrance McSwiney's *The Revolutionist* in which Erin McCann had played the main character, Hugh, five months prior at the Abbey Theatre. Robert had only heard about Erin from his uncle's description of the actor-activist's performance and looked forward to meeting him in the future. Eamon had often pondered the play's message as well as Erin's challenge for Eamon to join the cause. Eamon had been particularly affected by the play's line, "Ireland is in small danger from traitors, but in grievous danger from fools." It haunted his memory of brother Robbie.

This Monday morning of July 3 found Robert walking with his uncle Eamon toward Queen's College.

"How tragic and foolish what has just occurred at Four Courts," stated Robert. "Was there no plan on the part of the Republicans? To lose a battle in just three days indicates there wasn't. And, now the history of Ireland has been sorely diminished. Can individuals not recognize the paradox of losing both lives in the present and ancestral lines to the past? "

As the two approached the college, Eamon responded to Robert's exasperation. "We are a nation of muddled contradictions, Robert. Ye will soon recognize that. Some of us act out our dreams by taking up arms, others by writing about doing so. Some of us do both and are considered traitors; some of us do both and are considered heroes. Many of us are also considered fools because we can't make up our minds on what to do or who to be. As ye read in McSwiney's play, we aren't quite sure what a *revolutionist* is."

In considering a response, Robert tried to balance his American forthrightness with the Irish circularity he knew from Gaelic mythology and storytelling. He wondered what his uncle Eamon considered himself to be. Before he could ask, the answer came, but not to Robert's satisfaction.

"What I find consistent," Eamon continued, "is that, in any Irish person, there is a passion for freedom to do and feel whatever he or she desires. How that has come about, I truly haven't a clue. Perhaps centuries of speaking, singing, and writing—the creative attributes we have inherited—have forged that passion into our souls. Despite centuries of battle or famine or poverty, we have kept it burning."

He noted Robert's frown and attempted to lighten the conversation. "Too much peat smoke, whiskey, and potatoes have probably also embedded it in our bodies and brains."

Eamon recognized his attempt at humor had failed. His nephew's serious nature had yet to be Gaelicized. Changing tactics, he offered, "Ye come from a country that is just coming of age so your experience of this passion may be new to ye."

Robert stopped and turned to his uncle, deliberating the best words to respond.

"Uncle, yes; I am from a young country, not yet one hundred fifty years old. But we have just come out of our own civil war; one that, like here, separated South from North, brothers from brothers, and free from enslaved. Sixty years on from that war, there is scant evidence that its causes have been addressed nor amity across differences attained. Rather, an exaggeration of prejudice abounds and tares men apart, even though many have just fought together in the most recent of world wars. I hope I can learn from my time here to return home and—"

Robert's words were cut short by a shot from across the street. Eamon pushed his nephew to the ground covering him with his own body. When one man fled away, a flurry of people ran toward the two.

"Professor Smiley! Professor Smiley! Are ye alright?" Two young men leaned down and reached under Eamon's shoulders, lifting him to his feet. Questions and witness statements were blurted out by the two rescuers plus several others. They ignored Robert who had righted himself physically, but not mentally.

"Are ye injured?" one lad asked.

"He ran that way; no, that way; no, the other way." Three bystanders argued among themselves.

"Calm thyselves, please," said Eamon, looking quickly at his nephew, discerning that Robert was uninjured, yet confounded.

The professor turned back to the others. "It seems we are both fine. Thank God, the culprit was a poor shot," he quipped. "I thank ye for your help and concerns."

The crowd dispersed, but the two young men insisted on walking Eamon and Robert to the Queen's campus. There, they gave their "good-days" and proceeded to their own classes.

Alone again and in silence, Robert and Eamon entered Lanyon Hall and climbed the oak-paneled staircase to Eamon's office. Robert stopped at the landing of the first level. He had much to say. His hands began to tremble. "Why were you shot at? What is happening here? How can you remain so calm?"

Eamon reached forward. He gently rested his hand on Robert's right shoulder, looking into the young man's distorted face.

"Ye are a strong lad, Robert. I fear the Four Courts debacle now ensures the South will begin what Collins and Liam predicted—a full-blown civil war. Ye saw its beginnings in Macroom. Now, ye have experienced its tentacles in partitioned Ulster. I promise ye that our Smiley family—which includes the Irvines and McCormicks—will do everything we can to protect ye, as we do to protect each other."

"But why were you the target today?" Robert insisted.

Eamon turned away to continue walking up the staircase. "Ach, I'll answer ye after this class."

Eamon needed time to reply. He was not certain he was the target. Instead, he feared it was Robert.

"Come now," Eamon continued. "It seems to me that ye and I have much to think about regarding whether or not our assailant was a traitor or fool and whether we just experienced a reprieve from destiny. Shall we ponder over those muddles later? First, though, we must hear how our students answer the question about free will and destiny. Trust me, they will teach us much."

The two proceeded upwards.

Thinking to himself, Eamon added, "Robert is surely going to be tested. How I hope he will make the right decisions and be a just person, not a fool or traitor like his father. Let that not be his destiny."

Chapter 72

Good News?—August 1, 1922

7 Riverview Rd.
Bangor
August 1, 1922

My dearest Margaret,

Finally, it is with such joy that I share some good news with you. For the first time in months, the family and country appear to be experiencing a period of peace. Of course, that could change quickly; but for today, you can feel the relief and cheer in our hearts and on our streets.

First, on the family front. All members are safe and healthy. As for the McCormick-Irvines, Thon and Jon are thriving at St. Enda's. The youngest babes, Wolfe and Kate, are growing so round that we call them our chubby cherubs. Billy and Agnes have reconciled the differences I described in my last letter regarding Agnes' actions at Four Courts. As I wrote, Billy was furious at first—as much as he ever can be furious. Agnes had never told him about her sister's relationship with Nathan Dickson. Nor had Agnes revealed her own desire for revenge. Once she conveyed both, Billie calmed down and accepted her decisions. However, the length of time secrets are concealed often hurts more than their content. Alas, I believe that was the basis of my brother's anger, now turned to disappointment. Fortunately, our dear couple have the gift of love to forgive, recognizing they may never really understand each other.

Liam and BB never seem to have such differences; they are so symbiotic. I believe BB has a direct line of communication with her God who graciously intervenes whenever there might be a diversity of thought between them. Actually, I think Bigger is a medium who carries messages of reconciliation from our dearly parted to our harmonious couple. The entire McCormick family has flourished—Ian and Morna McNulty plus tiny Kieran and Maggie. As for Rachel, she remains consistently herself, an enigma of sorts to me. She is again seeking her role in the Cause—this time with the Nationalists. Thank goodness, her sister Shelley has spread eagle wings over our flighty sparrow, always flying to new ground for a nest and nourishment. I must admit that I worry about Rachel more than any other member of our family.

Another about whom I worry, but less so, is Ian. You and Francis are saints sponsoring his medical studies in America. Hopefully, he can replace your own Robert in any family gatherings. He is such a wonderful young man who has found his calling in healing others rather than hurting them. However, I am afraid to say that he may be healing himself since Rachel and he now have more than the pond between them. Perhaps you can find him a suitable American bonnie—although I doubt anyone can replace Rachel! Once he mends from her change of heart and finishes his studies, I know he will be an incredible asset to our country upon his return.

Speaking of filial exchanges, Robert has become an integral part of our Smiley family, coming from yours in America. He is now teaching with Eamon at Queen's in the Philosophy Department and tutoring Neil at night. Devin listens in. Both boys, in turn, are teaching Robert Irish Gaelic. You can imagine the breakfast conversations when all four of our "bucks" are together. Liza and I are left out too often, so I supplement her learning by reading parts of the *Táin Bó Cúailnge* in Irish and singing songs like "The Cows Are In The Clover." She giggles in delight. Her sweetness reminds me so much of Mother and Nanna Bella . . . and of you.

Regarding our dear homeland, you'll be pleased to know that BB and I are still writing joint articles for *Our Ireland*. We take the pulse of local and island-wide attitudes when visiting the Gallagher clinics and reading the response letters. Those indicate a great need for peace, which we believe is contributing to the current lull in fighting and disbursement of Republican fighters—both in the Free State and our six counties of Ulster. Since the Southern Ireland general election on June 16 that overwhelming (2 to 1) accepted the Treaty, there have only been small skirmishes in the South—Bruff and Kilmallock, for example. After the August 2 landing of the Free State navy in Cork and Kerry, the Republicans seem to be running away. I pray they are not regrouping.

BB doesn't say much about what Liam is doing with Collins. It may be that, like my Eamon, Liam wants to protect her. For the moment, silence is comforting. I do know that Mick and Liam will be traveling to the South soon to seek a formal peace with the Republicans. Pray for them.

In closing, please let us know how you and the children are doing. We look forward to Francis' visit next month and only wish that you could join him. Perhaps you can change your mind? I would welcome a long conversation about raising children, especially our girls, while serving our community. I trust you understand my need.

Until you may be here again, please write and give my love to Ian and the rest of your dear ones.

Most affectionately,
Your sister with love in service,
Kat

Post-Script: Have you heard anything about Francis' niece Molly? Hers is the only news about which I must admit being ignorant and, thus, fearful. She seems to have completely disappeared.

Chapter 73

Resting on an Unassured Axis—August 18, 1922

"The war is almost over," said Collins to the newspaper reporter. "Rest assured, once the last bullet is spent, we will be looking at the Irish countryside and towns of the future—prosperous and peaceful."

Liam and Erin pulled the Big Fellow away from the crowd that had gathered around him in Greystones, just south of Dublin. Despite the general public approving of the Treaty as indicated in the recent plebiscite, both Collins and Liam plus most of the Provisional Government Executive Council knew the anti-Treatyites were becoming more desperate in their opposition. With desperation came accelerated actions, more often and more intense, more spontaneous and more unregulated.

"Come, Mick," urged Liam. "We need to move on," urged Erin. He grabbed Collins' arm and guided him into the row house of his brother, Finbar McCann.

The three friends, plus two secretly armed companions, entered the narrow hallway leading to the kitchen at the rear. Daguerreotypes of the McCann family graced the walls on both sides. Mick paused at a small painting encircled by the framed faces of grinning yet departed love ones.

"Ach, if this isn't my hero, Theobald Wolfe Tone." Mick sighed. "I know what he would be saying today if he were still alive."

"And what would that be?" came a voice from the kitchen. Agnes McCracken-Irvine, carrying little Wolfe, approached the men.

Mick smiled. As both a storyteller and historian, he knew the ancestry of the McCrackens. "And don't we have his namesake right here today." Mick reached out to Agnes and captured the exuberant, three-year-old boy in his arms.

Now that the little one was listening, Mick altered his intended words. "Your namesake, Wolfe, would say that the sight of the eagle flying above, the sound of the wind and the smell of the sea are all a good Irishman—or woman—needs to be happy." Mick swung the child through the air like an eagle in flight and whooshed the sound of the wind. He scrunched his nose as though he were inhaling the sea. Wolfe giggled, and the adults smiled.

What Mick had wanted to say, however, was the statement that thirty-five-year old Tone declared during his Dublin court-martial on November 8, 1789, for his role in the United Irishmen uprising against the British: "After all I have done for a sacred cause, death is no sacrifice. In such enterprises, everything depends on success. I know my fate, but I neither ask for pardon nor do I complain." Tone died in prison eleven days later.

Mick said the phrases to himself. He knew his own life was targeted and had been for more than ten years, threatened by the British during the 1916 Easter Rising and the War of Independence. Since signing the Anglo-Irish Treaty just ten months prior, his British assailants had now been replaced by his Irish brothers, the Republican anti-Treatyites. On this very day, his Salmson car had been ambushed and driver shot, just one of many attacks the Big One had been threatened by.

Resuming his walk down the hallway with Wolfe held tightly, the Big One's thoughts reverted to the purpose at hand. Returning the child to Agnes, he and his companions settled around an oaken, kitchen table festooned with specialties prepared by a dozen women whom Agnes had mobilized for this brief meeting with Mick.

"My ladies, most gracious and beautiful," he began. The men and women tittered, some condoning and others forgiving Mick's amorous proclivities. "I thank ye for gathering on such short notice. As I have just been saying to those outside, ye and they are the backbone of our new Free State government. Soon, we will no longer be a provisional government, rather a permanent one leading to our future republic. The war among us is almost over, rest assured. Until then, I know ye will share our mission with yer menfolk and young lads and lassies."

The ladies nodded, as did the men. For the next hour, all shared their commitments. Mick listened, offered encouragement, praised their bravery, and cautioned them to be vigilant and careful.

"As I said in Tralee last week, there seems to be a malignant fate dogging the fortunes of Ireland, for at every critical period in her story the man whom the country trusts and follows is taken from her. Ye must not be among those taken."

Collins continued, "Despite the passing of our dear Griffith last week from a brain hemorrhage due to his extraordinary commitment to our cause, let me leave ye with this thought: We are free now to get back and to keep all that was taken from us. We have no choice but to turn our eyes again to Ireland. The anglicized person completely lost in Ireland will look to Britain in vain. Ireland is about to revolve once again on her own axis."

Mick rose, shook hands with each of the women. He raised Agnes' hand and kissed it, leaning toward her right ear. He whispered, "Tell BB to rest assured, I will protect Liam when we're in Cork next week."

The *Cork Sentinel* would have a headline a week later of those same two words: "Rest Assured."

CHAPTER 74

Let Us Pray—Sunday, August 27, 1922

"Let us pray." Father Sullivan bowed his head and took several moments to speak.

It had been five days since the news of Michael Collins' death on Tuesday, August 22. The news had spread from Cork to all parts of the island. People claimed that birds had stopped singing, flowers had wilted, and sheep had lain down in fields, unmovable by collies who had themselves, stationed stock-still beside them. A silence enveloped street and pub; faces were drawn tight and cheeks lined by tears; families drew inside their homes to embrace newborns and the elderly. The island was in mourning.

The Catholic church of St. Mary Immaculate Refuge of Sinners in Rathmines was filled by young and old, Catholic and Protestant, partisan and uncommitted. Every pew witnessed more than the normal number of attendees as though congregants and non-members needed to be touching each other for both physical stability and emotional comfort. The overflow listened through the open transoms of brightly colored, stained glass windows. Standing mothers and fathers held their young while leaning in to hear whatever words of comfort carried from the inner sanctum to them across the warm, evening breeze. Widows and disabled, who would learn of the words from their families later in the night, leaned on wooden canes along cemetery rows and parameter paths leading to Rathmines Road Lower. That road, too, was covered by mourners. All—inside and outside the church—wore traditional black ribbons and carried lilies, the symbol of innocence restored to the dead. All were hushed.

Father Sullivan raised his head.

"My brothers and sisters in Christ. Tomorrow will be the grand funeral of our nation's hero Michael Collins at Dublin's Pro-Cathedral. Today, however, in our small family church, we will honor him as our brother: the Big Fellow around our tables and in our hearts, the storyteller, the humorist, the soldier for our freedom. Each of us has a memory of him that will stay with us forever—a memory of his strength, his brilliance, his kindness. Let us summon our recollections, remembering a time he was with us in the flesh."

Muted sobs and reticent moans gave somber background to intermittent chortles of muffled laughter and whimsical sighs. Tears reached down to emerging smiles; chins reached up to eyebrows raised in pride. Many a heart beat in time with its neighbor's, known and unknown.

Two pews were filled by the Irvines and McCormicks. Kate and Wolfe settled between Billy and Agnes. Next to Agnes sat Jon and Thon. Behind them were Liam and BB. Morna and Rachel bookended the little ones, Kieran and Maggie. Next to the aisle sat Shelley and Stuart, the extended McCormick siblings. If memories could have been captured in a crystal chandelier above these two pews, it would have been etched in fine designs of elks, wolves, and moles, selkies and fairies, kings and queens.

BB held Liam's hand tightly. He had been with Collins at that fateful bend of the road called Beal na mBlath.

He had sobbed in BB's arms describing the death of his dearest friend, "We had told him not to follow the same way back to Cork from the tavern at Sam's Cross where he visited with his brother Johnny. And why didn't he sit in the armored car like Johnny told him? Ach, I am sick in my heart as I promised him I would protect him with my life, but I didn't.

"It was around 7:15. We were ambushed by so few men. Despite us telling Mick to stay in the touring car so we could drive on, he said we needed to fight the culprits. He thought they were fleeing so into the road he went unprotected. He took aim. Then, he fell. It was awful, BB, terribly awful to hear him cry out that he was hit. And, indeed, he was. I can't bear to tell you what followed as we carried him back to the car. O'Connell said an Act of Contrition. I think our Mick was already gone by then."

As Liam had with Michael, BB held Liam close in her arms until the sobs subsided. In today's memorial service, she could feel him tremble again.

Father Sullivan's voice brought BB back to the present.

"As ye remember our brother today, may I ask yer eyes to lift up to the cross before us? Behold—it is made of two pieces of fine cedar wood that cross each other, one vertical and one horizontal. Ye may not know the symbolism of our cross, but today perhaps its history may give ye comfort. The vertical piece connects our common ground here on Earth to God in Heaven above. The horizontal line reaches out to connect us on Earth to our brothers and sisters around us—here in Rathmines, in Dublin, in the North and, yes, even to the enemy we have fought for so many years across the sea. Ye see the small central area where the two lines cross? That is the cross' heart. That is where our God tells us to be—to know the blessings he offers us every day from Heaven to Earth and the free will he expects us to use in sharing those blessings with others.

"Today, if our brother Michael could speak to us and comfort us in his passing, he would say, 'Sit thee down in the crossroad of God's divinity. Place your heart in the center of the cross where God reaches down to us, lifts us up, and requires us to reach out to our fellowmen and women in peace, not in violence.' "

Father Sullivan made the sign of the cross before the congregants. "Whenever ye think of Michael, think of that place on the cross—its heart, his heart, yer heart—where ye join God and reach out to others. Michael will be there reminding us of what a righteous man—and woman—is."

The moans and sobs, the laughter and sighs, rose. Again, Father Sullivan raised his hand to quiet the crowd. It obeyed.

"Let us end our tribute to him by singing one of his favorite songs. I know ye know it by heart."

In his full-throated baritone, Father Sullivan began to sing Thomas Osborne Davis' "A Nation Once Again." The mourners—inside and outside the church—joined him, loudly rejoicing in and celebrating the Big Fellow.

"When boyhood's fire was in my blood
I read of ancient freemen,
For Greece and Rome who bravely stood,
Three hundred men and three men;
And then I prayed I yet might see
Our fetters rent in twain,
And Ireland, long a province, be
A Nation once again!
A Nation once again,
A Nation once again,
And Ireland, long a province, be
A Nation once again!
And from that time, through wildest woe,
That hope has shone a far light,
Nor could love's brightest summer glow
Outshine that solemn starlight;
It seemed to watch above my head
In forum, field and fane,
Its angel voice sang round my bed,
A Nation once again!
A Nation once again,
A Nation once again,
And Ireland, long a province, be
A Nation once again!

It whisper'd too, that freedom's ark
And service high and holy,
Would be profaned by feelings dark
And passions vain or lowly;
For, Freedom comes from God's right hand
And needs a Godly train;
And righteous men must make our land
A Nation once again!
A Nation once again,
A Nation once again,
And Ireland, long a province, be
A Nation once again!
So, as I grew from boy to man,
I bent me to that bidding
My spirit of each selfish plan
And cruel passion ridding;
For, thus I hoped some day to aid,
Oh, can such hope be vain?
When my dear country shall be made
A Nation once again!"

Una's Epilogue to Part VI

Let Us Rejoice for Now—Tuesday, May 1, 1923

We welcomed Michael eight months ago with a rousing craic. He appeared tired, yet relieved, to be among those who loved him and after whom he had modeled himself throughout his short, thirty-two years. Brian Boru raised his sword and gave a warrior's cry; Wolfe Tone offered an eloquent speech; Pádraig Pearse read a beautifully lyric poem; Parnell expounded (a bit too long and too late for any mortal souls) justifying his policies. Griffith embraced Collins, their bodies still warm from the August, Irish sun.

We other spirits surrounded the Big Fellow and outnumbered the fifty thousand that had flocked to the streets of Dublin to attend his funeral on Monday, August 28, of last year. But, of course, being wisps of the wind, leaves on the trees, and songs of the sea, we had already surrounded him throughout his life. He realized our presence.

Consistent with his humble character, he raised his pint of beer to all saying these words: "I am honored to be among ye whom I have cherished since a laddie. Yer bravery, brilliance, and love of our Ireland have guided me. It also appears that ye have kept me out of the reach of the devil or I wouldn't be here addressing you."

We all chuckled.

He continued, "But more importantly, ye have taught me the following: We have to build up a new civilization on the foundations of the old. And it is not the leaders of the Irish people who can do it for the people. They can but point the way. They can but do their best to establish a reign of justice and of law and order which will enable the people to do it themselves. I hope I have been that leader. Ye must now in this next life, give me yer thoughts how, together, we can influence those new leaders."

He then imbibed—and we with him—in the nectar of the Irish kings and queens.

It did not take him long during this gathering to approach our dear family. He enthusiastically shook hands with the men—William Irvine, his son Will, Bella's brothers Aiden and James, Patrick McCann, Lizzie's brothers Anthony and John, and Ryan McCormick. He even greeted Robbie Smiley, but with a frown.

Then, he turned to the women and graciously kissed their right hands—Bella McKnight-Irvine, Sister Bridgette McCann, Bella's daughter-in-law Lizzie Gallagher-Irvine, Lizzie's mother Kate McGregor-Gallagher, and old Eve McCann. She made him bow to her, kiss both of her cheeks after she reached up and pulled his shoulders toward her—ever the strong-willed matriarch. Christine O'Leary held back, watching from the sidelines of the family gathering. Mick turned to her and motioned her to him. Without a word, he kissed her right hand and turned back to us.

For the past months, we have given him our thoughts. We all have held counsel on the next steps our good countrymen and women must take. Despite the Civil War ceasefire declared yesterday, we know troubles still brew. Who will ensure this next phase upon which our Free State will travel to become an independent republic? Who will lead the reconciliation of those who have been on opposite sides of the road and now must travel it together? How will we again become a nation?

I trust in those around and below me—those of the past, present, and future. No matter what the troubles, we will survive them and thrive. With our Mick finally among us, let us rejoice for now.

Endnotes

1 Michael Collins (1890–1922). Known as the Big Fellow, Michael Collins is considered one of the heroes of the Republic of Ireland's independence movement from Great Britain during the first two decades of the 20th century. Most notably, he was a lead negotiator with the British government in 1921 on the Anglo-Irish Treaty that ended the 1920–21 War of Independence and secured the Free State of Ireland as the precursor of the Republic. A brilliant tactician who organized the intelligence wing of the Irish Republican Army, he was also a formidable politician, chairing the Irish Free State's Provisional Government until his assassination by anti-Treaty advocates in 1922.

2 Arthur Griffith (1871–1922). Writer and newspaper owner and editor, Arthur Griffith founded the Sinn Féin movement in 1905 and *Sinn Féin* newspaper in 1906, promoting the principles of independence from Britain through absention and dual monarchy, separating Ireland's and Great Britain's parliamentary structures. He founded the Irish newspaper *The United Irishman* in 1899 which became *Sinn Féin* in 1906 until 1914 after which Griffith became the lead editor for the journal *Nationality*. Griffith led the Anglo-Irish Treaty negotiation team with Collins becoming the president of the new Free State's first Dáil after de Valera stepped down as president in protest of the treaty. Being warned that he was working too hard, Griffith died of a cerebral hemorrhage ten days before Collins was assassinated.

3 Sinn Féin Party (circa 1930). Standing for the English words "Ourselves or We Ourselves," Sinn Féin was a leading party of Republicans during the War of Independence until the Civil War. It was in leadership turmoil during the 1930s: split by

those for and against the Irish-Anglo Treaty, political and military agendas, and Free State and Northern Ireland alliances. After the Civil War, pro-Treaty Sinn Féin members sat in the Free State Dáil, anti-Treaty members did not. In the 1930 Free State election, Sinn Féin did not offer any candidates. IRA members withdrew from any party affiliation with Sinn Féin, returning only in 1947.

4   Eamon de Valera (1882–1975). Born in America but raised in County Limerick, de Valera (aka the Tall One) served from a distance as a key player in the 1920–1921 Anglo-Irish Treaty negotiations that eventually created the Irish Free State in 1922. He was criticized during the deliberations for his conflicting messages to the team representing Ireland in London. He objected to its rejection of an established Republic, to the required Oath of Allegiance to the British King, and to the division between the North and South. These objections were taken by him despite his acknowledgment that Britain would never accept Ireland as a republic and, thus, would continue the War of Independence unless a treaty to that wit were signed. He supported the Anti-Treaty Sinn Féin party during the Civil War and founded the Fianna Fail party in 1926. He served as the first President of The Republic of Ireland when its constitution was instituted in 1937.

5   Ard Fhies. Annual political conference; On October 25, 1917, the Sinn Féin Ard Fhies created a republican constitution rejecting Griffith's dual monarchy approach to Home Rule and replacing it with a republic, totally independent from Great Britain. Eamon de Valera, Michael Collins, Countess Markievicz, W. T.Cosgrove, and Arthur Griffith served in leadership roles, albeit oppositional at times, in the reconstituted Sinn Féin.

6 Hanna Sheehy-Skeffington (1887–1946). A leader in the women's suffragette, feminism and republican movements, Hannah Sheehy-Skeffington was jailed several times for her activism, including a 1917 incarceration in Holloway Prison for her pro-German sympathy. She was a member of Sinn Féin and then Fianna Fáil. She contributed to the IRA publication *An Phoblacht* and founded *The Irish Citizen* feminist newspaper in 1912. She also founded the Irish Women Workers' Union and The Irish Women's Franchise League.

7 Sir Edward Carson (1854–1935). A Dublin-born Unionist, Edward Carson served as a lawyer, politician, and first signatory of the Anti-Home Rule, 1912 Ulster Covenant. In 1915, he was the Attorney General under the British government of Prime Minister H. H. Asquith and First Lord of the Admiralty under PM David Lloyd George. As an MP in the House of Commons and leader of the Ulster Unionist Party, he supported the separation of Ulster's six counties in 1921 from the Free State but felt betrayed by the Tory government and he stated that Catholics should not be made to fear an N.I. government.

8 Sir James Craig (1871–1940). Elected in 1906 as the Ulster Unionist Party MP from East Down, Craig went on to be the second signatory of the 1912 Ulster Covenant. To insure the safety of Protestants and to support the partition of Northern Ireland from the Free State, he founded the Ulster Voluntary Force and developed the proposal for partition from the South. In January 1921, he became the first Prime Minister of the Northern Ireland Parliament in which he served for 24 years. During this time, he advocated for the Ulster Special Constabulary and the Royal Ulster Constabulary.

9   Jeremiah O'Donovan Rossa (1831–1915). A leader in the Fenian and Irish Republican Brotherhood movements, O'Donovan Rossa espoused violence, including the dynamite campaigns, against the British in order to form an independent Ireland. He won a seat in the British Parliament in 1869 while serving a lifelong prison sentence life for treason, felony, and previous crimes. Given amnesty in 1870 based on his promise to leave Ireland and never return, he spent the rest of his life in Staten Island, New York. There, he founded *The United Irishman* newspaper that raised funds for the Ireland-based, independence efforts. Upon his death, his body was returned to Ireland for a patriotic, celebratory funeral in 1915 that supposedly contributed to the Easter Rising of 1916.

10 Judge Daniel Cohalan (1864–1947) and John Devoy (1842–1928). These two Irish-Americans were born in Ireland and exiled to the U.S. in their early years for anti-British activities, including armed insurrections. In the U.S., they were key figures in the Irish-American support of the Republican movement and the pro-Treaty side of the Anglo-Irish Treaty.

Judge Cohalan, born of Irish immigrants who fled the famine of 1847, was the U.S.-based leader of the Friends of Irish Freedom, founded in support of Irish republicanism against the British. He was a lawyer, New York State Supreme Court judge and political insider in the New York legal circles, particularly in its Democratic party Tammany Hall activities. He was against Home Rule as he favored a more collaborative relationship with Great Britain that would ensure that Ireland (and Irish-Americans) would gain London's respect and profitable economic ties. Cohalan never lived in Ireland but had a summer home he visited in County Cork.

A friend of the Irish Republican Brotherhood founder James Stephens, John Devoy served as recruiter of Irish soldiers in the British army into the IRB. He was imprisoned in 1866 for this and his role in a planned insurrection by Fenian members of the British Army. Like O'Donovan Rossa, he was released in 1871 as part of the "no-return to Ireland" amnesty and became a leader of the Glan na Gael, the U.S. partner of the Irish Republican Brotherhood. He became a journalist for the *New York Herald* and owned *The Gaelic American* newspaper from 1903–1928.

11 Joseph McGarrity (1874–1940). Another Irish-American who immigrated to the U.S. at age 18, McGarrity never lost his own father's love and interest in Fenian politics. Joseph settled in Pennsylvania and joined the Clan na Gael. He founded the *Irish Press* newspaper in 1918 and supported the War of Independence. McGarrity managed the American tour of de Valera in 1919, during which de Valera spoke against the positions of Cohalan and Devoy. McGarrity was an Irish-American anti-Treaty advocate of the Anglo-Irish Treaty but did not support the partition of northern and southern Ireland. As the chair of Clan na Gael in the 1920s, he led the organization in its alliance with the IRA's pro-violence, Republican movement.

12 James John O'Shee (1866–1946) A labor lawyer, O'Shee founded the Irish Land and Labour Association (ILLA). He served as a member of Parliament from 1895 to 1918, advocating for changes in land and labor laws more congruent to citizen needs. He did not support partition during the Anglo-Irish treaty negotiations but did support the Irish participation in World War I, believing that aligning with Britain would be an economic necessity for Ireland's survival. His legal acumen greatly assisted in land purchases by tenants and land owners and in legislation on social issues.

13 Countess Markievicz (1868–1927). Born as Constance Georgine Gore-Booth, the Countess Markievicz was an actress, republican activist, soldier, and politician. She helped found Fianna Eireann, Cumann na mBan and the Irish Citizen Army in the early 1900s. After being jailed in Holloway Prison for her role in securing St. Stephen's Green during the 1916 Easter Rising, she returned to Dublin to become a member of Parliament from Dublin's St. Patrick's district in 1918. During the pro- and anti-Anglo-Irish Treaty conflicts, she joined Eamon de Valera's Fianna Fail party and, in 1919, became the first woman in Europe to achieve a Cabinet post, being the Minister of Labour for the Free State.

14 Anglo-Irish Treaty 1921. The Anglo-Irish Treaty, signed on December 6, 1921, ended the Irish War of Independence and secured "home rule" for Ireland. It stated that Southern Ireland would take on the status of a Commonwealth Dominion within Great Britain with a dual parliamentary system. Elected Irish members of the two governing bodies (a Dublin-based parliament and the British Parliament in London) had to take an oath of allegiance to the British crown; i.e., George V. It also required that six Ulster counties comprising Northern Ireland be allowed to approve or reject their participation in the newly established 32-county Irish Free State structure. Elections in the six Northern Ulster counties held on May 3, 1921 resulted in citizens there voting against joining the Irish Free State, cementing the current partition between The Republic of Ireland of 26 counties and Northern Ireland of six. In the remaining Southern counties, a vote by the Dáil Council of the newly formed Irish Free State approved the treaty on January 7, 1922 leading to an 18-month Civil War in the Irish Free State between pro- and anti-Treatyites.

15 Rory O'Connell (1883–1922) and Eoin O'Duffy (1890–1944). Both O'Connell and O'Duffy were anti-Treatyite Brigade Commander members of the IRA during the Civil War.

O'Connell—Educated as an engineer and key in the Dublin General Post Office actions of the Easter Rising, Rory became the Director of Engineering during the Irish War of Independence and, subsequently, as an anti-Treatyite, he took on the key role of Commandant General during the Civil War, particularly in the failed anti-Treaty's siege of the Four Courts in Dublin. Captured by the Free State Army, he was executed on December 8, 1922.

O'Duffy—Land surveyor and engineer, O'Duffy became a leading member of the Gaelic Athletic Association. He was first a member of the IRB before taking on various positions in the IRA as a Brigadier. He was well versed in intelligence tactics concerning the Royal Irish Constabulary from which he had to flee in 1919. He organized a number of attacks on Protestants supporting unionism in N.I., becoming the IRA Chief of Staff in 1921. After the Civil War, O'Duffy leaned toward "nationalist facisim" and, in 1932, formed the Blueshirts to defend against IRA incursions. Seen as too violent and, thus, threats to the political reputations of de Valera and Cosgrove alike, the Blueshirts were declared illegal by deValera in 1933. In 1933, O'Duffy became the first President of the Fine Gael party, with Cosgrove as his second. Many Blueshirt members stayed in the Fine Gael party but the organization, as such, disbanded in 1935 as did its alliance with Fine Gael.

16 Cumann na Poblachta. Founded by Eamon de Valera in 1922, this political party stood for republicanism and transitioned into the Fianna Fáil party in 1926, de Valera's new alternative to Sinn Féin.

17 Special Powers Act of 1922 (Flogging Act). Known also as the Civil Authorities (Special Powers) Act (Northern Ireland) was passed by the Northern Ireland Parliament to secure the peace and safety Stormont members thought was being threatened by treasonous individuals and groups deemed treasonous. It was specifically used to stop any IRA-associated, Nationalist, or Catholic individuals or groups from meeting, publishing, or conducting any acts assumed to foster anti-British or republican sentiment. Violations resulted in indefinite internment, arrest without warrants and without trial.

18 Ernie O'Malley (1897–1957). O'Malley was considered the second to O'Connor during the siege of Four Courts. A member of the Irish Volunteers in the War of Independence, he became an anti-Treaty republican afterwards. Favored by Collins during the War of Independence, he turned against Collins and focused his paramilitary efforts on the anti-Treaty IRA efforts during the Civil War. He was injured, arrested, and imprisoned in Mountjoy Prison where he held hunger strikes in 1923. Upon his release, he spent the rest of his life traveling in Europe and the U.S., writing histories of the War of Independence and other military incursions. He returned to Ireland in 1934.

Also available from Margaret McLaughlin on Amazon:

*Beloved Reconciliation
Book 1: 1820–1916*

Publisher: Moore Media, Inc.
Language: English
Paperback: 454 pages
ISBN: 979-8-9852789-8-9
Paperback: $30.00
Kindle: $9.99

Made in the USA
Columbia, SC
10 October 2024